BULLET
HEART

BULLET HEART

MICHAEL DOANE

Alfred A. Knopf
New York
1994

THIS IS A BORZOI BOOK
PUBLISHED BY ALFRED A. KNOPF, INC.

Copyright © 1994 by Michael Doane

All rights reserved under International and Pan-American Copyright Conventions. Published in the United States by Alfred A. Knopf, Inc., New York, and simultaneously in Canada by Random House of Canada Limited, Toronto. Distributed by Random House, Inc., New York.

Library of Congress Cataloging-in-Publication Data
Doane, Michael.
Bullet heart / by Michael Doane.
p. cm.
ISBN 0-679-42507-1
1. Indians of North America—Civil rights—Fiction.   2. South
Dakota—Fiction.   I. Title.
PS3554.O143B85   1994
813'.54—dc20   93-37263
CIP

Manufactured in the United States of America

For Eric Ashworth,
sweet friend, who swore to me that I wasn't crazy

ACKNOWLEDGMENTS

High-wire artists and novelists are only marginally more courageous than actors, who have stunt people to take their falls. We take our own falls but there are often nets to catch us. Ever stumbling, I wish to thank David Kemp, for finding me wherever I wander; Dave Geisler, for lifting the "tourist" cataracts from my eyes; Gary Fisketjon, for his bracing wit and faithful support; my wife, Claudine, for the listening; Kevin McKiernan, for his remembrance and compassion. In memory of Mark Rosenberg, gone to blue. Also to D.B. and E.T.S. on opposite sides of the ancient war, for lending voice to their sorrows.

Delores
Her Many Horses
August 1973

The dry Dakota wind is howling against Delores Her Many Horses'
ear. Yet when she awakens, she hears only the breathing of the white
man next to her in bed. His smell has changed through the night
from Old Spice to sweat to beer.

She sits up and cold air settles around her like a silk blouse. With
one hand supporting her large belly, she swings her legs outward and
her feet touch the floor. Beyond the bed the air is wet and black with
darkness. "I'm leaving," she says aloud.

There is no answer.

"When I'm with you, I'm always out of breath. I need air."

His breathing is unchanged, his arm still reaching toward her
pillow.

"Anyways, a white man and a Lakota woman won't go. You don't
hear the dumb things people say, not like I do. They look at me like
I'm on fire and don't know it."

For a moment she thinks she'll be hysterical, the way they say
pregnant women sometimes get. She is tempted to start hitting him
just to get his attention. "You have your secrets, too," she says. "You
and Gaetan Avril."

She dresses in jeans and the western shirt he gave her, with a shattered mother-of-pearl snap over her left breast and the elbow patched with denim. "The shirt I'll wear for the rest of my life," she said when he plucked it from a Salvation Army bin and paid a dollar for it. She got her jeans from a woman with four children who has since had her tubes tied. Though oversized, the jeans are too tight over her stretched belly and she leaves the top button unfastened to let the baby breathe. She slips her feet into black leather flats and stands. Without looking back at him, she goes down the stairs to the main room, which smells like everything about him: wood smoke and alcohol, leather and oil and fresh sweat. She was drinking wine all night, but Tyrone had one beer after another and spilled one on her when they walked in the door.

She scrapes the door open and steps outside, where the moon is greasy yellow. Tyrone's mud-spattered Delta 88 is parked in front of the porch. The window on the driver's side is broken and she can see that rain has blown in and soaked the upholstery. The first rain in weeks had started to fall when they came home the night before, and the yard has turned to mud. That same night, the men in Choteau didn't believe Tyrone's version of events. They think he's from the FBI or something, so they took two-by-fours to the car. *You want to be a Indian, Tyrone? You gotta have a Indian car!*

She makes it to the far end of the yard then stops and turns around. Built upon a short rise, the house looks larger in the darkness than she knows it to be. From where she stands it seems taller than the trees to either side, and for a moment she thinks she sees a light in an upstairs window. Her feet are cold and she regrets having left her socks behind, but no longer wants to risk waking him. He'd have convinced her to stay put, stick around, we'll talk in the morning. Circling her in his arms and hypnotizing her.

She picks her way over ruts and mudholes for half a mile before she comes to a dry gravel road where Tyrone's mailbox stands. She opens it just to see the emptiness inside and leaps backward when a sparrow flies out. No, she says to herself. I'm only dreaming of a sparrow. But for a panicky moment the bird swoops around her head before flying across the road toward a stand of trees. It disappears in the darkness and the falling rain.

The soft light in the distance will be the sunrise and she walks away from it, toward Choteau. Her face is wet from the rain and her hair hangs in strings across her forehead. Her looks are going down that hillside, the far slope after twenty-five. The first signs of crow's-feet are at the corners of each eye, her skin dries out more easily now. She spends more than she should on creams and oils, Tyrone says. He says she shouldn't worry so much about her face. You still have a pretty mouth, and brown eyes that are deep enough to drown in if I look.

Don't look, Tyrone.

But the baby has made drums of her skin and filled her breasts to the point of aching. She knows that when it's over she will feel like a sack that's been casually emptied, but SheHe will be there, HimHer, as recompense for the lost blood and hanging skin.

She walks another mile and begins to wonder why she is doing it this way, leaving on foot. Choteau is another four miles unless she cuts across the old Averill fields, and at this hour there isn't a chance in hell of finding a ride. On late summer Sundays, the farmers sleep in, hung over after getting their harvest checks from Sioux Falls or Sioux City or Chicago and taking their money into town or out to Smoky Corners. Not even a lonesome priest would be out this early.

But then she hears an engine and instantly she struggles over the ditch and into the cornfield. Crouching between the rows, she can see a pickup on the road ahead. Indians. Two up front and three in the back, their rifles upraised like antennas. Ours or theirs? she wonders, and as the truck roars past she sees that they're goons, Lonetree's boys from Ree. They're heading east, away from Choteau, where she imagines those guns have been fired into windows and at parked cars.

She rises slowly. Fields of red and black Missouri basin mud and towering stalks all around. Behind her, a few miles over the horizon, is the river itself—jet black this time of night, when the sky turns silver and the first bronze shadows appear in the east. She moves along the rows, a woman alone among the stalks, a crowd of darkness moving around her according to the rules of wind.

Up ahead is the remainder of a house that burned almost thirty years ago, leaving only a red brick foundation that still delineates walls of a living room, a bathroom, a kitchen. When she was in high school, she and Elizabeth Bordeaux often drove out here when the weather was good. They would bring beer and push down the grass in the space that once was a living room. They would undo their braids, letting their hair hang loose down their backs, and recline in the grass to pass a bottle of cherry vodka and watch the stars. They would make up stories about the family that once had lived there, a white family, probably Swedes or Norwegians, Ulff and Birgitta and five flaxen-haired daughters to spread the chicken feed and milk the cows. Birgitta read her Swedish Bible on Sunday mornings and after lunch she and Ulff would climb the stairs for their once-a-week while the girls chased rabbits and squirrels in the fields. It was a place of mystery and secrets for Delores, there in the middle of what otherwise seemed endless prairie and desolation, distances that never ended in anything but sky. Inside the brick markers of the ghost house was the radiance of what would be on the other side.

One time Elizabeth took a rusty nail and carved *Let that man come this way just once* on the highest wall that remained. It was a strange thing to write, Delores told her, but Elizabeth just said, "Not if you know what it means."

The foundation is covered with a sheen of rain and, coming close, Delores thinks she can see animal tracks, then decides she dreamed that too, like the sparrow. But the tracks are larger than a dog's or a coyote's and lead to the grove of fruit trees north of the house. She cuts off the road and picks her way across the ditch, watching for dry ground. Once she's standing in the ghostlike living room, she swears she can feel the wind pick up and thinks immediately that she shouldn't have come here, that she should be back out on the road to Choteau. The wind blows from the north and she turns her back to it before looking at the brick wall. Other messages have been written over Elizabeth's wish: initials, dates, hearts with arrows in them, balloon breasts, and rocket-shaped dicks, but Elizabeth's cuts were deep, as if there were greater sincerity in her wish. *Let that man come this way just once.*

After high school, Elizabeth moved to and from the reservation almost every six months, unable to make up her mind where to put her feet, in the world where time is circular or the world where time is a straight line. Now she lives up north in Pierre, the state capital, and is married to a Crow named Russell. For a while she wrote letters that said *He drinks all the time and beats me*, then she wrote *He treats me like a May queen and is a good father*. She doesn't write anymore. Delores doesn't either. They call each other from time to time, though, and it always seems to be in the middle of the night.

The ground around her is strewn with broken beer bottles, food wrappers, discarded condoms. This always happens in abandoned places, the middles of nowhere turning into meeting halls for the adolescent and the depraved. This is where she meant to lose her virginity, back when she would come here to dream and watch the stars grow larger with each swallow of cherry vodka. She is looking at the messages on that wall when out of the corner of her eye, she sees the shadow. Ten, fifteen yards ahead of her, near a lone tree in a bare field. A wolf. She didn't dream it. For a long moment, she and the wolf contemplate each other. He will go for her throat, she imagines. If he's starving, she won't have a prayer. But the animal neither advances nor retreats. It crouches with head bowed, one forepaw slightly raised as if pointing at her. Then, suddenly, it turns and leaps away and in three quick bounds has disappeared.

Shivering with rage, she stands in the darkness of what used to be a house. *I am dreaming this. As I have dreamed Tyrone. As I have dreamed of leaving. I dreamed my own life to the beginning of old age and came face-to-face with the rest of me, what even the wolf will not devour.*

She arrives at her mother's trailer before seven in the morning, her flats soaked through and covered with red Missouri mud.

"Well, this is a surprise!" Helene peers across the five feet at her daughter. She isn't wearing her glasses and seems to barely recognize her.

"Won't you let me in?"

"Not a surprise, a stunner. I am stunned, Delores, to see you at this hour."

"I'm coming in, Helene. Before my feet fall off."

Helene looks over Delores' shoulder and her small eyes sweep the road in search of a car. "Did Tyrone bring you in?"

"I walked."

Delores reaches a hand to the doorjamb and pulls her weight up the three steps and into the trailer. Though Helene had been awakened by Delores' pounding, the television is already turned on. A skinny man in glasses is quoting yesterday's Chicago stock and grain prices with a nasal, disinterested voice. Yearlings and heifers. Barley, winter wheat.

Delores limps into the tiny bathroom where the tub is the sit-down kind, the porcelain curved into a seat. She takes off her shoes and massages her feet. While the tub fills with steaming water, she shucks the western shirt and maternity jeans and can suddenly see all of herself in the full-length mirror on the back of the door. Her black hair is wet and clings to her skull like a tight cap. Her makeup is smeared from the rain and the night so that her lips look askew and her eyes bruised. Her skin is soaked and her breasts are bursting, the nipples ever darker and with wider roseates. She gazes down at her belly and extends a leg, finding, oh Lord, a thin trace of Tyrone on the inside of her thigh.

"Did he beat you?" Helene is asking from the other side of the door. "Is that it, Delores? Tyrone beat you up?"

"No, Helene. He just got drunk and passed out."

She waits until the tub is filled and then sets herself down into the water, allowing herself a single tiny scream of pain and joy. The water rises to her breasts and stops there and she lays her head back against the wall and closes her eyes.

Helene knocks and then walks in. She has found her eyeglasses and looks ten years younger without the squint. She is wearing her hair in braids like some woman from the old times but Delores knows that it's just how she sleeps and that she will have combed those braids back out before she's finished her toast. She is as vain as I am. Maybe more so.

"I had my heart set on a wedding," she tells Delores. "A name for the baby."

"I know what you had your heart set on. It's not that easy, having a name."

Helene sits on the toilet seat as though it were an easy chair, one arm draped over the sink. "This have anything to do with that council business?"

"Could be."

"I heard there was FBI come to arrest Russ Poor Bull for digging up those graves."

"More likely they were looking for guns. I saw a pickup full of Lonetree's goons on my way here. Was there any shooting?"

"Not that I heard."

"They think Tyrone's a spy."

"Who does?"

"The council boys. Frank, Gene Fast Horse, the others. Because he's white and won't carry a gun. And because he's friends with Gaetan Avril."

"What about Noah Lame? What does he think?"

Delores squeezes the soap and it slips from her hand like a fish. "Noah's confused," she says.

Helene looks at herself in the mirror then reaches her fingers to undo the knots at the ends of her braids. "So you and Tyrone had a spat."

It is not a question, just another of Helene's flat facts. She always seems to say things that would float if they were objects.

"I saw a wolf," Delores tells her.

"In your dreams."

"At the burned-down house. I stared him down."

"Delores, they killed the last wolf in these parts about the time you were born. Must've been a coyote."

"It was bigger than a coyote."

"Danger always looks bigger when you've been drinking." The mirror above the sink has fogged over and Helene reaches her fingers to wipe away a spot so she can see her own face.

"I need some money," Delores tells her. "For a bus, I was thinking."

"To go where?"

"Up north where I don't know everybody and not everybody's looking at me to know my tribe or my politics."

"That baby could happen any day now. But I guess you've already thought of that."

Delores nods. The water has begun to cool, the chill of her having soaked in all the warmth. She can feel her heart beating and the baby turning around inside of her. SheHe feeling the lapping of gentle waves. HimHer. "I can pay you back," she says. "Next week the check's due."

"But you quit your job weeks ago."

"It's a maternity leave, Helene. This is a new age. The Great Society? We get more than just Indian money nowadays."

The water has gone plain cold on her, so Delores stands and reaches for a towel. Helene gets up to go into the next room and returns with a brassiere in her hands. "One of mine but it ought to fit you. I was always lots bigger upstairs."

They sit at the little table in the main room where Helene counts out one hundred dollars in tens and fives. Delores can see over her shoulder and out the window to the middle of the trailer park. This time of year, her mother's is the only trailer occupied. The other eight have been abandoned long since, but Toby Johnson rents out a few to hunters and fishermen during the open seasons. *Sport* hunters and *sport* fishermen, they have taken to calling themselves. To distinguish them from Indians, perhaps, who aren't very sporting about these endeavors and actually eat their catch and kill.

On the television a skinny gray coyote chases a skinny gray road-runner.

"If you've just got the moods, why don't you paint something?"

"Helene, I haven't painted anything for three years."

"One of those portraits you did so well. Like that one of your father that won a prize."

"It didn't win a prize. It won a scholarship."

"You *do* split hairs, don't you? I was only making a suggestion."

Delores takes the money, then stands and pulls her sweater over her shoulders.

"I don't expect letters, just send word of where you end up so I can sleep nights. Stay away from those AIM people and the council boys." She hands Delores a postcard with a stamp already on it. "Be careful about what you eat and drink and don't be smoking anything rolled by hand."

It isn't until she is alone at the Wilma bus terminal that Delores looks at the picture on the postcard. It is a jackalope, a mythical hybrid of jackrabbit and antelope that Dakotans are forever fooling tourists about. Another creature that doesn't exist. A pipe dream.

The Greyhound's floor is dirty and littered; someone's matchbox, a cinema magazine, cigarette butts, and a dismaying wad of Kleenex she would like to point out to the driver. She can't get comfortable. The bus is three quarters full and she takes two seats midway to the back where she can slide her legs to the side and take the wear off her knees. Across from her, a middle-aged man with slicked-back hair and a paisley shirt eats one doughnut after another from a brown bag. The only place where she could stretch out is the back row, and that's been taken up by an overweight farm wife whose feet are propped up on the seat. When she asks to switch with her, Delores feels it's necessary to point out that she's pregnant. The woman's sniff answers that Delores is also an Indian.

At ten in the morning they stop for a few minutes in Parkston and arrive an hour later in Woonsocket. She's been in both towns before and isn't far enough away yet. When she lifts her hands to her face she can still smell wood smoke, leather, Old Spice, sour wine. When I get north, she thinks, I won't smell of anything but baby oil.

The sky is overcast, Dakota grays mixed with roiling black clouds moving in from the west, and the sun burning orange on the other side of that screen. When the bus lurches, Delores swears she can feel the baby's fingernails inside her, holding on. She feels a constant urge to pee but the doctor tells her that's just the weight of the baby on her urethra. The bus motion makes it worse and, illusion or not, she gets up again and struggles down the aisle to the john. Closing the latch, she lifts her sweater to below her breasts, peels down her jeans and underpants, and sits. The metal toilet is cold and for a moment the urge leaves her but there it is again, a burning down low. This time it ends in a trickle, a small spill. She leans her head against the frosted window and just breathes in and out. The hurt is everywhere, in her belly, her head, behind her eyes. Even her clothes are hurting her. She wants to take off the sweater, the blouse, jeans, sweat socks, muddy flats, the double-D brassiere she's had to wear to harness her swollen breasts. Her breasts ache. They're not mine, she keeps thinking.

After a long while, she stands, zips halfway up, pulls the sweater down over her jeans, and staggers back to her seat. There is a second dirty Kleenex next to the first one on the floor and she casts a look of loathing at the man across from her.

The bus rumbles north on Highway 45.

There is nothing out the window but white grass, mud, corn, and barbed wire.

She struggles off the bus at Miller, and after another trip to the Ladies', orders a lunch of split pea soup and tossed salad at the bus terminal counter. The sun has come out, burning the clouds like tissue paper, and the air is so clear it sparkles. The sky outside the wide window is a hopeful blue and there is a cheerful bustle in the bus station cafe. The waitress' apron is clean and crisp, her hands are washed, her hair is in place, and she smiles while she pours Delores a second cup of coffee.

Delores is surprised that she still hasn't slept. Not after the five-mile walk from Tyrone's farm into Choteau. Not during that four-hour bus ride. Across the street is a Qwik Mart and she wanders the rows until she finds a bottle of red wine for a dollar fifty. It will be sleep medicine, she convinces herself. If she doesn't sleep she will weaken, will turn around and find herself in Tyrone's arms.

She rearranges her makeup and address book and angles the bottle until it fits into her purse. Then she boards the three o'clock bus bound for Pierre.

She gets out at Blunt for no reason she can think of.

She has traveled close to three hundred miles and is only seventeen miles from Pierre where she's planned on calling Elizabeth. But just when the bus is about to pull out, she stands on weak legs, reaches above her seat for her leather bag, and tells the driver, "Wait! Hold it. I'm getting off here."

Her room at the Medicine Knoll Motel costs $6.15 a night. On the nightstand there is a black telephone that looks like an antique. The stained wood floor is covered with fake Navajo-pattern rugs around a queen-sized bed with one flat pillow. On the pine wood wall above the bed is a Remington reprint of buffalo hunters and redskins pointing toward the far hills. The bathroom is tiny, with a sink and a showerhead, but no shower curtain. The TV gets the main channels, KELO in Sioux Falls, KORN in Mitchell. The lamp on the nightstand is a carved wooden Indian holding up the shade with the tip of his feathered lance.

Delores showers and then lifts her hands to her face. Lifebuoy and the barest trace of wood smoke. She wraps a towel around her middle and sits on the edge of the bed. An old film about American college girls on holiday in Rome is on the television. She stands and looks out the window into the parking lot and beyond. There is a hole in that window the size of a BB and the wind whistles through that hole, so she closes the curtains and returns to the bed. She turns out the light but lies propped up with her back against the wall, drinking from the red bottle.

SheHe is moving inside of her, preparing to migrate outward. She cups her hands between her legs as if to catch him. Her body will be emptied like a paper cup. SheHe will be like wet film, an oozing plant, and Delores will swell a last time and then go empty, smelling between the legs of—what do the men always say?

Fish. They always say fish.

Near dawn the bottle is long empty. She can hear "The Star-Spangled Banner" and when she opens her eyes there it is on the screen, a flag flapping in the breeze and men in uniform, white men, black men, Mexicans and Chinamen and not a single Apache or Sioux among them. The wind is like a bone flute through that hole in the window, a sound that rises and falls. The screen shows the flag in a freeze frame and then turns to snow.

She decides to settle on the fact that Tyrone is just a man who's floated upriver and drifted to her shore. In the litany, the winter count, he followed Willard Tree, Donny Ingersoll, Colin Yellow Bird, Rafe Diggers in Minneapolis, some man she met in a bar all the way up in Duluth, and another man she met at an Indian survival meeting in Omaha. Before Tyrone there was John Fire Smith. Each winter brought a different man to blanket me, to warm my feet.

By the winter, she thinks, Tyrone will be forgotten.

He's told her almost nothing about his past. Before he came to Choteau, he said, he drifted, and went off to the war before she ever set eyes on him. By the time she met him he was ten months out of the army, had bad teeth, bad dreams, and a talent for fixing whatever was broken. His breathing is funny, always that rattle when he sleeps. He says it's the Agent Orange he's inhaled, and at first she imagined white blossoms that he held to his nose, not knowing they were poison. He wasn't her first white man. He must have been her third or fourth.

The Choteau people weren't exactly taken with the idea of the two of them. Her blood mingled with theirs, they claimed; with Tyrone she could only share spit. Gene Fast Horse mentioned her grandfather and said he dreamed of him riding a cloud horse in the sky over Tyrone's house. "We don't know anything about Tyrone, Delores. We have things to do and he's always here watching us, trying like hell to be a part of things."

John Fire Smith looked at her and looked away. More sadness than anger. Eyes of rain and hailstones.

She told Tyrone she loved him but she didn't tell him everything. Stories and plans of what we would do, what they would do, the council of warriors.

Tyrone had his secrets, too. She wasn't the only one.

The sun is still in the sky and SheHe is no longer moving. If SheHe can sleep, so can Delores.

The wind blows, speaking through her window in the northern voice, the voice of warning. Delores sleeps and doesn't hear anything.

When night has fallen, she awakens. The parts of her are gathered round her belly like stones around a campfire; arms, legs, head, her chin tucked to her breasts. She unfolds herself, stretches, and rocks her weight forward until she is standing. Once the water from the shower has turned from cold to warm, she steps under the spray and stays there until her head clears, then dries herself, dresses in the same jeans, a red blouse with a white sunburst, white socks, and the same muddy flats.

She takes a pen and the postcard from her purse. The postcard is yellow and had probably been sitting in Helene's drawer for ages. *Stopped here instead of Pierre,* she writes. *Will find a job if I have to. I can still type eighty words a minute.*

She drinks tap water to rinse the taste of pennies from her mouth, then shrugs into her coat, takes her purse, closes the door behind her, and is halfway to the road when the motel lady comes out of the office and calls to her. She is overweight and is wearing an ugly green bathrobe, her hair in tight curlers.

"You got to leave the key!"

Delores crosses the lot and takes the key from her purse. The plastic oval keytag is the size of a playing card. She gives the woman the key and the postcard. "It's already got a stamp."

"I can see that."

"I might be back late. I didn't want to wake you."

"You won't," the woman tells her. "Keys are on the wall behind the desk. Serve yourself." When Delores turns to go, the woman adds, "Your room is a single. I'll know it if you don't come back alone."

. . .

When the Shot and Spot closes and her head is heavy as a river-bottom stone and she can taste the pennies again, she comes back to the room and counts her money, spreading the coins and bills across the bedsheet. All she has eaten are some beer nuts, a pickled egg, two Slim Jims. She met a man named Kissel, rhymes with whistle, who gave her a dollar for a kiss. She dropped twelve quarters in the Whirlwind pinball and never won a game, not even a match. On the television over the bar was a baseball game being played out in silence.

"I don't know you," the bartender told her.

"I don't know you, either."

"I don't got any wine here, lady. This here's a shot bar."

She counts the money and there are sixty-seven dollars left. After the bus, lunch in Miller, the bottle of wine, the beer nuts. Kissel paid for the egg and the Slim Jims. He offered two dollars to feel her breast. "For luck, the bosom of a woman with child." She said he should seek his luck elsewhere.

An Indian wearing sunglasses sat in the corner of the bar and she thought he was watching her through the dark lenses. When her legs began to ache, she sat at the bar and watched the Indians play pool on a table worn white around the pockets.

I won't go back there, she decides in the motel room. But the next night she drinks three beers and a half dozen shots of Wild Turkey until a fire is lit behind her eyes. Kissel says the baby will be born with the DT's, but she ignores him. At closing time she stands in front of the Whirlwind and watches the steel ball bounce and rattle, rebound, slide, and fall.

On her fourth night there, she is sitting alone at the bar trying to imagine how much is left in her purse when Harold Bad Hand comes in. It takes her a moment to recognize him and then she tries to shrink inside herself. Just five nights ago he was beating on Tyrone's car and screaming obscenities.

"Delores Her Many Horses," he says, and there is no surprise in his voice. He is wearing new jeans, a clean shirt, and has a shiny silver belt buckle that says Lefty. He takes a seat next to her and buys himself a beer.

She picks up the glass and drinks half of it before looking him in the eye. "Are you following me?"

"Hell, no."

"I'm not going back there."

"I ain't asking you to. I just got out 'cause of all the trouble."

She shakes her head. "You like trouble, Harold. You are trouble."

He was a basketball star at their mission school in Ree, the year they won the B tourney. 'Sixty-three, 'sixty-four? She remembers his face ten years ago, how his features already seemed carved, like that Indian on the back of the old nickel, his long hair trailing behind him when he ran the length of the court. But he is a half-breed, *iyeska.* Most of the Choteau people, like Delores, are full-blood Oglala.

He sips at his beer and looks at himself in the glass. "So where's Tyrone?"

"Mind your own business, redskin."

"That's what I always do. What in hell else is there to do in Blunt?"

He orders two more beers and Delores tells the bartender, "And some Slim Jims? I got a taste in my mouth."

"I'm paying," Bad Hand says, showing a wad of fresh bills. Then he turns to Delores who is staring at the money. "You here alone?"

"No," she says, looking down at the bulge under her sweater. "I came with a friend." She remembers that the team he was on made a name for itself. Five Sioux, never any substitutes, running full bore the entire game, shooting the ball from anywhere, playing no defense to speak of, just run and shoot, shoot faster than the others and keep running. The white players called it Indian ball and the mission Indians called it victory.

He studies her for a moment as if trying to dislodge a detail about her face. "You don't look all Indian," he says. "Anybody ever tell you that?"

"Not lately."

"Not all the way. Like you got blue eyes but they're not blue. I knew a Hunkpapa chick once, had blond hair." Then he shakes his head. "I guess that sounds like bullshit."

"Sure does."

Kissel steps in and sees her with Bad Hand. "Well, I see you hooked up with one of your own."

She ignores him. Lifting a glass of beer, she raises it to her lips and drinks it down. Beer only makes her more thirsty than she was before.

She wonders how SheHe is taking all this abuse, then decides she'd rather not think about it. "Why'd you really leave Choteau?" she asks.

"Didn't you hear?"

"Hear what?"

"About the shooting?"

"What shooting is that, Harold?"

There have been shootings and beatings for weeks on end, local whites and Indians in pickups cruising dirt roads with deer rifles at their sides. The Indians are split into two camps, those who prefer the old ways and want the land back against those who want the money doled out by the Bureau of Indian Affairs. The traditionals call the others goons and hang-around-the-fort Indians. And the whites in the area—particularly those from Wilma, on the west edge of the reservation—don't seem to mind getting help from the goons. Tyrone had come down from the Twin Cities after getting out of Vietnam and for two years has used his time and money and skills to help out the Choteau people and the others who'd joined them. Some Choteau people, including Harold, called him Wannabe behind his back and whispered about some FBI connection. Even though they couldn't prove anything, these people she's known all of her life threw him out.

Harold looks over his shoulder then back at her through the mirror behind the bar. She can only see one of his eyes in that mirror. The other is blocked by the jar with the pickled eggs. "You know. The bones thing."

She knows it is not a circle that she wanders, but a triangle: the country, the town, the reservation. In the center of her triangle is the perpetual war between the new ways and the old ways, between television and Lakota sing-chanting, between land that has dotted lines around it and land that is just land. Now she is in town and wants another Slim Jim to get rid of the taste in her mouth. She wonders what words he'll use when it comes down to what he wants from her.

"Have another beer," he tells her.

She stares at her beer, watching the bubbles that appear from nowhere, rising, rising. She feels the familiar burning and struggles off the barstool. "I'll be right back."

This time there is nothing but the burning, no release, not even a trickle. She waits until the burning passes, contemplating the names and dates scratched on the door in front of her. Women don't make drawings like men do. They sign their own names with loops and curlicues and hearts that dot the *i*'s.

The door opens inward and a white woman says, "Sorry, oh shit," and closes it again. In that second, she can see Harold at the pay phone, his back turned to her. She reopens the door just a crack.

"I said she's here. Up in Blunt." The ceiling fan is bent and the loud clicking noise muffles his voice so she can only hear broken phrases. ". . . hasn't got out of my sight . . . on a postcard, yeah . . . tell him I'll keep her here until he comes."

That fucking jackalope turned me in.

When Delores steps out of the Ladies', she can't find a back way out of the bar. In her purse, she has nothing like a weapon unless she could stab him with her pen. She can't count on the men in the bar to protect her.

The Indian with the sunglasses is sitting in her spot when she returns. He gets up to give her the stool. "This is Dennis," Harold says, one hand clapped on the man's shoulder. "He says on the face of it he's been drunk for a week."

"Why's that?"

"Ask him."

But she doesn't want to know. "I'm leaving now," she announces. "I'm done drinking."

"Because of the sickness," Dennis says as she goes out the door. Which sickness goes unspecified because no one is listening to him.

Harold grabs her arm above the elbow and pulls her close. Then he takes her hand and presses it to his pocket. "Feel this?"

She nods, feeling the gun hidden inside his shirt.

"Right," he says.

She looks around wildly for Kissel but sees only the Indian with the sunglasses and a few white people she doesn't know. The bartender is bent to the sink, rinsing beer glasses, and doesn't look up until Harold has already pushed her into the back room with the pool table. He points to a chair in the corner. "Sit still and don't talk. We're gonna be here a while."

She watches for movement in the bar, anyone coming in the door. But it's still early, just past eight-thirty, and the bar is seldom crowded until after ten.

She can feel her heartbeat for a full hour, each beat drumlike, rough wood on leather. Harold knocks down stripes and solids, muttering to himself.

"Who's coming for me?" she asks.

"The trick is, don't use the side pockets. They're smaller than the others. I figured that out."

"Is it the goons, Harold? Or did you sell out to the marshals?"

She gets up from the chair and stands over the jukebox where she reads the names of songs and singers, most of it country western or rockabilly. She reaches into the pockets of her oversized jeans but can't come up with a quarter.

A cool wind blows inwards. The door is open and no one is there to close it. Delores feels a chill at the back of her neck and she turns, prepared for anything—marshals, goons, the FBI.

It is Tyrone. At first she mistakes the gun in his hand for an auto part or a heavy tool, the way he holds it with both hands. His eyes move slowly around the room and lock into hers for a long moment and it is like looking at the wolf from the ghost house. She holds her hands flat against her belly, one over the other. Then Tyrone turns his eyes to Bad Hand. He's only a few feet away and shifting to her, moving back until his shoulder bumps her. He is trying to hide behind her, but she has pinned herself against the wall. "Move away," Tyrone says, but Harold reaches under his shirt for the pistol. Tyrone's first shot splits the plaster wall and the second, aimed lower, catches him in the chest. A third bursts into his stomach and he falls backward and then sideways to the floor. Delores watches him fall and then looks up at Tyrone who is staring at her, his pistol still upraised. He opens his mouth to speak, but no words come.

When she looks down, her hands are wet with blood. She lifts her palms to her eyes and finds that there are holes in each of them. The bullet has passed through Bad Hand, through her hands into her womb. Into SheHe.

And the bullet lodges in a cavity of the child's soft chest, as into wet wood, next to his beating heart.

PART ONE

The Bones War

Noah Lame

The summer they found the bones, I was living on the northern edge of Choteau, too close to the highway, in a four-room house with electricity but no plumbing with my wife June, son Herman, and daughter Jana. I was forty-seven years old and for two years I'd been out of work, so I was planning on applying to the reservation council for a job over in Ree where they were said to be looking for certified schoolteachers. I'd been gone from Choteau for close to twenty-five years, living in various places in Iowa and Illinois. It took me seven years instead of four to get my degree at the University of Illinois in Champagne. Some Indians tend to describe the reservations as concentration camps. My mother thought of them as earthly chambers of purgatory. She sold everything she owned to pay for my first year of college and I felt like I had to continue to the end to make sense of her gesture. So for six years I worked part-time jobs to get my way through. And for all that effort, I was a history teacher for one full year in a Chicago high school. That year was the basis of a long-lived lie. The rest of my years away from Choteau, except for the occasional substitute teaching, I worked construction or cleaned toilets, hauled trash, drove a taxi. The year Herman was born, I had a temporary job helping out in a county welfare office. When they say temporary, you get your work in twelve-week shifts at a minimum wage with no benefits at all. Twelve weeks on and twelve weeks off.

The last place we lived before coming back to Choteau was Des Moines, and it was there that June's drinking went from bad to worse. She started having black spells and the doctor said she had a liver that was shrinking up in its juices and I should get her into the AA right away or she'd die. She lasted less than a month at that and came out worse than before, as if she had to drink extra hard to get the taste of healing off her lips. I'd hoped that bringing her home would be the remedy and for a time it was. But going home only cures homesickness and in Choteau there were plenty of people to drink with. There's nothing like the res for the sight of drunks. The day we drove back into town we saw some dirty clothes lying on the street. When we drove closer we saw there was a body inside those clothes. We got out to see what was the matter and saw that the girl was dead drunk. She was eleven years old.

You think you've seen trash and then you see a Sioux Indian reservation. Tar-paper shacks, scrapped cars, mounds of tires and rusted appliances. Garbage higher than August weeds. That was Choteau in 1972. Stray dogs and swooping crows loved the place. I wasn't convinced I'd made the right decision.

I didn't have the courage to tell everyone how I'd failed in the white world. Instead I made it sound as if I was a schoolteacher the whole time I was gone. The shame of it is that even my best friends believed me. So in the spring of 1972, to make the lie true again, and to find a way to make ends meet, I applied for that teaching job. In the meantime, I was drawing welfare checks and getting by with odd jobs and wishing I could trade half of what I knew about American History to understand the rudiments of roof repair and in-door plumbing.

The Clay Creek Reservation barely even makes the maps, that's how small it's become over the course of ninety-five years. It once stretched seventy miles east to west and twenty miles north to south. When I was a child, the western boundary stretched all the way to Wilma, but that boundary has been nudged and scraped a full six miles east. By 1972 we were cramped between the Missouri River to the south, Wilma and Blue Eye Creek and the redrawn Wilma County line to the west, Highway 50 to the north and another county line to the east. Five miles north to south and thirty east to west. Ree, where the tribal council and BIA hang their hats, is at the other end of the res, twenty-six miles east. Choteau sits on the northwest corner. The way my house is situated, I can walk a hundred paces either north or west from my front porch and find myself on the other side.

In late April of 1972, the Wilma people started to break ground for the golf course. Gaetan Averill, Albert Roebuck, Jack LeHavre, and Stuart Baumgartner over in Wilma had got up the bank money and sufficient membership and already had a pool and bar and clubhouse. They bought out the Reeves and Almondinger farms but were still short on space, so Gaetan Averill sold off some of his land west of Blue Eye Creek. That put the site of their country club right up against the western boundary of the reservation and there was even some pressure on the council over in Ree to sell off more land so the Wilma folks could have a bigger golf course. They hired the contractors to plow down the fields into dust. They said the place would be called Eagle Reach and we couldn't figure out why since all the eagles were gone, ever since they dammed the river up past Wilma where the Missouri River swings north and cuts the state in half.

Some of the workers were Indians from the area, Russ Poor Bull and my son Herman among them. Herman needed living money to go with what the state would give him for tuition at the University of South Dakota and he was signed up as a bulldozer operator at five dollars an hour, which was great money in those days. Building a golf course is a big project and the land had to be leveled here and banked up high there, new trees planted, old trees cut down, the earth moved every which way. So it figured that Herman would have a full spring and summer of work, forty or maybe fifty hours a week.

One morning in May, only a few weeks after they'd started the digging, Herman hit into something solid with the blade of his bulldozer. When he stopped to check it out he found that he'd uncovered the tip of a gravestone. He called the foreman over and the foreman called Albert Roebuck. The stone was old, older than anybody knew right away, and it had only been buried about three feet under the soil. Roebuck was riled about the lost time this involved, but he called up a company in Sioux Falls and told these people they should move the grave. So in came some gravediggers to get to work on it and right next to that first grave they found another one.

The construction crew huddled up and decided to just carry on. If the gravedigging went on much longer they'd be late on their work schedule and they decided to keep plowing and hush it all up. The Indian workers weren't a part of this decision. They were moved off to another section on the site where they couldn't get their long noses into the business. They didn't know just why at first, but soon enough the truth came out.

When those first two graves were dug up and moved, the white workers started the bulldozers, but right away they ran into more tombstones and then everything ground to a halt all over again. Some professor from Yankton College was called in to take a look at things, and after pawing through the dirt a bit he came up with some beads and some brass finger rings and then he declared that one of the skeletons therein belonged to a young Indian girl. When he looked around some more, he figured that there were whites buried there as well.

State officials were invited to look over the site and they counted sixteen graves from about a hundred and ten years back. Only the one grave had beads and brass finger rings in it and they concluded that the other fifteen of those graves were filled with white people. As the digging continued, they found some of the bodies were just seven or eight inches under the ground.

Albert Roebuck had his construction company stopped cold, but the non-Indians were union boys and had to be paid whether they worked or not. Gaetan Averill and Stuart Baumgartner were doing the bank work and Baumgartner was asking all of a sudden for a guarantee bond in case the whole project was called off. There was a deal cut, it turned it, with Jimmy DeWare and the country club people that meant a bonus if the course was ready by the spring of 1973. Herman overheard the foreman suggest to Al Roebuck the possibility of just digging around the gravesite and Roebuck said, "Who ever heard of a graveyard hazard in the middle of a danged fairway?"

The South Dakota Archaeological Society wanted to dig up the place for artifacts. That was the year a lot of people in Choteau learned that white bones are sacred and Indian bones are artifacts. The county hired specialists to rebury the bones of those fifteen white people up north of Wilma with marble tombstones donated by the Jaycees and the Kiwanis Club. But that left the Indian girl's bones. Herman went to see Al Roebuck to make the case that this girl should be given a proper burial just like the whites, and Roebuck said it was too late, the state people had already cleared it with him to take possession of the bones and all the rest.

Mention that these bones would be hauled away as artifacts led to the first meeting we had in Choteau, at Toby's bar. There were plenty of other meeting places around, since Indians love to hold meetings. In the back room of Clarence Kills First's hardware-houseware store were a table and chairs where card games were sometimes played. There was the abandoned laundromat, a building that my mother had sold off to send me to a year of college, but the place smelled of mildew and was a haven for spiders. There was my house or Poor Bull's or any of the others', but they were all pretty short on elbow space. There was a proper meeting hall at the Church of the Redeemer if you didn't mind being surrounded by posters and signs telling you what a vile piece of business you were without Jesus Christ in your life.

So we ended up at Toby's the way birds end up in trees at sundown. It was our "short straw," the only place in town to get a beer, and in those days not many meetings were on the dry side. Toby's was a counter grill where you could get a soyburger or a chili dog and potato chips. Liquor sales are banned on the reservation and you aren't even allowed by law to buy alcohol outside and then bring it back in. If you're an Indian and want to stay legal, you have to drink your liquor in Wilma and *then* drive home. You can imagine Saturday nights on the highway from Wilma to Choteau. And with all those accidents, we get one hell of a reputation, partly deserved, as wicked boozers and lousy drivers. Toby's served hamburgers and soup and sometimes chislie, barbecued rabbit. The fact that he also sold beer kept lots of people off the roads and, since he didn't deal whisky, the state people left him alone.

The Crazy Horse Council must have met five hundred times in the next three years. Crazy Horse had been Oglala Sioux as were most of the people in Choteau, pure-blood or mixed-blood, though Pete Scully is a Burned Thigh, or Sicangu, and Toby Mad Bear Johnson is a Yankton. We still meet to this day, and the subject has never changed. The subject is how to resist becoming an artifact when you know you're a man.

Frank Poor Bull and some others were hot about the whole business, especially when the state boys came in and hauled the bones up to Pierre. There were about a dozen of us in the group, including John Fire Smith, Darryl Kills First, Pete Scully, and a white guy who'd moved into a place that used to belong to Gaetan Averill Jr. and had taken to hanging around with the Indians. The Averills were one of the richest families in the county, with thousands of acres that once were part of the Clay Creek Reservation. I knew Gaetan Jr. when I was a boy. We're about the same age, and while I was off living like a white, he'd changed his last name from Averill to Avril. He's the one who gave the farmhouse and land to this white guy, though none of us understood why.

The American Indian Movement was getting up some serious steam about then and we heard from one of their people that this gravedigging was also going on in New York, Oregon, Utah, and New Mexico. Sitting in Toby's night after night, we had plenty of arguments about whether or not to throw in with these AIM people who wanted to make a big protest at the state capitol in Pierre. The leaders had come down from Minneapolis and most of them were breeds, mixed, and we didn't know much about them except that they spent a lot of time in jail. The Bureau of Indian Affairs figured AIM as competition, so there was a lot of bad feeling going around. The reservation authorities over in Ree made it clear that anyone associated with AIM would be barred from government work on the reservation. And since eighty percent of all reservation work is government funded and supervised through Ree, that news had a real chill to it for some of us.

At the time, I wasn't interested in joining city Indians in any protests. I concentrated on the fate of those bones and after a number of phone calls and some sketchy reports from Indians in Pierre, we figured out that the bones and the beads and brass finger rings were destined for a new museum out by the Black Hills. That galled us, every one of us. We had another meeting and that was the night Frank Poor Bull showed me a loaded rifle.

"Who do you plan on shooting?" I asked him.

"The first white sonofabitch with a shovel who crosses my path."

Pete Scully came in with his boy, Gerald, who was fidgety as anything and seemed like he was not of this earth. He was pretty windy-headed and couldn't learn anything at school. We sat Gerald at the counter, and Toby gave him a few crackers to ponder and chew while Pete joined us at the table.

"Only reason I'm here," he said, "is I feel like shit and wanted to share it with all of you."

He had grown up in Choteau, like me, and was getting too old for battle. I couldn't bear the look on his face that night. Pete was always the go-get-em type. Even lately he was after us to all play baseball, though we already had creaky knees and bad eyesight. Just takes four, he'd say. One at bat, and three in the field. Pitcher, right side and left side. No mention of a catcher. If the batter missed the pitch, or worse, hit a foul ball, he was supposed to go after it as penance. Pete grew up in every other way. But he never forgot those games we had as kids when four was the least number we'd have. Usually five or six to a side and the team at bat supplied the catcher, so stealing bases wasn't allowed. Leonard Rocking Boy, Pete Scully, Frank Poor Bull, Clarence Kills First, and myself. When we were healthy reservation boys instead of worn-out reservation men.

While I was off at college, Pete went into rodeo work and did all right, traveling to Wyoming, Texas, New Mexico, Saskatchewan, Colorado, all around the west. Then he fell from a horse while calf-roping, broke a hip that wouldn't mend all the way, and came home with some disability money to a wife who was drunk nonstop and a ranch that he couldn't make go. His wife died young, leaving him with Gerald. Time passed the way it always does, like sandpaper. By the time I got back to Choteau, he'd settled into government checks and his pipe and his memories.

"This country club business is stealing my sleep," he said. "My people come from right near here and I keep getting this dream, like the bones they found are my grandmother's."

Gerald jumped down from his stool and came to sit on Pete's lap. Twelve years old and he shifted from one of Pete's knees to the other. Then he stood up and ran outside where we could see him chasing Toby's Labrador up and down the parking lot.

Pete turned to me. "You been to white schools, Noah. You got your degree. Whyn't you go up to Pierre and talk to these crazy people?"

Gene Fast Horse snorted. "Talk to them? I say we burn down Roebuck's house!"

Darryl Kills First and Frank Poor Bull thought that was a great idea.

All evening long, Clarence Kills First hadn't said a word. Now he erupted. "Bullshit! What's the matter with all of you?"

"We're trying to defend ourselves, Clarence."

"With guns and fire? All you're gonna do is get people killed."

Toby brought along a pitcher of lemonade. "This is real whirlwind talk if I ever heard it," he said.

Pete was still looking at me. "I'm waiting for an answer, Noah."

"What can I do? At the university I learned a little French and got a degree in American History. You think it'll cut any ice with the attorney general if I recite the Bill of Rights in perfect French?"

John Fire Smith cracked a beer and said, "Well, Noah. Look at it this way. You could talk to them in their own terms, show them some dignity. They might feel shamed enough to give us the bones."

Next thing I knew we had an argument, a perfect split down two sides. Some of us were for tongue-wagging and others for arson. Clarence railed against the city Indians that were holding so much sway over us. Nobody listened to him, so he stomped out of Toby's. Like half the people on our little res, he sympathized with the cause but not with the use of guns or fists. He never joined us again.

When he was gone, Toby suggested we put it to a vote. Without Clarence, we found ourselves in a four-four tie and went right back to arguing.

Around midnight, Toby threw a towel on the table. "Wipe up the spills, boys. Time to clear out."

Darryl Kills First laughed. "Hell, Toby. You never close up till we all just crawl out on our own."

"We keep saying the same things over and over," Toby answered. "The words are all used up. I think we ought to leave this up to Touch the Sky."

There was a moment of silence. Then Frank said, "It's getting real late and we aren't drunk enough."

Darryl Kills First reached across the table for a full can of beer and punched a tiny hole in the bottom with his penknife. "Try this." Holding his finger over the hole, he shook the can awhile then lifted it to his mouth, wrapping his lips over the hole. With his free hand, he popped the top and the beer shot out that hole like from a hose, straight down his throat. He set down the empty can and smiled at all of us.

"Beer shoot," he said. "Fast drunk."

Everyone but Toby had two or three beers in the same fashion and then we all stumbled outside.

"We'll take Pete's pickup," Toby said. "It's got the worst shocks on the res. And I'm driving, so one from the other team has got to ride along to make things even."

Frank was the drunkest, so Gene said he should be the one to sit. Frank took a long look at the pickup and just nodded. Then the rest of us piled into the truck and left the back gate down.

Toby got behind the wheel. "No holding the sides and no grabbing on to each other!"

So it was John Fire, Pete, and me against Darryl, Gene, and Frank's boy, Russ. We all stood up in the back of the pickup and crowded toward the middle.

"I don't even want to go to Pierre," I said to John Fire.

"I'll ride along with you, Noah. But first we got to make these warriors here touch the sky."

Toby pulled away and drove east. We all knew he was headed for the old river road. When we got there, he turned south. "We're off!"

The road flooded every spring, and when we hit the first deep rut the pickup jounced and I was the only one to fall. I scrambled to my feet and John Fire shouted at me to bend my knees. I shouted back that I knew how to play the game and just then we came to a series of ripples that shook my teeth. We hit one hole after another, right and left, and the six of us were bouncing around like loose change. Pete kept shuffling his feet and held the middle and after another hundred yards, Fast Horse slid backwards and then, as Toby drove over a high mound, he flew from the truck and landed on hard dirt. I didn't have time to laugh before I felt myself take flight, my head suddenly rising above a tree branch. I landed hard on a patch of weeds, scraping flesh from my elbow, and thought right away of June's face when she saw the torn shirt. But I didn't hurt anywhere— that was the point of getting drunk first, it makes you loose. Fast Horse caught up with me and we hurried up the road and then saw that Toby had circled around and was coming our way. We moved off to the side of the road just in time to see John Fire take to the air. Russ Poor Bull went right after him and that left Kills First and Pete. Toby turned the truck around one more time and the two of them stood side by side in the middle. Toby sped down the road and when he hit a tree root, Kills First was thrown like a sack of corn. Toby hit the brakes and Pete jumped from the truck with a whoop of triumph and came straight to me.

"Rodeo man," I said.

"Shit, Noah . . ." He spit blood and his smile showed a bloody broken tooth. "It wasn't hardly the Calgary Stampede."

I wore a blue suit with a vest that everyone chipped in for and I looked like one of those wooden mannequins in a Woolworth's window except for this wrinkled Oglala face. I'd seen a thousand pictures of Indians dressed up to go to Washington to see the White Father, but I failed to see that I looked just as silly and would have done better to wear jeans and boots and a beaded shirt. Before leaving, I looked at myself in the mirror with my shirt buttoned to the top and the green tie with the knot in a perfect triangle. My daughter Jana said I looked like a white lawyer and I shooed her away, but then June got up from her sickbed and packed some bread and biscuits and canned food into a brown sack. Then she folded her arms around my waist. She was a short woman and I was a tall man. She looked up at me like to the ceiling and said, "Be proud to be the son of Jim Lame." Which meant I was to show them that I wasn't a firewater Injun straight off the reservation.

I felt this was what my learning had prepared me for, to face down white men and beat them at their own game. I was vain in those days. And this was the journey that turned my head around and beat humility into me, a raw kind of humility that was sobering and useful and has remained intact to this day.

John Fire Smith drove us through a blinding rain. I didn't know him well until that drive and since that red Rambler of his wouldn't do more than forty-five miles an hour, we had plenty of time to shoot the bull. He was a man with an easy humor punctuated by long stretches of silence. And although time passing has given him the image of having been a leader, I never thought of him in those terms. He was too much of a loner and a brooder. When we made that drive, he wasn't yet thirty, there was a look on his face, something in the eyes, that made him look older, and he had long ago grown his hair long. Sometimes he wore a pair of braids, sometimes just one, and at other times he let his hair flow free from beneath a baseball cap with a B on it. Not everyone recognized what the B stood for and he told us Brooklyn, where a baseball tribe had gone extinct. That was the kind of humor he showed me through the few years I knew him well. He had a weakness for irony and jokes that he could turn back on himself. All the same, if I'd never asked him anything during that drive, I'm convinced he wouldn't have said a word. Once, before the shootings happened, he told me that he suspected that talk itself was life-sapping, that each word of English he spoke was weakening. Maybe that was why he said so little during the trials. I don't know for sure and would like to ask him, but I haven't been alone with him since they captured him up in Washington State.

But I was nervous as hell and ended up talking more than usual. Maybe it was my chatter that loosened him up, or maybe it was that boring drive. The terrain you see along I-90 at forty-five miles an hour is relaxing but monotonous. Once the rain let up, we were surrounded by cornfields and power lines and all these billboards for Wind Cave, Mount Rushmore, and the antique car exhibit in Murdo. The sight of those perfect green corn rows either drives you deep into your own heart or outward to another human being. By the time we got west of Chamberlain he even began to say a few words about himself.

He's from up north originally, from the Turtle Mountain band in North Dakota. His mother was Ojibwa and his father an Oglala who fought in France and died there when John Fire was just born. When he was three he went to live in Montana with his grandmother and she's the one who raised him until he was fifteen. A lot of Indian families still followed that tradition of grandparents, *unci* and *tunkasila*, doing the child rearing, so it was nothing unusual. John Fire spoke Ojibwa then and hadn't learned Lakota yet. He'd worked potato farms and ranches, mostly, and had shown up in Wilma to look for construction work. I asked him if he'd ever poured asphalt, and he said no but he could learn. We all knew that he was wanted in Montana and had taken to using various made-up names. We never questioned his story, that he was driving a car one night through Butte with two Crows who told him to pull over at a pharmacy. While he sat in the car, they robbed the place, taking mostly pills and anything that contained alcohol, and a pile of petty cash. When they came running outside he knew what they'd done and began driving at high speed in the direction of the northern border. He never made it. All three of them were arrested and the Crows told the authorities that John Fire had put them up to it. He took one look at his lawyer and decided then and there he wasn't going to get a fair shake, so he jumped bail and headed to Canada. That was about a year before he drifted south again and landed in Choteau. His story became all the more credible to me when I saw how his car-driving left a lot to be desired. He gripped the wheel until his knuckles were white and had a hard time aiming the car on even the flattest Dakota stretches. It was only later, when he was on the run, that he finally learned to manage a wheel.

What I remember most about that day was John Fire telling me about seeing his first sun dance. All these other things he may not have even told me about. They're all known facts now that he's famous, and I might be skipping around in my memory. Anyway, when he was about thirteen, he said, they were having a sun dance on Turtle Mountain. He and the other kids had heard about them before, but the sun dance was outlawed and so of course there weren't any road signs showing the way to the tipis. He and a friend sneaked out of town and crept up on the camp where the dance was being done. The way he told it, you could tell it was like the first time he saw magic or felt love. He described how the men stood straight and kept their eyes opened wide when the knives pierced the skin and the eagle claws were passed through the wounds and attached to rawhide thongs dangling from a pole. As he told me this his eyes were fixed straight ahead, not at the road, but beyond the road.

Then he went silent again until we were at the town limits of Pierre, the state capital.

I stepped out of John Fire's car and there was a face right next to my own, an Indian asking if I wanted directions out of town.

"No thanks," I answered. "I was aiming to go into the statehouse."

There were maybe twenty people in a circle around the two of us, and I had my first inkling that something wasn't right. The Indian threatening me was named Jerry Lonetree, I found out later, and it would not be the last time we ran into him.

My bag got knocked out of my hands and I was bending to pick it up when Lonetree raised his arm up high over my head. He was holding an empty bottle and was ready to skull me with it, but John Fire jumped him from behind and wrestled him to the sidewalk. After that there was mayhem, news people and police running up and down the street, sirens going off. I was knocked to the pavement, and when I got up someone knocked me down again. Then a white woman in a blue dress took me by the elbow and led me up the steps into the statehouse. A trooper at the door tried to stop us, and she told him off until he let us pass. Once we were inside she looked at me and said, "Are you wounded?" I said I was not. "This is as far as I can take you," she said. "I'm only a secretary." Then she just disappeared but I have never forgotten her face. During the worst years, I would sometimes see her face when I was in the sweat lodge doing my damnedest not to hate the face of whites. "Are you wounded?" she asked me, and I had no way to give her a clear answer.

John Fire saved my life that day and I have to wonder how many times since then he's done the same thing for me and many others. And him half Turtle Band Chippewa, an old enemy of the Oglala. He figured that was a part of his destiny, his being two halves of ancient enemies.

I got nowhere with those people at the statehouse. They said I had no jurisdiction or authority, that I didn't know the law. We went from office to office and the conversations were all the same. I wasn't even on the tribal council. The bones belonged to the state and were part of South Dakota heritage, and no out-of-work schoolteacher could change that. One well-meaning young man told us he was trying to save our culture, not destroy it. John Fire asked if we could put his grandmother's bones in the same glass display case, and I saw a flash of hatred in his eyes.

The third night there, John Fire and I ran out of money. We ate the last of the biscuits and soup June had packed for us, ate the soup straight uncooked from the can, and slept in the car and the next day my blue suit was a mass of wrinkles. We asked to see the governor and were told he was out of town. We said we would wait and we waited ten days without ever seeing his face. In the daytime we hung around the statehouse lobby and waited for various people to agree to see us. We were a nuisance and knew it, but through those ten days John Fire was calm while I was losing my temper every five minutes. It was my pride that was wounded. I had lived the white life according to the white rules and those ten humiliating days took that pride and wrinkled it worse than my damn suit.

But we didn't starve. After our fourth day of getting nowhere, we walked out of the statehouse and a fifteen-year-old boy was sitting on the hood of John Fire's car. He said his father was waiting for us. John Fire drove and the boy gave him directions to the edge of town, through rough dirt streets to a ramshackle house no better than my own. We were met at the door by a man in a beaded shirt that was open at the collar. The marks of his piercing were white in the light of the new moon.

His name was Kevin Walking Horse, he said. Join us.

So we spent our days waiting for the governor and our nights at the Walking Horse home where the pipes were passed. I did not join in, too embarrassed to give it a try, though John Fire passed the pipes and joined in the singing, adding his Ojibwa voice to the Oglala and Sicangu and Hunkpapa voices that surrounded us. The singing seemed to last until dawn. They were blessing the bones of that unnamed Indian girl into the arms of the Unknowable Great.

Kevin and Anna Walking Horse did all they could to make us feel at home. Anna was thirty years old and already had five children. She's the one who did all the reading. The tiny house was cram-med with books, mostly history and sociology, though I noticed that each evening before the singing she would sit down in the kitchen with mimeographed sheets of Lakota phrases spread before her. She was learning by correspondence with a Black Hills woman the language that her grandfather had spoken but no one else in her family. I sometimes joined her and struggled through the phonetic interpretations. I felt foolish at first and Anna smiled at my poor attempts. *Wikoni kini*, come to life. She repeated the word to me. Wi-koni ki-ni. And when I said it to her satisfaction, she moved on to a new word. After three evenings, I knew twenty words and the vowels no longer lost themselves in the tunnels of my throat and heart.

I was like a newborn. I knew the names of the presidents, dates of Civil War battles, and countless details about the Louisiana Purchase. I knew nothing that would put air into my lungs and turn me into an instrument. So I spent those evenings sitting against the wall and watching. I learned many things through the long years of learning agriculture and history and driving taxicabs and cleaning toilets, but mostly I learned that I had become an orphan, severed from my people. Kevin Walking Horse sensed what I was feeling and he offered me a strange gift: the skin of a drum. It was nothing but a blackened sheaf of hide with rough edges. I said I didn't understand.

"Strike this skin," Walking Horse said, "and it won't make a sound. It has to be stretched."

After the tenth day, John Fire told me we could stay to the end of the year without seeing the governor and that the girl's bones were still headed for the museum. "Besides," he added, "this suit's beginning to smell like roadkill."

That night we said goodbye to the Walking Horse family and started back south. After we'd only gone a few miles, I told him to stop the car. I got out by the side of the road, took off that blue jacket and the matching vest and pants and threw everything into a gully. Then John Fire unbuttoned his shirt and gave it to me so I wouldn't have to ride home in just my drawers.

I felt the last of my pride running down the gutter. When we were twenty miles from Choteau, John Fire stopped the car and flicked on the light so he could roll one of those homemade cigarettes he smoked back then. He had to roll his own, he said, because the chemicals in store-bought cigarettes had an additive that he was allergic to. Once he lit up, I thought we'd be heading out again, but John Fire said, "Got a Indian joke for you, Noah."

"Shoot."

"How many Indians," he asked, "does it take to change a light bulb?"

"I don't know."

"Sixteen," he told me. Then he took a drag off that cigarette and blew white smoke out the window. "One to rob the gas station for the money to buy the light bulb. One to spend the stolen money on liquor. One to beat up the guy who spent the stolen money on liquor. And one to drive the beat-up guy to the hospital."

"That's only four," I said.

"Yeah, but the other twelve are in jail."

"What about the light bulb?" I asked him.

Smoke surrounded John Fire's face and he shook his head and smiled. "What light bulb?"

Back in Choteau, I understood the joke. Poor Bull was still carrying his loaded gun. He wanted to shoot Albert Roebuck or maybe even the attorney general, and though I talked his ear off it was John Fire who finally convinced him to put the gun away. An AIM organizer named Willard Bent passed through town on his way to Denver and gave a talk about how tribes from around the nation were becoming unified. Communication between the reservations hadn't ever been much to speak of but nowadays there were newsletters and guide-books on Indian rights getting passed around and he told us the South Dakota office of the American Indian Movement would be pleased to have our support, an offer that split us in two. Though I was still burning from my humiliation at the state capitol, I sat on the fence. Bent said we shouldn't be using the name of Crazy Horse if we didn't intend full-bore resistance, and Frank Poor Bull told him we could call ourselves whatever we wanted and no city Indian was going to tell us otherwise. He was talking brave that night but before the meeting was through he was so drunk we had to carry him to his car and get Pete Scully to drive him home.

After a couple of days, Willard Bent drove west and left us to arguing at Toby's place. Sixteen Indians unable to change a light bulb. And we still had this strange white man among us. He didn't say much and I noticed that he hung back one day when we all went off to the sweat lodge. He was a soldier, that's what Pete Scully told me, and had been all the way to Vietnam and back.

We went to the sweat lodge without him, Frank, John Fire, Pete Scully, Gene Fast Horse, Darryl Kills First, my son Herman, and some man from Ree I didn't know much about. It was new for me, the smoke and the fire and the enormous silence that filled us to the edges of our skin. And even though we came home feeling better, I don't believe any one of us felt clean. We didn't notice that the white guy was gone.

The next morning, Herman came to the side of my bed to tell me he was going west to Pine Ridge to see Brings Yellow, whom we all knew to be a wise man of the old life. By this time, Herman was done with going to university. He was letting his hair grow to Indian length and was eager to tie his braids. Once he saw those bones and the brass finger rings, he gave up any thought of continuing in the white man's schools. I expected my heart to be broken but instead I felt a surge of pride. My days at the capitol had relieved me of the last of my illusions. And it was my son who later taught me all that I had forgotten and more than I'd ever learned at the University of Illinois in Champagne.

. . .

Judy Poor Bull told me. She heard it on the radio and came over to my place in Frank's beat-up car. The bones had been taken straight out from under the noses of those state boys. Nobody knew by whom, but there were long stories in the Sioux Falls *Argus Leader* and the Yankton *Press and Dakotan* the very next day. A white man, they were sure of that, had broken into the statehouse and made it up to the second floor where the bones were boxed and labeled in some locked-up office. One of the night watchmen got a glimpse of him on a back stairway but he was almost out the door by then. One paper said there was a car chase, another said he escaped on foot.

It was about noon when Judy brought the newspapers and by three o'clock most of us were gathered at Toby's to talk it over. We didn't know what to make of this news.

"We should expect a visit from the authorities," John Fire said. "They're not likely to forget Noah and me."

Gene Fast Horse said, "I could get you to Mexico in less than a day."

John Fire shook his head. "That would only make us look guilty, Gene. Anyhow, Noah here's got a family to look after."

"That don't matter," Gene told us. "They'll want some guilty Indians to put in jail before the weekend. You think it matters to them if you did it or not?"

After a few hours, all I could smell was tobacco smoke and alcohol. That was the night I learned the phrase "Saturday night warrior," used to describe Indians who would drink and talk about land swindles and Indian rights and brag about what they were going to do for their people. And what they'd do is get bulletproof, meaning dead drunk, maim each other in bar fights, then drive around dirt roads in pickups shooting at the moon and the stars. I wasn't a Saturday night warrior; I wasn't a warrior at all. I went home early and was in bed with June, staring at that drum skin that I had hanging on my wall and wondering how in hell to stretch it. It was maybe ten o'clock and there was someone knocking on my door. When I went to answer it, there was the white man looking me in the eye.

"Come outside," he said.

I followed him out to his car, a powder-blue Delta 88, the best-looking car on the res. In the backseat were two polished wooden boxes, each about the size of a small TV.

So it was the soldier who stole the bones back for us, while Frank was cleaning his rifle and Gene went out and beat up some white kid in Wilma who had nothing to do with it. To some of us the soldier was a hero, a great warrior, but Gene Fast Horse told me and everybody else at Toby's that the whole thing looked like a setup, and hadn't we ever heard of the FBI?

I didn't know what to think. I'd been to the statehouse myself and seen all the police, and I admit that I had my doubts about a man getting in and out like they say he did. Delores Her Many Horses stood up for him, though. And John Fire Smith did too. Which, when you look at the long face of things, was something you'd remember, since Delores had gone straight from him to the want-to-be. It was that day I fell in with John Fire Smith and heard the first sounds of that drumbeat, when I saw him defend a man who'd just won his woman away from his bed.

It wasn't the beginning of our troubles. The Lakota of my century were born with those troubles and will die with them. But Frank Poor Bull is right about it being the beginning of the new wars. There was only craziness that followed the finding of those graves. Craziness, murder, and Indians killing Indians. Just what happens when you bother the resting places of others.

I steered clear of Wilma from that time on and stuck close to Choteau. While waiting for word about that job in Ree, I was teaching local kids how to read English and their families paid me with chickens or tobacco or firewood, and sometimes with money. I still had my relief checks and we all survived, though no one was getting fat. I kept writing letters to Leonard Rocking Boy who was supposed to be my reference, but I didn't hear a thing from Ree. John Fire and Gene Fast Horse and the white man said they were thinking of joining up with AIM. Pete Scully drove up to Minneapolis to see about what they called an Indian survival school. June went to a no-more-drinking meeting in Wilma and said it wasn't as bad this time since it was mostly other Indians. I didn't want to get my hopes up, but when she went a second time I began to hold my breath.

The old burial place that caused so much trouble and grief is said to be a tee box on the golf course for a fourteenth hole. I don't know the game and don't catch the significance.

When we felt it was safe, we all gathered at the spot where Blue Eye Creek runs into the Missouri. Myself with June and Herman and Jana. Frank and Judy Poor Bull and their son Russ. Darryl Kills First, John Fire Smith, Pete Scully, Gene Fast Horse, Delores Her Many Horses, and the want-to-be whose name was Tyrone. We made a fire from willow wood and lit a high fire near where we buried the girl. When the fire had died down, we scattered the ashes across the ground by the river, down at the far edge where the golf course ended and the reservation began.

Helene Her Many Horses

When Myrene Tall Bull moved out of her trailer and into one of those abandoned east-side council houses, Helene was the only one left in a trailer court that had been jam-packed after the Korean War. That way she lived alone, separate from Choteau even if she was still within the town limits. There were nine other trailers, but only two were habitable. Indians hate glass, she'd always wondered why. The closest neighbors were the Poor Bulls, two hundred yards across a weedy field and a stand of elms, but Helene wasn't the type to socialize. She didn't rub elbows with Judy Poor Bull or Olive Kills First or June Lame. Judy thought she was snotty because she wore short skirts and makeup instead of tattered jeans and long-sleeved shirts. With June there was a grudge that went back to high school when Helene lost a game of strip poker on purpose. And with Noah, June's husband, there was a thistle, a cut, a sharp bone.

The other Choteau men said hello when they passed her on the road, and sometimes said more. She still had her figure at forty-eight, and that galled the women, so the most they'd do was nod or wave fingers. Except for June Lame, who always looked right at some spot above her head.

They went way back, June and Helene, from childhood playmates to adolescent sisters to adult rivals. After twenty-odd years, when June came back to Choteau with her two children almost grown and her good looks lost to whisky, Helene felt tugs of pity and sparks of wicked pleasure at the same time.

Judy had a house, Noah, no money, and alcohol poisoning. Helene had her television and the rosebushes and tomato plants out back, her daughter Delores, and a thousand dollars gaining interest in the bank since way back when Reynold died. Reynold was a veteran even if he never got closer to Japan than California. Between the BIA and the VA and all the jobs she'd taken on through the years, Helene had done better than anyone in Choteau at hanging on to her money. She'd had the trailer for close to twenty years. There was no land attached; that's the bottom line when it comes to trailers. But when those Wilma people sold the title to the trailer court to Toby Johnson, he said she could stay rent free.

There were plenty of empty houses in Choteau, mostly to the east, and Poor Bull once asked her why didn't she get out of that trailer and move across the road. She pointed out the clean blue carpet in her living room and the fresh rose wallpaper over the panels in her bedroom. She made him look at how the morning sun filled up her yellow kitchen and the way the tap water flowed easily and didn't leave rust in her white sink. She was close to the water main and knew that none of those empty houses had plumbing you could count on. The older people in Choteau lived west of the main road, in houses scattered around by time and circumstance. The houses to the east were government-built in the forties and fifties, arranged in perfect rows with the front doors facing the road and trees in all the wrong places and every damned one of them looked the same.

Helene never imagined herself in houses that made the pictures in magazines. She dressed herself nicely but ate and slept and dreamt alone, and had no need of more living space. She was queen of the trailer court and had her privacy, except for now and then when a hunter rented out the trailer close by and tried to look in her windows.

Delores didn't share her distaste for the Eastside and moved into one of those empty houses with John Fire Smith. John Fire was good with his hands and, three months later, Delores invited Helene over to admire the stone fireplace and the pine cabinets. Helene nodded her head and wrinkled her lips into approving smiles and didn't point out there wasn't a single butterfinger of sunlight coming through the front windows or that smoke and grease from the stove would blow straight into the living room if they didn't fix a ventilator to the wall, or that the tiny bedroom was on the north side and would take the brunt of the winter cold. Instead she said, "That bed looks hard, but I suppose you two will do whatever it takes to soften it up."

Helene had thought of Willard Tree as marrying material or even

Colin Yellow Bird, who never came around Choteau after Delores spurned him. John Fire was a good enough man, polite to everyone, and didn't drink like so many of the other men. But he was a warrior, an agitator, and would surely be in prison or have his head busted in by the authorities before too long. But she didn't talk about that with Delores that day. When they sat down to coffee, they had subjects on the table between them that they had to cover with their elbows. Instead Helene asked Delores what he was like in bed and Delores gave her a look that said *Please*.

"Go on," Helene insisted. "You told me about Willard Tree and that white kid up in the Twin Cities."

"John Fire's different," Delores said.

"How different?"

"Well," she said, taking a deep breath. "He makes me do all the work."

"The seducing?"

Delores smiled. "I wasn't talking about the housework. He thinks loving is building kitchen cabinets. And he won't leave the lights on in the bedroom."

There was worse. Until she started with John Fire, Delores didn't think much about being an Indian, an Oglala. She'd thought about her painting, her books, how to fix her hair, whether to dab perfume behind the ear or between her breasts, or how to scare up the money to go to whatever movie was playing in Wilma. She should have had a brother, or a father who didn't disappear for six long years and then die just after coming home. She spent most of her childhood alone with Helene and had always looked upon men as something more mysterious than they really were. She didn't understand that, compared to women, men are as plain and as seeable as the prairie: all you have to measure in them is their distance.

But with John Fire, Delores had become Indian through and through and for the first time felt the confusion that other Indians had felt their whole lives long. Helene had raised her white, dressed her white, never using the language that her own parents sometimes spoke, and sent her off to the mission school in Ree when the time came. Helene never saw the point in having ancient feathers or drum skins on the wall next to the refrigerator, of hanging on to a past that had been burned to the ground and shoveled over. Once, when Delores was ten, George Brings Yellow had come around wanting to know if Helene was telling her daughter about the old ways. Back then, he was thought of as the crazy man who'd squat in the middle of the prairie for days on end making embarrassing hoots and howls. Helene chased him from the house like she would have chased a brush salesman.

But the day she went to visit Delores in that asphalt-shingled house, they sat in her airless kitchen and drank instant coffee while Delores explained they weren't Sioux and they weren't Lakota. They were *Ikce Wicasa*, she said, the natural humans. "Free and wild," Delores said. "That's what we are. And when we get back the land we lost, we'll be a nation again."

Helene had heard that more often than she'd heard the weather report. Next thing, she imagined, Delores would be ghost-dancing in the altogether, gathering warriors to her side. She thought that if Delores split up with John Fire, she'd forget about the council and the agitation and maybe go back to Minneapolis to her painting classes and settle in with a passable white. It was almost what she wanted for her, a breaking of the branch to start a new tree. At least that was better than getting drunk at Toby's and watching the boys beat each other half to death when the liquor or the money ran out.

Ever since they built that sweat lodge behind the Poor Bull house, she could hear them singing. Their voices were loud enough and the sound carried across the field to her bedroom. She'd lie in her bed at night unable to sleep, but couldn't summon the will to close the window against that song. Though she didn't understand the words, the music was sweet on her ears. Turning down the bed at night, she began to look forward to hearing the first beat of the drum.

The week they discovered the bones at Eagle Reach, Delores dropped by to take her to the river. "Everyone's coming," she said, but Helene knew that it wasn't so. There were close to a hundred people living in Choteau and you could count the ones making a stink about those bones on two hands.

"There's a movie I want to see," she told Delores. "*North by Northwest*, so go on ahead." She didn't mention that she'd seen the movie twice before. It was the only one she knew of with South Dakota in it. Her favorite scene was the one where Cary Grant was all on his lonesome in the middle of the prairie and when the plane came to dust him, he had nowhere to hide. That was a fact of things in those parts. You can't hide in a prairie the way you can in a forest or a city.

There were knots in her that couldn't be undone, knots that had begun to feel as natural as her hands and feet. If Noah hadn't been among them, maybe she could have loosened those knots and in time been invited to the Poor Bull house for Sunday dinner or wandered over to Toby's on a summer evening to have a beer and talk about the weather. But Noah was there and was said to be one of the leaders. So she didn't go to the river to listen to the speeches and the singing. Instead she sat in the living room and turned up the volume, a tribe all to herself, and watched a movie where a white man fell off George Washington's nose, and died.

Delores Her Many Horses

They can whisper all they want, but she isn't an easy lay. She has to feel love in her bones before her flesh can be melted down. And if love comes wholesale, if love comes as easily as taking a breath, where's the harm? Even the homely nun she knew at the mission school said love was the greatest of the virtues. Love and humility. Delores confesses to one but not the other.

By the age of sixteen, she already had a reputation, even though she'd only bedded down with one man. She knew there was something in her face that gave her away. It was plain as day that she wasn't going to pick and choose like some of the girls at the mission school.

Then she moved to Minneapolis to study painting. During her first winter, she met a white guy in a Dinkytown bar. She was easily fueled by impatience and rum with Coke, and felt she needed less than clear blue skies. He took her from the bar to his apartment across the river in St. Paul. It was the dead of January, thirty below outside, a hundred above in the boy's creaky bed. She was too drunk to do anything other than stroke his back with her fingertips. He smelled of hair oil and alcohol while he lapped against her. Once he was finished he turned into a stone and sank to the bottom while she floated upward and out of the bed. Her feet touched the frozen floor and she awoke. The room was littered with paint cans, turpentine rags, balls of paper, bits of junk. She dressed and went to the window to see her face in the frost. *Now I'll have to nitpick my way into heaven. There'll be an asterisk or check mark beside my name.*

After the white painter was Willard Tree. He didn't much care about her, which got her hackles up. So she used her body like a lasso to drag him in. If he'd married her she never would have stayed, and all the while she wondered what the point was but was powerless to stop herself. For a time he hungered for her, struggled with her, and she felt sorry for continuing to lure him to her bed. One night, in a rage, he screamed that he had to breathe or he was going to die, so she backed off. By the time he caught his breath, she was gone.

She lasted two years in Minneapolis before deciding that painting was not for her and neither was the city. Before leaving, she was fitted with a coil and for days she felt its teeth clamp down with every step. "For Christ's sake, Delores," Helene told her, "it's your body, not a gearbox." So she took the pill and felt the waters surge in her bloodstream and saw her face go round as the moon. After that she tried a diaphragm, but the gestures it required infuriated her and she threw it in the trash, knowing she'd be taking risks for the rest of her life. What Helene called going barefoot.

Years passed and, even so, she didn't become pregnant. But Elizabeth Bordeaux was in the family way and had married a Crow and moved to Pierre.

"What about you?" Helene asked. She was seated at the kitchen table, bent over the papers in front of her. With a fine black pen, she filled in the missing crossbars of her typed capital H's.

"What about me?"

"By the time I was your age, you were in the second grade."

Helene is the only Choteau woman who doesn't look older than her age. She manages her face and body the way she manages her money. The Her Many Horses have never been as poor as the others because Helene has never let things slide. But she has had a penchant for the kinds of jobs that are advertised on matchbook covers, like the year she wore herself out stuffing envelopes. Then she saw an ad on TV for a correspondence course in writing greeting cards. She learned cake decoration and was sometimes called in to the Dee-Lite Bakery in Wilma to decorate a cake with sugar roses that no one else could duplicate. But the surest and steadiest money came from taking in typing and she'd forced Delores to learn the same, just in case. She still did all her work, mostly legal documents, on a used Olympia electric with a capital H that didn't cross. She had to go back with a fine black pen and fill in every bar.

"I'm still barefoot," Delores told her. "Maybe I'll have an accident and then what'll you say?"

"There are no accidents," Helene answered, "when it comes to the sex act. Only wishful thinking that we won't admit to later." And she bent and squinted at the page, and crossed another H in the word Heretofore.

Thinking wishfully, she was with John Fire for six ragged months. He came and went, but was upright and always stood his ground. She mistook his early shyness for indifference. She was only his second girl and the first had said goodbye years before. What he liked most was to hold her hand in both of his or to put his face between her breasts and breathe in deeply. He had an easy humor and a way of always turning the joke back on himself. It felt strange to be courted like a young girl. If she asked him for flowers, he gathered dandelions; if she was thirsty, he gave her a kiss. There were all the earmarks of impending marriage and she accepted him as her future. The neighbors approved of him and her reputation lost its taint, like a polluted river refreshed with clean rain. He seldom spoke to her when they were not alone. He was working for the council, or for AIM, or for whatever Indian activist group reared its head. She had a disquieting vision of sewing curtains for a kitchen with lemon yellow walls while John Fire went to jail for whatever crime could be dreamed up.

The longer she stayed with him, the more she felt the color leaving her, as though her leaves and petals were being stripped away one by one. When she showed herself naked to him it was as though she was still clothed. He didn't want much. He was a once-a-week man and even then his loving smacked of consent rather than desire. I'll scratch your back but mine don't itch.

She left him on a midsummer night that began at Toby's, where Gene Fast Horse, Darryl Kills First, Toby Johnson, and Noah Lame played poker for matchsticks. The air in the bar was stale even with

the windows wide open and a fan blowing from a shelf behind the
beer cooler. She sat at the bar with June Lame who was drinking
lemonade and going on about how her son Herman had changed and
now Noah too. "All this nonsense about those bones," she said. "Just
look at him. He used to play cards with a smile on his face." She
looked back at Delores. "If I go back to drinking, do you think I'll
start having fun again?"

Delores was on her fifth rum and Coke, having brought a bottle in
its brown bag. Toby had gotten tired of pouring for her and had just
left a bottle of Coke and a bowl of ice on the counter. The ice was
melted now and when Delores reached into the bowl all she had were
wet fingers.

Now and then June glanced at the bottle but said she wasn't
tempted. "My problem was bourbon. Is, I'm supposed to say because
they say I'll always have the problem, another drop or not."

June had one eye that looked straight at you while the other looked
askance. Delores hadn't noticed this before. It wasn't all that evident
unless you were up close. And her breath was like mint from all the
lemonade.

The poker game went on and on as the winners gave the losers a
shot at breaking even. Delores scratched away at a crossword puzzle
while June adjusted the television over the bar. The men never turned
it on except to watch the livestock, grain, or weather reports. Local
commercials for neomycin, pesticides, farm implements. "Living on
a shoestring," June said.

"What's that?"

"A three-dollar tube would fix this. Look at that. A color set and
Johnny Carson looks as green as those curtains."

Delores needed a five-letter word meaning *indolence*, but didn't
know exactly what that meant. She swiveled her stool and faced the
table. "Do those matchsticks mean anything, or is this just for brag-
ging rights?"

John Fire looked up and winked. "Think of all the fires we can
start."

"I want to go home." He had turned his attention back to the
cards. "I said I want to go home." She poured more rum into her
Coke and drank it down. Sixteen down: *indolence.* Someone, she
can't remember who, once tried to convince her that her name meant

sorrow. Dolor, from the Latin. She'd answered that she spelled it with an *e* and it meant "made from gold," so go fish. Twenty-one across: *inebriated*, five letters. She filled in the letters, stood up and told June she was going outside for some air.

That was all she intended at first, to seek out a breeze and stretch her legs. But as though a rope were tugging at her, she kept moving her feet until she was past the trees and out of sight. She'd walked halfway toward Highway 50 before she finally stopped. She looked up and noticed how the stars had grown long and thin and she knew it was a trick from the drinking. When she squinted, the stars moved up and down.

It was too far to walk the six miles to Wilma, and the bar where she might find some friends, so she stopped in the middle of the road and turned around. But she didn't want to walk home either, not to the house with the cold bedroom and the dark living room, where every time she got out a cookbook and struggled to cook a nice meal for herself and John Fire, the smoke filled the kitchen and burned her eyes. Where the bed stayed cold though her blood was hot. She took a few more steps in the direction of Wilma and stopped short again. Then she decided she'd camp at Helene's. John Fire would know where to find her in the morning. And then she could decide whether she'd go back to him.

She aimed herself in the direction of Choteau and had gone less than half a mile when headlights filled the road from behind her. She moved to the side and then her foot caught in a rut and she stumbled. A blue car came to a stop and the driver stuck his head out the window. In the darkness, she thought it was the Averill kid, but as he came closer she saw it was the strange white who was always hanging around with Indian families.

"I'm not lost," she told him. "I know where I live."

He later said that from a distance he'd taken her for an old woman, slumped over as she was, falling off the road as though down a flight of steps.

She felt his arms around her waist and the ground moved away from her. She was swinging in midair and then was in the front seat. The dash was lit up amber and she could smell tobacco and spilled oil. After driving a few miles down the road, he turned and looked at her. "A drunken Indian," he said. "God, how original."

A year later, she is still unable to unravel how it happened. Being drunk and falling in love bear a faint resemblance, and both defy memory. He drove her to the house on the east side, but she refused to get out. "Take me to the trailer court."

"Why?"

"I'm on fire."

He stared at her and she stared back.

Then he put the car in gear and drove. Though the trailer court was west, he drove east to his house. While he carried her to the front door, she didn't know exactly what her affliction might be. She meant to say something, to complain or to resist, but all she said was "I'm not broken. I can walk." And then she passed out.

Late that night, she woke and found herself in his bed. He was sleeping on the floor beside her, and she was halfway out of the bed to join him there before she remembered that she barely knew him. She slept, and in the morning the sunlight undid her. In the place where he'd slept was a folded blanket. She rose on cat feet and descended the stairs to find him sitting in the kitchen with his back to her. He wore jeans but his chest and back were bare. She could just see over his shoulder where radio parts were spread across the table. Of course she knew she was stark naked. She could feel the air on her skin while she stood in the doorway and waited for him to turn around. He might have heard the floor creak or felt her eyes burning into him.

When he turned, there was only a flicker of surprise. His blue eyes took all of her in.

"Who would ever believe this?" she said.

He followed her back up the stairs. When he climbed into bed with her she thought it was too soon but it was never too soon. She arched her back upward and he slipped into her like into velvet.

The Choteau boys waited for John Fire to kill the two of them. Tyrone anticipated a crippling of some kind, but feared his exclusion from the council even more. He hadn't planned on this, he told her, and neither had she.

It took her a week to summon the courage to drive to the house to get her belongings. John Fire helped her pack everything into cardboard boxes and his eyes avoided her while she gathered clothes and books and cosmetics. He insisted that she take a rocking chair he'd restored. "I don't rock much," he said and for the first time she wondered if she was doing the right thing.

When the car was fully loaded, John Fire looked at her face as if to frame it for memory. "Thanks for leaving the toaster," he said.

"John—"

"Don't explain and don't fret. I had six good months and neither of us broke any promises. You can come back for anything else whenever you want. There's no lock on the door."

The following morning brought rain that plunged from clouds the color of a gun barrel. She drove Tyrone's Delta 88 through the downpour to get her books but John Fire wasn't there. At Toby's, she found Judy Poor Bull and June Lame sharing a pot of coffee.

"They've gone to Pierre," Judy told her. "Noah and John Fire."

"To ask for the bones," June added.

Delores shook the rain from her hair, awaiting their judgment and an offer of coffee.

"That girl needs burying," Judy said.

The women were watching the rain and hadn't even glanced at Delores. She reached behind the counter to where Toby kept his cups and, with measured gestures, took a seat at their table. Wind blew a slant of rain against a cracked window. Delores heard a scraping sound; Judy pushing the sugar bowl in her direction.

By the time she got home, the clouds were spent and the sun came out. Tyrone was in the kitchen, poring over maps of the Clay Creek Reservation. She folded back the northwest corner, took his hand, and led him outside.

A humming filled the air; insects, the breeze in the corn, distant cattle chewing the earth. The yard in front of the house was littered with shallow puddles. When she looked down, Delores could see a dozen of her reflections. She led him down the road and across a bare field. The sun was hot and she unbuttoned her shirt and showed her breasts. "It's all right if you stare, Tyrone."

He stared and smiled.

They came to the burned-down house, and Tyrone stopped cold. "Not here," he said.

"Uh-uh. This way, *Che Maza*."

Farther on was the cornfield bordering the unfinished golf course. Delores shucked off her jeans and turned to kiss him. "Doing it in the cornfields is an old Dakota tradition."

Tyrone began tearing cornstalks to make a mattress over the mud, but she stopped him. Smiling, she lay down in a shallow puddle. "It's warm, Tyrone. Soft."

Naked, he leaned over her. "What's that mean, *Che Maza?*"

"Iron prick."

When he was inside her, she shifted her hips back and forth, sinking into the earth. A crow swooped overhead. Her hands grasped red mud and she lifted her fingers to his chest and face. Sweat ran down his nose and rained on her. Her mouth closed around his and she bit until she tasted blood. Tyrone cried out and when he tried to pull away, as he'd done before, she seized his hips and held him there, squeezing her thighs to take his seed deep.

He rolled away and said, "You'll have a baby."

"I hope so." She reached a hand to his face. "With that mud on you, you look like an Indian."

He turned away and reached for his pants. His eyes rested on a puddle and she knew he was looking at his reflection. He looked for a long time. The want-to-be.

And then, very deliberately, as if performing a sacrament, he wetted his hands in the water and washed the mud off his face.

After being gone for close to two weeks, Noah and John Fire came home empty-handed. The next day Tyrone disappeared.

She went looking for him. Toby said he hadn't seen him and Darryl Kills First just glared at her. "I saw him headed west," Gene Fast Horse said, "burning rubber like the law was on his tail. At most, I figure you'll get a postcard from California."

She knew it was a lie and slept crosswise in their bed, occupying both of their spaces, and three days later he was back, greased and painted in Lakota glory.

The evening they buried the girl's bones by the river, a strong wind blew from the southwest and the dust in the air made the sky turn red. Even the ripples on the water led to the burial place. Everyone took this for a sign and the old superstitions ran rampant before the

e Andrew in the space of two hours. He married my mother
e was twenty, got her pregnant with my older sister Ruth, and
ned up to fight in the European war in 1918.

man that he was is a man I never saw. All I grew up seeing
empty clothes. After coming home from Europe, he gradually
sense of who he was or who he had been and stopped being
sible for my mother and sisters. I was born in the seventh year
decline and my sister Theresa came along a year later. With
w children, I'm told, my father perked up for a stretch, enough
a steady job as a farmhand. The joke was he was working for
on land that belonged to him. He had sixteen of his own acres
never had the ambition to cultivate, leasing them out to white
s, and when we needed fresh money he'd hire out for a week
onth at a time.

d been moved around when he was young and an uncle of his,
n Parmelee, had taught him about the old religion, but my
r had been raised by the Little Sisters of Mercy (at school we
them the Sisters of Little Mercy) and didn't allow talk about
underbirds in the Black Hills or how the *siyotanka*, the flute,
be used to conjure love from young girls. She kept us on a
ian path, the one they'd laid out for us more than a hundred
ago and was meant to lead to a sacred state called assimilation.
ce you get the Christian hook in your mouth, there is almost no
go.

netimes in the summer, my father would drive over to Wilma
ang around in front of the Gem Bar and crack jokes with the
s. He often took me along and we'd make some money cutting
with a hand mower, or we'd carry groceries home for women
et paid with loose change or hard-boiled eggs he'd peel with his
bnail and never once break that white skin.

e Choteau people called him Wishbone. As opposed to Back-
He was too easygoing, even compared to any number of shiftless
on the res. The people in Wilma treated him like a firewater
, a bum, and he just took it, swallowed their guff the way he
owed their hard-boiled eggs, all at once, with a smile that didn't
water.

dmit I've heard and seen worse. My mother's parents just ran
and left her at the mission school. June's dad, Clarence Little
spent a good part of his life in prison but when he was home he

sun went down. Pete Scully handed th
to light the ceremonial fire. She hearc
Darryl Kills First just shook his head w
prayers were finished, John Fire approa
an eagle feather. Then the two of then

Noah Lam

Some people are born to responsibility.
a flat tire or a baby needs feeding, so th
ask why no one else did it in their place

My mother was born a Poquette. Her
her mother a Yankton, and they both we
six. So she was raised at the mission sch
up doing everything on her own. But
through and through.

I grew up in Choteau back when there
us there. Like nearly all of the children,
Ree when I was six. Father Albert used to
me to spread my fingers. "Look at that,"
spread of an eagle." And he'd tell me ho
look wrapped around a basketball, or ma
wrestling team?

I didn't join anything. I'm not a joiner.
and faster than most boys my age, I didn'
sports except when Pete roped me into a g
was young, the only activity that got me b
books and my hands the size of eagles had
wore my eyes out before I was twelve years
in poor light or from a bad diet like a docto
wearing glasses ever since, the kind with th
eyes look bigger than they really are.

Before I was born, my father was a hard
one of the handsomest men on the reserva
fourteen and went to work first as a ranch h
elevator operator. There wasn't anything he
baseball and shot pool with the best of the
fishing contest when he was only thirteen, brir

used to beat on her two older brothers, Leroy and Dennis. Frank Poor Bull's father was a drunk and so was Pete Scully's uncle. James Harrison Lame was just a little windblown is all. Not knowing exactly why he even got out of bed in the morning.

The only time I remember seeing him work hard is after my sister Theresa died of pneumonia. It was January and he had to dig a grave in the frozen earth. A priest was supposed to come over from Wilma but he never made it, maybe because of the blizzard that was coming. I was only seven at the time but I can still remember standing outside watching my father, his hatless head bent to that ground as he lifted the pick and threw it back downward. Sparks flew when the pick struck rock and though it was freezing cold, sweat was pouring down his face and his black hair was slick and white from where the sweat had frozen. The ice gave way and the ground was like black iron that came away in hard plates. When the cold got to me I went into the house and watched from the window. After an hour, my father came in to warm his hands. He wiped the sweat from his eyes and drank a cup of cocoa, then went back out again. Half an hour later he came into the kitchen with snow and dirt on his boots and said it was done. But when my mother and Ruth and I were bundled up in coats and scarves and we went out to lay Theresa into the ground, the grave was too shallow, maybe only three or four feet deep. My mother looked at that grave and then at my father, and the cold day just got colder. She told my sister and me to go back inside but I stood with her while she reached for the pick and stepped down into the grave. After a while the wind began to blow from the north and I couldn't stand it any longer and went back into the house. My father was already in the kitchen loading wood into the big black stove.

We sat by the stove and waited for my mother while my father stared through a hole at the flames. The sky grew dark all at once and then it was night and my mother came in to say it was time. Snow was falling and had covered the dirt so that the hole had turned white. We buried Theresa in the dark and my father put a wooden cross in the ground to mark the spot.

The next morning we saw that the cross had blown away in the blizzard. We went back out and cleared the new snow as best we could, but we never did find the exact same spot and didn't know if we were putting that cross at her head or her feet.

The doldrums set in again. Instead of leasing out his sixteen acres, my father sold them to Gaetan Averill and signed on as a farmhand for a dollar a day. This was in 1933, when I was eight. Averill fired him after two months and that severed our connection to that land for good. The rest of that year, my father roamed around or went duck hunting or fishing for perch. If work came along, he'd stick with it for only a week or two before packing it in. "I'm sunk," he'd say to us after quitting another job. "I'm just all busted up, I guess." But he wasn't a drinker nor did he seem much interested in other women. He hadn't been wounded in the war, hadn't even shot a gun or been shot at. But the way my mother put it, after he'd had a bit of money and driven a white man's car and seen cities like Chicago and Minneapolis and Memphis, the reservation was never enough for him again. He was drunk on that other world and the war was over. So he brooded.

My father went away about two years after Theresa died. After a few months he wrote to say he was living in Minneapolis, so my mother took a bus up there to bring him home. A week later she came home alone and said he wasn't there anymore. With the little money left from the sale of that acreage, she bought part interest in a launderette where there were two washing machines and a spin dryer. After that, I had the cleanest clothes in Choteau. And I'd watch her wash and dry and iron the clothes of friends and neighbors, even their private underclothes, though if she ever caught me staring at the brassieres I'd get a hand across the face.

We got a postcard from my father from Omaha and six months later another one from Saint Louis. He was living in the cities, one after another, from the north to the south. He was marching a straight line to the Gulf of Mexico and the day I turned thirteen we had a letter with a postmark from Galveston. It was the last we ever heard from him, and I imagined he must have walked right into the sea.

Though it was my mother I admired, I lived a number of years in the shadow of my father, knowing all the while that I was following the wrong example and being helpless to change it. My mother gave up everything in life but Jesus on my account and sent me to college on the premise that I should never return. My mother died without knowing that it all only added up to one year of schoolteaching and then the familiar city-Indian shiftlessness. And after long years of keeping my promise and staying away from the reservation, I came back. My hands were as soft as April snow. I'd never plowed a field or cut down a tree or dug a grave.

When the girl's bones were found at Eagle Reach, I remembered Theresa and how my father had sat in the kitchen watching the fire while my mother had finished digging the grave. The snow on his boots melted and there was a puddle of mud and water at his feet. I felt his shame and then I felt my own. When I came back from Pierre with John Fire, June said that I was beating my breast too hard. I couldn't tell her in simple words how it felt to have walked out of my body for close to twenty-five years, trying to be a schoolteacher to whites, and even longer trying not to be an Indian anymore. I tacked the drum skin Walking Horse had given me to the wall and waited for it to stretch and to sound. And it mattered enormously that the want-to-be who rescued those bones brought them to me first. He had shown me respect and that was all the beginning I could ask for.

I learned how easy it is to be two places at once. It's only a question of ignoring time. I worked with kids who were slow at reading. I helped find odd jobs for people who were out of work and Pete Scully and I raised money for the Indian shelter in Wilma that was in dire straits. I had an old Smith-Corona typewriter and I began to correspond with Indian activists from all over, from Sacramento to Saratoga. The Crazy Horse Council newsletter was my doing, though most of the articles came from other writers and other sources.

It was good to sit in a chair next to a boy or girl and watch them pass their eyes over the black words. I had spent too much of my time with older children and had forgotten how wonderful it could be to see the meaning of a string of letters as ordinary as "see Jane run." A lot of those kids with so-called reading disabilities had fewer problems with the words than they did with the stories. Dick and Jane and Spot and green lawns clashed mightily with Lakota myth and the Old Testament, not to mention life on the res. So we took to reading cereal boxes, labels on soup cans, or even articles from my own newsletter. I looked everywhere for storybooks with Indians in them but couldn't find much besides Hiawatha or Tonto, so I had to write the stories myself. June helped out and after a time her stories were far better than my own. I typed them up on the Smith-Corona, leaving spaces on each page for drawings that Jana added with a black pen. First we paid a penny a page for a mimeograph print and then stapled them into booklets, then Tyrone got a machine of his own and we did the printing out at his house.

These booklets got passed around and more of them were printed up on a press up in Minneapolis. In years since, the stories have been misinterpreted by white folks as being true Lakota myths. I have even seen books from out east that included "Indian legends" that June wrote in 1972 and 1973. One of these told how the Indians had begun to despair. They were losing their land and the sacred buffalo, the eagles no longer flew in the skies, and the wind blew away the soil in which the grasses grew. In need of a hero, they gathered the red mud from the banks of the river and fashioned it into the likeness of a warrior. They placed this likeness on a mound in the middle of the high grasslands. The winds blew soil and dust from all four directions and covered the warrior and as the years passed he became a mountain. When she wrote this story, June was making a real effort to get off the bottle. She had in mind a high hill that you could see from the kitchen window and wanted to take her strength from that sight, but a journalist wrote that she was probably referring to the Black Hills.

Another story, more contemporary, recounted how the Pope had gone fishing with a Lakota medicine man. At one point, the medicine man had jumped out of the boat and walked on the water to retrieve a fish that threw the hook. The Pope thought to himself that if an Indian medicine man could walk on water, then he could too. So he jumped out of the boat and sank straight to the bottom. When the medicine man fished him out, the Pope said he never would have guessed that the medicine man's powers were so great. To which the medicine man replied it was only a question of knowing where the rocks were. This one got us a letter from a priest down at the mission school but we left it in all the same.

Herman came home in early December after three months at Pine Ridge and I hardly recognized him with his long braids. He was as quiet as ever, but not fidgety quiet like before. As a child he'd tended to stutter, always trying to get his words out in a rush, and that stutter had led to shyness. But now he spoke slowly, parceling his words. He never smiled much and I couldn't tell if he was happy or not to have come home. The gray clouds that had persisted through November had finally melted from the sky. Up on the north edge of Choteau, there was more sky than land and looking at blue is always a great pleasure at the end of a long stretch of overcast. I assumed it was Herman's coming home that had brought out that blue. Of course, all parents think that way about their children.

June baked bread with raisins in it and roasted a chicken and we had supper with lit candles and a big roaring fire. We ate with our hands and drank water from a jug, but June allowed herself a glass of elderberry wine.

Afterwards, Herman and I went for a walk on the road that led to the river. Herman said that he'd had a hard time following what George Brings Yellow had taught him. Too much of it was foreign to him and many things, including the sun dance, still struck him as pointless, though no more meaningless than the transformation of wine into blood.

"I feel stupid but not ashamed. Like a real young boy all over again. How come you never taught me these things?"

I answered that I had taught him what I'd learned myself. I had gone to mission schools and to church with my mother. I was damn close to being assimilated.

"How many Yanktons are left?" Herman asked. He was thinking about my mother's mother.

"I don't know. A few hundred, maybe." Yankton means end village and I figured that was about the size of things. Some tribes, like the Santee, had been almost entirely wiped out.

Herman said he was the only one with a trace of Yankton blood at Pine Ridge. "It makes a difference to some of those people, whether you're a blood or not. Oglala, Hunkpapa, Sans Arc. Some of the tribe members there don't want to hear about AIM because the leaders are all Ojibwa and from the cities. The BIA people don't want AIM or the traditionals to have any say in matters. But George Brings Yellow says the tribes are all coming together into the same circle. He treats me like a Lakota and calls me his son."

I spent a long night rubbing a bruise that didn't show on my skin, reminding myself he meant he had a spiritual father, not a new one. The drum hide hanging on my wall glowed blue in the dark of the room.

The next morning, Herman began building a sweat lodge in the open field behind the Poor Bull house. The one we had used before was built by Frank Poor Bull and hadn't been kept up. Herman gathered willow sticks from close by the river and planted them in a circle, bending the upper edges. Then he covered the sticks with old blankets and gathered sage grass, sweet grass, and green cedar from the fields north of Choteau and several smooth round stones from the banks of the river.

It was curious to watch him, and even more curious to see a true sweat lodge in that field. My life was changing fast and I had a hard time recognizing what had once been so familiar: my leather reading chair with the table and lamp beside it; the high rows of books over my desk, books I'd gathered and read and arranged by subject over the years. I removed the pictures of the apostles that my mother had left to me. They'd hung on various living-room walls in the fifteen years since she died, and their mournful gazes had finally got too burdensome.

When the sweat lodge was finished, Herman invited me and John Fire Smith, Gene Fast Horse, and Pete Scully. Just outside the lodge, willow sticks had been placed for the fire, four of them running east and west and another seven running north and south. When the flames began to lick, we went inside. This sweat lodge wasn't anything like the one I'd been in before. The floor was covered with sage that was warm beneath my feet. Herman carried the stones into the lodge, holding them in deer antlers, and they made a crackling sound as he placed them in the center of the floor. Gene Fast Horse sprinkled sage-grass cedar on them and the lodge filled with a magnificent odor, though it irritated my nose and I had a hard time breathing. Then Herman poured water onto the rocks and as steam flew upward through a tiny hole in the top blanket, I swear that my heart went with it. I'd been to the sweats four or five times before, but in a way, this was the first time. The other sweats had been makeshift and not up to snuff. We'd used tap water instead of water from a stream and carried the hot stones with a pitchfork instead of deer antlers or a fork of wood. John Fire had pointed out to me that the entrance to Poor Bull's lodge faced north and not west, as it should have.

Herman sprinkled more water from a leather pouch onto the stones, then he began the prayers. It was a hotter sweat than I'd ever had before and I was dizzy from the smoke and steam. Herman opened the blanket and let cool air in four times, but we sat silently, passing a pipe filled with a tobacco called *Chanshasha* that he'd brought back from Pine Ridge.

I had my misgivings then and I have them to this day. Any ritual takes getting used to and will seem like hokum if you look at everything through the eyes of a skeptic. But that day I was filled with pride for my son and for all of us there in that lodge. There was a moment in which I was gone, taken, clasped to a dream I didn't understand, and I felt that each of us had become confused with one another. I felt that we were becoming a tribe. Only Herman was apart from us, ahead of us, as if higher up a steep hill. It may have been dizziness from lack of air or my weakened state from sitting so long on the ground. I had felt light-headed in church during Communion and sometimes wondered if it was from the fasting that preceded the sacrament. I don't know what to say. I don't know who God is or what color his skin is, or how to find him, and the words that I'm given to sing, either English or Latin or Lakota, never come close to saying what I would like to hear said. I came out of that lodge feeling giddy and harebrained, and the feeling lasted a lot longer than I thought it would. In fact, I've been light-headed to this day, which I consider a mixed blessing. But since that day of steam and smoke, my skin has grown red again. The mysteries have been soldered to the Mystery and the sweat of my whiteness has dried in the wind and become dust.

Herman returned to Pine Ridge and a week later there was a march down in Des Moines that some committee Indians joined up with. The point was to spread the news that Indians had it even worse than Negroes and that civil rights in the upper midwest should be as important as in Mississippi. After the march, there was a rally at a big auditorium, where there'd be speeches and singing, but state troopers had set up at the door and insisted on searching people for liquor and weapons. Gene Fast Horse objected to this and a fistfight broke out and then a general ruckus that made the six o'clock news. Fifteen people were arrested, twelve of them Indians, and Fast Horse was charged with incitement to riot.

They couldn't make the charges stick, but it was about this time that I noticed how much he liked the limelight. Alone with us, he made more noise than sense. But whenever the reporters and camera crews came around, he'd change his voice and words to fit what he felt was a dignified and angry tone. The white folks thought he was a good interview and went to him instead of John Fire, which always disappointed us. And I admit I never liked Gene Fast Horse. I didn't appreciate the sex jokes he was always making about Delores, and I knew he called me a diploma Indian behind my back.

It's since been written and said that John Fire was at the Des Moines march, and I know for a fact that's not true. He was in Pierre with me to see a lawyer about a water rights problem we were having on the northern part of the Clay Creek Reservation. But he was a part of the incident two weeks later at Mount Rushmore. I can swear to it because I was there too.

It wasn't much as "Indian incidents" go, and compared to what followed, it was only a brushfire. John Fire had gone to live at Pine Ridge for a time and he called Choteau a week beforehand to tell us that he was helping organize this rally at the park. We drove out west in Frank's pickup and met up with him in Hot Springs, south of the Black Hills. I'd never seen so many Indians in the same place. There were Cheyenne, Crow, Ojibwa, and people from all the branches of the Lakota. George Brings Yellow was there, as were a few of the AIM leaders I'd been hearing so much about. All told, there were maybe five hundred of us. Our little group was made welcome and we camped out by the Cold Brook Reservoir. There were a half dozen troopers on the ridge overlooking the reservoir, and with our tents and campfires we must have given them a real scare.

It isn't easy to get to the monument. The main road is narrow and has a control point where tourists check into the parking area. Early in the morning, we had a caravan of about a hundred cars and pickup trucks. Although we opened up the trunks and glove compartments to show we had no alcohol or firearms, we were told that we couldn't enter all at once. Some of the AIM people and John Fire, who hadn't yet joined up, thought we should just bust our way in, but George Brings Yellow had another idea. We backed everybody down the mountain and got the wives and children settled into another campground, and then fifty of us were chosen to form an expedition. Pete Scully and Frank Poor Bull had to stay behind, but I went along with Gene Fast Horse and John Fire. I don't understand why I was chosen. I was neither young nor strong and until very recently I hadn't shown much interest in the affairs of my people. Maybe George Brings Yellow and the AIM man from Minneapolis, Willard Bent, had pegged me for the leader of the Choteau group. It was the kind of mistake that happened all the time.

Tyrone was there as well, one of the few *wasichu*, or white men, allowed in. Another was a photographer named Clyde Bennett who worked for the Rapid City *Journal*. The smartest thing we did that day was to let Tyrone bring him along. His photos made all the papers and turned this bittersweet little skirmish into a memorable event.

We rode in seven pickups, seven men to a truck, and circled around behind to the foot of the mountain. It was a hard climb up, through a pine forest that was dusted with snow, and the footing was slippery. We started up at noon and it was well past three in the afternoon when we crawled through three barbed-wire fences, and ended up standing on top of Teddy Roosevelt's enormous stone head. This was trespassing, though in our statements we pointed out that, as far as we were concerned, the Treaty of Laramie of 1868 was still in effect and it was the tourists who were trespassing, not us. George Brings Yellow stood right out on the edge of that head. He was wearing his eagle feathers and beaded shirt and he spread his arms wide and lifted his head to the sky and reclaimed the Paha Sapa, the Black Hills, for the Indian people. This is where Clyde Bennett took the picture that became so famous, of Brings Yellow with his arms outstretched, while below and beyond him are the huge faces of Jefferson and Washington and a panorama of the Black Hills.

We stayed for two hours. Some of the traditionals danced an eagle dance and smoked pipe but most of us just stood around laughing and joking to hide our nervousness. A helicopter circled overhead the whole time and now and then a man would get on a bullhorn and advise us that we were trespassing on government property and would be prosecuted if we didn't leave immediately.

Someone suggested that we light a ceremonial fire, but Tyrone pointed out that one spark could light that forest up and then they'd all be writing news articles about firebug Indians instead of peaceful demonstrators.

It was getting close to dark when we finally abandoned the monument and slipped back through the barbed-wire fences. By the time we got back to where we'd left the trucks, it was pitch-dark and we were all tired and thirsty, our euphoria spent. A dozen patrol cars were waiting for us. Some of the windows on our trucks had been shot out and three had slashed tires. The men left guarding the trucks, including Pete Scully and Frank Poor Bull, had already been arrested. Troopers in riot gear were above us, where the road looped up around the mountainside. They advanced at a slow, deliberate walk and we were grabbing at rocks, sticks, pieces of glass, anything to defend ourselves with. George Brings Yellow stepped forward and motioned for the troopers to stop. For a moment, confused, they obeyed him. "We are leaving," Brings Yellow told them. "We will not fight you."

A sheriff came forward and informed him that he was under arrest. The charges were trespassing and incitement to riot. The Indians started screaming and a few rocks were thrown, but nobody was hit. Brings Yellow was handcuffed and escorted to a squad car, then the sheriff called out five names and asked those individuals to step forward. I could barely recognize my own name being called. It was too unbelievable. Before I could react, Tyrone Little walked up ahead and said he was me. I broke from the group I was standing with and ran toward him, my tongue still stuck to my teeth. Maybe because I was running or maybe because of the wild look in my eyes, the troopers thought I was going to do something dumb and just like that they had me down on the ground and were beating me with their damn sticks.

I wasn't a witness after that point. Everything that went on had to be recounted to me later and none of the stories is quite the same. A fight broke out between the troopers and a handful of Indians, people throwing rocks and swinging clubs. John Fire told me that Tyrone jumped into the circle of the men who were beating me and even took the stick from one of them and started hitting him with it. The troopers had to retreat and then they fired canisters of tear gas, which drove the Indians a hundred yards down the road and pretty much put a stop to the fighting. Gene, John Fire, Tyrone, that AIM man Willard Bent, Brings Yellow, and myself were all taken into custody, and the others were escorted back down to the camp east of Keystone. Bent had a knife on him and they tried to get him on a weapons charge, but all charges were dropped two days later. I think they didn't want it coming out in court how their boys had used tear gas and those wooden clubs, though word got out anyway because some trooper had smashed Clyde Bennett's camera and the photographer sued the state over it.

I had a broken rib and an ugly face. My glasses were smashed— they always go by the wayside in a fight—and a tooth came loose, but it was already rotted and about to fall out.

I was the one who'd been beaten up. Coupled with my letter writing, that made me a leader as far as the whites were concerned, though few of the Indians I knew would have agreed. There were other leaders among the traditionals or in the various tribal councils and of course in AIM. George Brings Yellow was a leader. So was Willard Bent. And John Fire led by example.

I never joined AIM. Not because of the violence but because they didn't seem unified in a way that inspired confidence. There was too much drinking and carrying on back then. I wanted things to change, sure, but I didn't want to have to pick up empty whisky bottles and spent shells while I was waiting.

Everyone heard and read about the ceremony on Rushmore, but the fight remained in the shadows, except for what came out during Clyde Bennett's court case. The Indians themselves were divided about it. Some of the traditionals felt the AIMers were stirring things up needlessly, to which Willard Bent answered that it was high time we started thinking about defending ourselves. "I'm not a new Indian," he told a reporter. "I'm that old bad news Indian you thought you'd gotten rid of."

George Brings Yellow didn't comment to the newspapers, but in the Pennington County jail we agreed it had been a good day for the people, a day of renewed pride. We shared a cell for close to three days, so I was finally able to observe my son's new spiritual father. "I always thought you were a crackpot," I told him.

His smile had a trace of weariness. "I used to be real lonely. Now everybody wants to speak with me, to help me preserve the old ways."

He took a long breath. "I think sometimes they care less about the old ways than they claim. I have this vision that I will be lonely again before I die."

Tyrone was accepted by AIM as a useful ally, a man who knew maps and firearms. Delores Her Many Horses had moved into the farmhouse that Gaetan Avril gave to him and for a while they were a part of every action that AIM put on. Once she was carrying his child, we took it as a sign that he had gotten past the want-to-be stage.

Gene Fast Horse got himself interviewed on the radio and gave a speech that was half cribbed from Chief Joseph or that movie *Cheyenne Autumn*. Then he came back to Choteau and in the space of an hour got into a fistfight with Darryl Kills First over a game of eight ball.

John Fire Smith was on a television show in Sioux Falls. He made a name for himself right then and there when he said the visit to Mount Rushmore had two purposes: first, to remind whites that the Black Hills legally belonged to the Indians, and second, to collect the rent. But he didn't scare common folk the way Willard Bent did, and he even told an old joke that got passed around the white papers quite a bit. "When the white man wrote up the text of the treaties, it read 'This land shall be yours as long as grasses grow and winds blow.' What we didn't notice was the small print at the bottom that said 'or for ninety days, whichever comes first.' "

I spent one day in the hospital and another two in jail. Then we all drove back to Choteau where the first thing we did was get into that sweat lodge. I breathed in the smoke as though it were the air that gave me life. The smell of the grasses was like a medicine and I forgot about the pain in my side and the cuts on my face. That night I asked Herman to explain the ceremony to me again. He walked me through it slowly and with patience, a good teacher. I asked why he had mentioned *six* directions.

"To the whites," he answered, "there are four directions and to the Indian there are six. We have the same north, south, east, and west, but the other directions mean just as much to us."

"Which are those?"

"Up," Herman said, pointing to the sky. And then his face broke into a rare smile. "And down."

Harold Bad Hand

The man in front of me looked like his hair combed itself when he woke up in the morning. I bet his suit never even wrinkled, so when he asked me about prison conditions, I stared back at him just to make his nerves jump.

The man wanted to know about before I went to prison. When he smiled I could see how big his teeth were. They were flat and looked like piano keys and probably weren't real.

In prison it's the same world, I told him. There ain't no difference between inside and outside for a mixed-blood. *Iyeska* is the Lakota word and I hear it plenty. It means those-who-speak-white. I get beat up drunk, poked and kicked and swore at for my mother's blood and I never seen her that I can remember. I've always wondered how come Indians think a themselves like cats and dogs.

My old man was a Sicangu, a Burned Thigh. He was good enough with a blade and his fists, but also drunk without a job or feathers or his own car. My mother was Czech and he used to tease her with the word—rubber check, checker board, check mate. She had me in a house in Choteau and passed me straight to my grandmother, Janine Bad Hand, who was blind in one eye. Then my mother went to Sioux City or somewheres. Checked out.

My grandma lost her eye to the nuns at the mission when she was about twelve, and wore a patch over the hole that was left. She took the patch off at night, and sometimes in the morning she'd be sitting in her chair and I could see that big red place where the lid was all shriveled up like a shed snakeskin. She blamed the nuns, she said, but not Jesus. She had pictures of Jesus all over her house, pictures and holy cards pinned to the walls, and in the biggest one, in the kitchen, he was real tired-looking and pointing to his bare heart. We lived in Pine Bluff where there was no school and nothing to do at all. The other kids went off to the mission school, but Janine kept me at home to take care of her. She drank bootleg whisky and got sick every morning. Sometimes she'd give me a little whisky, even when I was seven or eight, for a toothache or a fever. I remember falling down once and Janine laughing at me while my cheek was flat against the cool dirt floor. Then she put me to bed and the bed tipped over it felt like. All my life I hate whisky and only drink wine and beer like my old man.

Janine died when I was ten. She had a rotten liver and went poky dot all over her face and hands and I wouldn't kiss her goodbye. My father was in the pen, I don't know what for, and I had to go to the same mission school where Janine left an eye behind. The priest called me Young Grudge and I was glad about that, it was a earned name and not a name stuck to my lips without my saying okay. I said I was a Sicangu blood but they knew I wasn't, not for real. The priest told us about heaven and hell and I knew where I wanted them all to go.

Until I went to the mission I didn't know about the *maza skan skan*, the clock. Like Janine, I ate when I was hungry and went to sleep when I was tired. But at the mission there was times for work and times for play and we ate when they said to or we didn't eat at all. Same thing in prison. All you do on your own time is breathe and daydream. I stole plenty in my life but I never stole nobody's watch.

All the time I said bad words, day and night, even to myself. Then a woman from Ann Arbor came to the mission and said she was a speech therapist and would I say the alphabet without a swear word and I couldn't. She said I had a speech disorder is all and for a whole year we met up in her office to make chitchat as long as I would say only soft words and not hurt words. Hurt words she said were weeds in the garden of my head and they'd die if I didn't say them. Russ Poor Bull said she was a head shrinker and if I talked to her my skull would get too small for my brain and I'd get headaches and go blind. So after I had a headache one time I didn't go no more. This woman came to the mission to find me, and I told her go to hell fucking white bitch. She went away but she came back with the priest who I said could fuck himself with a bent rake. I guess I stayed in school because it was the mission where they can't kick you out except for rape or murder. The bad words stayed in my head like weeds and I still say them all the time.

I was no good at anything, not school or with girls and my face isn't pretty like Russ Poor Bull's or Darryl Kills First's. But I am the best at basketball ever from the mission, twenty-three points a game my senior year and All State B team, and would've made All State A team if I played at a A school. We were too good for everybody my last year with me at guard and Russ at forward, we never used no substitutes and played fastbreak the whole game long. Nobody called me breed for the whole season and even the priest stopped calling me Young Grudge. They called me Shoots Dead then and we won the South Dakota B school tourney over them white schools. It was Indian ball, they called it, not Breed Ball or Blood Ball. I sometimes didn't even feel that ball in my hands, I just lifted and let fly. I shot with my left hand on a dead run, I ran flat out and the ball went up and down into that hole for me, the only time I ever was good at something except for shoplifting. I got hands so fast they blur. And in the final game of the tourney I put up forty-one points and was alone on TV with a man who said I was not stoppable.

So that year I was a Indian even to Indians. But I couldn't play in college with no money and no grades better than maybe a C, so I got a job cleaning toilets in Wilma and was a breed all over again. I used to play basketball with the men at the Wilma high school, but those guys never passed me the ball and we had a few fights so I couldn't go there no more. I drank more than before and hung out with Russ and Darryl and a guy named Fast Horse who'd come over from Pine Ridge.

I got wild like they knew I would. One time at a bar in Wilma I got in a fight with two guys who damn near killed me. The police took us all out a there and stuck me in a clinic instead a jail because my face and head was all beat up.

Delores Her Many Horses had a typing job at the clinic and sometimes came to see if I was all right. It was a summer job, she said, she was going back to college in the fall. I was so weak in my bed I couldn't move my head or my legs and I couldn't hardly talk back to her. I knew she was seeing Willard Tree but I didn't care, I wanted to touch her and smell her hair but she never came close enough and I couldn't get out of that bed to follow her. I had a concussion and had to lie still. She said I should keep my eyes on the ceiling or my brain might slide out my ears. One time she came and sat in a orange chair by the bed and said it was her last day, take care now. And the next week when they took off the bandages a lady said there was mail for me and there was a get well soon card and inside a pencil drawing of my face without scars or zits and my hair combed back and my teeth all straightened out. Like she was wishing me handsome and she wrote I shouldn't drink and fight so much.

But once I was cleared out, I drank the same and got into more fights. And even when I got cut or kicked I felt fine inside, letting off steam and hurting back. Russ's old man said I was a brown-bag Injun and didn't want to see me at his house. One night I was drinking wine that I took off a old man and went by that house and threw rocks until Russ' mom came out front and I shouted every slut bitch word I knew at her and drove away. I got fired from my job and that was fine with me, but I still smell shitpot in my sleep even if I never cleaned another one. Darryl and me went all the way to Sioux City and robbed a gas station and both got caught and went to jail for a year in Iowa. Darryl went back to Choteau when he got out but I went on to Pine Ridge where they didn't want to see a breed from somewhere else make good. I got stabbed in a fight in White, South Dakota, the knife hit a rib or I'd be dead now, and I was in a hospital only for a week before they put me on the street with a bandage tied around me like a rope. It was a blood who stabbed me and the res police let him go so I knew the score in that town. Before I left I stopped by his woman's house and raped her good, holding my knife to her neck and telling her to shut up or I'd cut her head off. She shut up just fine but I cut her a little anyway just to see a full blood bleed. I took her car and drove west to Wyoming and then got to Fort Collins in Colorado with no money and that car all broke down.

I don't know what year, it must be wrote down someplace because in Fort Collins I took the biggest car I could find, a Lincoln Continental with white walls, and robbed three houses that same night and filled up the car with TVs and a stereo and food and all the liquor cabinet. It looked like a whole Kmart inside that car. I meant to head straight back to South Dakota but was sick as a dog. It should have been fun taking all that stuff, but it wasn't. I felt like shit, my skin itched, and there wasn't no one to beat up except pictures on the walls and this woman that was in one of the houses. There was all this wine and beer in the front seat but nobody to drink it with and laugh and pal around. I drank what I wanted until the sick feeling was gone and then I blacked out. When I came to I was in jail and then they sent me to prison for sixteen years.

It was Cheyenne in there, and Crow and Arapaho from up south.

Denver Indians is from all parts, so I fit right in, breed or no. I had a knife I made with glass from a bottle and a handle of wrapped-around twine and pieces of my clothes. It was good for cutting but not for stabbing and one night I lost it in a man's neck, they called him Henry Four but that was made-up.

We heard about how all the South Dakota Indians were in a new group called the American Indian Movement and had a riot in Sioux Falls and some of the prison Indians started calling themselves brothers and organizing meetings and shaking fists at white guards, but I didn't go along with that. I'm still a breed and nobody's brother. And one time there was these letters passed around the prison, trying to get Indians to join up with AIM. Somebody passed one of them to the guards and Henry Four said it was me so I cut him.

One good thing about white men is they don't think a me as a breed, just a Indian. Henry Four didn't die and I got moved to a place by myself. A white lawyer said I was one tough redskin and he meant I was mean. My sixteen years went up to twenty-one, but that didn't make no difference. I like to eat and there was food there and a mattress to sleep on better than I had even with Grandma Janine. I stayed alone in a cell for two months but then got moved back to the same block and had to watch my ass because Henry Four's friends was waiting for me. I quick made a new knife to keep my brothers from stabbing me.

They said I sold them out but it wasn't me. Even the guards thought I was a snitch and for the first time I got to play basketball outside on the court with no net, but it was just me shooting around and nobody to play against. I stopped being Indian. I stopped being anything. Another AIM letter got passed around again and it said we were all bloods who lived like Indians and the only breeds were the ones who lived like whites. I threw it in the trash.

Henry Four came back to the block with the stitches still in his neck. I waited for him to come after me, but he just hung out with the bloods. I knew I was nothing when he didn't try to kill me. Sweat and spit and piss and not even worth stabbing.

And one day I had this visitor I never saw before, a white man in a suit and tie who said he wasn't a lawyer, he was a agent for the FBI and could he talk to me. Talk, I said, but we'll see if I listen and I gave him that smile I got that says, You prick, you better fucking hope I'm still smiling when you turn your back.

He said I was in trouble and inside I thought don't I know it and then he said I could die right there in prison and wouldn't I like to get out.

I said sure, but I had a hard time to keep smiling.

He had a paper and he looked at it and said, "Aren't you from Choteau?"

I said, "A long time ago, yeah."

He said I could go back there and live and I said no way, not there, there's no jobs.

"I can arrange for you to have some money and a roof over your head."

"And who do I gotta kill?" I asked him, and laughed real loud. I thought he'd get mad like I wanted, but he just put his papers on the desk and said I should sign this one here and this other one there.

"You got a name?" I asked him and he said, "William Person, call me Bill."

Delores Her Many Horses

She has gone barefoot since the day she met Tyrone and the baby is due at the end of the summer. When the doctor in Wilma gave her the news, she'd felt tears spring from her eyes. I am not barren. Her crying surprised her. She'd never before wept from joy.

But then the doctor reminded her that the baby would be a mixed-blood.

"What does that matter?"

"To me, not much. But I hear being a full blood is a big deal with you people."

While Helene drove her back to Choteau she worried how Tyrone would take the news, heads or tails. She found him bent over a Wilma County map he'd marked with circles and dotted lines. At first he listened as if her news were a distraction, then his blue eyes went gray. "A baby," he said, the words as flat and disinterested as if he'd said, "A rake." But he stood up and crossed the floor to come close to her. He touched her face and her closed eyelids. Then he leaned his weight downward to join his head to hers, danced her in his strong arms and squeezed her lightly before letting go, as if not to damage anything.

He is not a simple man to love but he is the father and that's a stone fact, and this helps her overlook his strangeness. He drinks too much, like everyone else except John Fire and Noah, and he never seems to entirely sleep. His muscles twitch, his legs shake, his lips move up and down. He did a full year's duty in a green jungle where one day he swallowed smoke. "No one knows about it but it's all over that jungle. We put it there so nothing would grow and the Cong couldn't hide themselves. It's a clear enough strategy. You win the war by destroying the battlefield."

She reads in a magazine about Vietnam vets and their hardships once they got home. How many of them became drug addicts over there, and how some of them killed civilians and livestock out of terror or simple boredom. But there are no marks on Tyrone. The skin of his forearms is clean and unbroken. There is only his occasional coughing and shortness of breath. She wants to know if he killed anyone—a man, a woman, a water buffalo—but she doesn't ask and he doesn't tell her. All he admits to is having been up north for weeks at a time. In the night, his coughing sometimes wakens her. He often leaves the bed and wanders from one room to another like a ghost, and at these times she thinks she knows.

At least once a month, they drive somewhere—Omaha, Minneapolis, Rapid City—to meet with Indian activists. Tyrone is counted on as a strategy man for every action: how to get a radio announcement out in time for it to be useful; which members of the press can be trusted as fairminded; how to plan on food and gasoline money and to organize places to bed down travelers. They borrow tactics from the civil rights and peace movements. An old mimeograph machine is set up in the room off the kitchen and Noah delivers the newsletter pages that Tyrone spends whole nights grinding out, and the next morning the kitchen always stinks of ink.

There are the day-to-day worries of unemployment, telltale cracks in June Lame's sobriety, marijuana in the mission school, the recent rape of a white girl in Arthur and the subsequent stomping of an Indian suspect by local high school boys. Money is always in short supply, bail money, money for ink and paper, for gas and postage. Tyrone doesn't have a job but always seems to come up with a hundred dollars or fifty or twenty when the need arises.

He keeps the eagle feather on top of the dresser, in a box with stray buttons, loose change, and a pair of cuff links she has never seen him wear.

The winter is cold but short on snow and the corn stubble shows in the fields, which glitter when the sun shines. Late February 1973. The book says SheHe will have lungs by now, a heartbeat, eyes that are closed but can see the backs of their lids, fingernails like insanely tiny moons. Anything is possible.

At the end of the month, she and Tyrone join the others at a weekend meeting in Sioux Falls. After the meeting breaks up, there are a half dozen cars in the parking lot, but suddenly there's only Tyrone's Delta 88 and John Fire standing there holding a brown bag filled with clothes and books.

"I was supposed to ride back with Frank," John Fire tells them.

"Hop in," Tyrone says.

The first miles are slow going. Tyrone is struggling for something to say while Delores, next to him in the front seat, looks out the window as though those shorn cornfields are suddenly the most interesting sight of all time. The overheated engine ticks and Tyrone wonders aloud if it might not boil over. He can't take it any faster than forty-five miles an hour, and Delores has the impression that they're moving underwater and straining every mile against an invisible current. Just past Beresford, thirty miles out, John Fire begins to mimic one of the lawyers, a man named Petersen who compared the Indian problem to a golf dispute. *You can't keep track of another man's strokes. If he says par, you write down par, even if you'd bet the farm that it was bogey.* Then he tells Tyrone and Delores a feeble joke, but their laughter is forced, and he sits back, silent.

Tyrone drives faster and then slows back down. Delores finds she's been holding her breath, so rolls down the window to take in some fresh air. When the sun is gone, the eastern corner of South Dakota is all horizon and white stars pulse in the black sky around them. She rolls the window closed and notices how their smells mingle. One prickly thought leads to another and not a single sentence completes itself in her mind.

Ten miles east of Choteau, Tyrone flicks on the radio. He's fixed every broken radio in town except his own and the reception is faint. They listen disinterestedly to a weather report and then the news comes on. John Fire suddenly asks Tyrone to turn up the volume.

They hear the phrase "Indian takeover," then "armed camp," then mostly static. Tyrone fiddles with the dial, but it only grows worse.

"About here would be fine," John Fire says as they approach Toby's.

"I planned on taking you to your door."

"Got no door left."

Delores hadn't heard that he'd moved out of his house and was sleeping on Toby's couch. They leave him by the side of the road, and when Delores glances back, all she can see is a horizonless darkness.

The next morning, John Fire hitches a ride west to the Pine Ridge Reservation to join a group of Indians who have occupied a village and immediately been surrounded by state marshals and the FBI. In Lakota, the place is called *Cankpe Opi*. But over the coming weeks, Americans would know it by the English translation, Wounded Knee.

The siege goes on longer than anyone would've guessed. And around the state, barbed-wire lines are drawn between Indians who support the takeover and Indians who are against it. That barbed wire will take years to come down.

On the Clay Creek Reservation, Reese Lonetree, the tribal president, has condemned Wounded Knee as a communist-inspired subversion of true Indian values. He prohibits sympathizers from gathering and enlists help from people on the BIA payroll to maintain order. Many of them, fearing the loss of their jobs, take up guns to patrol the reservation. Roadblocks are thrown up to keep supporters from hauling food or supplies to Pine Ridge. And because the takeover is being led by "traditionals," anyone performing ceremonies or rituals is subject to harassment.

During the first week, Gene Fast Horse wanders into a pool hall in Pine Bluff and is beaten up by three mixed-bloods for having praised the leaders. A few days later he goes after them with his deer rifle but can't manage to shoot anything other than the tires and windshield of their car. The next day a pickup comes barreling through Choteau, the masked men in the back firing at houses, dogs, and parked cars before driving away in the direction of Ree.

Negotiations break down and by late March, a month into the siege, word reaches Choteau that there is no food left. Tyrone spends a morning in Wilma and an afternoon at home on the phone, and a few days later he and Delores drive south into Nebraska and then west. Just below the reservation's south border, they come to a flat place near the sandhills where a dozen cars and trucks are gathered. Men are loading canned food, powdered milk, coffee, cigarettes, bandages, and antibiotics onto a flatbed truck. Tyrone helps another man haul a huge spool of industrial tape from a pickup to the flatbed. Delores has never seen these men before. Most of them have long hair and there isn't a single Indian among them. "Who are these people?" she asks Tyrone.

"Friends," he says. Then he gives her directions to a motel nearby and tells her to wait there. "I'll be back by midnight."

She is alone with the television and a vague sense that he will not return. The television flickers like a poorly lit fire, but she watches an entire movie and then he is back with her, his presence making the room suddenly smaller. He smells of car oil and smoke when he bends to kiss her. "Have you eaten?" he asks.

She points to a takeout pizza box on the small table by the bed.

"I could drive you somewhere," he offers. "There's a truck stop about ten miles west of here."

She shakes her head. "I'm not hungry. I wanted you to come."

"And here I am." He undresses and climbs into a hot tub.

"How'd it go?" she asks.

He doesn't answer her.

"Did you get into the village?"

"Didn't try to," he says.

"Then who were those men and what were you doing all this time?"

He dries himself and climbs into the bed as if into a boat. They make love, although her mind is elsewhere, and when he sleeps she cannot. The boat drifts and she spends long hours wanting to awaken him and hear him speak.

They rise at dawn for the long drive home to the house Gaetan Avril gave him, though he has never explained just why. The old Averill, Gaetan's father, had thrown a fit over the affair for ever having put those acres in his son's name.

"Just who is Gaetan Avril to you?" she asks.

"We're close friends, from a long time back."

"I've lived here most of my life and it's a *very* small town, so how come I never heard of you until a year ago."

He doesn't say another word and the silence burrows under her skin like a chigger, reaching straight to where the blood flows.

"And I wouldn't mind knowing where you were last night while I sat in that motel room."

He flicks on the radio and tunes it to a Sioux Falls station. The first update is always about Wounded Knee and Delores listens to the report of an airlift, a pair of Piper Cherokees that flew in low and dropped supplies estimated at one to three tons. Powdered milk, coffee, flour, bandages. No arrests had been made and the wings of both planes had been taped over to cover their numbers.

When they cross the bridge at the Missouri, she reaches to set her watch back to Central time. West of the river is ranchland, and east is where the cornfields begin. She remembers the night she and Elizabeth Bordeaux drove back and forth across the bridge, ten o'clock, nine o'clock, ten o'clock. "We're Indians," said Elizabeth, crossing to the west. And when she drove east again she said, "No, we're just dark-skinned white chicks out on the town." Elizabeth is a half-breed; white father and Oglala mother. Bloods, breeds. Ranchland, farmland. Central, Mountain. And then Elizabeth stopped the car right in the middle of the bridge where it was neither one time zone nor the other, where it was only night and too dark for them to see the water moving beneath them.

At Wounded Knee there are exchanges of gunfire, sympathetic press reports and press reports that make it look as though every man, woman, and child in the Wounded Knee settlement is intent on the overthrow of the United States government. Negotiations collapse when the occupiers insist on discussing the Treaty of Laramie of 1868, the piece of paper that ceded the Black Hills to the Sioux for all time. By early May, the siege has attracted close to two thousand Indians from sixty-four tribes, but is coming to its end. Talks are promised and by the ninth the last Indians still in the settlement give themselves up for arrest.

A week later, rainwater spills from the eave spouts and Delores risks her neck to climb up a ladder and clear the gutters of dead leaves. She takes pride in doing what pregnant women aren't supposed to do. But the life inside her is growing outward, making her fingers tingle and adding a sting to the air she breathes. Tyrone has taken a gym bag filled with clothes and shave kit and driven alone to an AIM meeting in the Twin Cities, where those arrested at Wounded Knee will be tried. Without him she finds that boredom strikes easily, so she gives herself a daily list of chores. She has just finished waxing the kitchen floor and has risen, her knees red and wet, when she finds Harold Bad Hand on the other side of the room.

"If you track dirt I'll call the police."

Harold's face is dark and his hair is slick with rain. "Red man come in peace," he says with a dumb grin.

As she circles out the back door and around to the front of the house, she wonders what on earth Harold would ever have to say to her.

He is waiting for her on the front porch and says right away, "You got to spy on Tyrone."

"Why would I do that?"

" 'Cause you're Sioux and he's a damned cheeseface."

"Is this a new way of saying Wannabe?"

Harold shakes his head. "Gene Fast Horse and I been talking it over. We think he's an apple: red on the outside and white on the inside."

"You're mixed up, Harold. He's white on the outside and red on the inside. What do you and Gene call a man like that?"

"He knows too many things. And with what we got planned, we damn better sort out the warriors from the whites."

"I grew up with you, Harold. Do you really think I'd take your word over his?"

"That's right, Delores. You grew up with me. We come from the same place and the same blood. This man Little—"

"He rescued the bones. He's paid more bail for Gene than the two of you've spent on liquor."

"Ask him where his money comes from."

"I lie down with him at night. That's kind of spying, isn't it?"

"Not if you don't tell us what he says in his sleep."

Two weeks later, she and Tyrone drive together to Pine Ridge for a weekend conference. On the way home, they stop for gas and she sees Tyrone take a fat roll of bills from his jeans pocket and peel off a twenty. When he's back behind the wheel, she asks him where he got it.

"What?"

"All that money."

He stares at the road for a full mile and she has to ask again. "And this time, Tyrone, I really want an answer."

"Gaetan gave it to me to use for the council."

"Gaetan Avril? What on earth for?"

Tyrone smiles. "He's like me, I guess. Just has a soft spot in his heart for the Native American."

In bed, he refuses to turn out the light and makes her tell him about her life, the Indian life, what she knows of the old ways.

She just laughs and says she didn't hear much about the old ways in Choteau. "Everybody was always dressed white, trying to look like they were from Omaha or Wilma. Like the people in Vietnam you told me about, getting plastic surgery so they wouldn't have slanty eyes. We couldn't go that far, but plenty wanted to. And at school they used to tell us over and over that we had to kill the Indian to let the man live. That's what we were trying to get away from—our Indian-ness."

"You must've learned something about the Lakota. Didn't your parents teach you anything?"

"Helene? Are you kidding?"

"What about your father?"

"He took off when I was a baby and didn't come back for six years. He was in the army and then he lived in California with a Mexican woman. There wasn't much about him that was Indian to start with. Anyway, he died not long after he came back."

"No one else?"

"When my grandfather was still alive, he taught me a few things, mostly fables of Coyote and Old Spider, lots of raunchy stories."

"What about the Little Sky family?"

"The only one left is June. Noah's wife."

"What about her brother Leroy?"

"I don't remember him. June says he and the other brother, Dennis, disappeared when she was about eleven."

"Disappeared?"

"Took off. Ran away. It happens all the time. You get to a certain age and start thinking of the res as hell. So you wander to one of the cities—Omaha, Des Moines, wherever—and then you find out it wasn't so bad after all."

"Who raised her? June, I mean."

"The whole village. She was with the Kills Firsts for a while, then at the mission school. I don't really know."

She wants to turn off the light and to slip over to his side of the bed. Though they're both naked, the pillow between them is like a large rock. She wants him to circle her in his arms and she will carve the questions from his mouth with her tongue.

"You never knew any other Little Skys?" he asks.

She sighs and shakes her head as if to rid herself of desire for him. "What's so important about them, Tyrone?"

When he doesn't answer, she feels her skin crawl. She shivers and he says, "I'll get another blanket."

"I'm not cold, Tyrone."

"I ask a lot of questions, is that it?"

She imagines him in the jungle with his rifle crooked into an elbow, eyes peeled for yellow men in pajamas. Orange smoke circles his head and he breathes in deeply.

"Too many questions," he says.

That night his coughing is like a bark and when he leaves the bed she is wide-awake, her eyes already accustomed to the milky light of the room. She waits until he has gone downstairs, then wraps herself in her blouse, leaving it unbuttoned, and follows him.

She can hear his voice from the bottom of the stairway. He's in the kitchen and at first she thinks he must be talking to himself but the telephone is on the wall by the table. She sits on the step to listen and after a few moments she realizes that he's talking to Gaetan Avril. They are discussing the situation in Choteau and she wonders why Tyrone is telling him so much. The rain is falling and the sound of it covers his words like radio static.

SheHe twists in her belly, tiny feet testing the walls of its small, wet chamber. Delores looks at her hands and sees in them what are called lovelines and lifelines and the broken lines of treachery.

Then she presses her palms to her middle, telling SheHe to read carefully, carefully.

Gaetan Avril

On a rainy April morning in 1973, I sold the family interest in the Ford dealership to Albert Roebuck. Albert clapped his hands before shaking mine, certain he'd just jumped on the back of a humongous cash cow, but he didn't listen hard enough for mooing or bawling. Before that spring rain dried on his lawn, Ford Credit roared in with a list of overdue debtors, many of them Clay Creek Indians whose credit I'd gleefully approved. My father had left me in charge of the dealership for the past ten years and I'd damn near run it into the ground. Repo men combed the res for Pintos, Mustangs, and Thunderbirds and mostly came back with hulks, shells, and scrap metal. Owning wheels is a big deal but I have yet to find an Indian who grasps the concept of tune-ups, lube jobs, and oil changes.

One Indian who slipped the repo noose altogether was Gene Fast Horse, who bought a red '71 Thunderbird, big horse of a car, nothing like they used to be. It turned out no one could ever find Fast Horse, either in Wilma or in Choteau, but at least once a week we'd see that red car flying down Main Street, radio blasting like summer thunder. The front bumper was torn half off, the windshield was cracked, the muffler riddled, and the driver's-side door bashed in like a beer can. By the summer I sold the dealership, we didn't see that car anymore, though we'd catch sight of Fast Horse from time to time. The Thunderbird just disappeared.

My father and I kept in-town offices off First Street. What separated us was the reception area where Janet Orbach's buns grew wider by the day and a Men's/Ladies'. One sweltering morning in early June, Janet had spent the morning sniveling about her workload and the toilets were in their third day of being stopped up when my father crossed that perilous divide and showed his face at my door. "I was thinking of lunch," he said.

I looked up from a scattering of geological charts for a waterland plot we'd had a yen for since long-term drought was the smart bet. The water was too alkaline, was the consensus. "It's only ten-thirty."

"My stomach can't tell time."

I found myself in a red Naugahyde booth at Scarlett's Inn Cafe, a menu close to my nose, and the stink of my old man's pre-meal cigar making my eyes water. The late-breakfast crowd was just breaking up and I was more than occasionally required to lift my head and nod a howdy to bankers or real estate neighbors with maple syrup drying on their lips. Scarlett's was my father's favorite lunch spot, a darkened room with plush red carpeting and fake ferns where he could order to his liking and get served before anyone else. "Small-town clout," he used to say, "is still clout. 'Course you don't subscribe to that, do you, Little G?" Big G and Little G. Pet names for the two of us that nobody used but him.

I ordered a club sandwich, knowing full well it was only a ham sandwich with canned turkey loaf and a rumor of lettuce. The menu was elaborately handwritten and spelled it "lettus," turkey was called "turkee," a touch of local phonetics for the less literate in our midst.

Vegetable soup arrived for my father. "You having any of this?" he wondered aloud.

I shook my head.

"So how's Sam? Still wants that hall light on when he sleeps?"

"Yup."

"Fear of the dark is curable, you know."

"He's only nine. Let's spare him what terrors we can until he gets to be my age."

"Your age is still scared. You give him that new rod and reel I dropped by?"

"He says, Thanks a bundle, Gramps."

"Maybe I ought to take him out next weekend, show him how to cast."

The waiter took away the empty soup bowl and the old man swapped his spoon for a knife and fork. When his chipped beef on mashed potatoes arrived, he finally got to the point. "You screwed Al Roebuck like a drunken squaw in heat."

After only one bite into that sandwich, I had a piece of ham gristle stuck between molars. I was working at it with my tongue, which put a garble to my response.

Jimmy DeWare stopped by the booth to remind us about the Lions Club meeting, six-thirty sharp. "Speaker tonight is Cal Dickerson from up Murdo way. The Dakota Hydro boys."

My father said we'd be there, though he knew it would take wild horses on drugs to draw me within five miles of a Lions Club bull shoot. When Jimmy was out the door, I asked, "Just who are the Dakota Hydro boys?"

"Enlightenment committee, teaching people around the state about how the Missouri water is ours to use or to lose."

"Another dam, you mean?"

"No, just dam management. Spillway levels and floodwater control. But don't bother feigning interest, son. It makes your eyes look the wrong color."

A light-haired young man came in and sat down at the counter. He was wearing a lumberjack shirt with the sleeves rolled up and oil-stained jeans. I could tell he wasn't a local because he wasn't sporting a cap. Wearing a cap with a baseball logo or cattle feed brand name was a must in the county's social scheme, though you can get away without one if you're dressed for business like Big G and Little G.

"What was it last month at the Lions Club—duck population? Geez, the backwater wetlands are lead-poisoned from decades of buckshot and everyone's wondering what in tarnation happened to all our feathered friends?"

My father waved a weary hand. "We're gonna have a conversation about Al Roebuck and that's all there is to it. Nothing else, not ducks, not water rights, and not the price of beans."

I took another wedge of sandwich and broke it apart to remove the turkey loaf. "Fire away."

"In recompense for the loss he's gonna take on this repo affair, I'm signing over half my share in Tom Tom Town. I just thought you should know."

Father and son, we owned four farms in the county, a ranch in the western part of the state, a filling station and convenience store alongside Highway 50, part interest in the Pheasant Run Motel, a sixteen-lot trailer court on the west edge of Wilma, and stocks and bonds too numerous to manage without a pair of full-time accountants. The lone business my father had outside our incorporation was a tourist trap called Tom Tom Town, purveyors of fine cowboy and Indian souvenirs and western literature. I hadn't wanted any part of it so my father went fifty-fifty with Al Roebuck.

"Been doing great business this summer," my father said. "But the Clay Creek people can't come up with enough beads and blankets and artifacts so we've had to order half our inventories from New

Mexico and Colorado. Folks from New Jersey can't tell Apache blankets from Sioux anyway."

"What's the point here?" I asked.

"Well, you're such a goldarned Indian lover, I thought you'd catch it with your bare hands."

I lifted my hands as if to pound my mitt but thought better of it.

"Look at it this way," he went on. "Your redskin friends bitch about unemployment to the tune of eighty percent. Fair enough, you figure. Then we give them work of one kind or another and what do they come up with? Zippo. Just like that meat-packing plant."

In the mid-sixties, encouraged by state-assisted financing, my father and Al Roebuck opened a meat-packing plant in Ree. The prospectus looked sound enough. Seventy-eight jobs at union wages, and the stockyards up in Sioux Falls were geared for delivery of steers at whatever rate the plant could operate. In addition, the state would kick in one dollar to the company for every Indian hour worked, a good deal for them if we kept the Indians off welfare. But Roebuck and my old man immediately ran smack into the thorny issue of "Indian time": the Sioux just couldn't seem to deal with a clock. Shifts were short-handed from the get-go, and employees wandered in an hour or two late if they showed up at all. Bonuses were offered to any man or woman who came in on time, but only a dozen of them ever collected. Then my father tried to fire the remaining laggards and found himself face-to-face with a troop of lawyers, so he and Roebuck were forced to compromise: shifts were changed and the Indians were allowed to come for any four-hour interval that suited them. Some days there were too many of them and other days not enough. Tools rusted, broken windows stayed broken, and the place began to stink of rotting meat. The health inspectors took one look and closed it down after only six months. Roebuck, my father, and the state took a big bath together.

My father pushed his empty plate aside and reached for a fresh cigar. He patted pockets for his lighter and couldn't come up with it, so he set the cigar on the edge of the fake oak table and leaned forward to look me square in the eye. "My point is this, Little G. Al Roebuck has been my friend and partner since before you were born. I guess that way you can count the years, huh?"

I nodded while he took a hundred-dollar bill and laid it on top of the lunch check. "Now you can piss down my leg till the cows come home and I'll just look the other way. You're my flesh and blood and that counts for me in ways I can't express." He found his lighter in his shirt pocket and whipped it out. Instead of looking at him, I watched the flame as he touched it to tobacco. When our heads were crowned with blue smoke, he went on. "Don't dick with Albert, son. Or I might feel it in my own behind, *compris*?"

The sound of that lone French word was still hanging in the air when the young man in the lumberjack shirt slipped up to the table and laid a hand on the hundred-dollar bill. "Finished, sir?" Without looking up, my father just nodded. I watched the man cross toward the register, but first he came to the door. After a swift glance in all directions, he rushed out.

The old man was staring at me. "What is it?"

"Uh, that wasn't the waiter, Dad."

He shot up from the booth and ran to the door as a pickup without license plates kicked up gravel and disappeared down the road. My father came back to the table red as a beet. "You know that guy?"

"Never seen him in my life."

"And you let him walk right off with my money? Just what kind of son are you, anyhow?"

I held my hands outward, palms up. "Your only son," I said, the smile breaking over my face like the yolk of a just-broke egg. "Your namesake."

My father came out west from Pittsburgh in 1931. He was a hydraulics engineering student on a field trip, studying the advisability of damming the Missouri in the vicinity of Wilma. The dam at Breakneck Point wasn't built for nearly thirty years, though he used to point out that his work had been used for the project manifest. He had already married Louise Martingale, who was carrying me at the time, and he had plans of becoming someone memorable. A hundred and fifty years ago, the Indians called Germans "the bad speakers" and French "the good speakers." My father, born in Quebec, was on the right side of the speaking fence but when he was twenty-four, he changed his name from Avril, Ayv-reel, meaning April, to the blander, easy-to-utter Averill. Having a straight American name was a big deal in 1931. For second-generation immigrants on the make, heritage sucked hind tit.

I was born in 1932, at the onset of the dust bowl years when there were more grasshoppers than blades of grass. All the same, when his fieldwork was done, my father bought twenty acres west of Blue Eye Creek and six miles east of Wilma, and announced his intention to turn them into a farm. He wanted to build an empire for me and my mother, and for countless grandsons to follow. He discovered, to his lifelong glee, that he had a gift for acquisition.

In those years, the General Allotment Act of 1887 was still in effect. Indians were given plots of land and a few supplies and could hold individual title to reservation land. They also had the right to sell it off as they desired and the land grabs went on at fairly regular intervals. Gaetan Averill, with help from his new pal Albert Roebuck, learned how to belly up to the bar with the best of them. In the family archives, I found deeds and transfers and liens as well as details of the sales transactions, some of them signed and others marked with crooked X's or drawings of feathers or arrowheads or the sun. On March 5, 1932, the Walking Horse family sold its last twenty acres for thirty-six dollars and was never heard from again. A month later, fifty acres were signed over jointly by Jim Little Sky and Francis Scully, who were promptly hired to farm the land they had just sold. Six months later, Jim's brother Sonny sold fifty of his hundred acres and another eighty it turned out didn't belong to him for ninety-four dollars and a truck. By the end of 1934, the Averill spread, half grazing land and half farmland, covered six hundred acres. There was another deal, a sliver of sixteen acres purchased from James Harrison Lame, that included a proviso that Lame could work that land at three dollars a day for life. By 1936 my father had more than three thousand acres and had spent only eight hundred dollars of his own money. The rest came in bank loans or from Roebuck, the last of which was paid off in 1964.

Traditional Indians argued that the land, once sold, could never be recovered. They claimed that the money they received would trickle through their fingers and they'd need to keep selling more land until it all would be gone. All the same, by 1943, the Clay Creek Reservation had dwindled to half of its initial size of eight hundred thousand acres. Albert Roebuck, Geoffrey Corbin, my father, and a dozen others owned land that straddled the Missouri along a sixty-mile stretch of sloping grassland, suitable for either corn and hay or for grazing, rich, black river-bottom soil that was easy to irrigate.

The first scam must be the hardest to close, though it's not likely anybody lost sleep over the plight of the red man. His face was on the nickel and if his descendants didn't know the value of those five cents, that wasn't Roebuck's or Averill's fault. They were men of their time and place, amassing land and capital in South Dakota when the prior tenants, losers of all battles, had become invisible to the public at large. Horning in on their property was just good business and admirable civic initiative. Anyway, those land archives don't tell the story of why I changed my name.

In the autumn of 1943, two Oglala brothers named Dennis and Leroy Little Sky were jailed for having threatened my father with a loaded rifle. Their reasons for doing so don't appear in the newspaper accounts. Six months later, Leroy, approximately thirty-one years old, just up and disappeared. The next fall, my mother left our house under circumstances that were never made clear to the people of Wilma. The night she left, our house burned to the ground.

But I knew why she had left, where Leroy had gone, and how the fire had started. My father couldn't look me in the eye, so he shipped me to a military academy in Wisconsin where I studied agricultural engineering and learned how to buff-shine my shoes.

Later, the day after my eighteenth birthday, I went to the county courthouse and legally changed my name to Gaetan Avril.

About the time I was having that lunch with my old man, the golf course at Eagle Reach was almost finished but people were slow to sign up as members. For one thing, the course was too close to Choteau. If you were standing on the tee at sixteen, your back was exposed to a treeline that might or might not be bristling with Indians toting deer rifles, which makes it hard for a white man to concentrate on his backswing. And the fact that they'd found both white and Indian remains on the fourteenth hadn't sat well with the locals. Roebuck and my father had financed a good part of the deal, and they were watching their investment go straight down the toilet. So while Tyrone and I were preparing to take them to court for ancient land swindles, they were trying to see if they couldn't push the western border of the reservation to the other side of Choteau with a swift buyout and they had more than a few greedy allies among the Indians in Ree. It started out as a local struggle and I thought it would stay that way. I didn't count on Wounded Knee or the American Indian Movement or the Bones War.

Once that war started, I had to stay clean away from Choteau. There was an influx of badges, both state and federal, like moths around a flame. The Indians couldn't always tell who the plainclothes fellas were but I knew them on sight and so did Tyrone. The FBI had added AIM to its list of "extremists," just like the Black Panthers and the Weathermen and whatnot. And though AIM was a national organization, the leaders somehow settled on the Clay Creek Reservation as a place to make their stand. Choteau was being watched night and day, and by the end of July the surveillance included regular flights of an unmarked Cessna that was taking photos from four hundred feet. I was trying to keep my sympathies under my hat but I suppose they were plain as day and had been all my life. To the whites I was an Indian lover and to the Indians I was my father's son.

But Tyrone was there on the inside where I needed him. For reasons of my own, I'd been looking for him for years and finally found him, in December of 1971, at the VA hospital up in St. Paul. I had land of my own, fourteen hundred acres that had once been in my mother's name, and I offered half of it to Tyrone, along with that beat-up house bordering the property. It was a widowed farmhouse, no farm left to it, and had just been swallowed up in the multitude of acquisitions. My father cursed himself for years for having left that land in his old name, but he'd been trying to water down his property taxes and hadn't counted on the way family events got out of hand. Tyrone wasn't all that interested in the land. He told me he wasn't a farmer and wasn't about to start. Though I offered him more, the house was all he accepted and he leased everything except five acres to the Ingersolls, a decent family that had been busting Choteau sod far longer than the Averills. And he made me swear to keep it a secret who he was and where he'd been. This made perfect sense at the time, given the social climate around Wilma, but it didn't do him much good as far as the Choteau crowd was concerned. They called him Wannabe behind his broad back. And once the plainclothesmen began to filter in, he had a gamey smell as far as the Indians were concerned, as though he was the advance man for the FBI.

Anyway, Tyrone was trying to convince the Choteau families to file court claims for the return of the property their parents or grandparents had sold. I was to carry the legal fire by providing the documents that would justify their case. We had a lawyer in Denver advising us on how to proceed, though we kept that fact between us. Out-of-state lawyers aren't well loved where I come from, especially those who specialize in land law.

Tyrone was trying to grease the rails in Choteau by doing things like helping out with home repairs or legal aid or bail money that he got from me. He didn't tell me in advance about going to Pierre to steal back those bones. I'd have tried to talk him out of it, though when I heard the news I danced Mary up and down the hallway and out the front door. My obsession over those bones terrified her. She knew it was hatred of my father and not love of Indians that stoked my fire. She grew up in Wilma and we'd been married for ten years, so she had a pretty clear view of my true battleground. Our son, Sam, was only nine and I was bursting to tell him the whole story but I worried that he'd tell his grandfather and then our paper war would be in ruins.

I hadn't expected AIM to get much of a toehold. Choteau town had been a sleepy little place for most of my life, a collection of houses and shacks that most of the county folks wished would move a hundred miles east. But by the spring of 1973, after Wounded Knee, it was a hostile beehive of redskin agitation. I think that's the phrase my father used. So, I took to meeting Tyrone on the sly. I'd dial his number and hang up after three rings so he'd know to meet me at the roadhouse up north of town. Two rings and he'd know I'd be at the secret place south of his house.

Now and then Delores answered before I could hang up, so I'd make small talk, inquire as to her state of health, the baby and all. She wasn't friendly or even polite. Though I'd long since changed my name back to Avril, she insisted on calling me Averill. Tyrone loved her but he kept his secrets to himself, his past and present and whatever he was aiming for. If he had just once confided in her, the years that followed would have had a different color to them altogether.

My father was keeping a close eye on my whereabouts. We didn't work elbow to elbow, but the family business caused us to cross paths once or twice a week. I had learned as a child that although he had his fingers in every corner of Wilma County and seemed to have eyes in the back of his head, there was a single blind spot, a point in the universe that he could never see for what it was: his son. He mistak-

enly assumed that the military academy had whittled the tree of my
hostility to twigs.

Once the FBI agents turned up, I started spending my evenings
out at the brand-new Eagle Reach Bar. There were card games almost
every night after supper, and I had plenty of money to toss onto the
table. About ten days after our lunch, I found myself in a game with
my father, Stuart Baumgartner, Jack LeHavre, Jimmy DeWare, and
a young guy with a wife and new baby girl and not enough ready cash
to hold his own. When we were alone, my father and I could talk
family business, land, horses, or the weather. I could sit in his office
with my feet up on his desk and crack jokes. But the one subject that
drove us both bonkers was the Indians, Choteau, the past, all that. I
knew the ropes and needed a crowd around us to loosen him up on
this subject. For weeks I'd been waiting for a game without Albert
Roebuck's big butt crowding the table. When he was around, I
couldn't pull any wool over my father's eyes and coil the conversation
in my direction. My reputation as a Democrat didn't help either, but
when men drink and win at cards they tend to forget themselves and
information slips out of their mouths like cheap fish hooks. And it's
easy to *lose* at poker if that's what you're aiming to do. All you have
to do is dump your best cards or ride a pair of eights against a strong
counterbet. Losers are closed-mouthed and surly, while winners are
generous with both alcohol and chitchat.

My father was drinking Manhattans. Jesus Christmas, there's a
poison to beat arsenic. He had fifteen percent of Eagle Reach and,
of all the partners, he was taking the bad news the hardest. He came
to that table to win back a piece of his losses and I decided to swing
the game in his favor as best I could. The fourth hand of the night,
Stuart tried his first transparent bluff, taking two cards and giving us
this Chinese-looking smile. I was dealt a pair of sevens and then drew
a third when there were already fifty dollars in the pot. The younger
guys all folded when my father tossed in a twenty. It was up to me
and I gave Stuart my look, the one that for years has put the chill to
him, and raised him twenty. Like I knew he would, he folded and
reached for the whisky.

Everybody knows someone who can weep on command, that
squeeze of the eyes and the dribble of teardrops. But as far as I know,
my trick's unique: I can sweat just by willing myself to. I went at it
after Stuart folded, erasing the look I had on my face and replacing

it with paleness. All I had to do was hold my breath and clench the muscles across my chest and shoulders. My father was looking at me and then at his cards. The pot was sugared up nicely and I felt the first trickle of sweat run from my hairline to my eyebrow.

"Call you, Gaetan. And raise you forty."

I pretended to think it over. Ten seconds, twenty. There was sweat on my nose and in my eyes. Then I turned my cards face down on the table like I was ashamed of them.

My father raked in the cash and I reeled him in like a tuckered-out walleye.

There's something to be said for making money hand over fist. No one blames you for it, but the general public appreciates it when you pony up for taxes come April. All the same, my father liked to play with crimped cards and he turned tax evasion into an art form. His first tricks were lacking in subtlety: the house was in my mother's name, for example, or a sixty-acre plot that showed up as twenty acres on the tax lien. Poor handwriting would have made a handsome alibi if the county auditor noticed 2's in the net payable column that were supposed to be 7's. It wasn't until the late forties that my old man saw the light and scrapped this penny-ante stuff in favor of broader, bolder strokes. He received a tax break for "consulting services" to the county water board. Several marshy acres were declared game reserves even though leaking pesticides had so sullied the water that no self-respecting mallard would dip a webbed foot in those parts. In 1952 the reserve was declared open to hunters and my father received the first of his annual rebates to the tune of five hundred dollars. That ended six years later when a hunting party from back east, five men who'd shelled out a thousand each for a week of pheasant and duck hunting, complained of headaches and nausea. Then there was his first five thousand acres, acquired while he still called himself Avril. After he changed the name, he conveniently forgot to alter the paperwork. When I turned eighteen and changed my name, he wrote off the gesture as sentiment or caprice. But thereafter, I had claim on those five thousand acres as well as another three or so he'd put in trust for me while I was learning to march in step at the military academy.

An hour into the poker game, my father was up close to three hundred dollars and the table talk finally turned to future prospects for Eagle Reach. We all agreed that the membership would fill out once the golf course opened in three weeks, but that the Indian troubles would squash any chance of making quota. Then I won a modest pot, thirty bucks and change. Jimmy DeWare complained that the pool-cleaning crew left a lot to be desired and the conversation drifted to gripes about the club services and the layout of some of the holes. It took another hour and sixty-odd dollars of personal losses before we came back to the real subject.

Stuart Baumgartner said he'd installed an electric fence around his house. "Fry any redskin to a cinder."

"Not to mention birds, stray dogs, and your own kids if you're not careful," Jimmy told him.

The new man said there was a rumor that John Fire Smith had been to Cuba to meet Castro.

Stuart said he'd heard the same thing from Special Agent Robbins. "He tells me it was Al Roebuck who made the call to the feds. Bull Smedsrud tried to put the skids to that idea. Said it was a state matter and he'd do the job with his own marshals."

Bob "Bull" Smedsrud, the state attorney general, was spearheading pressure against the AIMers. "What about Smedsrud for governor?" Jimmy asked, and our glasses were briefly raised in tribute.

"I wish to hell he'd bottle up Reese Lonetree's goons," my father said. "They been drifting off the reservation a hell of a lot more than they used to."

"They're attracted to Choteau," I told him. "Target practice."

He shot me a glance.

Jimmy DeWare, showing off his human side, pointed out that he used to work at the clinic with Delores Her Many Horses. "I know this won't sit well with all of you, but there are women and children out there."

"And a shitload of firearms," Stuart said.

My father reached his long arm to his tumbler. The ice had long since melted and his drink looked like gasoline. "Our troubles will soon be over," he said.

How's that, I wanted to ask, but I knew I had to leave that to someone else. While my father dealt the cards, Stuart Baumgartner did me the favor.

"The FBI boys," the old man told him, then finished off the Manhattan. For a moment I worried that he wasn't going to complete the thought, that the vermouth had numbed his tongue for the night, but he merely paused to let out a bit of air. "All this time, it turns out . . ." He shut up again and reached into his shirt pocket for a cigar, not realizing his cigar pack was sitting on the table. I reached across and handed it to him, then he lit his cigar.

"All this time we been fretting and they got an inside man." He breathed out a blue Panamanian cloud. "In Choteau itself. Son of a gun. Three cards, Stuart? You ever take less than that?"

"Inside man?" It was me pushing him; my first mistake all night. "An Indian?"

"Got him in from Denver. Some lame buck, I guess, got his dick in a knot and had to play ball." He was looking closely at his cards, then remembered I was there and the color returned to his ice-blue eyes. "What's it to you, Gaetan? You in or out?"

I was in and threw away a queen and an ace. My father tossed me two cards, a seven of diamonds and another queen right back. Now the sweat on my face was the genuine article. The bet went to forty dollars and I called for no reason I could think of. Jimmy showed a pair of tens with a king kicker and Stuart had red aces. The new man was beat and had that look on his face like he was trying to figure out what to tell the wife. My father smiled and murmured, "Harem," then fanned out three queens for all to see.

My man in Denver was slow to answer my questions. He had a contact at the FBI office in Denver, not to mention access to Colorado state prison records. He'd already helped us out by passing on some useful hearsay, but this time I needed the straight dope. I mailed him a list of all the Indians I knew to be in Choteau and waited more than two weeks for him to get back to me. When he called me at home, I told him to sit tight and I'd call right back. It took me ten minutes to drive into Wilma where there was a pay phone they'd just put in by the Texaco station.

"Twenty-eight-year-old with a mean streak," he said. "He pulled a year for armed robbery in Iowa. A bungled burglary, evidently, but the file doesn't say much more. Then they got him for breaking and entering, full-scale burglary and assault, you name it, here in Colorado. He had more than twelve years left to serve on a sixteen-year term, but they cut him loose nine months ago and nobody's saying how come."

"What's his name?"

"When he got arrested, he was going by the name Bobby Small. You know the Indians, Gaetan, they take names like racehorses. During his trial they found he had a dozen AKA's."

"Let's hear them."

"Bobby Stars Come Out, Dennis Dog Moon, Jerome Draper, Clarence Draper, Del Winter Camp. You want to hear all of these?"

"What's his real name?"

"The file says it's unconfirmed. But I guess that doesn't matter to you, does it?"

"I'm holding a pen to paper."

That was only a figure of speech. When he told me the name I didn't need to write it down.

A few weeks later I told Tyrone that the marshals were planning a raid. "I overheard the old man on his telephone. He's got one of those intercom sets and he's none too careful about the wiring job."

"What're they after?"

"The guns, of course. I have the impression they know just where to look."

I didn't have details on the arsenal that was out there. When I found out later that there were more than forty-five rifles and half as many sidearms, it occurred to me that the mass arrest of the adult population of Choteau was averted by a margin of about eight hours. But the fact that Tyrone tipped them off put him in even a worse position. How had he known? That was a question he couldn't answer to anyone's satisfaction, and given the heat he was taking, I didn't even try to get in touch for the next two weeks.

But then I got another call from my Denver man. It was close to midnight and I didn't bother getting dressed and racing to the pay phone.

"My guy at the Bureau," he said, "mentioned reinforcements coming straight at you. An assault group, evidently."

"What the hell does that mean?"

"Listen, Gaetan, he didn't spell it out and I was in no position to ask."

I woke Mary up and told her to get herself and Sam dressed. Then I packed bags for both of them and loaded them into the Chrysler.

Under normal circumstances, our house wasn't in any line of fire, but it was getting harder to judge just where that line fell. "Drive straight south," I told her, "until you get to Nebraska, then take Highway Twelve all the way to Sioux City. Check into a motel and stay there. Don't come back to South Dakota until I say so."

"Where will you be?"

"Driving in circles. But don't worry, I'm nobody's idea of a target. I'm still white and still my father's son."

I followed her car as far as the state line then turned around and hurried back toward Wilma. The town was dead quiet and although I cruised around for a good half hour, I didn't see a single car on the streets. It was past two in the morning when I drove out of there. I took the dirt roads well north of Choteau and skirted back south to Tyrone's place. I banged on the door until they woke up and Delores came to the door. She was wearing a pink housedress and looked huge in the moonlight. She stared at me as if I was a bug and then Tyrone was behind her, in jeans and boots, buttoning his shirt. "Let's go for a drive," he said, "and leave Delores in peace." He didn't have to remind me of Delores' feelings. As far as she was concerned, I was the reason everyone in Choteau mistrusted him.

Tyrone was in the mood to drive around and he took to the dirt roads. Everyone but tourists—and there were damned few of them— was avoiding Highway 50. Though he didn't say so, I knew he was heading to wherever the guns were hidden. After about half an hour, he turned into a rocky field and the next thing I knew we were on a road I never knew existed, heading south. Tyrone switched off the headlights but there was a bright fat yellow moon and after four miles or so I saw we were coming up on the meeting hall by the Indian cemetery. We were within two hundred yards when Tyrone pulled over. There was a light-colored car parked ahead of us, along the road that bordered the cemetery. The front door was open but we couldn't see anyone inside. Tyrone asked if I was armed and I shook my head. "Jesus Christ, Gaetan. You must be the only unarmed white man in the damned county."

We sat there in the gray darkness for a few minutes, then Tyrone edged the car forward until we could see into the cemetery. There was a man with a shovel and he was digging like hell. He had his back to us and all I could see was his long braids. By the way he was stumbling around, I gathered he was drunk.

"We ought to stop this," I said.

Tyrone lit his lights and gunned the engine and when the car bounced onto the cemetery road the man turned around. He threw down that shovel just like that and picked up a rifle. Tyrone yelled to get down but I was frozen in my seat. The first shot missed us altogether, but the second banged off the mirror on Tyrone's side. The next took out a tire and we spun sideways and slid into a ditch right next to the church. Tyrone put his foot to the gas but the wheels just spun in the air. His door was jammed against the ditch, so we climbed out my door and by the time we got out the man had leaped into the car and driven off.

I recognized the car and so did Tyrone. It was one of those pale blue jobs that the FBI were driving, though it was pretty beat-up. "So now they're dressing up like Indians," I said.

"Nope," Tyrone said. "That *was* an Indian. Your man in Denver had it right."

I wanted to get the hell out of there, but Tyrone went into the cemetery to look around. A lot of gravestones were kicked over and Tyrone stopped at one that looked like it had just been dug up. "That's where the rifles were," he said. It was a fake gravesite and now it was just a hole in the ground littered with bullets. Tyrone stuffed a few into his pockets and stood up. We were heading back to the car when all of a sudden he stopped short. Another grave had been dug up, and this time it wasn't a fake. There wasn't a headstone with a name or anything, just a tipped-over cross. The casket was made of pine and a layer of tin and was half rotted away.

We knew we had to get out of there, so I sat behind the wheel and rocked the car while Tyrone pushed. The soil was dry but the car was tipped at a bad angle and we could only get one of the rear wheels to touch ground. It was no go. We gave up and decided to just leave the car in the ditch. It was six miles west to my house or eight miles east to Tyrone's, and we hadn't gone east along the dirt road more than a hundred yards when we saw headlights coming our way. We turned to run in the other direction, but the road was cut off by a pair of cars that spun sideways on the gravel. To either side of us were empty fields, no corn to hide in, and not a single tree.

Tyrone took the bullets out of his pocket and tossed them casually into the weeds. "Hold your hands real high, Gaetan, so they'll know you're not armed."

A moment later we were surrounded by state marshals and there were rifles pointing at my eyes.

Noah Lame

In peaceful times, the howling of a wild animal in the night is almost magically comforting. You lie in bed and listen to the coyotes or a wild dog and the last of your waking dreams is laced tight. But when the times themselves are wild, as they were the spring and summer of 1973, the same howling will set you on edge; it's the sound of a bad omen, of worries just up the road, and the feeling of being watched by unseen eyes.

Reese Lonetree was no friend of AIM or of our group at Choteau. There were only twelve hundred people on Clay Creek and he had about a hundred of them on the council payroll, plus full control of the BIA police, and he was leaning on us with all he had. We knew he was getting support from the state. There was the attorney general, Bob Smedsrud—Bull they called him—a fat little guy with round eyeglasses who used to work in legal aid around Wilma County and sometimes on the res. The Choteau crowd knew him from the years he was lawyering for Indians. Frank Poor Bull says he was hell on wheels back in the early sixties, a white man working for the red man day and night with low pay. But then there was a story about how he raped this one Indian girl and got off for lack of evidence. I don't know if it's true or not. All the same, no one saw Smedsrud around after that. Now, ten years later, he was making hay up in the capital by throwing legal and police support behind Reese Lonetree's private army. He called himself an "Indian fighter," which went over even better in places like Sioux Falls and Rapid City than it did in Wilma, where people knew at least some Indians and didn't want all of them dead.

Our newsletter expanded from six pages to twelve. Donations went up, including an anonymous gift of three thousand dollars that I suspected came from Gaetan Avril. We'd never had so much income but it was all going for gas, food, legal bills, and self-defense. Lonetree's goons—led by his son Jerry—were roaming the reservation and harassing any AIMers and traditionals they could find, and one of their chief targets was the Choteau group. If they found anybody out alone and unarmed, they'd handcuff them and make them lie facedown for hours at a stretch. Another tactic was to drive into Choteau and shoot off their rifles into houses where there were women and children, then drive away. John Fire had always been against our having guns, but now he agreed there was no other alternative. He'd slipped out of Wounded Knee before the feds moved in, but they knew he was there and had him pegged for one of the leaders. So now he was wanted in both South Dakota and Montana, so I advised him to lie low out west for a time. He just smiled and told me he'd joined up with AIM at Wounded Knee. "I'm on the defense committee, Noah."

I don't know who we got the guns from though that's where an awful lot of our money went during the spring of 1973. At first I argued against the idea, but once those goons knew we were armed they sure were a lot less bold about shooting at houses and cars. By the time summer rolled around Choteau was quiet for a while, but the tension only got worse.

It was during the spring that we noticed the FBI people hanging around Wilma or cruising the outlying dirt roads in their sky blue cars. I'd be sitting on the porch with a book and my coffee and could see the dust in the distance and it was always Russ Poor Bull on that motorcycle of his or one of those blue cars. I think they were Thunderbirds or Firebirds. I don't know cars, I just know they were named for birds. The man we saw the most of was Special Agent Bill Person. He was fond of wearing golf shirts with those turtles stitched on the breast and except for his dark glasses he looked like some golf player. We got used to him a lot faster than I would have thought. He used to come out and visit like he was a neighbor or something. When a kid from Lake Andrew was accused of raping a white girl, Person poked around until it came out that there wasn't any rape at all, those two had been meeting up for weeks in the backseat of a parked car. For a while he bewildered us. Fast Horse was in favor of running him off since the FBI has no legal jurisdiction on Indian reservations, but we didn't go along with that kind of talk. There were more agents where he came from, and anyway, he didn't seem too bad, though I don't remember anybody inviting him over for Sunday lunch.

One chilly April evening, he drove up and I came out on the porch to see what he wanted. I wasn't surprised when he got out of the car but left the engine still running. That's what Indians sometimes do when they go into towns where they know they aren't welcome.

"Are you Noah Lame?"

I said I was.

"Sorry to trouble you," he said. "Dinnertime and all. My name's Bill Person and I'm an agent of the Federal Bureau of Investigation." He extended his hand as if Indians have been shaking hands with the FBI for years and years.

I shook his hand, but didn't invite him in. I told him I'd noticed his car more than once.

He nodded. "I was in the neighborhood and thought we should meet."

I wanted to be polite, to show that I had good manners and an education that must have equaled his own. But we were out there in plain sight of everyone coming to or from Choteau, and it made me jumpy having him on my property. "No can talk now," I said. "Wife cook buffalo tongue. Me go eat."

He ignored the sarcasm and said he was sorry. I noticed he was always sorry about something. And he had a way of changing his voice from a folksy voice to an FBI voice, and I quickly got into the habit of listening for one or the other. "I just thought I should warn you," he said. "Your property has been targeted for a health inspection. Even though you're on the reservation, the county commissioners have the authority to fine you."

That fast, I dropped the Hollywood Injun talk. "Fine me for what?"

He nodded toward the north. "Apparently that outhouse is too close to the county road. I believe the regulations require a distance of fifty feet. We could always measure if you like."

"Who told you about this?"

He spun out his folksy voice. "It's a real small town, Mr. Lame. You can hear all kinds of things at the Eagle Reach Bar."

The country club had just opened and they said the golf course would be ready in the summer, as soon as the grass grew in.

"Why're you telling me this?"

"Because it smacks of harassment. There's bad blood in the area, Mr. Lame. You don't need me to tell you that. Ever since Wounded Knee and that business with the bones at Eagle Reach. My duty is to observe the situation and provide assistance when jurisdiction permits me."

"Are outhouses your jurisdiction?"

This won me a smile that sure as hell looked sincere. "No, I'm afraid that's simple friendly advice." He reached into his breast pocket and pulled out a card that had his name and number on it. The address was Minneapolis but he'd penciled in another phone number. "That's Pheasant Run Motel. I'm there most evenings. Either myself or Special Agent Cale or Robbins. If you ever need anything, don't hesitate to call."

Christians make mention of cold days in hell. I chose diplomacy and didn't bother pointing out that I didn't have a phone.

"A pleasure meeting you, Mr. Lame. I'm sorry again to have disturbed your dinner."

As he turned his car around, I could hear the radio was tuned to a ballgame, bottom of the sixth and the Twins still trailing.

The spring was long and wet, which meant the mosquitoes were worse than usual. By the time June rolled around, they were everywhere. It gets humid as hell where we live, the kind of heat that promises rain that never comes, and the air was hard to breathe. My wife June was serious about her gardening that summer, though, and the humidity was great for her tomatoes. You could almost see them growing out of the red clay of our front yard and she'd made a little border of marigolds around them. She said marigolds kept the bugs away.

Choteau was attracting quite a crowd since the end of the Wounded Knee occupation. People were drifting our way and settling in. Kevin Walking Horse, who'd given me that drum skin in Pierre, moved down with Anna. They installed themselves in an abandoned house close to Toby's that was covered with asphalt shingling and didn't have any heat or water. Tyrone hooked them up to the electricity, and June and Jana helped them find furniture. Once they got settled, Anna started giving courses in Lakota while Kevin Walking Horse and George Brings Yellow organized daily prayer sessions for the traditionals. A man called Jim Bordeaux, who'd been at Alcatraz in 1969, pitched a tent behind Pete Scully's house and spent most of his time working on all the cars that were getting worn down from all the driving east and west.

On the one hand, Choteau was becoming a spiritual and cultural center. On the other hand, it was an armed camp. There wasn't any and I held on to June so she wouldn't get hurt. When I heard Jana scream, I let go of June and climbed up the ladder and I found Lonetree beating on Herman with his gun. He stopped when he saw me coming, then he very slowly raised the barrel until it was touching my chest. There wasn't anything in his eyes that I could read, neither hate nor anger. They were like wet stones shining at me while he mulled over whether or not to pull the trigger. Over his shoulder, Jana was clutching a towel in front of her.

"Get dressed, Jana." I heard the terror in my own voice. "This man is leaving."

Lonetree rested the gun on his hip. "I guess this room is clean," he said. Then he smiled as though he'd said something funny and shoved past me down the ladder.

I followed him down and found that they'd kicked over the tomato plants and the marigolds and even the sunflowers that by this time of year had grown to almost six feet tall.

"State property is missing," Blue Suit told me before leaving. "Property that you were inquiring about for quite a spell just last year. If you have any information as to the whereabouts of two parcels marked with the state seal, it's your duty to notify us."

I told him to go to whichever hell he believed in, but all he did was turn around and get back inside Gaetan Averill's blue car where the windows were rolled up tight to keep from losing the air conditioning.

By the end of the morning there wasn't a house in Choteau that hadn't been ransacked. Toby's place was almost totally destroyed, all the windows broken or shot out, his chairs smashed, plates and glasses all over the floor. They even tore apart the brass bed at Helene Her Many Horses' trailer, though by some kind of merciful oversight they left her television intact. Some Indians from the reservation were right there with the marshals, helping them wreck things. We'd seen these BIA guys before and it was the first time we truly understood how split up we all were, Indians helping whites to clean us all out. Sure, they were under government's thumb and afraid of losing everything they had, but it was hard to remember as much that particular morning.

Willard Bent and John Fire escaped by going out the back of

Toby's and cutting across the row of trees that border the dirt road. From there they made it to the river and even swam across to Nebraska. They hid out on the other side and then snuck back to Choteau once they thought the marshals were gone. This was a route they'd figured out awhile ago and it wouldn't be the last time they'd have to use it.

What got our attention was the way they looked in places where we'd kept guns before. And each time they came up empty-handed, we noted their surprise. Willard Bent and John Fire had moved those guns just the day before without telling a soul. If they hadn't, we'd have all been up on charges of one kind or another.

Out of pure frustration, they took Toby into town and grilled him for three hours. He had to walk all the way back to Choteau because they wouldn't let him use the phone to call for a ride. He told us that they'd taken him to Albert Roebuck's boardroom behind his office because there wasn't enough room at the town hall to accommodate everyone who was there. He said besides the marshals, there had to be a dozen BIA police and a number of white men from the Eagle Reach crowd, including some guy from the local newspaper.

"Them marshals thought I was John Fire Smith, but Gaetan Averill set them straight. They was madder than hell and started shouting at those BIA boys for giving them smoke. But once they had me, no way they'd let go without asking me some questions. Like, had I ever gone to Cuba and was I friends with Weathermen. Nobody beat on me but they didn't pop me no cold beer either. By the time they finished with me, they was throwing papers and shouting and fighting about who was doing more to screw up our lives."

We all got a good laugh out of that, one of the few times we didn't feel that what we were up against was invulnerable. All the same, we knew we had to get assembled in a hurry and sort out what we were going to do.

Toby's place couldn't hold us all, so we met up at the old church hall on the old Wilma road. It used to sit squarely on the reservation but over the years the land around it got swallowed up by the county. There were more people at the meeting that night than there'd ever been, not just from Choteau, but from Wilma and Lake Andrew. It was stifling hot and we hadn't thought to bring enough water and lemonade and sandwiches. There were cardboard banners on the wall proclaiming Christ's mercy, and pictures of lambs and clouds and verbs that ended with eth. Cometh, sayeth. The old line gets used at such times, about how, when the missionaries came, they had the Bible and we had the land and now that we've got the Bible, *they've* got the land.

Gene Fast Horse had his braids tied back with red cloth to show he meant business. He came along with his friends from Minneapolis and Omaha. Indians who barely knew what life on a reservation was all about. Between Gene and Frank Poor Bull's boy, Russell, it was harder and harder to have a proper meeting. Russell had been fired from his job at one of Roebuck's farms when they found out he was on the Crazy Horse Council, and he kept telling us the first thing we should do was to burn Roebuck's place to the ground and then that country club. Harold Bad Hand wasn't much help either. He usually broke up meetings with his shouting and swearing, but that night he just sat in a corner drinking wine in a brown bag and glaring at all the older men.

Just before we got started, Darryl Kills First came inside and said there were about a dozen cars outside, people from the BIA and the tribal council and two cars that he was sure were FBI. A man in a suit was writing down license numbers.

Some folks had brought their children and it was taking some doing to get them to stop running around the hall and to sit quietly in their chairs. Gaetan Avril was there—the son, of course, not the father. He and Tyrone were the only whites and they sat off to one side with Delores Her Many Horses. I recognized Leonard Rocking Boy sitting not far from Harold. Leonard and I grew up together but had grown apart, like a pair of sticks floating down the river, one in the current and the other swirling off toward shore. We'd both been to college and now I was tutoring school kids for apples and pennies while he made a good living at the Wilma electric plant. He was on good terms with the BIA and the Wilma town council, had five children by the same wife and put them all in the public school system. It was said he gave a third of his earnings to the children's fund on the reservation, and I knew for a fact that he spent every Sunday as a volunteer at the retirement center. It was obvious he didn't much care for the proceedings.

The journalist who'd been along at Rushmore, Clyde Bennett, was taking pictures of everybody. Gene Fast Horse offered his best profile but it made me glad when Bennett didn't bite. He wanted something real, not cheap glamour. Then Gene stood up and started giving us a loud inventory of the damages done to Choteau. While he spoke, Leonard Rocking Boy stood and waited for him to finish. He folded his arms and I was reminded of a picture I once saw that showed on one side the bad Indian with a gun in one hand and a bottle of whisky in the other, and on the other side the good Indian with a Bible and pitchfork. Leonard looked a hell of a lot like the good Indian just then.

Gene was still talking up a storm when John Fire jumped up and shouted, "Hey, the cow is dead!"

We sat there in stunned silence, then Gene said, "What the fuck's the matter with you?"

"The cow's dead," John Fire repeated, with that silky tone he sometimes used. "We don't need your bull."

That's when Leonard Rocking Boy shouted, "You AIM people are crazy and all you're gonna do is get people hurt!"

Gene sighed and looked out at the crowd. "Will someone tell this hang-around-the-fort redskin to go home?"

"These aren't the old days," Leonard said. "Those days are gone. We can preserve our culture without all this violence!"

"You're barking up the wrong tree, Leonard." It was Delores.

John Fire added, "We're just trying to hang on to our dignity, Leonard."

"Guns and alcohol won't restore your dignity."

Leonard left shortly after that and half the crowd went with him. The meeting split into separate conversations and arguments and people gradually drifted out. When we were the only ones left, the Choteau group moved a circle of chairs together and we continued. Harold said to Gaetan Avril, "You got no right to be here."

"It's all right if he stays," Tyrone answered. "He's been a big help."

"He's been a big help to you," Gene said. "Giving you that house and land."

"He's not on the council," Harold said.

"He's his father's son," Darryl Horse added.

Gaetan nodded to Tyrone. "Evening, everybody," he said, and Clyde Bennett followed him out.

When they were gone, Tyrone turned to Fast Horse. "He didn't repossess your car, Gene. Roebuck's the one on your tail."

"Where in the hell is that car?" Poor Bull asked.

"I got it stashed where nobody's gonna find it," Fast Horse said, and he smiled as if he'd just swallowed something that tasted good.

"This church isn't even on reservation land," John Fire reminded us. "We can't be splitting up into small bands. They can come any time they want, and we're alone here."

"We got to organize our own defense," Frank said, "just like they're doing in Minneapolis. Not just with guns, but witnesses, too. They keep themselves out in the light where if someone gets beaten up, it makes the papers."

"That won't happen here," Tyrone said.

Delores Her Many Horses was looking over my shoulder at her reflection in a window. She'd always been on the north side of vain, and ever since she got pregnant she seemed to be in a panic over her looks. I wanted to ask her how she was feeling and to tell her to stay out of harm's way with the baby so close, but conversation never was easy for the two of us. I'm a diploma Indian and she prefers to hang with the warriors. Catching me looking, she said, "Where's June?"

"June's in no mood to talk to anybody. She stayed home to clean the place up."

The marshals hadn't called on Tyrone, so it was no surprise when Gene brought it up.

"You might have noticed," Delores told him, "we're almost three miles away and they must've thought the bones were in town."

"This raid didn't have anything to do with those bones," Pete Scully said. "It was revenge is all. Just plain spite."

"I don't know why they didn't hit my place," Tyrone said, shaking his head. "I just don't know."

Harold snatched at the air, then slowly opened his palm. But there was no fly inside.

We were talking in swirls and mixing up our subjects, but John Fire and Tyrone held us together as best they could. They both argued that the best course was to hang on to the land we had and to fight to recover the hundreds of thousands of acres that had been whittled from the res. After that, we could govern ourselves rather than leave our affairs to Reese Lonetree and the breeds in Ree. Tyrone was always making the same point: retrieve the land, the land is forever. It's an old idea and no one disagreed. And John Fire told Gene Fast Horse to stop comparing the reservation to a concentration camp. "It's our land," he said, "and you shouldn't degrade it."

Fast Horse backed down there, but I can't say we all pulled in any one direction. Gene and Harold had their point of view and Tyrone and John Fire had theirs—like two racing winds coming together to make a cyclone. Herman took faith in the prophecies of the ghost dance, in which the ghosts of all dead Indians would rise up and join us to wipe out the white men.

That's something I never believed. I don't want to see the white men annihilated any more than I want to hunt buffalo with a bow and arrow.

When the meeting finally broke up, I walked home with Herman and Jana and we could hear the coyotes howling up north beyond the trees. The night was warm and our house wasn't far, maybe four miles down a dirt road, but in the darkness the distances were stretched. I was seeing marshals and confused Indians behind every tree and the wind picked up at our backs, hurrying us home while those coyotes only yelled louder. Jana said maybe they had a rabbit on the run.

When we got to the porch all the lights were on and the front door was wide open. Dirty dishes and ashtrays were piled up on the table and June lay facedown on the kitchen linoleum. She was back on the bottle and the howling just wouldn't quit.

There were no seams in the weather, nothing to mark one blazing white-sky day from another. There were bills I couldn't pay and the well behind the house was giving up yellow water that tasted of sulphur. When I told Herman to learn a rain dance or two he felt an insult where I meant to lay on some humor. Before they'd found the bones at Eagle Reach, I'd been a prime candidate for a teaching job at the secondary school in Wilma, but not long afterward, Leonard Rocking Boy called to say I'd been passed over for someone with better qualifications. I set down the phone as if putting a stone over the hole where all my hopes were buried. At least there were still some vegetables in the garden that the marshals hadn't stomped over, so we had carrots and onions and green beans.

Then, one evening, Gaetan Avril came by with a box filled with canned goods that he said were in excess.

"In excess of what?" I asked, and he just shrugged. He was trying to get on my good side, though I couldn't guess why. I invited him to sit on the porch for a beer and a smoke. That way we were facing the highway and couldn't be easily seen from Choteau. We silently watched cars pass from east to west. It was bowling league night in Wilma and the farmers from north and east of the reservation were heading in. Gaetan had a thirst that wasn't surprising considering the heat and when he finished his beer I was ashamed I didn't have any more to offer him.

"Plus the water's gone yellow," I told him. "Maybe I could send Herman over to Toby's for a take-out."

"Never mind. I can't stay long." He looked out toward the highway where a car whipped past.

"If you're wondering, I didn't touch Ida Andersen's grave." A white lady's grave had been dug up out at All Souls.

"I know you didn't, Mr. Lame." Then he said, "What do you know about Harold Bad Hand?"

"Not much," I admitted. "I knew his grandmother when I was a boy. She died when he was about eight or ten, I think. He got raised at the mission school, but I wasn't living here back then."

We weren't friends in those days, Gaetan and me. In years since, he's become as close a friend as I ever had. He has a fire in his heart that burns hot every day of his life and I suspect he's the type of man who never sleeps well but never complains about it either. Years ago I looked at him as a rich man's son and I couldn't fathom what he was doing with the likes of us. The way his father was and his relationship with Tyrone Little made everybody a little uneasy. So I didn't tell him that night about how we all thought Harold was a little touched in the head, that ever since he'd gotten out of high school and his basketball days were ended he'd been drinking too much and smoking weed, or that he stole people's change off bar counters and coffee shop tables.

"This council of yours," Gaetan said, still changing subjects according to his mood, "why don't you get serious about it and find some legal advice?"

"Advice for what?"

His eyes moved from left to right and then right to left. "This land," he said, and I was surprised to hear him laugh. "Almost everything west and north of here belongs to my father and Al Roebuck, according to the law. Some of it used to belong to you."

I never owned a square foot of dirt but I knew his meaning. My father had sold off his land as part of what they called his patents-in-fee. To own land back then meant you were an American citizen. It also meant you could do what you wanted with that land. When June's brothers both disappeared in the same year, she signed over the Little Sky property and she was only eleven years old. It hadn't occurred to me until young Gaetan brought it up that night that the land where they'd found those bones used to belong to the Lames.

"I've seen the books, as they say. Your father never signed his name. Not even an X or a thumbprint that was witnessed. A lawyer with good lungs might argue your way back into those sixteen acres."

I shrugged this off as whirlwind talk and Gaetan didn't press me on it. As the sun was going down, he said he'd best be off, and I walked him to his car. We shook hands that night and I didn't know if it was to thank him for the canned goods or just for passing the time. I noticed his car looked kind of beat up, with dents all across the hood and some serious cracks in the front windshield. When he saw me looking he said, "Damned town kids. You never see them but they're always there."

Later I found out that Kills First had made those dents with a baseball bat, out of sheer idiocy.

Once Gaetan was gone, I called out for the family and we sat down to a dinner of Dinty Moore beef stew and peaches for dessert. Later that night, I was standing on the porch looking west in the direction of the land Gaetan had mentioned. I caught June throwing up out back of the house. "Peaches and bourbon don't mix," I told her. Then I helped her up to bed and sat and watched as she lay with her mouth wide open like before, sucking wind from an empty sky.

Two nights later, Herman was arrested in Wilma. He'd gone into town to buy groceries and some pest killer for June. Those marigolds weren't panning out like she'd thought. Anyway, there'd been some trouble between some white kids from the high school and a group of Indians who'd driven over from Ree, and all of the Indians got locked up. Frank drove me into town in his pickup and we spent about four hours at the police station trying to find out what had happened. They were asking five hundred dollars for bail money which of course we didn't have. When we got there they said Herman was at the clinic, though they wouldn't say why. An hour later they one of us who was the leader. That leadership thing is something the whites usually get mixed up about, and this confusion came out during the trials. They kept insisting John Fire was like a general or something, and that just plain wasn't true. When it came to self-defense, we usually listened to Willard Bent. John Fire had the quiet sense of humor and was everyone's big brother. My son Herman and Kevin Walking Horse were spiritual leaders and, even though he wasn't trusted by everyone, Tyrone Little taught us how to get things done.

In late July, the hot spell broke and we had two days of rain that cooled the earth and our blood all at once. June was off the bottle and it was like having a new wife, this woman who for so long had slept unmoving on the other side of the bed. Herman continued with his spiritual training and was in the sweats every day. I had to admit he was becoming a man with more wisdom in him than I'd ever hoped for, though his faith in the Great Spirit reminded me of my mother's in the Blessed Virgin. June said every time she licked her dry lips with her tongue, missing the alcohol, she thought of Herman and what he'd become. "Then I don't feel the need so much." My daughter Jana was a little like me. She turned to books at an early age and by this time was almost sixteen. Although no one had told me face-to-face, I knew she would be marrying up with Toby Mad Bear Johnson. Which might have condemned her to a life of working in his bar and grill and never leaving Choteau but I've heard of worse things happening to a man's daughter.

The bones of that nameless girl were resting near the river, and on the first anniversary of her burial, we all met at the same spot. The men passed a pipe that had been prepared by Herman and then all of us got into the water and swam and joked around under the moonlight. I went home with June and we had a long sweet tussle, love sprung from relief and a touch of surprise in the way she was wanting me. Nothing infirm in life was remedied between our hips, but for a few minutes I didn't really care. When I moved away from her, she fell instantly to sleep, but I couldn't. Instead I laid there and listened to the wild dogs calling from the north.

The next morning, I was sitting down to breakfast with June and Herman. It was one of those white-sky August mornings that hold the heat close to the earth and all the windows were open wide. Our kitchen looked out on Highway 50 and we could see a pair of cars

come in toward us, then they swung around and blocked the road. I
got up and counted half a dozen other cars, all marked as state
marshals or highway patrol except for two, which I recognized as
belonging to Gaetan Averill and Albert Roebuck. A white-haired man
in a blue suit stepped out of Averill's car and came straight for my
house flanked by two marshals with shotguns on their hips. I was still
wearing my pajamas and June was in her bathrobe. I didn't have the
presence of mind to send Herman upstairs to wake up Jana and tell
her to get dressed. Instead, I stepped out on the front porch to meet
them. The man in the suit had an envelope in one hand and a briefcase
in the other. He asked me, "Is this the residence of Noah Lamer?"

"Lame," I corrected him.

"Are you Mr. Lame?"

"Yes I am," I said. "Who are you?"

He didn't answer, so I didn't know until the next day that he was
sent by Bull Smedsrud. All he said was that he had a search warrant
and would I please comply peacefully.

I asked to see the warrant and saw it was handwritten legal language
with the state seal at the top. "I don't see the point," I said, but one
of the marshals was already pushing up the porch steps and brushing
me aside with the butt of his rifle. "My wife's not decent!" I shouted
at him. "Give us two minutes to get dressed."

"In two minutes," said Blue Suit, "you could remove those bones."

I knew they didn't care much about the bones, and figured it was
my trip to the statehouse that still had them riled. I was looking
around for Special Agent Person but didn't see his car, and then
those two marshals and a few of the BIA fellows, including Jerry
Lonetree, went through that house like a cyclone. They started in the
kitchen and made a shambles there before going into the living room,
where they turned over the sofa, dug up floorboards, took apart the
lamps, and tore long strips from the wallpaper. I'd always hated that
wallpaper but I hated them worse for spoiling June's nice walls.
Herman got out his camera and tried to take a picture of what was
going on, but one of the marshals cuffed him and smashed the camera
against the stone fireplace. After that, the search was pure sham; all
they wanted was to point out who was in charge. Lonetree went up
to the attic and busted in on Jana who was almost naked. Before she
could get the bedsheet wrapped around her, he was kicking over the
mattress and tearing around underneath. Herman went up after him

of his brood and they were what you'd expect, snapshots of two little boys in shorts playing softball, eating hot dogs, or just smiling straight out at you. His wife was real pretty, which didn't surprise me since SA Person was a good-looking man even if his hair was prematurely falling out. We could hear static and cloudy voices drifting across the police radio. At the same time, he had the AM radio tuned to the news. He was waiting for the scores of the ballgames and wanted to know whether I followed any teams.

"Ever see any Indians in the professional leagues?" I asked him.

"Sure. Jim Thorpe. And there's a guy on the Padres name of Gene Locklear." Then he laughed this short laugh and said, "There's always the Cleveland Indians."

"And the Braves, the Redskins, and such."

"The Redskins are a football team."

"What's the difference?"

He turned off on the dirt road that leads straight south to the Missouri. The Wilma people call it Gaetan Road but we just say the river road. About half a mile from the water, he stopped the car and turned off the lights.

"What's this?" I asked him. "Am I under arrest?"

He was still using his friendly voice but you could hear the FBI training in every phrase. "I'm grateful you called," he said. "No reason we can't work together, you and I."

"To do what?"

"Make the peace."

"Will you prosecute the police for brutality?"

"Be damned hard to prove."

"Not if it was the other way around."

"Listen. As far as we can figure it, you're the only one of the Choteau people who's been to college. You've lived in white communities before. And I understand Indians listen to their elders. That's three reasons why you should be a leader. And as such, we ought to be able to reason together, you and me."

"I don't know what you're talking about."

"We've had reports that there are guns stored in the vicinity. There's a rumor that your son's hiding them for the AIM people."

"You'd better check your sources, Mr. Person. Herman's in spiritual training." I was dodging the question and trying not to look shifty-eyed like guilty people always do on television. That there were guns in Choteau was no secret within the council, but I didn't know where they were exactly. I was afraid of guns and up till then wouldn't touch one.

"The situation is obviously getting out of control—all the shootings and the drinking."

"Counting Eagle Reach," I told him, "there are seven bars in Wilma and only one in Choteau. You're new around here. Temperance isn't rampant in the great state of South Dakota."

He turned to face me. "I don't understand you people. The government builds a school for you and in six years it's so trashed you need a new one. That hospital in Ree is as good as any in Sioux Falls or Minneapolis and even has an Indian on the staff, and still no one wants to set foot in the place."

"Indians don't trust Indian doctors. Or Indian lawyers, for that matter. We tend to think of those as white occupations."

"Close to fifty percent of the adult population on the Pine Ridge Reservation is alcoholic. The figure's lower in these parts, but it's still ridiculously high."

"Here's a statistic for you. Indians make up six point five percent of the South Dakota population. But we're pushing forty percent in the prisons."

Agent Person pressed the button that lowered his window and lit a cigarette. "Listen, Noah. Mr. Lame. We've been around this town long enough to know that your people are in serious trouble. Guns and alcohol are causing the problem. That liquor store in Wilma does hellacious business, even in the early mornings."

"I've been to that liquor store, thank you, and I've read all the statistics and I've got one or two more right at home if you'd care to look. One alcoholic Indian, recovering nicely until a few nights ago. And one battered Indian male. Now you write that down, or turn on that tape recorder in the glove compartment!"

He gave me the look I'd been waiting for since the night I met him, the police look that showed me what he thought I amounted to.

"People are going to die if we don't do something soon. You've got all the locals against you, not to mention the BIA and Reese Lonetree's bunch. My people can't control all these elements. And as you already know, we can't protect you. Once your friends in Choteau started carrying guns, this all got out of hand. Neither the BIA nor the FBI can tolerate an insurrection."

"We're defending ourselves. We don't like being shot at."

"These AIM people are allied with outside forces hostile to both state and federal peace. If they'll lay down their arms, we can negotiate."

"I don't know anything about outside forces. You must have the wrong end of the stick."

"John Fire Smith," Person said. "We understand he's a part of your band."

So it was John Fire they wanted.

"He's wanted in two states and that gives us all the jurisdiction we need."

"John Fire's out west," I lied. "Last I heard he was in Washington."

"That's not what we hear from witnesses."

"What witnesses?" I knew he was talking about an inside man.

He said something back at me but I didn't hear him. Between the police radio and the news on the AM band, that car was full of voices. Then, though I couldn't tell where from, I heard someone say the name Little. I didn't hear anything else because Person snapped off the police radio and said he wanted to listen to the scores.

"What I'm trying to tell you is that you don't have a chance. They have the numbers and the guns and public sentiment."

Then he started up the car and drove me back toward the highway. I didn't want anyone seeing us together, so I told him to let me out when we got to the intersection. "I can walk from here."

Before I got out, he remarked on what a beautiful night it was. "Out here, where everything's so flat, it's all horizon and sky wherever you look. I'm used to living in cities and feeling surrounded. A place like this, you couldn't hide from God if you tried."

"Have you tried?" I asked. Then I turned my back and faced the road home.

Judy Poor Bull was sitting in the kitchen with June. It wasn't any longer June's habit to get to bed early, so I wasn't surprised to find her up. She was in her nightgown and had a glass in her hand. I was too tired to be angry, so I just sat down and took off my shoes.

"It's orange juice, Noah. What's in this glass."

All I would have had to do is taste it. Or put my nose to it and smell what a lie smells like. All I did was ask if there was coffee, and June got up real fast and said she'd make some.

"What brings you here, Judy?"

"Since that white lady's grave got dug up, the goons and some locals are back cruising the dirt roads. Willard Bent's organizing the men for a night watch."

June poured hot water through a filter and steam rose toward her face. I saw how pale she was and how much thinner she'd become. I almost never saw her eat. Like she knew that eating was a waste of time, since she'd only get hungry again later. "Nobody's seen Tyrone Little," she said.

"A few days ago," Judy added, "Harold Bad Hand said he'd seen him skulking around the cemetery out on the west road."

"Harold Bad Hand," June said, "sees Tyrone Little in his sleep."

We didn't hear a car pull up. I was busy with my coffee and wondering if I shouldn't head over to Toby's when we heard a racket out front. It was late and I was dog tired but I shot up out of my chair and made it to the door in time to see taillights disappearing down Highway 50.

Sitting on the porch was a cardboard box the size of a small TV. On the outside was printing that said Del Monte Tomato Paste 72 Containers This Side Up. But there was an earthy smell and what looked like wood ash had leaked out a hole.

I closed my mouth and held my breath, then bent to open it. Inside there were bones.

Judy ran to Toby's to fetch the men and they all came running. We didn't exactly know what we had and knew we'd have to get out to the cemetery to find out. Frank went for his pickup and I sat in the cab with him at the wheel and Willard Bent on the other side of me. Frank had his deer rifle and his pockets bulged with shells. There were four more of us in back and everyone but me had a firearm.

Even before Frank pulled to a stop, we could see that at least a dozen gravestones had been knocked over. I waited by the truck while the others were running through that yard like crazy men. No, I was thinking, you can't hide from God out here. Then Willard Bent gave a shout and I crossed the road toward the south corner, where the stone wall was partially collapsed. I could tell where Willard was standing when I was still thirty feet away. My mother's stone cross had been shoved to one side and raw soil was piled high around it.

The eagle screamed. I fell into that empty hole and dug with my fingers to find her. Her name was blood on my lips and I tasted the earth that held her. Frank climbed down and grabbed me and held me to his large chest. My nose and mouth were filled with soil. My glasses were broken. I could neither speak nor see and I spat and swallowed until at last I could breathe.

Mitakuye oyasin. All my relations.

No hiding from God. *Wakan tanka.*

I stopped thrashing. Frank lifted me out of the grave and wiped the dirt from my brows and forehead. I could see his face. I was not blind.

There were seven of us there that night and we fought an Indian war that no one saw. Frank had an extra gun for me in his pickup and we piled into the back while Pete drove around in wild circles. We didn't know where to aim or who to kill so we stopped back at Toby's and picked up Harold Bad Hand. Then we drove toward Wilma and shot up the sky and the cornfields, a stray dog, and every road sign in sight. I don't know what would have happened if we'd come across any of those goons. It's hard to aim a rifle when you're being jounced around in the back of a pickup on a dirt road. At one point I heard Bad Hand shouting to Frank to turn back east and the next thing I knew we were driving up to Tyrone's place. He wasn't there, but Bad Hand and Darryl Kills First took a few shots anyway. I don't remember much after that. Willard Bent took the wheel and got lost for a while. Not being from Choteau, he didn't know one dirt road from another and finally just pulled over to the side of the road. Nobody had the energy to drive so we all just slept like that, sprawled in the back of that dirty pickup.

The next morning, when the sun came up, we were all feeling the sting of humiliation. Back in Choteau, John Fire and Kevin Walking Horse were madder than hell that we'd left the town unguarded. No goons had been spotted, though Pete Scully had seen a few cars driving on the roads north of the highway. They found three kinds of footprints and made drawings to show us. There was still no sign of Tyrone Little and everyone took that news in his own way.

I didn't listen to Gene Fast Horse or to Harold Bad Hand. The men I trusted most in the council were Pete Scully and Frank Poor Bull and John Fire Smith. I didn't listen to the river and I didn't listen to the wind. Nor did I follow the path of Helene Her Many Horses, who used to throw sticks into the air and then read what they said after they fell back to the ground. I was dog tired and instead of sleeping I worked the problem out like a crossword puzzle and then remembered the name I'd heard on the police band. And as much as I liked the man's manner and the way he'd helped us, I settled my sights on Tyrone Little all by myself. Arrows were being flung into the air and every one of them pointed in his sorry direction.

Frank and I went back to my house and we washed up and put on clean clothes. Then he helped me carry the box down toward the river where we cleaned those bones in Missouri water, rib and skull and clavicle. We arranged them into a circle and lit a fire of willow sticks over them. Frank and Herman and I kept that fire burning high until the sun was directly overhead and our shadows had disappeared into ourselves. The wood burned hot and I grew dizzy from watching the flames. The bones and ash were indistinguishable. Native dust. Dakota topsoil.

There were plenty of sticks nearby and any two of them could have been fashioned into a cross. I held one in each hand while Herman stood off to one side and sang a song to the sun.

I threw the sticks into the flames and they burned white and she was resurrected.

Harold Bad Hand

Blood don't matter to me and not even skin now that I seen what they come to. I dig up them bones and they all look the same, white or redskin, they're all rotten and there ain't even a smell anymore except kind of like wet leaves. It's funny how a shovel and a half hour's digging can get them all so riled. I listen to these old men talking in Choteau about the red man and his dignity and I want to puke but I just nod and reach for the wine and think about rattling those bones in their faces. They want to bring back the old ways and they talk about Crazy Horse and Gall and all these Indians that I know ain't nothing but bones and maybe not even that much. Cale and that other man, Person, they didn't count on me going both ways and when they let me out of that prison it was a surprise to me that I'd fight them all, red and white. You got to kill the Indian first. Oglala and Brule, all the bloods.

Me and Russ took them old lady's bones. I did the digging while he stood watch and only one time a car passed us. I had to only dig a little, that grave was old and worn down but the dirt was hard and full of rocks. The casket was caved in and when I hit it with my shovel I could smell them leaves. I knew who she was, she was one of those sisters from the mission school from back at the beginning. They had a picture of her on the wall in that priest's office that I used to see over his shoulder while he was telling me how to kill the Indian in me to let the man live.

It sure spooked Russ, though. And before we could tell anybody back at Choteau it was us that done it, we found out they was *mad*. Noah Lame said it was a crime and even John Fire Smith, who I pegged as a real warrior, swore that no Indian would do such a atrocity, that was white man ugliness.

I heard they give the white man a eagle feather for saving redskin bones up in Pierre and I was after one for my own hair. That white man was more Indian than me. He had a Indian woman in his bed and that feather. And after that meeting at the church hall, Russ Poor Bull stopped going around with me. I got him alone one night and told him about what happened to Henry Four with just a glass knife. He's bigger than me but that's only on the outside and I knew he was plenty scared.

She didn't ask me to come but I came anyway one night after a meeting at Toby's to Myrene Tall Bull's dirty house. It was on the east side and there was no electric lights. She didn't have no wood for a fire so we just sat in the dark fooling with each other through our clothes. She had beer and some wine but it was homemade and sour and after drinking some I felt my head come open and we both was sick.

"I got money," I told her and she just looked at me. "I can get you money, too."

"You can?"

"All you gotta do is keep your eyes open and tell me what you see."

She drank more of the wine and nodded like a dummy.

"You listening, Myrene?"

"Show me some money, Harold. I want to touch it."

I gave her a five and she shrugged. Then she got up off the floor and took off her jeans and fell asleep on the couch. I crawled over to her and shook her to wake her up but she was out cold from the homemade wine. I touched her wherever I wanted but she was acting so dead that it made me mad. I took my knife out of my boot and held it in my hands. There was dirt and rust on the blade and I thought about my old man who said to keep a knife clean and sharp. I stabbed the dark but there was no blood at all, just more dark around me and I couldn't stab it all. I saw my shadow from some moonlight against the wall and I shoved the point of the knife at the head but it moved so I stabbed again for where the eyes would be and missed every time. Then all at once I felt real tired like after a fight and remembered about Myrene lying there. Her legs was pale and hanging off the couch like she was gonna fall if I didn't catch her. I wasn't mad anymore, I felt like crying. She couldn't help it, Myrene, if she wasn't Delores Her Many Horses. She was dumb, dumber than me, and fat and drank worse than any Indian in Choteau. She and me could of been married we was so alike. So I put away my knife and then laid my head on the floor that smelled like dogs had been there and I guess I passed out.

Person told me my contact would be Special Agent Cale. I had to meet up with him about once a week to tell him what I seen and heard and it was like telling fish stories, like how there was not only the rifles but making them out to be automatics when they was mostly single shots or old .22s, and then telling him we had grenades from this Vietnam guy but I didn't know where they was hid. Don't forget the cash I'd tell him every time and he almost never did, but sometimes he gave me bills that was too big to use, fifties and hundreds that I had to go all the way to another county to change in at a bank so nobody'd see I was flush. One time in Toby's I slipped up. I was reaching into my pocket for matches and all them bills fell out on the floor and Noah Lame saw me stoop to pick them up. He didn't say nothing right then, just gave me a real hard look through them fat glasses. A few days later, I heard he was trying to get me kicked out on account of my drinking. The old men wanted us sober and to sit in the sweats and say hey-ya, but Fast Horse and Kills First stood up for me and said I was a warrior, so Lame had to swallow me down.

I knew where the rifles was hidden and I told Cale. I thought they'd go in themselves, but it was state marshals that tore up the whole town and came up empty. Cale swore at me and said he wasn't gonna wait forever. He kept asking what they were going to *do* and there was nothing to say. All I saw was people writing things and fixing cars and going to the sweats. John Fire said the guns were for self-defense. Cale said no ticky no washy, whatever the fuck that means. And a few weeks after that I heard John Fire telling Willard Bent about the fake grave out at the Indian cemetery.

I drove out there late at night and parked. Then I just sat in that car and drank all my wine and tried to think. The wine was squeezing on my brain but I kept on drinking it. I figured I'd take those guns to Cale myself, there was more where they came from. Then I'd tell him I quit and I'd just go off somewheres, maybe Canada, where he wouldn't find me, him or the bloods, up north where I'd live like a wolf. I was seeing three stars for every one by the time I got out but the dirt over that fake grave was still soft and I found the guns about four feet down. They was in two wood crates and I put the first one in the back and was going back for the last one when I saw the grave marker. It was just a stone cross but there was a name scratched on it, Pauline Lame. I had a crate a guns in my arms and I just kept on walking and put those guns in the car with the others.

I was wearing those old black boots that Cale bought me. He bought me that blue car, too, the same color as his. I had my eye on a red Camaro but Cale just said let's take a car like Indians got and he even beat on it with a crowbar to make dents and cracked windows so it looked like shit. I went back to get my shovel and passed that gravestone again and it was easy, easier than digging up the old white sister. I had a cardboard box in the trunk that was big enough to hold the bones after I broke them up some and I stacked that box in with the guns. Then I thought about them bootmarks all over the place so I went back with my shovel to cover them up. I didn't hear the car until I was almost done and when I heard the noise I dropped that shovel and picked up the rifle and started shooting. My aim was bad but the car hit the ditch and spun over. When I saw that white guy Tyrone climb out I fired till the gun was empty but I missed him every time. Then I ran to the car and started it up and drove like hell without the lights on.

Back at Choteau I dumped them bones on that bastard Lame's doorstep and then hid the guns up by the highway, off in a cornfield. Then I went back to my place to change into my new shoes. I threw the boots and the shovel into the gully out back and then went straight to Toby's where people were screaming about how the whites had dug up old lady Lame's death place.

Frank drove by in his pickup and I could see Gene Fast Horse and Darryl Kills First standing in the back. "Are you with us?" Gene shouted to me.

I nodded my head. I was with them, I was a warrior, I was blood. Gene reached out a hand to help me into the truck and Kills First put a rifle in my hands. We drove off to I don't know where, shooting guns in the air like to kill the stars and saying hey-ya and haka-yé and kill them all and I fired my gun and loaded and fired again and said let's kill them, let's kill them all.

Gaetan Avril

The FBI boys took Tyrone and me to Albert Roebuck's boardroom, where there was a headquarters of sorts, with a bank of telephones and wall maps of the county and the reservation. From where I was sitting I could see the map of the reservation and I was trying to note where the colored pins were placed while Special Agent Cale was asking me what in the hell I was doing out by the cemetery in the middle of the night. A woman in uniform noticed me looking at those pins and she bent over to whisper something to Cale, who nodded to her. Then she turned and removed those pins from the map.

Tyrone was in the office next door, and I assumed they were keeping us apart so they could trip us up. I was with Cale most of the time and his tape machine kept jamming, so the interrogation was moving along at a snail's pace when my father came in. He stood across the conference desk from me and just stared as if to convince himself that he wasn't seeing things.

"The sheriff called. You're in a real sorry state, son. Boyd Sumter's on the way over." Sumter was his real estate attorney. "Four in the a.m. is not his best hour."

The woman served me coffee in a Styrofoam cup. "Cream or sugar? All we've got is Sweet'n Low."

"Police brutality," I said, and smiled to make sure she knew I was kidding. She frowned all the same. "Black, thanks."

Cale lit one L&M with another and told my father he'd have to leave. "This is federal business, not some country dustup."

"You call Mary yet?" my father asked me.

"She's out of town. Sam's with her."

"First blessing of this shitty night."

When he was gone, Cale offered me more of that weak coffee.

"Am I under arrest?" I asked.

"Not technically speaking, no. We just wanted to ask you some questions." He reached to open a thin little file at his side. "I assume," he said, "we're on the same side of the fence, Mr. Avril."

"That remains to be seen."

Boyd Sumter came in and laid a briefcase on the table in front of him. Despite the hour, he was wearing a tie and I could smell fresh aftershave. "Criminal law isn't my strong suit, Gaetan."

"Don't worry, Boyd. This is just a fishing trip."

Cale was asking me the same questions over and over. What roads had we driven on? What time had we started out? How did the car get stuck in that ditch and what about those bullet holes? The other fellow, Person, came in after about an hour and looked like he'd just gotten out of bed. He said, "We noticed the citizen's band radio in your car. How come you were tuned to the police band?"

"Factory default when the battery's disengaged."

Like everything else I told them, it was the truth and nothing but, though I did neglect to mention rifles or a fake grave. Mostly they wanted to know what we'd seen out there. Had we passed any other cars, seen any headlights or people? I told them we'd seen nothing but corn and starlight, and it turns out Tyrone said pretty much the same thing.

At around seven in the morning they gave me toast and more coffee and let me go. Agent Person apologized for the inconvenience and said he hoped, under the circumstances, that I understood. My car had been towed out and while I drove Tyrone home we compared stories and concluded that we hadn't given them anything they didn't already know. As I drove up to Tyrone's house, Delores came out on the porch in her nightdress. She didn't even look at me. Tyrone got out of the car and I noticed for the first time that he still had dirt all over his shirt and pants and his hair was going every which way. He walked up to Delores and she started to back away, but he came close and put his arms around her. After hesitating for a moment, she lifted her arms around him and held him tight.

Delores Her Many Horses

"When your tits go south, sleep with your head to the north and lift your feet with a cushion or two. Gravity lifts the milk backwards to that bone there, the whatever."

"The clavicle, Helene."

"When I was carrying you I got so big that my shoulders were rounded with muscle. I looked like Jayne Mansfield except I wasn't blond and was never quite that dumb."

"She wasn't dumb, Helene, she was exploited."

"You have a way of turning comments into arguments."

Delores rises from the kitchen table and turns down the volume on the television set. There is cardboard over the window where once there had been glass.

"It wasn't the marshals," Helene says. "It was that Indian boy, Jerry Lonetree, who broke the windows. The marshals just pretended they were looking for something. It was that Indian who hated me having glass windows."

"Let me buy you some clear plastic to put in here," Delores offers. "It lets in the light."

"You try looking through plastic and you get a headache. Anyways, I don't need to look outside. I got my television for that." Helene reaches for the coffeepot. "More?"

Delores shakes her head. Her nerves are already jumping in her arms and legs. When she shifts position on the kitchen chair, SheHe moves with her. Sleeping, she guesses. Even though she hasn't slept more than three good hours at a stretch all week.

She reaches into a cupboard to where Helene keeps the wine and pours herself a large glass. There are houseplants yellowed and dying on the kitchen shelf near the window. Helene can't be bothered to do more than water them and she always gives them too little or too much. "The pothos is dead," Delores tells her.

"Which one is that?"

"The one that looks like rope. Why didn't you give it a new pot?" Delores loves having houseplants and has taken to lecturing friends and strangers on the proper care and feeding. She takes the pot down from the shelf and pokes a finger at the hardened soil. "The dirt's all white from calcium. I suppose you just used tap water."

"Whatever was at hand."

Delores considers telling her how Tyrone went off with Gaetan Avril last night and didn't come back until morning. While he was gone she had been awakened by gunshots, someone firing at the house, probably Lonetree's goons. When Tyrone finally came home he was covered with dirt and wouldn't say where he'd been or what had happened to him. Just some throwaway joke about pheasant hunting. But it's never an unburdening, talking to Helene. After the revelations will come advice and making a throw of the sticks to determine what to do next. She's been throwing those sticks for years, her own made-up version of the I Ching mingled with poorly understood Lakota lore. Helene has been making up her own religion for as long as Delores can remember, but it's hard to say whether or not it's an improvement over Christianity. Neither seems reliable.

Her glass is empty so she fills it with wine. The label says burgundy but that only means it's red. By now it's nearly eight o'clock and through the lone unbroken window she can see Tyrone walking up. The council will be meeting again tonight, at Toby's. Tyrone fills the doorway and his smile undoes the knot of worry that has formed at the corners of her mouth. He bends to kiss her and then plants a kiss on Helene's forehead. In his beaded shirt and summer tan, he almost looks Indian. Even his hair is Lakota black. It's only in his blue eyes and compact nose that he shows himself up as white.

It's nearly time to go but she wants more wine. She feels the weight in her middle and legs and wants at least to feel light-headed, to have the illusion of weightlessness.

Tyrone helps her out of the chair and they head down the dirt road to Toby's. When they step inside, it is eight sharp, but it's clear that the others have been there for some time already. Empty beer cans are scattered across the table and the air is thick with cigarette smoke.

The mood is ugly. Frank Poor Bull doesn't even call them to order before announcing that Tyrone's car, just last week, was spotted at the Gem Bar two nights running.

Tyrone reaches across the table for the water pitcher but can't find an empty glass. Sitting next to him, Delores can smell the cologne she bought him the week before. On her own skin it had smelled like the spices listed on the bottle, though on Tyrone it smells of wood smoke. She is uneasy at the sight of a trickle of sweat on the back of his neck.

"It's a democratic place, Frank. They serve Indians *and* whites."

Frank looks down the table at Noah whose glasses are broken, and Delores studies him. He squints through the cracks and looks as though he has a headache.

"The bar," Noah says to no one in particular, "isn't the real question. The real question is the *location* of the bar."

"Meaning next to Averill's town office," Frank says.

"And Albert Roebuck's car," adds Fast Horse.

Delores notices that Harold and Russ are standing by the door. Darryl Kills First is sitting next to Frank, playing with his hunting knife.

Tyrone is looking at that knife and his smile is frozen. He coughs and says, "It's a damn short street. If you park your car anywhere in that town you're right next to everything."

"What we're trying to figure out," Noah says, "is your relationship with young Gaetan."

Before he can answer this, Frank says, "Why'd you come here? A white guy like you showing up fresh from the army. All the rest of us was born and raised here or close by."

Then they're all asking questions or pointing fingers. Frank asks why young Gaetan gave him that land and the house. Gene Fast Horse asks where he gets his money and his eyes have that dull wildness to them, dark water that won't focus. Frank has some papers in his hands but from where she sits Delores can't see what's written on them. Frank says they've also noticed his footprints—"those army boots nobody else wears"—down by where the bones were buried.

"I go there a lot," Tyrone says.

"What for?"

"To think straight and to keep watch over her."

This is news to Delores.

Tyrone asks, "Why do I have to answer these questions? I've been with you. I am with you, so why are you doubting me now?"

Pete Scully says, "You never come to the sweats with us."

"I've never been invited."

They're asking him all the questions Delores wanted to ask. Tyrone has had money and information for as long as they've known him, and nobody knows where he gets either one. And she's seen papers in his desk drawer, official-looking letters postmarked from Denver. There's an FBI office in Denver and she nearly says so out loud, but just as suddenly she feels a rush of shame.

Gene says to Tyrone, "You took John Fire's woman away from him."

"He didn't *steal* me," Delores snaps. "I'm not a car."

"He didn't need to steal her," Kills First says. "Delores'd fuck a rock pile if she thought there was a snake in it."

Too late, she touches Tyrone's arm just above the elbow. He stands and pushes the table backward. Kills First reaches the knife in his direction but Tyrone has him by the wrist. When he twists, the knife clatters to the floor. When Delores tries to get up she's knocked flat by Bad Hand. Instinctively, she turns so that she is resting on her side, her hands protecting her belly. From where she is lying all she can see is dirty boots in a circular dance. It takes three of them to haul Tyrone outside. She can sit up but doesn't have the strength to stand. Then she feels arms beneath her own and Noah pulls her to her feet. "Best stay inside," he says, but she pulls away and heads out the door.

Russ and Darryl are holding Tyrone while Harold bends down to untie one of his boots. He yanks it off and carries it over to where Frank is standing with his papers. She can just see over his shoulder that he has a drawing of a footprint that matches the bootsole, heel and toe.

"It's him," Frank says.

Immediately, Harold and Gene start stomping his car, jumping up and down on the hood, and then Gene takes a two-by-four to the glass. "Hey hey, Tyrone. What do you think now?"

"Do something," Delores begs Noah, but he just stands there inside the door of the bar as though he's afraid.

"You want to be a Indian, Tyrone?" Fast Horse swings the two-by-four and demolishes a side mirror. "You gotta have a Indian car!"

Then he goes to work on the front grille while Harold Bad Hand does a mad dance on the roof. His foot slips and he falls to the ground but gets right up and casts his eyes about the yard in search of a club. John Fire moves to the front of the car and tells them that's enough, but nobody's listening. The car seems to sink, though the tires are intact. Frank starts shouting at them to stop and in frustration he grabs Fast Horse by the neck. The younger man spins around and his fist sweeps the air. Then he rights himself and swings again, catching Poor Bull flat across the cheek. Poor Bull goes down like a tree then sits up. Fast Horse towers over him, both fists ready. John Fire steps between them and so does Pete Scully. "Nobody asked for this," Pete says.

The men help Poor Bull to stand. His left eye is already swollen shut and he turns to Tyrone and points a finger at him. "What do we do with him?"

"We waste him, that's what." Harold is waving a pistol around and John Fire takes it away from him.

"That's up to Noah," Frank tells them.

Noah stands a short distance from Tyrone. "You were there," he says. "At the cemetery."

"Yeah, and I saw plenty of footprints."

"Yours and those FBI people," says Fast Horse.

"Check Harold's shoes," Tyrone says.

Everyone turns toward Bad Hand, who only smiles bitterly at Tyrone.

"I saw him there," Tyrone tells them. "Gaetan Avril is my witness."

"He's lying," Harold says.

John Fire says, "Only one way to find out."

"Take off your shoe," Frank tells him.

"I wasn't fucking there!"

"You weren't with us at the cemetery," says Frank. "We picked you up here about an hour later."

"He's lying," Harold insists. All the same, he bends and removes a tennis shoe. "They're new shoes," he tells them.

Frank looks at the bottom of that shoe and then at the drawings that Willard Bent made that morning. Then he hands the shoe back to Harold and looks across at Noah. "It's up to you, Noah. That shoe don't match."

"Let him go," John Fire says.

Noah turns to Tyrone. "Go away," he says. "Take your blue eyes and your Vietnam as far away from here as you can get."

Russ and Darryl let go of Tyrone's arms. For a moment he stands in the same spot. He looks at his car and then at Delores. She knows he's wondering what she will do and she doesn't know herself. Though he's limping slightly, he manages to open the door on the driver's side. Delores hears someone yelling in her ear to stay put. But she crosses the yard to the car and when she sees that the passenger door has been caved in, she goes around and climbs in the driver's side, sliding her heavy body to make room for Tyrone. He gets in and closes the door, the keys already in his hand.

There is almost no darkness to the night, as though the cloud cover has absorbed the light of day and held it there. Rain clouds, Tyrone had said that morning. He drives the dirt roads, away from Choteau, aimless west, north, west, south. Neither of them speaks. Near Wilma, he stops at a roadhouse and goes inside. She knows he's calling Gaetan Avril. Then he comes out with a six-pack and a bottle of red wine. He is unshaven and his eyes are yellow. His beaded shirt is torn at the shoulder.

The wine she drank at Helene's has dried in her mouth, so she drinks deeply. This is almost marriage, she is thinking, when you follow your man out of the place where you were born. And if he looked her in the eye, she'd look right back to see what's there. Tyrone doesn't talk, and she doesn't talk to him. "Silence," Helene once told her, "is the marriage talk that counts most."

He drives back to the house and parks, then goes inside to make sure they're alone. The front windows are shot out and there is broken glass on the couch and end table. She follows him upstairs to the loft bedroom. She doesn't want to undress, she wants to sleep in those same clothes, but Tyrone suddenly has his arms around her and it's clear what he's wanting.

"Drunk," she says. "Both of us."

"Sure are," he agrees.

She unsnaps the mother-of-pearl snaps on her shirt with a single gesture and sits on the edge of the bed. It takes a long time to get those maternity jeans over her belly and then she gets under the covers without taking off the rest. Tyrone is behind her and is already warm. She can feel how hard and big he is through the material of her underpants.

It's too close to the day, she's thinking, only another month or so. "I can't," she says. "You know I can't."

He pulls down the material and moves against her. He doesn't enter her, he only begins to. The depth of a kiss. It doesn't take long before he erupts and rolls away. Sinking, he lifts one arm to cover his eyes. She can smell that wood smoke. In the spring the room smelled so strongly of lilacs that it made her dizzy and she got Tyrone to trim the bushes. Then it was summer and from her bed she could smell hay, cut grass, and pine from the new boards across the ceiling. Tyrone found moths in the closet and put cedar chips across the floor to drive them away and for the first few months that was all she smelled.

"Where will we go?"

"Go?"

"Where will we live?"

"We'll stay right here," he says. "We have to protect them."

"Protect who?"

"Poor Bull. Lame. The others."

"I don't think they need you to be their guardian angel."

"Angel?" he says. He doesn't understand, and she can see he's pretty drunk.

"Protect them from what?" she asks.

But he's asleep and she can hear the wind at the window and the first slaps of rain on the roof. She sleeps and awakens and the room is hot and dark. Tyrone's breath has that rattle that it often has. Her mouth is dry from the wine and her head hurts, so she turns and wills herself back to sleep. But it's shallow and brief, and when she awakens this time she knows she will not sleep again.

"I'm leaving," she says aloud.

PART TWO

Mitakuye Oyasin,
All My Relations

Frank Poor Bull

I'm not one to leave junkers out to rust on the front yard. I don't
have much except crabgrass and high weeds but that's just nature's
mess and no sign of laziness or neglect. And all these years that Russ
has been dead, I keep his motorcycle in the shed back of the house,
way toward the back where Judy won't see it even if she goes in there.
I don't shine it up or oil it or nothing but it's out of the rain. Birds
get in through a hole in the roof and leave white and black droppings
all over the seat and the mirror and sometimes I break down and get
out a rag and brush that bird crap off the seat. That crap is dried to
dust, dry as grief. And the chrome has gone to rust but it don't matter
a damn.

We loved Russ too much and from the time he was fourteen we
watched him skip school and get in fights and water himself into
stupors and I hardly ever raised my voice. My own mother was a
drunk and I should have known better than let Russ go down that
same path. But he was the only child we could ever have and we
spoiled him. I gave him that motorcycle for his fifteenth birthday and
it cost me more than a horse would have. I could have bought a horse

and clothes for Judy like she needed but she said no, let's get the boy a motorcycle.

I spent my whole boyhood believing what my mother and others like her told me about Indians and alcohol, how we was born with the land taken out from under our feet to justify any kind of drinking or hell raising. As though there's no place to put a foot down and grow roots so we naturally just drift through life like thin air. My mother was fifty-one when she died and was so dried up and skinny that the coffin, made to adult size, looked too big for her. The only real friend she ever had was Pauline Lame. The winter my mother died, Pauline starved herself as penance 'cause she never converted my mother to the Christian church. She said my mother's soul would just float around in space forever. One night she was delirious from no food at all and was trying to tell us she'd seen Jesus out on the cemetery road, going to weep over my mother. She didn't drink, Pauline, but she never acted exactly sober either.

It was terrible what they did to her grave. Like all that was human in them was peeled away and gone. When I saw Noah chewing roots and earth like a crazy man and I saw the moon turn red and my own face was hot to the touch.

Gene Fast Horse was a noisy sonofabitch but he had spirit and that's what I seen in Russ, a boy hellbent on not being a sit-down Indian like me. I quit school in the fourth grade and lie to people about reading and writing. In my heart I feel like a cow that gets led from barn to pasture and back again. So I got mixed up that summer and instead of watching over Russ I was listening to him like he was the older one, like he could teach me. He was a part of the group that wanted us to get rid of Tyrone Little. Noah and John Fire and me took Tyrone's side, though. I liked him. He'd always been handy with tools and advice on what to do. He hooked up the electricity for the Walking Horses and when Noah needed to move his outhouse, Tyrone contracted for all the digging equipment and fixed that broken hinge on the door. Once when somebody poured sand in Willard Bent's car, Tyrone took that engine apart down to the last pipe and laid all the pieces out on newspaper. Then he cleaned and oiled every one of them parts, using his fingers to get to the narrow spots. We'd have left that car for junk, but at the end of the day I started that car up and it hummed.

But then we found those footprints and even Noah said we had to run him off.

I thought we'd put a lid on the troubles that were hounding us the night we kicked him out. But not two hours later, that FBI man came out to Choteau and drove straight to my house. He stood in the doorway and looked over my shoulder to where I had the AIMers symbol, a U.S. flag hanging upside down, on the wall next to my single-shot Remington. "It's loaded," I told him.

Though it was almost sundown, he was wearing his dark glasses like they always do, but he didn't have no summer clothes on. He had a suit on and was sweating real bad. He said he was looking for Russ.

"What for?" I asked.

"We have evidence that Russ was knocking over the graves out at All Souls."

I'm a bigger man than he was. People think I'm taller than I am because I got a high round chest. Like a tree, they used to say. He was afraid of me, I guess, the way I was standing up real tall and him sweating while I was cool as a cucumber in the shade. "You're a liar," I said.

"It'll go better for him if he gives himself up. Do you know where we can find him?"

Right then he was at Toby's with the other young warriors. "He's out west," I said, "visiting people at Pine Ridge."

He told me they'd seen Russ just that morning, racing his motorcycle through Wilma with Gene Fast Horse riding on the back.

Maybe he wormed his way into Noah's good graces, but damned if I was going to listen to him. Truth is, I knew he wasn't lying. It was Harold Bad Hand and my own son digging up them bones. Special Agent Person said he had plates of tire tracks that matched that motorcycle.

I could hide my son but I couldn't hide my shame. My mother used to hit me with whatever was handy—broom, kitchen things, a hairbrush, once even a plate that still had food on it. I'd never laid a hand on Russ and now he was twenty-two, full growed, and it was too late.

"Your son would do better talking to me than to Sheriff Merchant," he said.

I caught myself looking at his shoes. They were black but topped with red dust like what you find along the river where the clay dried out. Shoes with skinny laces and not at all the kind of shoes you used for walking around. I said as much and he looked at me all surprised. Then noises started coming from his car. He turned to the car and then looked at me and he was mad.

"The shit's piling up, Frank, and we're gonna need more than wings, if you get my drift." Then he turned his back on me to answer his radio and I knew it wasn't me he was scared of.

Pete Scully

After we kicked Tyrone out, the skies opened up and the rain come down looking almost white and turned the roads to mud. We didn't give a hoot. We was just happy to get rid of the dry dust and of Tyrone Little.

John Fire drove out with Willard Bent to one of the other places where the guns was hid and hauled them all back into town. They parked Willard's car in the yellow grass in front of Frank's house. He had that Chevy Bel Air that was more rust than white and he used to joke it was a car that wanted in the worst way to become red. Anyway, John Fire wasn't there until well after the shooting started. He spent the night watching over the cemetery. That one FBI man, the one who always acted so friendly, came out to Choteau around nine-thirty looking for Russ Poor Bull, so John Fire made Russ go along to the cemetery just to keep him out of town for the night.

It isn't true what got reported, about how everyone in the village was dead drunk. Kevin Walking Horse never touched a drop and neither did his wife. Noah Lame had a long drink the night before, but after what he seen nobody could hardly blame him. It was only about seven or eight of us over at the Poor Bulls' house where Judy was going to fix dinner. Poor Bull cracked out a jug of cider and poured all around. When June Lame took a cup I saw Noah looking the other way.

We started out slow and built steam as the night lengthened. After the rain stopped, the sky was torn, the clouds like broken skin. When everybody else went off to bed, I took the last of that cider and settled into Willard's car to finish it off. The homemade mash was so sour it hurt your eyes, and I opened the door and started throwing up. I remember looking down at the weeds and wondering if it'd still show up in the dust the next day or would I have to go down there and kick dirt over what I'd done. No dinner in me but I was throwing up my breakfast, my guts, whatever was in there that wasn't fastened down.

The last thing I remember about that night before was seeing Willard up front, sitting at the wheel with a rifle by his side. He hadn't been drinking with us, but had spent the whole time looking out that front window toward the road that led straight to us.

I was still asleep in the back and woke up when I heard some shots being fired. By the time I sat up and looked out the window, Willard was already out of the car and had his rifle aimed to the side of us. Then he squeezed off a couple shots at the trees there, but I couldn't see what he was aiming at.

Harold Bad Hand

Just before sunup, Cale and Robbins came out to the house and rousted me, told me to get behind the wheel. I didn't have time for coffee or even to take a piss. I lit a cigarette and followed them out of Wilma. They was driving west on Highway 50 and we passed at least a dozen marshal and BIA cars out along the highway. We drove on past Choteau until we got to Tyrone Little's place. They was in their fed cars and I had my blue Dodge and I parked a ways off in case any of the Choteau crowd was around. Cale told me to wait outside but after a few minutes I went inside anyhow, where they had Little handcuffed while they was going through the drawers and all. They had him in the kitchen with his back turned to the door so he didn't see me. Delores was gone, like you'd figure after what we done to Little the night before. Cale and Robbins was looking for the grenades I'd made up but all they found was papers and money and parts for electric stuff. Robbins was cussing a blue streak and I went up the stairs to where there was a bedroom with rainwater on the floor and the bed all torn up. There was a big dresser against a wall and the drawers were all opened and on top was some cuff links, a comb, a framed picture of some old-time Indian I didn't know, and that eagle feather. It was a big one, mostly white, and just sitting there like it was forgot. I heard footsteps on the stairs and grabbed that feather quick and dropped it down the front of my shirt. Cale came into the bedroom and saw me and said I should get the hell out. He was shouting and all hot about something.

"This house is clean," he said. Then he came over and looked me in the face and said he knew I had the guns. They had my bootprints, the boots he'd bought me. I should of knowed the shitsucker had them marked. He said, "If you don't turn the guns in, you're going straight back to Colorado and we'll make sure you bunk with Henry Four."

"All right," I said. "They're hid somewheres."

"Where?"

"Come meet me east of Choteau."

"I'm not meeting you anywhere. Just bring the guns in and leave it at that."

I said, "I got a whole lot more to tell you, but you won't hear a word if you don't show up."

"Don't push me, Tonto. I know who dug up those graves."

"It wasn't me."

"Like hell." His voice had a sound in it that I didn't like.

He had to take Little into town and I told him to meet me at eight-thirty out by the highway east of town where there's a sign for a deer crossing. I knew he'd slow down and pull over to the ditch. There's no place to park there, just that ditch. Robbins put Little in the car and I came outside too fast. Little was in the back and he looked out the car window and saw me standing there on his porch. Then Cale got in and drove away. I jumped in that blue car they gave me and parked across the cornfield where I'd hid the guns. It was still early morning and the shadows was long. I checked the firing lines to make sure the sun was at my back, not in my face. I had two deer rifles and three shotguns all loaded when I saw two cars. Robbins drove on ahead toward Choteau but Cale slowed down and pulled over right by that deer sign. I had a nest made in that cornfield and was sitting pretty. Cale rolled down his window and lit a cigarette. My first shot hit him in the arm and I kept on firing. He got out of the car and then reached back in so I knew he was on the radio. Those rifles was three-shooters and I emptied them and then tried my hand with the shotgun but it wouldn't carry. Cale was crouched down behind the car and I had to move around to get a better look at him. After I reloaded one of them rifles I got off a shot that hit him square in the neck and down he went.

Willard Bent

I was just about awake, sitting kind of hunched against the door when I saw the feds coming up the main road. They were moving real slow and nobody was around so I shook my head and slapped my face and reached for my rifle. Then the car stopped so I opened the door and got out. I could see it was Robbins and when he saw me, he stepped out of his car. It was maybe twenty yards from him to me and he didn't seem ready to come any closer.

"I'm looking for Russ Poor Bull! I got a warrant."

"Let's see it!" I shouted back.

"First you put down that gun."

Back in St. Paul, I swore to myself I was through putting down my gun for white men. "I'm a city Indian, Robbins, and I know about the law. Let's see the warrant first."

I don't know who was more nervous, him or me. He turned like he was going to get back behind the wheel. Then we heard the shots.

I didn't know where they were coming from. It was far away but not that far. I wasn't thinking straight. Then Robbins had his gun out and was shooting at me. On instinct I fell to one knee and raised my gun so I was shooting from between the car and the open door. Robbins fired back and then Pete started yelling in the backseat. There were tents with people in them about twenty yards to the right of us and those people needed cover. Robbins scrambled up into his car and I knew he'd be on his radio and we'd be overrun in no time.

Noah Lame

When the shooting started, I rolled myself onto June to keep her covered. There were two shots, maybe three. I was barely awake and wasn't counting. When I heard more shots, I knew they were coming from far away and not into my house.

I roused June, who was half dead from whisky. She was still in her clothes and I found her shoes under the bed. Herman was already up, wearing only his jeans and those bandages around his ribs. "Where are they?" I asked him.

His eyes were wild. "I don't know!"

Jana helped June into the kitchen and I told them to stay on the floor. We heard more shooting and when I looked out the window in the back of the living room I could see a car in the ditch west of the Choteau road. The door was swung open on the passenger's side and a man was kneeling behind it and firing a rifle in the direction of Poor Bull's house. As far as I could tell, that was the only shooting going on. I told Herman to get the women to Toby's and keep them there in that big basement where he keeps his supplies.

When they were gone, I went to the attic and watched out the little window. My glasses were still broken—one lens was gone altogether and the other was cracked—so it was like looking through an empty bottle, but I could see the cars coming along the highway from the east. After counting ten of them I quit watching and went out the back way toward the trailer court. Running from tree to trailer, it took me five long minutes to get to Helene Her Many Horses' front door. What I saw busting in was a blur I've never forgotten. She was stark naked, standing by the television that was blaring away. I stood there and gaped at her. She didn't even try to cover herself, she just blinked at me through her glasses and said, "You're twenty-eight years too late."

"Get down," I yelled. "They're shooting out there!" Just then a bullet came through the window. We both hit the floor and I crawled over to Helene in a hurry. A few more shots hit the trailer and we squirmed into the kitchen.

"Delores isn't here," she said.

I couldn't make any sense of that, so I didn't answer her.

"She came by this morning and left about an hour ago. She'll send a postcard."

I told her to stay put and slithered on my belly across the tiny living room and into her bedroom. There was a bathrobe hanging on the door and I yanked it down, then crawled back to the kitchen and told her to cover herself.

"Who's shooting at us?" she said. She was looking over my shoulder and her eyes were excited. I turned around and saw she was watching the television. A man with white hair was holding a microphone to his lips and singing a love song.

Bill Person

That morning I had an eight o'clock breakfast meeting with Special
Agent Cordray in Monowi, Nebraska, about thirty miles south of
Choteau. We finished at 8:35 and I had just gotten into my car. I was
due to drive west to Spencer and then northwest to Bonesteel to
question a man named Draper about a gun purchase that had been
made in his store. I had driven perhaps five miles when I received a
radio message from SA Robbins. The contact was bad and I couldn't
hear him clearly. He sounded very nervous and at first all I could
understand was that there were Indians with rifles. He also mentioned
a white Chevrolet Bel Air.

I turned the car around and sped toward the bridge at Yellow Fox
Point. The roads on the Dakota side down that way are not in good
shape and there'd been rain the night before, so they were still muddy
and hard to navigate. I asked SA Robbins to tell me where he was.
He was shouting that he was taking fire and he told me to come
quick. I repeatedly asked him to tell me his location. I could hear
what sounded to be gunshots but whether they were from his own
firearms or not was unclear. He did not give me his location. He said
again that he was taking heavy fire and to send help.

SA Cale was on the radio line and informed me that he was east
of Choteau and was hit. There were other voices on the line and I
was ordering everyone to clear that line so we could communicate. A
few minutes passed before I heard from Cale again, who said he was
approximately one-half mile east of Choteau.

Frank Poor Bull

When I was arrested they said I was the one who fired the first shots
but I didn't have a gun until about an hour after the attack started.
The only place I knew there were rifles was in Willard Bent's trunk
and I could see easy enough that he and Scully were pinned down
there. I sent Judy out the back way and told her to get to Toby's.
There's a basement there and I thought she'd be safer than in our
little house. I watched out the back window until she made it past

the trees and to the front door, then I went back to the front of the house and crawled onto the porch.

There was some tents pitched about ten yards past where Bent's car was sitting and I remember thinking there was families inside and how tents don't stop no bullets. I wasn't thinking too good and ran north when I should've run east. I was trying to get to those tents, but I don't know what I was thinking I'd do if I'd made it. I heard some shots I knew were meant for me, so I fell to the ground and just laid there for a long time and prepared myself for dying.

Judy Poor Bull

I'm an old woman now and I was an old woman that morning. I ran till my legs quit and my heart burst open. When I got to Toby's place, June and Jana Lame was already there. I didn't see Toby but they told me he was out back with Herman. June was crying and Jana had her arms around her and was telling her to shush. For a long time we didn't hear no shooting so I went to the window and could see out to Willard Bent's car. Willard wasn't there no more and I didn't know where he'd gone. One of the back doors was open and Pete Scully was crouched behind it. I didn't know they was FBIs until Jana told me. We was all so scared we didn't move. I was the only one who even looked out the window.

Frank Poor Bull

I had dirt in my mouth and my nose so I turned on my side and tried hard to breathe. Then I crawled ahead until I came to the main road. Toby's was about thirty yards to my right and in between was the car they'd been shooting at me from. The front door was open and a man was lying on the ground beside it. I got to my feet and ran across the road toward the tents. There were three of them all out in the open, in the big space just past Toby's parking lot. I tore through each of those tents, feeling my heart about to burst, but there was nobody inside. I found out later that they'd run east to the Walking Horses' house and got arrested there later on in the morning.

When I came out of the last tent, I heard Gene yelling at me from

Toby's. He was up front, behind the windows that looked in on the bar and grill, and was waving a rifle back and forth. He shouted at me to cover the road from my house. I guess he didn't know all I had to shoot with was my fingers.

I jumped into clear ground and all of a sudden a man came out of the tall grass. I thought I was done for, but it was that newspaper guy, Clyde Bennett, and all he did was take my picture.

Noah Lame

The shooting stopped for a while, so I took a carving knife out of a kitchen drawer and told Helene we should get out of there. I was convinced that Choteau was surrounded and the safest place would be toward the center of town. Helene didn't have any shoes so I gave her mine. We waited in that kitchen for about fifteen minutes and then I said she better give me her glasses. "They won't fit," she said, but I put them on anyway and could see a little better. When I poked my head up and looked out, there were a few cars about fifty yards west of us but nothing to the south or southwest.

"So when are we going?" Helene asked.

We crept out the door and slipped between the two rusted-out trailers south of Helene's. I was encouraged when no one fired on us. Just past the last trailer was the laundromat and right when we made for it the shooting started up again. My heart was paining me and I stooped down to the floor of that laundromat and caught my breath. I looked at that carving knife in my hand and felt so stupid I just threw it away.

"We're going to have to run now," I said. "We're going to try to get to Poor Bull's. Can you run that far?"

She nodded and we stood up. I peeked around the doorway and couldn't see anyone. Then I felt Helene's hand on my shoulder and I instinctively reached back and took it into my own. "Don't let go," I said.

"I never have," she replied.

We ran west to a stand of trees and circled back south to that tar-paper shack where Poor Bull kept an old car he could never afford to fix up. That FBI car was sitting on the road about forty feet straight to the east of us, sort of tipped back into the shallow ditch, and I could see a man's body lying next to the front door. He looked dead. My heart was about to burst and I was tempted to stay inside that shack, but we just caught our breath and then were off again for the last twenty-five yards, right through Judy's corn and carrot patch.

We burst through the back door into the Poor Bulls' kitchen and Frank and Willard Bent couldn't believe what they were seeing, me with Helene's glasses on and her wearing nothing but a ratty bathrobe and my black lace shoes. Willard handed me a rifle but I said I didn't know how to aim. Willard said that was okay, I should just pull the trigger to make noise and not waste too many bullets. One of those blue cars was coming up the road and we fired out the window. It stopped short, then backed up like crazy until we couldn't see it anymore.

Harold Bad Hand

When I got to Cale, he was just lying there breathing in and out and he looked up at me with these eyes like the Jesus on my Grandma Janine's wall. I aimed the shotgun at his head and pulled the trigger but there was no shell in the gun so I had to go back to the cornfield for a deer rifle. When I got back to the car he was already crawling up to the road. His blood was all over the weeds and his arms and face and I didn't even have to aim.

Bill Person

Robbins had no business there as far as I knew. We were looking for Russ Poor Bull because we had tire tracks out by All Souls Cemetery that matched his motorcycle. I assumed that Robbins had discovered he was back in Choteau and went to pick him up, which he shouldn't have done on his own.

I was still about five miles east of Choteau when I heard SA Martinez shouting over the line that he could see Robbins' car. He said he was taking heavy fire and asked how long it would take me to get there. I told him only a few minutes and he informed me that he was withdrawing. I asked if he could see Robbins and he told me no.

As I turned off the dirt road onto Highway 50, I saw that there were two state marshal vehicles just ahead of me. Until I reached the area north of Choteau, I had no idea how many marshals had already arrived in the sector. I had lost contact with Cale and had no idea where he was at that point. We were using the radio line to coordinate a blockade. It was a few minutes past nine when I arrived at the outskirts and spotted SA Cale's car resting in a ditch on the north side of the road. The car was shot up and all the tires were flat. A cornfield ran along that road and the stalks were high. Given the placement of the bullet holes in the car, I assumed that the shots had come from that field and I approached the car with caution.

Judy Poor Bull

When close to an hour went by and we didn't hear no more shooting, we didn't know what to make of it, but we knew it wasn't over. Gene said he had a car hid in some trees about two miles east and he was all for heading that way. But first we had to get the children out.

Kevin Walking Horse drove his station wagon up the street and back, but didn't draw any fire, so he drove around behind Toby's and loaded up the young children in the back. That was the first time I saw John Fire that morning. He was out back where Toby's shed is, talking to Kevin Walking Horse. I called out to him about Russ but he couldn't hear me. I thought Russ had come back into town with him. I didn't know until later that John Fire came into Choteau alone and left Russ to keep watch over the cemetery.

Kevin Walking Horse took the back road that leads toward Gaetan Avril's farmhouse. Not ten seconds after he was gone the shooting started up all over again and we was sure they was firing at the station wagon. There wasn't any way we could make a break for Gene's car. John Fire and Darryl and Gene went to the front window of Toby's and fired their guns to the north where there was at least twenty cars lined up on the other side of the trailer park.

Gaetan Avril

I didn't need a radio to know that the war had begun. My house is only a few miles from Choteau and when the shooting started, I was already dressed and about to get into my car to go to work. I ran back into the house, dialed Tyrone's number and listened to it ring twelve times. Then I got back into my car, but instead of driving to Wilma I cut across the north edge of Eagle Reach—down the four- teenth fairway and straight through the fence—and headed up the river road toward the highway. Even before I got there, I could see the place was fairly well surrounded by state marshals, the local cops, and some of Lonetree's men in their pickups.

"What in hell's going on?" I asked Sheriff Merchant, who looked scared to death.

He pointed to the marshals. "It's out of my hands, Gaetan."

I tried to nose through the roadblock onto the highway, but two marshals drew their pistols and put a stop to that right away. One of them was real nice about it, saying of course he wouldn't shoot but it wasn't advisable all the same. So I sat at the junction of the highway and the river road and fiddled with my CB until I was on the party frequency and another hundred people must've shown up within the next half hour, including my father and Albert Roebuck and a number of their Eagle Reach pals, all of them with deer rifles. My father pulled his car over next to mine and leaned out the window. "You'd best clear out, Gaetan. You're not equipped."

I started to ask him about this army all around us but Roebuck clapped him on the shoulder and he edged the car ahead toward the roadblock. One of the marshals nodded and waved them through.

I sat in my car and concentrated on the CB chatter. As best I could tell, there were two FBI agents inside Choteau and Bill Person out on the northeast corner. The north and east of Choteau were blan- keted by marshals and sharpshooters and I could see for myself that the west route was flanked by marshals and Wilma people and Lonetree's goons. I listened to the radio for a good forty minutes and only once heard any reference to the south side. South of Toby's is a road that runs east to west and borders a rocky field where nothing much grows. The field is about fifty yards deep, then it's three miles of trees and scrub to the Missouri River. Given all the screaming and yelling on the radio, I figured that the attack wasn't half as organized as a Lions Club picnic. Any cars to the south of Choteau would be fully exposed to the back windows of Toby's place, and nobody seemed to want to play that position.

I drove away from the checkpoint, backtracking toward my house, but stopped the car where the road bent closest to Blue Eye Creek. To the west was Eagle Reach and to the east a cornfield. The trees along the creek provided cover and I followed the creekbed as it swayed eastward. Now and then I heard gunshots to the north, but they were far away. It only took ten minutes to cross from the creek to the trees southwest of the field. There was still too much open ground between myself and Toby's, so once I caught my breath I decided to stick to the treeline as long as possible. I angled northward until I could just make out the back of Poor Bull's house. There was an elm tree about ten yards closer in, so I crawled over and dug in at the base of the trunk. A station wagon was coming down the south road, which ran within twenty yards of me and I could see it was filled with kids, but the driver wasn't anyone I knew. Someone was shooting from a long ways off, though I couldn't see any traces of bullets hitting around the station wagon. At Gaetan Road, it turned down in the direction of the river.

After waiting for a long time at the edge of that slope, I stepped out into open ground and began to run straight for Poor Bull's house.

Harold Bad Hand

After I shot Cale, I heard on his radio how a whole army was coming to Choteau. They were heading east from Wilma and I was clear on the other side of town. I ran back north across the cornfield to where my car was on the dirt road. Two cars was coming toward me from up north so I gunned it west. I was running north of the cemetery and could see John Fire's car heading south toward town. I knew what I had to do. Nobody'd seen me shoot Cale and that left just Russ Poor Bull who knew about them bones.

Bill Person

I radioed to Martinez that I had arrived just north of town and was still on Highway 50. Then I got out of the car and approached the ditch. SA Cale had crawled about fifteen feet from his car and was lying faceup in that ditch. He was wearing a white shirt with blue stripes and one of his arms was bloodied and wrapped in what appeared to be a T-shirt. He had taken a bullet to the left arm and another in the neck. The blood around his head was already dry and thick. His right arm was crossed over his face and I could see that his hand had been blown off.

Noah Lame

Around ten that morning, John Fire made it over from Toby's and told us all the women were inside. Kevin Walking Horse had driven the children out the back road though nobody knew if he'd made it.

The rifle box was sitting on the floor in the kitchen and John Fire counted six rifles but only fifty rounds or so. Frank took half the shells and two of the rifles and hurried out the back to Toby's. John Fire and Willard Bent stayed near the front of the house and told me I should keep an eye out back, so I leaned over the kitchen sink and looked out the window. There were only half a dozen trees between the yard and the dirt road that led west toward Eagle Reach and I had a clear enough view. There were little pots of herbs and flowers ranged along the windowsill and the faucet had a bad leak to it. I'd taken my eye off the road and was looking at those pots when I suddenly noticed something moving to the southwest, somebody coming through the trees straight at the house. I raised the gun to my shoulder and fired, but with Helene's glasses I couldn't see where the bullet went. I could make out it was a man carrying a box. I must have been yelling because then John Fire was beside me and I was about to shoot again when he clapped his hand on my shoulder and told me to stop.

The man made it up to the back door, and when John Fire opened the door he fell right in.

Judy Poor Bull

Anna Walking Horse and I went through that whole kitchen trying to make weapons in case they attacked the house. I had some Coke bottles we filled with lamp oil and stuffed rags in top for flame bombs. Anna tied a butcher knife to a broomstick and when Frank saw it he said, "That's one mean lance, little sister."

Then Darryl came back into the kitchen and said they was low on bullets. Frank had only brought shotgun shells and they was using straight rifles. Darryl said he had ten shots left and Anna said he should stop shooting at the trees and wait for targets. Darryl told her to shut up and then Herman stood up and said he'd go. I thought it should have been Fast Horse but nobody was listening to me.

Darryl took a bullet out of his pocket and gave it to Herman so he'd know what to bring back. Herman went out the back door and we could see out the window after him. He had long legs but with those broken ribs he was kind of bent over and couldn't move all that fast. He was trying for the elm trees to the west, where there was a tire swing and a junked car, but he just seemed to stop. He looked like he was walking, took a few slow steps, and then he went down. I hadn't even heard any shooting so I thought maybe he'd just stumbled, though he never did get up.

Bill Person

I radioed for an ambulance, anyway. God, I was sick to my stomach. Cale had a wife and a little girl back in Denver and whoever had shot him had obviously just finished him off. It was more like an execution than a murder.

I took an M-16 and two boxes of ammo from my trunk and placed them in the passenger seat, then drove west until I came to a roadblock. At least a dozen people, only two of whom were in uniform, waved rifles in my direction. I stopped and identified myself. On the other side of the roadblock, approximately one tenth of a mile from Choteau, I found several Indians being held prisoner by a group of marshals. Some of them were grown men, but most were women and children and they were all standing in the hot sun with their arms raised to their heads. A tall young man with long hair was running around taking pictures of everything in sight. I didn't know who he was at the time but found out later it was Clyde Bennett, the journalist who'd been trailing AIM around for months.

I could make out Sheriff Merchant in a crowd just ahead of me. He was in a complete panic and tried to order me to stay clear of his police line. He was busy directing his town "deputies" to take up positions along the highway, the limit of his legal jurisdiction. After five minutes, I returned to my car and contacted SA Martinez. He informed me that he had penetrated Choteau and was heading up the main road toward the bar and grill. I advised him to wait for me but he continued ahead. I could hear firing both over the radio and in the near distance. SA Martinez shouted that he was taking fire but didn't answer when I asked if he could identify the source. Less than a minute later I saw his car backing up the road and onto the highway. I ran to meet him and found that he was unharmed, though his car had taken at least half a dozen shots across the hood and front.

To my knowledge, only Robbins and Martinez had entered Choteau by this time. It was close to ten a.m. and although the highway was crowded with armed men, no one had attempted an assault on the town. I relayed Sheriff Merchant's claim about the high number of armed Indians in town and Martinez said it was probably an exaggeration. Twenty or twenty-five, was his estimate. He sketched a rough map on a scrap of paper and showed me where he believed the shooting had originated. We decided to forget about using the main road and approach the bar and grill from the northwest, which would require a vehicle other than the sedans we were driving. I made a radio request to SA Cordray to bring an ATV and assault gear up from Monowi. The attorneys for the Choteau defense later maintained that we already had this matériel in place, which was untrue. They implied that we had planned a morning attack. But if that had been the case, I would not have been thirty miles away when the shooting started and SA Robbins would not have gone alone into the heart of that town. I waited with SA Martinez for over an hour, during which time we took crime-scene photographs of SA Cale and scoured the area for evidence. There were a number of footprints that bore what appeared to be markings of tennis shoes around the body. It was an easy imprint to read due to the previous night's heavy rain. The shoe tread was deep and there were few marks from wear; they were new shoes. A second pair of footprints belonged to SA Cale. We needed more than that hour to cool off. The sight of Cale with his face already bloated by the heat and his hand blown off gave us both thoughts we didn't want to have. We found empty shell boxes and expended shells, broken sunglasses that I knew had belonged to Cale, and in the car were road maps, a .32-caliber revolver, and suntan lotion. The floor and front seat were littered with gum wrappers, a newspaper, various shells, and orange peels.

I asked SA Martinez if he'd had any contact with our informant, and he replied that there'd been no sign of him since early in the morning.

At five minutes to noon, we had our ATV and assault gear. I again advised Sheriff Merchant to clear the civilians from the area or to confiscate their arms, but he was in contact with Bull Smedsrud and wasn't taking orders from me. At approximately twelve-fifteen, SA Martinez took the wheel and we entered Choteau from the northwest corner, about two hundred yards west of the Lame residence. We skirted west and then south behind the trailer court and, as we approached the Poor Bull house, we could see Robbins' car. All the tires were shot out and the door on the driver's side was open but neither SA Martinez nor I could see Robbins. To the east of his car were a few tents and a white Chevrolet which I assumed to be the car Robbins had mentioned over the radio. Both doors were open, as was the trunk, but the car appeared to have been abandoned. To the west of the Poor Bull residence were several large trees and a wrecked car. I directed SA Martinez to drive around those trees and approach the bar and grill from the west. As we came around those trees, we could see a man running hunched over from behind the bar and grill. He was heading toward our position. I stepped out of the car and fell to one knee and trained my sidearm on him. I could see that he wasn't armed, so I simply followed him with my aim. There were two shots, but not from my gun nor from SA Martinez'. To this day I don't know who fired those shots. There were at least fifty people in the sector by that time since the marshals and locals were flanking us and I wasn't in control. We saw the man go down but didn't wait to see if he got up again because we were taking fire from the north side of the bar and grill and had to withdraw.

Judy Poor Bull

June was crying and screaming and tore herself out of my arms, trying to run out after Herman. Jana helped me hold her back and then we seen Helene Her Many Horses walk out the back door of my house.

I couldn't believe it. She was moving through the tall grass like she was in some kind of trance. I yelled out the window to tell her to go back, but I don't think she heard me. She walked straight to where Herman was lying and bent over him. We could see men coming from the other side of the trees. At first we only saw a few but then there was more, at least twenty. Gene went out the front with his gun but then he threw it on the ground and raised his hands. Darryl Kills First followed him out and did the same thing. I was hoping they'd defend us better than that, though I can't say I blame them. Frank still had his gun and he checked and seen there was three bullets left. "What time is it?" he asked me.

I told him it was past noon.

"They've had more than two hours," he said, meaning Kevin and the children.

Toby's place was surrounded by men with rifles and a row of cars and trucks was coming up the main road straight for the front door. Frank set the rifle against the counter and stood up.

Noah Lame

Willard Bent was holding the barrel of his gun to Gaetan Avril's head while John Fire tuned the CB radio to the police frequency. Gaetan was saying there was only one way out of Choteau and that was to go directly south. Willard told him to shut up and then yelled at me to keep watching out that window.

I could hear voices and knew that John Fire had found the frequency, right where Gaetan had told him he would.

"This is a setup!" Willard shouted.

"Why'd you come?" John Fire asked Gaetan.

"Personal matter," Gaetan answered.

"Where's Tyrone Little?"

"I wish to hell I knew."

We listened to that radio for close to half an hour and figured that between the FBI, the SWAT team, the state marshals, Wilma police, and Lonetree's goons, there had to be close to two hundred of them in all. We heard they had Myrene Tall Bull and maybe thirty other people from the houses on the eastside. They were throwing around words like *deploy* and *flank* and were even arguing some about who was in charge of what. That made us all smile a little, but only in the way you do when you know you're about to die. There were too many of them to kill, even more were on the way.

Gaetan had brought along a county map and, once Willard put the gun down, he asked for a pencil. He drew what he'd seen from the highway and added X's where he thought the marshals and BIA police were at. He also drew a circle near the east hook of Blue Eye Creek and said, "My car's parked there, if you find yourselves out that way." He gave me the keys.

Next thing I knew John Fire was opening drawers and cupboards. I thought he was going to pack some food but all he took was a little bottle of black pepper and one of those cans of ground red pepper, the hot kind. There was more shooting, but when I turned back to the window I couldn't see anything. The shots seemed closer than the others we'd heard so we assumed they were closing in. I could see a man on the ground to the southwest corner and he was firing toward the trees west of us.

"They're coming," Gaetan said.

Helene came into the kitchen and just stood there. I still had her eyeglasses but she was staring at me with wide eyes. My first thought was she'd been hit, but she shook her head. "Noah," she said. I was distracted by more shooting and ducked my head down behind the sink. A few shots hit the house and John Fire started firing out the window. When I lifted my head, Helene was gone. I stood and looked out the window and could see her heading south. Then I couldn't see her anymore and so I went to the bathroom on the south side of the house and smashed out the window with the butt of my rifle. She was standing in the middle of the yard and looking down but I couldn't tell what she was looking at. Then she bent to her knees and just stayed there. I hollered even though she was probably too far away to hear. John Fire was shouting for me, so I went back in the kitchen. The door was open and he said I could stay or go along.

"What about Toby's?"

"They're taken," he said.

Willard went first and John Fire said it was time to go.

I looked at my bare feet, but it was too late to cover them. I followed him out the door.

Bill Person

Someone was shooting at us from a position southwest of the Poor Bull house, so we fell back to the trailer court and waited for the wave of marshals to join us. When Sheriff Merchant radioed for all points to move in, I knew it was time to piece together a cohesive stranglehold. There were BIA police covering the east side of town, and marshals were to the north and west. I asked Merchant who was covering the south road and he answered that Lonetree's men were headed that way. I asked him to confirm their position. "If we push down from this direction, they can only go south and we'll lose them."

Sheriff Merchant didn't answer me but I could hear someone with him shouting that they should saddle up. I took this to mean they were beginning their assault, and I directed SA Martinez to return to the main road of Choteau and proceed toward the bar and grill.

Frank Poor Bull

We saw them coming through the trees to where the tents were. They were like ants, there were so many of them. I saw two men in black jumpsuits and wondered who they were, and then I spotted at least twenty more off to the east. I fired my rifle without even aiming. I could have killed any one of them but didn't see the point in it. The fight was gone from me after what happened to Herman Lame. Gene Fast Horse ran out of bullets and Darryl Kills First lost his nerve. Everyone was looking at me and all I saw were people close to death. Maybe I had it in my head that if I put that gun down everything would work itself out.

When they came into the house, we had our hands in the air but all the same they threw us to the ground and clapped handcuffs on us. I was pulled to my feet and yanked out the front door and it was crazy to see marshals all around me and men in jumpsuits all looking at us while behind their backs I could see Willard and John Fire and then Noah running like mad for the back road. I started laughing and then had to look away so the marshals wouldn't see. I didn't even care when one of those marshals cuffed my neck, I was still laughing like a drunk man and saying *run run run* to myself when they shoved me into that car.

Noah Lame

We made it to the barbed wire at the edge of the south road and still no one had shot at us. On the other side of that fence was a shallow ditch and we climbed in there to catch our breath. Across the dirt road was a naked field for about fifty yards, then the trees that ran down to the Missouri. We discussed the best way to clear that space and decided to go together rather than one at a time. By now there were cars on that road, but they were all coming from the east and stopping at Toby's. "Imagine that field is shoulder high with corn," John Fire said. "To us it looks empty, but to anybody else it's full of tall corn and they won't see us."

It was his way of hypnotizing us and he picked up on that all through the day, telling us we were ghost runners, we were eagles, we were wind. We made it through that bald field to the treeline and kept on going. We heard later that someone had seen some Indians running south, but they didn't come after us.

After about a mile, John Fire waved for us to stop. "Listen," he said.

I bent my ears to the wind and heard nothing.

"Dogs," Willard said.

John Fire nodded. Then I heard them for myself.

Reaching into his pockets, John Fire pulled out the red and black pepper he'd taken from the Poor Bull kitchen. He emptied the pepper into a small pile in the dirt and said, "Anybody feel the need to take a leak?"

I said I was bursting and he told me to pee on that pile. I left a stream that would have made a stallion proud and then John Fire stomped his feet into the pile and told Willard to do likewise.

"The dogs trailing us will come across this scent and stick their noses right into this pepper. That ought to fuck them up good." He laughed louder than was safe.

"Where'd you learn that?" I asked him.

"Tyrone taught me."

Willard had left the CB radio back in the ditch so we didn't have any way of knowing where they were. We headed off again and the sun was well on its downward swing by the time we came within sight of the river. We were still about a hundred yards away when we noticed a white pickup parked down by the edge of the water. Standing next to it was an Indian with a rifle in his hands.

"A brother," John Fire said.

Willard laughed. "You're crazy, John Fire. He's one of Lonetree's goons."

"Well," John Fire said, "maybe so. Let me go talk to him."

He left his gun behind and just walked out from under the trees and headed for that pickup. Willard Bent crouched low and aimed his rifle at the other guy. When John Fire came up close, he raised his arm high in the air and shouted howdy. The two of them talked for a while and then John Fire signaled for us to come down. It turned out the boy was supposed to be guarding the river but his heart wasn't in it. "I hear they shot an Indian back in Choteau and now they're all crazy because some FBI guy got wasted." We wanted to know what Indian but he didn't have a name to give us. He told us there were BIA police and marshals both east and west of us and probably a dozen men at the bridge. "You thinking of crossing here?"

"How deep's the water?" Willard asked.

The boy just laughed. "It's the *Missouri*. You don't even have to swim."

Willard wanted to take his gun from him, but John Fire said no. "If his gun's missing, they'll know he let us through."

It was another five hours before sundown and we decided to wait right there. We moved back into the trees and kept an eye on the pickup. Once a car came by and someone talked out the window to the boy. I held my breath and then saw the boy shake his head.

That part of the river was about a quarter mile wide and so shallow that we were just wading with our heads bent low so we wouldn't give away our profiles. We only had to swim the last thirty yards.

Gaetan Avril

When they started shooting, I holed up in the closet for a while and then in the bathroom, where the walls seemed to be more solid. Nobody counted afterwards, but I'd guess they put a few thousand rounds into that house before finally busting down the front and back doors and storming the place. The marshals didn't know what to make of it when they found me sitting on the toilet. One of them asked me, "Where are the Indians?" So I said, "What Indians?"

Their disappointment was monumental. They were sure they'd trapped a whole nest of Sioux and all they got was a white man sitting on the john. I must've been the only one who saw the humor in it since a couple of them were waving their pistols in my face. I was taken into the living room and cuffed, then one of those men noticed the photographs on the wall over the couch. They were family pictures, mostly, of Frank and Judy Poor Bull and their relations. That guy started shooting at the pictures and then they all were, Lonetree's punks and some BIA police and a number of marshals. They shot every picture off that wall and when only glass and shot-up plaster was left, they dragged me outside to where they were herding up the last of the Choteau people.

The Indians were just as surprised to see me among them as the cops had been to find me on the crapper. Everyone looked bewildered by the sunlight, and we were looking at each other as if we were complete strangers. June Lame was raving, and I saw one of the BIA police tying a rag around her mouth to shut her up. George Brings Yellow had a cut across his forehead and looked like they'd punched him around more than a little. As they pushed me along to a patrol car, I saw Frank Poor Bull sitting in a car just to the left of me, grinning like nobody's business.

Noah Lame

It's hard to run in wet clothes and we had to wait until we were all dried off to get moving again. From the Nebraska side we could see the activity back in South Dakota, where cars and pickups were cruising along the river's edge, their headlights showing them off.

We didn't have any food, but I'd gotten a number of swallows of Missouri water so at least I wasn't dying of thirst like before. John Fire's gun got soaked during the crossing, so he dug a hole and buried it. Willard had lost his rifle as well so we were down to a pocketknife and our teeth for self-defense. My bare feet were bleeding and John Fire offered me his shoes, but I wouldn't take them and we ended up making me a pair of slippers. I put on John Fire's socks and then Willard's and stuffed leaves between them, under my heels and toes, to make soles. Then we crossed through a sorghum field to a wide pasture where we had to walk real slowly so as not to startle the cattle. At the end of that pasture was a barbed-wire fence and beyond that a field of corn where we tore off one ear after another and chewed the corn. It was field corn, meant for cows, and tasted bitter, but I could feel the strength return to my body and my head cleared.

All that night we walked through corn and sorghum fields, avoiding the dirt roads. Just about sunrise, we came to a small town called Monowi. I stayed back with Willard while John Fire went ahead to take a closer look. When he came back, he was driving a blue pickup.

"Hotwired," is all he said. "Hop in."

The gas tank was only half full and Willard was kidding John Fire that he should have at least found us something with enough gas to get out of town. We drove right alongside the Niobrara River, which takes some doing when you consider the trees and then the sandhills and all the ridges and gullies. By midmorning, my bones were so bounced around I couldn't feel them anymore. I felt soft as a fish and I was getting headaches from looking through Helene's glasses, so I took them off and stuffed them in my shirt pocket. We kept the radio on and the KELO news was that there'd been a gunfight in a South Dakota reservation town. Two FBI agents were dead and all kinds of Indians arrested. Bull Smedsrud was interviewed by KELO radio, and in his version of events, Indians had ambushed one agent in the heart of Choteau and another along Highway 50. Cold-blooded murder, he said. He added that most of the leaders had been rounded up but John Fire Smith was still at large, armed and dangerous. Willard laughed and wondered why in hell nobody mentioned him.

We made it to Spencer near sundown and ditched the pickup in a ravine on the outskirts. Willard went into town alone to make a phone call and came back a couple hours later with a man I'd never seen. He wasn't Indian and by his clothes I took him to be a farmer. We didn't trade names so I still don't know who it was. All Willard said was they'd been in jail together a number of years ago for stealing cars and he was willing to drive us as far as Casper, Wyoming.

Before heading that way I said goodbye. I knew I had to get back to Choteau; I had June and Jana and Herman to look after. Willard thought he'd get out west and John Fire chose the north where there were lots of people in Canada who could hide him. They figured they'd start west together and split up in Idaho or thereabouts.

They left me a canteen and a bologna sandwich and I spent the night sitting alone in a cornfield. I made a supper of two ears of corn, that sandwich, and water, then I settled down into a ditch between the rows like I was a pheasant and watched the stars. The mosquitoes were bad and the blue flies were biting, but after a while I was too tired to swat at them. I didn't want to sleep but there was no stopping it and I didn't wake up until the next morning. I still smelled like river and dirt, and my whole body hurt. My legs felt like old wood and it took a long time of stretching before I could start walking.

I stepped out of that cornfield and headed for the road. Spencer isn't a big town but I'd never been there before, so I stopped in front of the drugstore to ask a white man in a baseball cap for directions to the sheriff's office. He took one look at me, at my filthy clothes and wild hair, and said, "Are you one of them Induns from Choteau?"

I nodded and said I was going to turn myself in.

"Right this way," he said and tried to take me by the arm. I pushed him away but he was shoving and poking me all the way up the street and around the corner. After a while I got tired of that and shoved him back. Right there on the steps of the sheriff's office, he jumped me and got me down on the ground and started punching me. I fought back as best I could, but I was short of wind. Just as the sheriff ran out to separate us, I felt Helene's glasses break in the pocket over my heart.

Judy Poor Bull

Before that day, my nights was always filled with visions that left me tired in the mornings. I always looked bad in the mornings but it wasn't alcohol, it was the dreaming. Those dreams were most always of animals, fox and coyote and eagle. There weren't many people in my dreams, not Indian or *wasichu*. They was good dreams, mostly, but they stole my sleep and most days I had to take naps. George Brings Yellow said those dreams were my roots and the rest of my life the trunk and branches of a tree. If that's so, this tree is dying. The roots are dried up and gone.

I was put in a makeshift jail cell with Anna, June, and all the other women they'd rounded up. They gave Helene a shirt and pants to go with the men's shoes she had on. I kept looking for Delores but nobody I asked had seen her. We didn't know where they'd taken the men and it's funny, we was more afraid for them than ourselves. Anna was the only one of us who'd fired a gun but they didn't know that. We was strip-searched and poked at and given back our same clothes. There weren't no showers but late in the afternoon a woman came with sandwiches and those little cartons of milk like at the mission schools. I stayed close to June who stopped crying but still wouldn't talk. They were taking us one at a time for questions and when they called my name I started to shake. Anna took my place at June's side and I followed a policewoman down the hall to a small room that didn't have no windows. Sheriff Merchant and another man was waiting for me. Like Anna told me to, I said I had the right to legal counsel and Sheriff Merchant said this wasn't an official interrogation and please sit down.

I sat on a wooden chair and leaned my elbows on the table between us. I wanted to show them that I wasn't afraid of them, that I wasn't one of those reservation Indians that turned to jelly when a white man stared at them. One of the deputies lit a cigarette and watched the blue smoke it made in that hot room. Then the sheriff looked at me funny.

"We found his body out by the Indian cemetery with two bullet holes. Whoever did it cut off his braids and stuffed them into his open mouth. I'm sorry."

The deputy kept blowing smoke rings that climbed to the ceiling and broke. I felt the rain inside me. Then the sheriff reached into a big envelope and took out a plastic bag that had an eagle feather in it. He said, "We found this near the body. Can you identify it?"

I said it was an eagle feather.

"Whose?" he wanted to know.

The Indians are closest to God, is what Brings Yellow said. It's a big-headed thing to say but I believe it, too. I knew whose feather it was. We all would know if we saw it. But I didn't say Tyrone Little to those men, I didn't say nothing at all. I watched the smoke that came from the deputy's pink mouth and listened to the thunderstorms inside my head that grew louder and I couldn't hear nothing else.

Gaetan Avril

They had me on a raft of counts. First I'd been seen trying to crack a roadblock and later I was caught on Poor Bull's porcelain crapper. Then they found my CB radio in the ditch by the south road with both John Fire's and Willard's fingerprints on it. When Noah gave himself up in Spencer, my car keys were in his pocket. The FBI people, particularly Person, wanted me locked up, but there were already too many prisoners, too many suspects. With half the state under arrest, I was let go after being held and questioned for three days.

During the trials, they made it sound like that FBI man went out there all by himself to serve a warrant on Russ Poor Bull. But no warrant had been issued and he'd driven straight past Poor Bull's house and gone almost as far as Toby's. They say he was killed some time between 8:30 and 9:00, but I was out on Highway 50 at no later than 9:05 and a complete assault force and roadblock were firmly in place.

The way I saw it, he went out to Choteau to serve a warrant that he didn't have on someone who wasn't there. He was trailed by another agent and behind them were a hundred or more armed yahoos who later opened fire on houses with women and children inside. To protect themselves, John Fire Smith and Frank Poor Bull and the others returned their fire. Two FBI agents were killed and two young Indians. It was the Choteau Indians who were attacked and the Choteau Indians who went to prison.

Bill Person

I had reports to file but there wouldn't be any making sense of the affair. More people wanted blood than could be arrested.

History isn't a dial that you can turn back and forth. Before coming to Choteau, I'd looked upon the Indians as a conquered people who refused to believe their way of life was extinct. And although the press gripped this story between its teeth, it wasn't a fight between the whites and Indians. In Wilma I met scores of people who actually liked the Indians but were rightly terrified by AIM and the violence they fostered.

The Indians have a Lakota word, *toka*, that means "outside Indian." I blame these deaths on the tokas, not the Choteau people. And I blame the idiots of this same state who passed guns around to the Ree Indians and the local whites and pushed the Choteau crowd into a corner. But as the years have passed, I've had to swallow what I feel and just plain do my job.

The night after the shooting, I drove out of Wilma toward Choteau. The town was still cordoned off, but I didn't want to go there anyway. I cruised the same dirt roads I'd already driven a thousand times. Though I was alone, the fear had finally left me, and when I came to a field near that Indian cemetery, I stopped the car and got out. I waited for nearly half an hour before my contact finally appeared. He drove the car we'd given him right up to the ditch and I saw he was armed as soon as he got out.

"You can put that gun right on the seat," I told him.

"What if you was some marshal?" he said, setting down the pistol.

"I'm worse," I said. "Where have you been?"

"Hiding out. And I didn't get my money before Cale died. You owe me."

"Not until the last ones are rounded up. We've got all of them but John Fire Smith, Willard Bent, and Noah Lame. And that woman has disappeared, the one who lived with Tyrone Little."

He nodded. "Delores."

"I want you back in Choteau right now, and keep your eyes peeled."

He shook his head. "I wasn't there for the fight and that's something they'll remember."

"Tell them you escaped."

I don't know why I trusted him. He was a killer and none too bright or stealthy in what he did. But I was counting on a clean sweep and the Her Many Horses woman hadn't been seen by anyone throughout the whole ordeal. "Just find her. And when you do, call that same number. We'll handle the rest."

"What about my money?"

I counted out two hundred dollars and told him there'd be more if we found that woman. He folded the money and stuffed it in his pocket and I had a feeling I'd never see him again. He got into the car and I felt my hand close over the firearm strapped to my breast, but I held myself back. He drove east toward Choteau. After that, it was too late to stop him.

I knew I should leave well enough alone. There was still a lot of shooting going on, mostly running exchanges between the Indian factions. With random shootings, no place is safe. I walked out into the cornfield and after cutting through a few rows I was startled by a pheasant that leaped from the stalks and then ran from left to right. I don't know what possessed me as I drew my gun and chased that pheasant through the field. I wanted to kill it but never got a shot because it refused to fly. It just ran from row to row and, exhausted, I finally gave up.

I holstered my firearm and leaned over to catch my breath. I was cursing myself for sending that Indian on his way when I should have held him in custody. And, as I'd been doing all day long, I thought about Cale and his blown-off hand. The hand of a man can't stop a bullet.

The corn was as high as my head but it didn't hide me. Out there you expect to hear the voice of God and you feel watched. I heard my name in the air, a voice drifting through the night. I headed out of the field toward the car, where the radio was calling my name over and over.

Helene Her Many Horses

When people sit in that yellow chair, they never seem to tell her anything and only listen. So now it's Tyrone with his hair all wild. Like the dirty Indian who came two days ago, he's pretending not to be in any hurry at all but she can see he's anxious for her to get to the point. But she has always told her stories the way she wants, in whatever order she likes. People tell her to start at the beginning, but the minute that just ticked by is no different for her from the beginning. She tries to tell things that the wind won't blow down.

For years she's been watching Indians get born, Indians get drunk, Indians get jailed, Indians come and go and come back again. They have no memory, and can't remember their own lives half as well as she does. Here's a fact: she has never been inside a hospital as either a visitor or a patient. Twice she's been inside a church but only because Reynold insisted they get married that way, and then later when Delores was baptized. And she never felt a thing inside those walls, not hot or cold or afraid or filled with ghosts. The priest was speaking some language nobody else understood, so they took his word for it that if Delores drowned in the tub or something she'd go straight to paradise. Like insurance, that baptism. Helene mentions this to Tyrone while he sits up straight in that yellow chair. He wants to know if she's heard from Delores but he'll only know the fingernail and not the whole hand if she just tells him flat out about the postcard.

"Did she tell you she was a painter?"

"Yes, she did."

"She won a competition in high school when she painted that portrait there of Reynold. As far as I can see, she got him just right except for the chin. Chins shouldn't be that hard to paint. Not like eyes." She stares at that painting of her dead husband until she remembers it's just oil on cardboard. The paint is beginning to flake off and the nose is missing its tip.

"It's a fine painting," Tyrone says.

"She wasn't too happy at that school in Minneapolis. What lies does she tell people about why she quit?"

"She says they tried to coerce her into doing abstracts."

That's two words Helene doesn't know in one sentence, so she lets it pass. According to the clock on the kitchen wall, it's three-thirty in the afternoon and she's missing the game shows. When that Indian in the golf shirt came yesterday it was about the same time of day and she'd missed all of "Jeopardy." He was wearing dark glasses the whole time, as if the sun was shining right in her living room. It was like talking to a bug. She'd like to catch "Jeopardy," and maybe if she tells Tyrone what he wants to know, he'll leave her be. But it's the first time she's found herself alone with him and she decides to hold him there for a while longer.

"They're looking for you," she tells him.

"I know they are."

"I threw the sticks and decided it's a boy."

He shakes his head.

"The baby."

Then he just nods. He's like a tired fish that she's holding on a strong line, but then her heart goes all soft because he's made her a grandma—*unci, grandmère.* "I'm the only one in Choteau," she says, "that doesn't hate your guts."

"I'm grateful for that."

"I bet she lied about her age."

"Delores? She's twenty-six."

"Like I said. She was born in 1945. Can't you add?"

No one asks anymore, but when they did ask she always used to say it was nine months to the day after Reynold Her Many Horses shipped out to the South Pacific. They got married in the church and had two days together. By the time he came home, Delores was walking and starting to talk. Helene's father was a Crèvecoeur and she was glad to give up a name like that, French and hard to spell and meaning broken heart.

"Where is she, Helene?"

"Pete Scully says they found your eagle feather next to Russ Poor Bull's shot-up head."

He nods. "It was my feather. But I didn't shoot him."

Helene tells him, "People's belongings tend to get passed around or misplaced. Noah's got my eyeglasses and when the FBIs caught me, I was wearing his black lace shoes."

"Did you tell them where she was?"

"They didn't ask. They didn't even want to know where my shoes came from, like it was normal for an Indian lady to be wearing a man's shoes. And they had a hard time writing down my name right."

Reynold used to have problems cashing his VA checks because, in the army, they'd skewed his name into Reynold Herman Horses. He spent six months in California and then more than a year on Guam fixing electric things like radios, oscillators, and toasters. When he came home to Choteau, he opened up a repair business, branching out from electric appliances to include gas motors, and Helene used to watch him oiling and wiping down his tools every night. He lost his business to drink when Delores was almost four, couldn't fathom the circuitry anymore. Then he disappeared for exactly six years and came home dried out. He didn't tell her in advance that he was leaving. She woke up one morning and was alone in the bed. Propped up on his pillow was the postcard. There was none of his handwriting on it, just the color picture of a damned jackalope and the caption

"THE LEGENDARY JACKALOPE IS HARD TO SPOT! HE COMES
AND GOES AND JUST WHEN YOU THINK YOU WON'T SEE HIM
ANYMORE, HE REAPPEARS!"

This was supposed to give her hope but instead it made her mad.
She found out that first day that he'd sold the shop for two thousand
dollars and left all but a hundred in the bank for Delores and her.
For the first three weeks he was gone, she didn't hear a word. Then
he wrote a letter with a postmark from Reno that said he was out
of money but had a hook out on a job and planned to reel it in.
The next letter took longer to come, almost five months. He was in
San Luis Obispo and off the bottle. Looking at his handwriting,
she doubted it. A month later he sent her a wristwatch with no letter
at all.

The nineteen hundred dollars lasted close to a year and a half,
which was when she got the third letter. By the love of sweet Jesus
and the Blessed Virgin, he had a good job fixing radios and hi-fi's in
Sacramento and here was a little of the fruits of his labors. Forty
bucks. Delores and Helene had moved into a tiny house on the west
side of town and she spent part of the money on a used radio. The
static was bad and all the stations were too far away to come in clear,
no matter how she screwed the dials. She was waiting for Reynold to
come home and repair it—that's what she started telling herself.
Reynold would come home and would spread his tools across the
kitchen table, then bend over the radio parts to find the flaw. She
would hear the music the way it was played and the voices would be
clear as a bell.

Delores was a noisy girl who acted up plenty at the mission school.
You could say Helene had her hands full. From the time she was
little, Delores was always in need of a hairbrush or lipstick or eyeliner
and was always after Helene to put curlers in her hair. She liked
hairspray, which gave her a headache, but she was good with books
and always made her grades, even later when she was drinking and
carrying on with Elizabeth Bordeaux. So it wasn't just boys that made
her sunup and sundown. There were books and her paintings that
filled up all the space on the wall by her bed and the refrigerator
door. Delores was already close to six years old when Helene finally
bought a refrigerator at a white woman's garage sale in Wilma. Frank
Poor Bull loaded it into his pickup for her and drove it into Choteau.

Her house was just one room though it had enough space for a bed for her and a cot for Delores, a burner for cooking, some shelves for her books, and a table where they could sit and eat or Delores could draw pictures on the brown paper they cut from grocery bags. Helene had tacked down the linoleum sheets herself. They were just scraps and didn't match, so she used different colors to mark the "rooms": green for the kitchen, white and red speckles for the bedroom, and a strip of eggshell blue right in front of the door. There was no plumbing and she had to haul water from the outside tap across the road. Everyone shared that water and didn't even know where it came from.

Frank couldn't haul that refrigerator all by himself, a Frost King model as tall as Helene. It was the first time she'd seen Noah Lame since before Delores was born and he was changed. Like her, he wore glasses and when he climbed out of Frank's pickup, they just stood there in front of the house and squinted at each other through their lenses.

Helene swallowed and took in air. Her voice cracked. "What brings you back to the res?"

"Just passing through," Noah said, but she already knew he'd come back to marry June Little Sky.

"Where do you want it?" Frank asked.

"There's a spot all cleared against the north wall. Where the plug is."

The two of them heaved and grunted while she held the door open wide. There was a roll to the floor that made the refrigerator tip forward and the door kept falling open, so they wedged a piece of wood underneath to hold it level. It was a good refrigerator for only fifteen dollars. All that was wrong was the handle was broken and the tray for vegetables was taped in a couple places. Helene plugged it in and heard the first hum of whatever inside was making it cool. Then she opened the door and began to set food on the aluminum shelves, an apple, a can of peaches, cereal boxes.

"No need to refrigerate canned food."

She turned and there was Noah at the front door.

"You're still here?"

"Or the cereal boxes. That won't change a thing."

She could see he was trembling, as though his legs wouldn't work anymore. She had intended to be like steel, as solid as that big refrigerator. He would have to take those steps across the linoleum, not her.

"After the wedding, I'm going back," he said.

"To Illinois," she said.

"I got a job teaching high school in Chicago."

She wanted to say something kind to him, to acknowledge his education. He had always seemed a failure, neither hunter nor fisherman nor handyman, so different from Reynold whose hands were always making something from nothing. The words rose slowly to the surface of her throat. "The kids there call you Chief?"

"Only when my back's turned."

She didn't know spit about the white world and was envious of June on that score. Noah was still standing there shaking like a leaf and she finally said, "Why don't you sit in that chair?"

He was so relieved that he let out a small laugh. So they sat together at the table and the sunlight glittered off his eyeglasses while he told her about the time he'd spent in Illinois, first in Champagne and later in Chicago working as a janitor and as a fry cook and then as a replacement teacher for a few months at a mixed high school. She had never seen a black person and was curious about them. He told her they were a lot like themselves, like Indians, but a lot angrier on the surface. Then she asked if he was hungry and he said no, but she took that apple from the refrigerator anyway. He took a bite of it and then set it back on the table. Finally he looked across the sunlight at her and said she sure was looking well.

How am I supposed to look? she wondered. Beaten down, gray, miserable? Her tongue was hot in her mouth and she knew that she wanted most of all to get up and move over to the wall where her bed was. No man had seen her naked in a very long time, like her body was a secret, her still slim legs and smooth skin. She didn't eat carbohydrates because that's what made so many Indian women get fat like they got. It was 1951 and she was only twenty-seven years old and no man's diddle in her would make her younger.

She thought all that but didn't say a word. What she did was reach her hand across the table and she put it like a gift inside his own. It hurt to know he'd come back for June and not for her. Before she'd married Reynold, she'd thought she'd won Noah. When she and Noah and June played strip poker that late winter night, they were eighteen and it was the last year of school. Cherry-picking season, is how the boys put it. They sat on the floor by the fire at Noah's house. His mother was sleeping in the next room and they had to play as quietly as they could. It wasn't easy to manage and June was giggling the whole time, but Helene did her best to hide her excitement in the shadows of that fire. She showed a pair of threes on the first hand and could have removed her shoes or the ribbon in her hair. But she was in a hurry, so she took off her blouse, and Noah's eyes got wide. Helene was drinking blackberry brandy, which made her a little sick, and even with the fire she was cold, so she knew her nipples were standing up. After that, June won almost every hand because Helene did her best to lose. The winner stays covered and the loser strips, rules of the game. And when Noah and she were both buck naked, June was still in her bra and skirt and Noah didn't even look in her direction. Helene had a boldness that June could never match.

"Now what do we play for?" Noah asked.

"Kisses," Helene answered. She lost again and Noah leaned in her direction. Over his shoulder, she saw June staring at her with hatred. June moved her hand toward a lamp and tipped it over just as Noah's lips met Helene's.

Within seconds after the lamp crashed onto the floor, Pauline was at the door. Her hair was wild and her eyes fixed on Helene's bare flesh. Noah leaped up and his mother brushed him aside and headed for Helene with a stick in her hand. "Slut!" she shrieked. "Demon!" Helene ran right out the door into the snow. She was still naked and could hear Pauline screaming at her son. The stars saw her, the trees. Snow was falling and it landed on her body like tiny stinging sparks. June came out of the house with Helene's clothes in her hand but she refused to wear them. June said she'd freeze to death but Helene didn't feel the cold. She felt plumes of fire coursing through her. Noah had seen her and could never forget.

She waited for him to come to her for the cherry picking. Spring and summer, she waited. Then Pauline sold that launderette and sent him off to the university in Illinois. Though he never asked her, she told him she would wait. The first summer he came home, he was with June or with her and never made up his mind. The next fall, he wrote her a letter saying he was dating a white girl named Carolyn and hoped she would understand. Three months later, he wrote a love letter and she guessed that Carolyn was out of the picture, but he didn't come back to Choteau that summer. He was working a full-time job to pay tuition for the coming fall, his letter said, and he sent along a photograph of himself in a brown suit. She burned both the letter and the photograph. The snow melted over her and she turned to Reynold the way the leaves of a tree turn toward the sun.

In her house that day, Noah gripped her hand and said he didn't understand how Reynold could stay away.

"You managed to," she told him.

He just shook his head. "Not entirely," he said. "I'm still sitting here." She thought he was going to weep, so she retrieved her hand. It occurred to her he still hadn't made up his mind, that his thoughts were swimming in circles. And now it was summer instead of winter, with sunlight instead of dark beside the fireplace, and Pauline Lame could not climb from her grave to stop them.

She rose from the chair and reached for her buttons. He looked at her fearfully and she unclasped the hook at the back of her skirt. It fell to the floor and she stepped out of it like she was stepping out of water. She saw on his face that he liked what he saw. "You're different," he said. "Slimmer."

She took a step forward so he only had to reach out to touch her. He put his hands on her breasts and then his head moved forward until his nose was touching her belly. She told him to take off his glasses, but he said no, he wanted to see things clearly. Then, in a hurry, he dropped his clothes on the floor. The two of them were naked except for their eyeglasses. She lay back on the table and felt crumbs under her skin and Noah lifted her a little to make room for himself, then she had to hang on to him to keep from falling off. He shook and she shook with him. Their bones collided and he covered her lips with his teeth. They shared a soaring and came to a high place and melted downward until his knees hit the floor. She sat up and his head was bowed close to her sex. They smelled hot and close, like summer. She touched the top of his head. "Now you can marry her," she said.

She thought he was finished, kneeling the way he was. But he stood up and helped her off the table and turned her around so her back was to him. There was something that he needed to know and he must have thought it was in her that day to answer him. She leaned to the table and he moved his hips forward. The pleasure was gone for her, she felt like butter, and her legs were pressed against the edge of the table where she couldn't move. "Noah," she said. "Noah, please." But he kept on, growing wilder. It was like being slapped and she lay her head to the table and waited for him to finish.

She doesn't know if she heard Delores first or just saw her. Delores in her little red dress that Helene had stitched back to life after finding it at the Goodwill. She was supposed to be at the Bordeaux house all day, but there she was with her finger in her mouth and looking at where Noah and Helene were joined. Noah stopped and leaped backward. "Turn around!" he shouted, but Delores stood her ground. She looked at Noah, who was scrambling for his clothes, and then she looked at Helene. Helene was still stretched across the table and she lifted herself onto her elbows.

"You hurt?" Delores asked her.

Helene said no and started to laugh. After a moment, Delores was laughing too. Helene felt past shame, her own daughter catching her like that. She hurt her stomach she laughed so hard and when Delores came to her, she took her in her arms and they just held each other while Noah put on his shoes and socks and pants and shirt. Helene thought he would leave but he just stood there and then she saw what transfixed him so.

Indian noses tell more stories even than eyes do. Helene's nose is flat and broad and it's hard to hold her eyeglasses in place, but Delores' nose has a tiny ledge. That morning she looked more like Pauline Lame than like Helene.

Noah was staring at her and Helene told him to stop it. "And keep your mouth shut," she added.

He just nodded, and combed back his hair with his fingers and turned away.

"Delores, go on outside and water the tomatoes."

"It's not morning," she argued. They always watered in the mornings.

"Just go," Helene said.

She reached for her skirt and pulled it to her waist. She could still feel Noah's fingers on her as she dressed. He wouldn't look at her. He was looking at the books on a shelf, Delores' books that Helene got for her at a discount in the used-book shop.

"She's like you," Helene said. "She reads all the time."

He said he was sorry. Just that, not what he was sorry about. Helene didn't bear him any grudges. They had met up just once after she was already married to Reynold, when he had gone off to the army, and it had been her doing more than his. She told him he should go away. "When the tomatoes are good and wet, Delores'll be back and this time she might ask questions."

She stood at the front door and watched him go while Delores hauled the water can around their little garden out front. When he'd disappeared down the road and into the trees, she turned back to the refrigerator and opened the door. The cool air surrounded her and she breathed it in. Her head cleared and she went to work, putting back the canned food, the cereal boxes, the fruit and corn and the apple that he'd only taken one bite of, and even that postcard of the jackalope, everything she possessed that needed preserving.

A few years later, Reynold came back to Choteau and she didn't bother making things hard on him. His hair had gone white and it was true he was off the bottle for good. What she didn't know until later was that his heart had quit on him out in California. He was weak and needed naps and had a hard time walking in snow. He took a job at his old repair shop but this time on wages. He never told her anything about what he'd done for those six years but a few months after he died, a Mexican-looking woman from Los Angeles showed up with a four-year-old girl and asked why she hadn't been getting her money.

Sometimes Helene thinks that the sperm that comes out of a man is like what webs are made of. To this day Delores thinks she has a Mexican half-sister and doesn't know that she's the daughter of Noah Lame. Though it didn't go unnoticed by the women in town that when the shooting started, he came to her place. She was in front of the TV doing stretching exercises with the show called "Five Minutes to Fitness." She doesn't have leotards or tights and does her jumping jacks in the altogether. That's how Noah found her when he came charging through the door and grabbed her and held her to the floor. And though she had sworn he would never again hold sway over her or get an elbow hold on her affections, she held his hand and ran with him in whatever direction he asked.

If Delores remembers what she saw that day, Noah bent over Helene and both of them red in the face, she's never said so. When she said she was leaving town, Helene gave her the jackalope postcard that had been sitting in her kitchen junk drawer forever. She didn't want Delores to have that baby by herself. She wanted it to have a name, not a secret, to carry through life. That's why she gave her that postcard, like a charm to make her stay close to her. Its power held and three days later it came back to her with a stamp and the words, *Stopped here instead of Pierre. Will find a job if I have to. I can still type eighty words a minute.*

"She sent you a postcard?" Tyrone asks her. "Can I see it?"

It's in the kitchen junk drawer, under string balls and pencils and an old *TV Guide*. It takes her a while to dig it out because she still doesn't have her glasses. She's been blind for four days and can't decipher how much money they're winning on the game shows. She hands the postcard to Tyrone and he reads it quickly.

"Up north," she tells him. "Look at the postmark."

"Who does she know there?"

"Not a soul. Unless that Indian boy made it up to see her."

"What Indian boy?"

"Harold. He came by two days ago, while you were in jail."

"And you showed him this?"

When she nods he grows small right in front of her. Or it is another trick her eyes are playing on her. She's nearsighted and Tyrone has four eyes and a mouth with a thousand teeth.

Bill Person

The Indian's body had been taken to Pierre and I drove up there alone to take a look at it. Two .45-caliber slugs. One pierced his right lung and the other went through his stomach, missing the spine, and exited through his lower back. That first slug was fatal; he might have survived the second.

The coroner presented me with the personal effects. Leather belt with "Lefty" engraved on the buckle. Blue Levi's, torn undershorts. A cowboy-style shirt with mother-of-pearl snaps. Seven hundred eighty-four dollars and thirty-seven cents. Mismatched athletic socks. A new pair of tennis shoes with near-perfect tread. I sliced the red mud from that tread, Missouri basin clay.

Gaetan Avril

The marshals found Russ Poor Bull's body out by the Indian ceme-tery. Whoever'd killed him had cut off his braids and stuffed them into his open mouth. He'd left Tyrone's eagle feather pinned to Poor Bull's shirt.

That, if anything, was proof positive Tyrone hadn't done the killing. No one's dumb enough to sign himself that way. But what made all the difference to Judge Anderssen up in Pierre was that the prosecu-tion's only other evidence was footprints from the cemetery the day before the murder. Between the time Tyrone and I had been arrested out there and the killing, a lot of rain had fallen. So he wasn't charged for that. Instead he was tried for the murder of Harold Bad Hand and the attempted murder of Delores Her Many Horses and child.

Unlike John Fire's trial, which lasted two months, Tyrone's was a three-day blow. He initially refused all counsel, including the pricy lawyer teams I'd lined up. The state appointed an attorney who, I realized too late, was in my father's pocket. He never called the witnesses who saw Bad Hand pull a gun, and he refused to put Delores on the stand, though that may have been Tyrone's doing. He wanted to spare Delores and didn't want to goad the prosecution into digging into his past. He wanted to be hung. His grief over what he'd done untied every knot that bound him to life. On the face of it, he'd shot a pair of Indians and in South Dakota that should have qualified him to run for public office.

The prosecution concentrated on a domestic angle. Tyrone Little was an out-of-control Vietnam vet who killed Bad Hand and wounded Delores in a jealous rage. I wasn't there, but I knew well enough why he'd nailed Bad Hand. The tragedy was how that bullet passed right though him and into Delores. But his defense lawyer kept Bad Hand's links to the FBI under wraps. As far as the public knew, he was just a poor slob of an Indian killed in a barfight.

I had troubles of my own in the year following the shoot-out.

Though I'd slipped the charge of aiding and abetting, I took on a fragrance that was not much loved in the town of Wilma. My boy Sam was harassed in school, and Mary was dropped by her gardening club because her husband was a noxious weed. Ever after, she abandoned the scientific approach and simply flung seeds in every direction, letting the onions grow between itchweed and the strawberries get tangled with the squash. What grew most rampant were the silences between us. She loved me and she always had. But I didn't listen to her pleas to leave the county and start a new life somewhere else. "Just look at what Sam's becoming," she told me. But I wouldn't. I lowered my head and went farther down an ever more lonesome road.

Despite all that happened, the golf course at Eagle Reach opened in the spring of 1974. I wanted to learn the game, but that meant weathering pettiness of the lowest order. At the clubhouse bar, my vodka martinis were served with maraschino cherries instead of green olives. I opened my locker one morning and found that my driver was bent out of shape and someone had pissed in my golf shoes. I think Sam's reluctance to know anything about Choteau or Tyrone Little dates to this miserable year and he has never forgiven me for sending him away to the private school in Minneapolis. Though it only lasted two years, he never entirely came home from that place and there is only a trickle of water flowing under this particular bridge of father and son.

The first year, I worried that Tyrone would hang himself or cut his wrists with a dinner fork or some damn thing. When I went up to visit him at the pen, he didn't speak and for a long time after that he just kept losing weight, as if his intention was to slowly fade and then vanish into the thin prison air.

Delores gave up the boy to her mother and began serving a stretch in Yankton on a weapons charge that was as bogus as anything going around that season. When she'd been there close to a year, I finally drove up and had to wait two days before she agreed to see me. She was in a minimum-security cellblock, but I wasn't allowed entry until I'd been finger-searched from my molars to my asshole. We sat in a recreation room that had Ping-Pong and shuffleboard as well as a black-and-white television and a machine that spit out watery coffee. I'd brought photographs of Joseph, and it was those color glossies that thawed Delores to the point where she'd at least look at me.

I handed her the sugared coffee she'd asked for and she took it with both hands. "What'd you come for?"

"To see how you're getting on."

"I don't play Ping-Pong, if that's what you mean."

"I meant your health."

She glanced downward toward her belly and then her eyes flickered upward and met my gaze. "Judy Poor Bull sent me a letter," she said. "She says you've been taking care of everyone, with money and all. They must love your ass in Wilma."

I laughed and told her about my screwed-up driver, but she didn't see the humor. I learned right then and there to never talk golf with Indians.

"Can I keep these?"

"That's why I brought them." She began to look through the pictures once again. "He's doing just fine," I told her. "The pride of Choteau. Do you know what they're calling him?"

She frowned. "His name's Joseph. Not that other name."

"They call him that with affection."

There was a long silence. Delores was staring at the Ping-Pong table and then suddenly she said, "I share a cell with a woman who murdered her husband."

"Is she dangerous?"

"No, her husband was."

She was wearing a necklace I knew Tyrone had given her and I took faith in that. I swallowed air and worked my tongue around my mouth for a long time and then asked her, "Why did he shoot you?"

I didn't expect her to answer. She drank down her coffee and crushed the paper cup in her fist. "There's a law against prisoners writing to each other," she said. "So he wrote me through my mother." She returned to her cell and came back with a box of letters. "You can read them," she said. "Maybe you'll even understand them. I can't say I do."

Each of the letters had been torn to bits and taped back together. The sight of them jangled my nerves, so I lit a Winston. Smoking was my newest filthy habit that wouldn't survive the year. But I needed something to occupy my hands and I liked the ritual of patting pockets for the lighter and then reaching into the pack for something I could hold to my lips. I smoked three Winstons while reading the letters, expecting that in at least one of them he would finally spill the beans.

Of course he didn't do that, and he hasn't to this day. He didn't even say outright that Bad Hand was a spy for the FBI. He didn't even try to defend himself. *It was my gun and my bullet. I shouldn't have pulled that trigger.* I didn't learn until some years later that he wrote to her almost every week that he was in prison. If that writing was like bleeding, it was a bleeding away of remorse.

"He had reason to kill Bad Hand," I told her.

"We all did," she said.

"And he wasn't with the FBI."

She shook her head, more out of irritation than disagreement. "Then why'd he come to Choteau? And who is he to you?"

I reached into my pocket, but the pack was empty.

"He was always asking questions," she continued. "He never shut up. In bed, at dinner, doing the dishes. All these questions about the families and what did I remember from when I was young."

I wanted to answer her in the worst way. But if Tyrone had written all of those letters and still couldn't find the words, neither could I. I told her I was sorry and she stared at me as though I was diseased. Before I left, I asked her if there was anything I could do for her. She said no and turned toward the door. Then suddenly she turned back to me. "There is one thing."

"Name it."

"Tell them I don't want them to cut my hair anymore. I look mean with short hair, like a criminal, and that's what they want. I want my braids back."

In the fall of 1975, my father and I went to court over land that was in both our names, a forty-acre stretch north of Highway 50 that the old man bought in the name of Gaetan Avril some months before he'd legally changed his name to Averill. So now I was the only Gaetan Avril in the county and although that parcel was titled in 1933 when I was still in diapers, the county clerk agreed with my legal loophole and the land belonged to me.

I immediately sold it to Kevin Walking Horse for twenty dollars and a beaded shirt Anna'd made.

This was only the beginning of applied revisionist history, and I instructed my lawyers to get a leg up on the old Poor Bull spread.

In January of 1976, Sheriff Merchant clocked me at ninety-eight

miles per hour on Highway 50 outside Wilma. He also could have
had me on the breath test, since I was driving on a full tank of vodka,
exactly the break my neighbors were looking for, a chance to put me
to sleep like a rabid dog. But Merchant wasn't the shitsucker that
everyone took him for. "You're a danger to the community, Gaetan,"
he told me.

I was in no position to argue, so I just nodded.

"But it appears to me you're already in a kind a jail, so let's forget
we ever met up tonight."

I drove the rest of the way home under fifty-five and made sure I
set the parking brake before I got out. It was the first moment of
kindness or mercy I'd been shown in close to two years of being a
madman. When I crawled into bed and found Mary wide awake and
anxious, I grew sober and tender all at once.

She was brave and she loved me and I didn't blame her when she
went to visit her sister in Denver for a few weeks or even when her
visit was extended by two months and then by two years. Life with
me was something short of hilarious in those years and I didn't even
want to live with myself.

Joe Merchant wasn't the only one in Wilma who was suffering
remorse over the Bones War. Jimmy DeWare quietly sold off his
shares in Eagle Reach and I noticed him spending less time with
people like my father or Al Roebuck. From time to time, I'd catch
him looking at me like he wanted to say something, but he couldn't
join me and we could never be friends. He was a decent father, a
citizen, and I was the town birdbrain.

A woman I barely knew, fiftyish and wearing more makeup than
should be legal, stopped me on First Street one day and went into
this long harangue about having always been able to drive out to
Choteau, her whole life long, and feel welcome among the families
there. "I didn't think of it as an embrace of cultures, Mr. Avril. I just
thought of it as neighborliness."

"So what's changed?"

"People like you who don't believe in God and yet insist on rewrit-
ing the subtle path of history he's laid out for us."

She was potty, sure, but I felt the bruise of her judgment layers
deep. I found out later she'd been good friends with Judy Poor Bull
and no longer felt safe in Choteau. I still rub at the bruise because
this woman with all her makeup had an undeniable point. Pursuing

my own aims hadn't done much for the men and women and children of Choteau and even less for my wife and son. You try to paint justice with a sword and all you get is shredded canvas.

The spring Mary left me, I continued to roam the golf course on my lonesome. When my application for the second annual club championship was mysteriously misplaced, I played my own tournament during the off hours, by myself, and beat Stuart Baumgartner's winning score by six unseen strokes. Day to night and fairway to green. Mary wrote letters with no news in them about when she'd be home. And when Sam cried out for her at night, finding me at his bedside was small comfort.

In the Indian summer that November of 1976, Bull Smedsrud was elected governor of South Dakota. The vote wasn't even close, though I was pleasantly surprised that he'd carried Wilma County by only a slim majority. We'd seen Bull up close and I wasn't the only white man in the county who thought the Indians got a raw deal. But there were fewer qualms elsewhere. He was for bauxite mining and turning over prairie lands as bombing sites and he had a speaking voice that inspired confidence in the future of the state that calls itself the Land of Infinite Variety.

There was a very effective TV ad that they ran over and over: a voice said, "When South Dakotans wanted law and order, he listened!" And in the background were pictures of Indians in pickups with deer rifles and shotguns at the ready.

Noah Lame

My son had a singing voice that I can still hear, a way of singing songs that made it sound more like a chorus than just one person all by himself. The day I turned myself in, I was taken in leg irons to Wilma County Jail and put in a room with a bench hanging from a chain. I tried to sing those songs and after a while the sound of my own voice was bouncing off those tight walls. I couldn't remember all the words in Lakota but I could feel Herman singing with me, so I wasn't alone.

Two days later, I heard they got Willard Bent in eastern Wyoming but John Fire was still on the loose. Sixty-three people altogether had been arrested by then and when the authorities finished sorting out their catch, they somehow settled on Willard and me as the guiltiest parties—maybe out of embarrassment that we'd gotten away. Frank Poor Bull, whose aim was even worse than mine, was given eighteen months for illegal possession of a firearm. Gene Fast Horse, Pete Scully, and Darryl Kills First, who among them had fired more than four hundred rounds, were let go for lack of sufficient evidence. Our wives were harassed and interrogated for three days and then released. Kevin Walking Horse made it all the way up to the Standing Rock Reservation on the North Dakota border, and when the arrests died down he just drove back to Choteau with a carload full of well-fed children.

June came to see me and her face was rain. I begged her to stay off the bottle but that juice was like Jesus to her and Judy Poor Bull told me that they'd taken to tying her to the bed so she could sweat the poison out. She was drinking wood alcohol, Sterno, whatever she could lay her hands on. If there'd been alcohol in snowfall, she'd have stood outside, her face turned up, catching it with her tongue. By the time I went to trial, in November of 1973, they had to give her up to the hospital in Yankton where the shook-up spirits go.

They moved me to the state pen on the north edge of Sioux Falls. There were plenty of Indians inside that place and I didn't lack for news and gossip. Willard Bent was there too, but they kept us apart except for our meetings with the attorneys. We had seven lawyers between us, all of them from out of state, and the trial was getting nationwide attention. We were accused of sedition, possession of illegal firearms, and a list of crimes as long as my arm. But neither of us was charged with the murder of the FBI agents. They were saving those for John Fire. If they ever caught him.

Our lawyers were as tough as the government's and a lot smarter. They got the trial moved out of state, which was the first piece of luck. No jury in South Dakota would've settled for less than a public hanging, but in Iowa we had a chance. The prosecution's evidence was mostly circumstantial. There weren't any witnesses who could say for sure they'd seen either of us fire a gun. All they had was our fingerprints on some of the rifles from Poor Bull's house and my footprints from behind the house. During the trial, one of our attorneys pointed out that Helene had been wearing my shoes, so they couldn't even prove beyond a doubt that I was ever in Poor Bull's house. Their mistake was trying to lump me in with Willard Bent. The truth was, we hardly knew each other, and if they'd concentrated on him instead of both of us, they might have nailed him for killing Robbins. But like I said, they were saving that up for John Fire. And after two months of trial, during which four of the prosecution witnesses were found to have been coerced into false testimony, Willard Bent and I were set free.

Locking us up hadn't stopped the war, either. Indians from Choteau to Ree were killing each other in drive-bys and knife fights. Two months after the shoot-out in Choteau, Gene Fast Horse was wounded in a fight just outside the BIA building in Ree. He took off for California and they put out a warrant on him. Figuring he was next in line, Darryl Kills First ran off to Florida where he got arrested for grand theft auto. He spent three years in a prison out there and moved back to Choteau when he was released in 1977. Fast Horse stayed put in California, which wouldn't extradite him, and went on being the media Indian he'd long since become.

Bull Smedsrud and Reese Lonetree teamed up to terrorize the reservation. Smedsrud was cruising around in an assault vehicle, organizing farmers and ranchers, and Lonetree's goons went so wild that even the FBI started to back away. As a gesture, they intervened to get George Brings Yellow released from the reservation jail. When he got out he found that his old house had been burned to the ground. His reaction to that was to arrange a massive sun dance that attracted Indians from all over the country, plus the usual surveillance squads from the FBI and the state marshals. Two of those marshals wandered into the middle of the camp searching for guns and George gave them food and water, everything there was to offer except the piercing or the sacred pipe, and sent them on their way. I was sorry to have missed all that. In prison, I'd heard the eagle bone whistle and smelled the burning sweet grass. My fingers touched the unbroken flesh at my breast and I'd decided it was time I was pierced.

Less than a month after I got out of the pen, they caught John Fire out in Washington State. We were all ashamed to hear it was an Indian, a Pullyap, who turned him in. Three days later, he escaped while they were transferring him to California, but it wasn't a week before they caught him north of San Francisco.

He had the same set of lawyers as Willard and I, but he didn't have the same luck. His trial was in Fargo and when it comes to Indians, the two Dakotas might as well be the same state. Myrene Tall Bull was the star witness and she testified that he'd bragged about killing

Robbins. His lawyers later proved that Myrene had spent the night in one of the tents out past Toby's and when the shooting started she'd gone east. She was in custody within an hour and had blessed little chance of having come across John Fire.

During the trial, they asked Pete Scully if he'd seen John Fire shooting a gun.

"Yes, I did," he answered.

"Can you tell us what or who he was shooting at?"

Pete no longer looked at his feet around white men. He looked that government attorney in the eye and said, "He was shooting at you."

"At me? I was a thousand miles from Choteau that day."

"Then how come you're so sure it was him who shot Robbins?"

When the defense asked John Fire if he'd shot Robbins, his answer was simply that he didn't know. When the shooting started, he'd told Russ Poor Bull to stay and guard the cemetery, then had driven into Choteau and entered town from the south road.

"Were you armed at this point?"

"I had a twenty-two rifle, a rabbit gun."

"Was this the only arm in your possession that day?"

"No, I also fired a shotgun."

They had the rabbit gun right there in court but no one ever found the gun that killed Robbins. My guess is that thirty-ought-six is still sunk in Missouri River mud, but they didn't ask me about that. All the same, if they had found that gun, they would've made it look like it was John Fire's anyway.

Bill Person testified over three days and he sure had a handle on the details. At 9:05 I did this and I heard that at 10:15. Before the marshals cleared all of us troublemakers from the courtroom, I did my damnedest to get him to look at me. His hair was even thinner on top than before and he wore a clean blue suit and tie, so I guess those golf shirts were put away for the year. He knew I was there but he wouldn't look my way. He just gave his testimony like he was telling us a recipe.

He was cross-examined by the defense for the better part of two days, which is when we learned that he and Martinez had taken Myrene Tall Bull to a motel outside Wilma and threatened to make trouble for her family if she didn't act as a witness for the prosecution. He denied it, naturally, but then they put Myrene back on the stand.

"Miss Tall Bull, did Special Agent Person ever threaten you?"

"Yes."

"Can you tell us what he said?"

"He said to tell how they was planning things with their guns and if I didn't say it he would hurt my family."

"Did he say how he would hurt your family?"

"My brother's in jail. He said he'd hurt him there."

The day before his sentencing, John Fire made a statement that gets quoted all the time. The judge got red as a beet toward the end and even started pounding his gavel to keep people from cheering. John Fire said that he was innocent of doing anything more than defending himself and his friends. That the judge had unfairly disallowed all witnesses in his favor while allowing all sorts of false testimony against him, including that of Myrene Tall Bull, who'd already recanted. That Indian grievances would not disappear by making a single Indian disappear. That he had no doubt whatsoever that the judge would give him a life sentence, or two or three, to satisfy the white racists in America. "You want our land for the gold and the uranium. And because the American Indian Movement preaches the preservation of our lands and culture, you are prepared to lie, steal, and kill to stop us. You say 'In God We Trust' and your God is now weeping bitterly as you turn the garden of the earth into a Kmart. The Lakota people have no belief in hell. That's a Christian invention and it comes from your hatred of the earth. There will be another trial and your hatred will be turned back into your faces. You think that time is a straight line but we know it's a circle and all of us will meet again."

After he was given consecutive life sentences for the murder of Robbins and Cale, I went home to Choteau and lived a ghost life. Food fell from my mouth and my sleep was as shallow as the river. My one best friend, Frank, was in prison and the other, Pete Scully, had gone to Minneapolis to work in an Indian survival school, where they teach how to defend their dignity in a white man's world. By now, there were schools like this in almost every large city with a significant Indian population—Tacoma, the Twin Cities, Los Angeles, Denver, even Cleveland. Pete wrote that I should join up with him, but I never did. I walked the fields between Choteau and the river and tried to sing with my son's many voices, though all that ever came out was a hoarse whisper.

I was alone for a long time and then June was let out of that place in Yankton. I hoped that she'd be cured but she was an empty dress who took to drinking at the first sign of rain. I didn't stop her. For a time, I thought it might be best if we drank together, husband and wife, but we always ended up crying ourselves sick and waking up cold on the kitchen floor. After a month of that I didn't have any more stomach for alcohol and June just drifted away from me day by day.

Toby wouldn't serve her anymore, so one spring night she hitched a ride into Wilma. When I saw she was gone, Toby and I went after her, but she must've hidden in the Ladies' or somewhere because we didn't find her at the Gem Bar. She was there, though, and at closing time they kicked her out with all the other drunks. A late snow was falling and the roads iced over. She decided to walk home and must have got lost. She was south of Wilma, on a county road that led to Nebraska. She got run over but nobody stopped. They might have thought they'd hit a deer or maybe they knew it was just an Indian. When we found her she was stiff as wood. I don't know how they ever fit the parts of her into that box.

The day they buried her, I did the last of my grieving. There was no bark left on that tree.

In September of 1974, Frank was given parole and after being held for an extra week of aggravation in Sioux Falls, he came home to Choteau. Within an hour we'd all met up at Toby's. Judy was there and Kevin and Anna Walking Horse. While I was in prison and her mother in the hospital, Jana had moved in with Toby, though the wedding wouldn't happen for another year. She was pouring lemonade and ice water for everybody and it was good not to see beer cans and liquor bottles on the tables. Pete Scully drove down from Minneapolis in that same white Bel Air that was mentioned so many times during the trials. He'd finally given up waiting on the rust, though, and just had it painted bright red so it looked more like a fire engine than a car.

Frank had managed prison better than I had. He'd been moved to

Lompoc, in California, to keep him away from me and Willard Bent and he had stories to tell, like about the time he cut a ceremonial pipe from a chair leg. The chair was from the block warden's office and a Modoc named Joe Kirrell had done the sawing. "There was no *chanshasha*," he told us, "so we smoked Bull Durham."

The cornfield across the highway belonged to Gaetan Avril and we had his permission, so Frank and I went over with grocery bags and yanked off a few dozen ears from their stalks. It was close to sundown when we got back to the house, and Helene Her Many Horses had come over to show us the baby. Though he was over a year old, it was the first time I'd seen him. He was a strong child with long black hair they'd never cut, but he couldn't walk yet. Helene held him up by the arms and he stood there on shaky legs and stared at all of us like we were the strangest folks he'd ever seen. It must have occurred to us that evening that a whole generation was missing. We were the grandfathers and grandmothers and here was a grandson, but where were our sons and daughters?

After supper, Helene told us Delores was being held in the county jail in Pierre on a weapons charge even though she'd been long gone when the shooting started. She'd only been home from the hospital two days when they came to take her away. She nearly bled to death but somehow held on long enough to get the boy into this world. She named him Joseph and in years since there've been arguments about who gave him his other name. I know it was me. It was the sight of that boy with his long hair and his clear eyes and the same nose as mine, the deep way he looked past your eyes. And to give him only a Christian name struck me as insufficient. Judy Poor Bull says it was Frank who gave him that other name and Toby Johnson claims it was Jana, who remembers no such thing. The whole town poured all its hope into him and as the years passed and he refused to learn to read or to add numbers, we were all convinced that it was a part of his calling.

Helene sat five feet from me with the boy in her lap. She looked my way and set him to the ground and aimed him in my direction. Then he walked as if born to it across the distance that separated us.

I held him in my arms and smelled the earth and sky in his long hair. You can't fly with one wing, but right then I felt my feathers starting to grow back.

I named him Bullet Heart.

Delores Her Many Horses

At the hospital in Pierre they put needles into her arm and she fell into a cloud. They told her later that they'd opened her belly and removed the child, then sewn her back up. He had lost too much blood, a baby only has so much, and the bullet had lodged itself next to his heart. Because of the blood loss, he had gone more than an hour without sufficient oxygen coming to his brain. They couldn't say for sure what effect this would have. He could be physically impaired, his motor responses, his nervous system. Or he could be an imbecile.

They could not remove the bullet. It was too close to his heart and he was too weak. A nurse showed Delores a drawing of a heart and placed her finger on an aorta, *here*. In an X-ray the bullet seemed as large as the heart itself, a black spider burrowed deep within him.

He survived one night and then another. There was some worry about blood poisoning, and one of the nurses came to see Delores to ask about medical insurance.

"There isn't any. Call the state people."

"We already have and your coverage is for childbirth only. The rest of this, the critical care and all, is adding up fast. Sign this, please."

"What is it?"

"Just a little insurance. It says you can be brought up on charges if you don't pay in full. If it's any help to know, they got the guy who shot you. He gave himself up right away."

Her own wounds healed slowly. She had lost blood and amniotic water but the hole in her stomach was smaller than the cesarean seam. When she hemorrhaged, her ovaries became inflamed and had to be removed. Each night they emptied her full breasts with a machine, cleaned her wound, and changed the dressing. After a week, the nurse snipped away her stitches, but she still wasn't strong enough to walk.

When he was two months old, Joseph weighed six and a half pounds and the fluid that had seeped into his lungs was gone. Helene drove to the hospital in Frank Poor Bull's pickup and took him back to Choteau in a driving rain. The baby never cried, she told Delores, either from hunger or wet diapers or fear or sorrow. He didn't walk until he was nearly two years old and spoke his first word at the age of four, but he grew up to be neither physically impaired nor an imbecile, though he was slow to learn things and was exceedingly, almost spookily, quiet and docile.

The bullet could never be removed without killing him.

He wears it like a seed beneath his skin.

The hole in her stomach scarred over, but all the same she felt there was a breach in her flesh and the wind was whistling through her hollow body. Joseph grew strong while she remained weak, and Helene took care of both of them. While she lay in that hospital bed, she had a visit from the FBI. There were no witnesses to place her in Choteau at the time of the shootings, but, all the same, could she perhaps answer a few questions? Hadn't she lived with John Fire? She didn't have anything to tell them. I was in Blunt, you can ask the lady at the motel. Ask Kissel, rhymes with whistle.

Two days after she was released from the hospital, they came with a warrant to the house in Choteau where she'd taken up residence, the place where she'd lived with John Fire. They found three empty Wild Turkey bottles, a spent shell they slipped into a plastic pouch, an ashtray filled with lipsticked Marlboro butts, twelve dollars in ones and change, and a pair of shotguns and a Colt pistol under her bed. She had never seen any of these guns in her life.

She was given a one-year sentence that would have been reduced to six months if she'd played ball. Her only news came from the outside, in cards from Helene or Judy Poor Bull, a package from Elizabeth Bordeaux that contained a short letter and a box of cheap cosmetics from Amway. She was assigned to dishwashing and once, after lunch, she counted three hundred eighty dinner trays but only three hundred seventy-eight forks. The block supervisor slapped the back of her head and said she'd better come up with those missing forks, pronto. But it was no use pleading with the women in the block. Those forks had probably already been fenced for cigarettes or sexual favors, and Delores wasn't responsible for the flatware count anyway. It was a white woman named Sandy Fox who took a week in the dark as punishment. And one of the missing forks, broken at the handle and sharpened down, was later stuck in her wide ass. The shank, they called it. Sandy Fox, went the word, was a snitch.

Delores worked lotion into her reddened hands each night after the dishwashing, but her fingers remained wrinkled and raw and sensitive to the touch. She'd been in prison for less than three months when she got the first letter from Tyrone. Her mother smuggled in carefully torn bits of it, paragraph by paragraph, during three different visits. In her cell she pieced those paragraphs back together again: *Dear Delores, don't burn this before reading it all the way through.* She read the letter three times but didn't answer it. There were a half dozen more before she was released, and she found another stack was waiting for her at Helene's.

When she tried to dig her heels back into the soil of Choteau, no roots sprouted and she began to drift. She'd go off somewhere, come back, then leave again. Years passed by, uncounted. Whenever she moved to a new town, her mother forwarded her postcards and letters in manila envelopes. On occasion she opened them and passed her eyes over the words, but most times she didn't have the courage to read what he had to say. There was more of him that could hurt her. Though she hadn't felt the bullet, she could feel the words.

Each time she moved, she considered burning the letters or throwing them out, but the words inside seemed to have become living things that would have to be killed first. Instead, she stored them in a shoe box.

She could not sit still. The ground beneath her was shifting, turning to sand. She followed paths that could not include Joseph, west to Buffalo Gap, Denver, and a bus ride to Fort Lauderdale for Darryl Kills First's trial. Then back west to Huron and north to the Standing Rock Reservation, where she had a job at the Indian Center. She fell in with a man named Garrett who got into the habit of beating her when he was drunk or out of sorts. After one of those nights she headed to Denver, where she worked the graveyard shift at a Qwik Chek that had been robbed ten times in the last year. The owner hired her with the mistaken impression that Indians wouldn't steal from another Indian, but she still had at least one night out of every month with her hands in the air and a knife or gun at her back while punks, Caucasian or Hispanic or Native American, rifled the register.

During her fifth month on the job, a young man came into the store. Though the weather was warm, he wore a plaid hunting jacket and Delores kept an eye on him as he strolled over to the vegetable freezer and pretended to examine its contents. He kept one hand in the jacket pocket and with the other he reached for a bag of green beans. *At one in the morning, he has a hankering for green beans.* There was a buzzer behind the register and all she had to do was press it with her knee and a patrol car would be alerted, but the cops always showed up ten minutes too late. The man approached the register and dropped the green beans to the counter. But instead of ringing up the sale, Delores opened the cash drawer and said he didn't have to use his gun. "Or your knife, or whatever you're carrying. Help yourself, I'm too tired to be threatened."

The young man was an undercover cop and there were two others watching from outside. The incident was made to appear as less than unique, and the judge took her previous conviction into account. Delores was given six months and served every one of them in a Denver jail.

She lost her unemployment and had to rely on her relief check from the state. She moved to Rapid City and lived in an abandoned car on the south edge of town. A fifth of Wild Turkey cost close to ten dollars, but Thunderbird wine could be had for less than three. Most of her possessions were stolen, her makeup and clothing and the books she'd carried with her. But in her purse she still had a drawing that Joseph had sent her; it showed either the Missouri River or a road to someplace in the sky.

One late spring morning she awoke and found herself covered with her own vomit. It was red and at first she mistook the blood for wine. She went to a clinic in Rapid City to quit drinking and stayed for nearly four months. She had a room with clean sheets and a photograph of Mother Teresa over her bed, and her window looked out on a changeless stretch of prairie. Only the sky changed, like a watercolor that never dried—the white clouds, the rainclouds, the burning sun. She read *Black Elk Speaks* after years of lying to others that it was her favorite book, and she read it again. A fat young girl from Lusk, Wyoming, played checkers with her before lights-out and Delores usually let her win because it gave her such pleasure. A kindly-eyed white man who worked there said that if she kept on drinking, the blood vessels in her face would break and she'd have a South Dakota roadmap in place of her beauty.

There were twelve steps. The second one said she had to give herself up to a higher power. It was not specified what that power had to be. It could be Jesus or *wakan tanka*, the counselor joked, or even the Republican Party. Delores plain skipped this step, though she had little trouble with the other eleven. When she left the clinic, a typist's job was waiting for her with a construction company in Rapid City. For three months she wore a print blouse and pressed jeans to the office, drank instant coffee from a Styrofoam cup, politely and repeatedly peeled the supervisor's hands from her buttocks, and typed bidding lists with three carbons for a hundred and four dollars net per week. She drove a ten-year-old Mustang with a broken window on the driver's side, a faulty muffler, and a cracked headlight. An Indian car. At night she made her dinner and took it to bed, from where she watched television or did crossword puzzles or read books that didn't have love or Indians or alcohol in them. But after four months of living this way, she swallowed the hook again, swallowed it whole. At the clinic they asked her why, but she could only tell them what she had told them before. *There's a black hole we're always staring into and after a while we just jump in.*

After a week, she simply walked away. A drunken Indian. God, how original. She found a bar called Smitty's where the lights went out for nearly a week, by which time she had no money, no car, no job, and only the dirty clothes she was wearing. She hitchhiked from Rapid City to Pine Ridge where a friend gave her a dress that was too tight on her and bus fare back to Choteau.

The three of them—Helene, Delores, and Joseph—lived for six months in the tiny trailer. Joseph was almost fourteen and had grown as tall as Delores and sometimes there were slivers of memory when she watched him move across a room or tip his head to the side before speaking, as his father had.

One spring evening, when the river was high and the scent of lilacs was overpowering, Gaetan Avril came knocking on the door. She hadn't seen him since she was in prison that first time, but he said good evening as if only weeks had passed. They sat on folding chairs in front of the trailer. When Helene offered coffee or cider, Gaetan said he'd pass. Why he'd come was to offer a house that was sitting on land he'd turned over to his son. "Sam's never there," he said. "He's gone east and sworn himself to metropolitan existence." He shrugged unhappily. "So, there's that lonesome house with no one for the mice to talk to. I'd like the three of you to have it."

Delores said, "We'd have to think it over—"

"What's to think about? There are two big bedrooms and a living room that could make a dance floor. The plumbing's sound and the kitchen's got all the appliances."

Helene said, "Wasn't that your father's old house?"

"He only used it for a while when he was building his second one. The first place burned down a long time ago."

Delores looked closely at him, remembering the foundation where she'd seen the wolf the night she left Tyrone.

"Those kitchen appliances are tempting, Mr. Avril," Helene said, "but you'll notice I got a few of my own."

There was another house, more of a shack, through the trees on the other side of the road. It had been built forty years ago for a farm-worker's family, and they decided that Joseph should have it for himself. To the west of the house, the land had been cleared, trees and boulders removed, and the earth scraped over. Some of those acres had been part of Eagle Reach Country Club until Gaetan Avril brought suit to revert title back to himself. When Joseph moved in, Gaetan paid to restore the fireplace and fix the damaged roof.

Delores had walked out on Joseph many times, but she took his leaving harder than she'd expected.

"It's only three miles," Helene reminded her.

"Miles is a notion given us by the English."

The day he moved out, Helene took a cardboard box out from under her bed. "Saved them for when you came back. I meant to give them to you soon as you showed up, but I didn't want Joseph to catch wind."

Fifteen letters from Tyrone, neatly typed on white bond. More words than the Missouri River had bends. *Still loving you*, he wrote with a pencil at the bottom of one of the letters. Though she'd forgiven him before the bullet left the chamber, his confession was still sweet to read.

PART THREE

The Want-to-Be

Joseph Her Many Horses

There are two worlds, his mother said. Listen to me, Joseph. The first world is as whole and evident as the wind, and the second, well, the second is less whole. You understand me, Joseph. I live in both worlds and therefore no world at all, no place, but you are strong and whole and your eyes are sharp. Poor Bull and some of the others think you are a spirit, a holy man.

He knows—and she does too, since he came from her body—that he is not only a spirit. He wears the dream-catcher around his throat and breathes in the smoke of the sacred fires, but there is the wound in his chest to tell him as he breathes that he was born and is still alive.

The first world you have to search for, Joseph, you have to listen for it, you have to close your eyes and seek it below your lids. The second world is always there, all the time, whether you want it to be or not.

When the sun lights up the tops of the trees, he is at his morning place by the river. The sky flies low and is blue and the heat is already sweltering. He's wearing his oldest jeans and the ground beneath his bare feet is warm and dry. The air is heavy and hard to breathe. Flies are exploding from the trees.

Downstream, the riverbank rises to a white bluff where the waters have exposed the roots of trees that shade Sam Avril's house. Sam wasn't awake when Joseph came to use the phone. He seldom stirs before the sun has climbed halfway up the sky. But Joseph rang the bell until, startled, he came to the screen door. Joseph apologized and Sam said, "No sweat. It's a break in my decadent routine that my father would approve of."

When he spoke to his mother, he could hear the whisky in her voice. She said yes, she would come, tomorrow, what should she bring? He told her he has everything he needs or wants.

The river is low and the shoreline has receded. Gnats hover and waterbugs skate over small pools left from the rain. Thin white weeds grow along the water's edge like hair on a girl's forearm.

Joseph hears the drums of hooves and a calf breaks from the trees and approaches the water. It is one of George Boy Kemper's and normally wouldn't have made it past the string of barbed wire along the treeline. The calf casts an eye at Joseph and bends its neck to drink from the river. Joseph watches the pink-and-gray tongue move in and out as the calf's eyes look upward, flies circling its head and ears. Then the animal spooks and its forelegs slip into the mud along the riverbank, its bawling tragic and funny at the same time. It struggles up and frees its legs, switches its tail back and forth, then bends again to drink. A moment later, when the calf has had its fill, it turns and heads back through the trees, taking a walking crap.

Joseph reaches a hand to the water, fills his palm, and drinks. Gil at the country club told him never to drink water from the Missouri River, not downstream from the dam. "All those chemicals in there, raw sewage. And the water doesn't flow fast enough or deep enough to clean itself. It's like drinking urine."

The water is warm and tastes of the soil and the roots of grass. He drinks again.

The red clay along the banks is as dry as toast. Noah Lame, or maybe it was his grandmother, told him a story a long time ago about a warrior made from wet clay. When the sun came out he was baked as hard as rock like a statue. Many years passed and the rains and winds covered him with soil, and now the warrior is a mountain.

. . .

He sits near a thin stretch of sand where years ago there was a boat launch and stoops to read the ripples. The water leaves him a message there every morning and he reads what can't be written or spoken. When the water is swift, the ripples make great swirls and circles in the sand. Other times there are knots or wrinkles, a worried scribble that seems like a warning. Or the sand is flat and clean and unbroken. When the waters have receded even farther, the sand grows dry and white and when Joseph sifts through it with his fingers he finds the bones of birds and fish or the slick shed skin of water snakes. The night writing has left many ripples but there is also a white film on the water and along the bank. He dips a finger and it tastes like paste or mucus. It is something he has never seen before.

He stands and walks upriver following the white threads until he comes to Blue Eye Creek, a narrow stream that trickles down from the north and drains into the river. The creek is low at this time of year, but the rains have fed the water bed. Not far away is a spot where Sam has put up some logs and dug a ditch to run water into a few rows of corn next to his house. Joseph slogs through thick brush alongside the stream until he comes to a pool by Kemper's barn where the water is white and thick, like paint. Next to the stream is a rusted tractor that's been sitting there for years, and a toolshed with a padlock and a wheelbarrow still crusted with white dust. He doesn't know what it is, but it doesn't mix with river water. George Boy Kemper is not like Pete Scully. Old Pete respects the water and would never dump this into a stream.

Joseph gathers stones and fallen wood and quickly dams the stream so the water from the pool won't get in.

Noah Lame told him that the soil on top is not soil but the blood and bone of their people. He thinks about this as he digs up earth from around the pool and pours it into the water. When the pool is filled, Joseph returns to his spot by the sand and sits for a long time looking out over the water to the cottonwood trees on the other side. The leaves are no longer green but they are not yet brown. When there is a breeze they are silver, and in another month they will be the color of Toby Johnson's homemade wine.

The water parts before his eyes and a gray pike shows a fin. He bends his naked back to look closer and the sunlight stings his flesh.

. . .

The sweet grass and cornfields abruptly end at a barbed-wire fence. Beyond is the strange place of mown grass, trees that grow in perfect rows, and scattered rippling greens carved from the earth. Joseph has only to walk a quarter mile along the riverbank and then cut across the eleventh and twelfth fairways until he comes to a footpath that leads to the clubhouse.

Despite the rain that fell in the night, the sprinklers are already in motion. They drift slowly from right to left, casting high arcs of spray across the fairways on the back nine. As Joseph crosses the twelfth fairway, a jet of water sways toward him. He stops to wait for it and feels the momentary flash of coolness as the water showers over his shoulders and chest.

Gil Dunham is waiting for him in the greenskeeper's office. He is wearing his tan slacks and white short-sleeved shirt with the ER insignia and a name tag. "You're all wet, Joseph."

"Sprinkler's on."

"Yeah. I came in early and started it up. Ten through fourteen. The timer ought to shut off any minute now and you can mow. Start with eleven 'cause it dries out before the others."

Joseph opens his locker and takes out his white shirt. They let him wear jeans or shorts if he wants, but the white shirt is part of the rules. He has two of them and twice a week he leaves a dirty one in the laundry hamper and it comes back two days later washed and starched. He doesn't like the starch, though he doesn't know who to ask to stop using it.

Another man comes into the office. Joseph has seen him before, out on the course, but doesn't know his name. He doesn't look happy. "Yesterday was junior tournament and the course'll be chock full of those pop cans and candy wrappers. We should be teaching these kids a little etiquette before setting them loose on the course, don't you think? Anyway, see that your redskin sweeps that shit up. We got a mixed best-ball this weekend and a few guests are driving down from Sioux Falls. I plan on seeing Eagle Reach looking sharp."

"Joseph?" Gil is looking at him, while the other man looks right through him.

Frank Poor Bull says I am a spirit. Only another spirit can see the flesh of me.

"You hear what Mr. Roebuck said?"

Joseph nods. "Teach a little etiquette to the kids."

Dunham smiles and the other man turns to look out the open door as if a vision awaits him there. He sighs and then slowly turns to face Joseph, though his eyes can't quite find the Indian's. "I want immaculate," he says. "I want manicured. Savvy?"

"Don't worry, Albert. Joe here's the best help I've ever had at greenskeeping. You can count on him."

"I never count on Indians, Gil. I'm asking you to ride point on this. Am I clear?"

"Clear as day."

The man proceeds to tell Gil a joke about a gorilla that learned to play golf. "First tee, par five. Hundreds of people in the gallery. Whack, five hundred yards straight onto the green."

Joseph buttons up his shirt which is now on its third day and the starch long gone. He takes his gloves, key chain, and baseball cap with an eagle stitched on the front and shuts his locker door. This man, he thinks, has the face of the coyote, his eyes always watchful even when he's pretending not to see anything.

"The gorilla steps up and looks over this two-foot putt. Everybody wants to see a double eagle, so the crowd closes in around the green. Whack, another five-hundred-yard drive."

Gil's laughter is like warm tap water.

Joseph puts his hat on and instantly feels a foot shorter. He goes out to the lot to find his golf cart.

"Immaculate!" the man shouts at his back.

The sprinklers have shut off and the grass is still moist, but the sun will burn it up in minutes. Joseph takes the electric cart out to the shed in the stand of trees near the twelfth tee. Though the river is close by, its smell is mixed with the sprinkler water. Bad golfers lose a lot of balls in the river to the right of the fairway, and Joseph often forages along the banks for stray balls. They pay him twenty-five cents each at the driving range but he doesn't always turn them in. He doesn't need new money every day.

He pulls the key chain from his pocket and opens the shed. Inside are bags of fertilizer, pesticide canisters, a half dozen varieties of grass seed, motor oil, dirty rags, shovels and rakes, a hoe, and a shelf of chemicals. He takes a can of Valvoline and punches the spout into its top then goes behind the shed where the tractor is parked under a plastic awning. He opens the hood, loosens a metal cap, and stuffs the can upside down into the oil drain.

After mowing, he needs to trim a tree on the fourth fairway. The branch of an elm has grown too long in the wrong direction and has to be cut back. Later on, he'll rake the sand traps and, if he has time, wash his tools with the hose behind the shed and scrape rust from the mower blades with steel wool. He hooks the mower to the tractor and then adjusts the blade height so that the cut will not be too severe. In dry weather, the low grass will turn brown in the sun no matter how many hours the sprinklers are on.

Joseph dislikes the cutting. Before starting up the tractor, he raises his head to the sky and closes his eyes. There are clouds in the west, moving toward him. High up, the wind is stronger than below, so there will be rain again tonight, or maybe tomorrow. The sprinklers will turn on anyway unless Gil shuts off the timers. One time he saw the sprinklers going during a downpour and when he told this to Noah Lame, the old man laughed until his face got red and his eyes were wet.

He rides across the bald field and already is thinking of the high place where the grass grows fast and long and the air is always cold. He will have to pass that way today, and he's afraid. There are voices in the river and there are voices in the trees, but they are voices without language. The grass that grows so fast swiftly out of the ground is almost words, talking, and the cold air is crazy on a day hot like today. The first time he cut the grass there he wasn't thinking of anything until he felt the cold at his neck. Feeling visited, he just shivered and kept mowing. Two days later, Gil said by God why didn't you mow out that way and he said he had. Like hell you did, Gil said, so he took the tractor back out and the grass was long as a woman's hair. He felt the cold wind again and the grass screamed beneath the blades.

He's scared to mention this to anyone, though the night before he almost told Sam. Sam is the only white besides Gaetan who really listens to what he says. And one time Joseph asked Gil if he could get somebody else to mow fourteen. Gil said something about Indians and firewater, though he knows that all Joseph ever drinks is water from the river.

He turns the tractor onto the eleventh fairway, where the sprinkler water has dried to nothing. He will cut the grass at eleven through thirteen and then will approach the mound from the east, downwind, as if that might make a difference.

He aims the tractor for the green-and-white flag four hundred eleven yards away. As he drives he keeps an eye out for the garbage the white children might have left behind.

Just before sunset, the bats are twirling in the trees, waving signals of warning. Smoke from a grass fire on the other side of the river rises over the ridge but where Joseph stands, shaded in the trees, it is already night and the river has changed from brown to bottle green.

Finished with his work at Eagle Reach, Joseph is hungry and wanders from under the trees into a pasture at the south edge of Gaetan Avril's land. The ground is soft and yielding under his bare feet, though the grass has grown dry through a blazing day. The cattle watch as he draws near. He is attracted to them, their fragrant heat, their laziness, the ripping sounds they make when they chew. Hey-ya, he calls out to them, and a few turn in his direction. A sparrow sweeps down low and then glides upward and disappears in the trees to the north. Beyond the pasture is a cornfield, the stalks already rising above his head. He pulls an ear from one of them and peels back the green leaf and golden hair that covers the meat. The corn is still young, the kernels like white teeth, but the sweet taste bursts wet over his dry tongue. He eats three ears and is reaching for a fourth when he sees the pheasant, a fat male, two rows away, its colors radiant in the dying light. Seeing Joseph, it runs across five rows to lead him away from the nest. But instead Joseph circles around to where he knows the nest will be and glances through the stalks to where he can see the head of the hen.

He is not a hunter. In another month, the hunters will be out and although Gaetan has posted all around his land, the men sometimes ignore the "No Hunting" signs and fill the sky with buckshot. Even after the first snows have fallen, Joseph avoids the fields. After the pheasant hunters come the duck hunters, the deer hunters, and the men in search of wolves no one has ever seen.

Beyond the field is a long rocky slope and then an empty pasture. Joseph crosses it and comes to a field of sunflowers that bend in the breeze. It is a place that attracts gophers and birds and in the midst of those sunflowers is a gravestone Joseph cannot read.

Stepping over a creek bed, he comes close to Gaetan's house. The earth is a riot of food and immediately a tomato bursts under his bare foot. He bends and finds another, half of it blackened with rot. He eats the sweet half and moves on. He stoops beneath a leaning elm to brush away leaves and sticks, then pries a radish from the soil. He chews and smiles. There are more radishes between bright blades of grass and beets bleed from a mound of wet clay. He digs with curled fingers and lets the earth fall away, leaving potatoes the size of small stones. He rubs them against his shirt to clean them and eats his fill, while darkness fills in the trees and the birds go silent. With his tongue, he nudges a radish into the pocket of his cheek and puts another handful into his jeans pocket. Then he turns back and heads across the pasture toward Choteau, a tomato in either hand for Helene.

Helene's trailer is shaded by an enormous elm tree whose lower branches brush the roof. The white paint is badly chipped and in some spots there are patches of rusted aluminum that look like burnt skin. There's no apron below the trailer and the undercarriage is exposed. Snakes nest there in the summers, and in the winter it's where roaming dogs take refuge.

He can hear the television from far away. Helene is hard of hearing and turns the volume up high so she can follow her game shows, but she rises from her chair to unlatch the lock when Joseph raps on the screen door. She takes the tomatoes in her bony hands and smiles vaguely, then sets them on the tiny table in her kitchen and returns to her chair. She is watching a show she'd taped on her VCR. She has nothing but these shows, tapes and tapes of them, "Jeopardy," "Password," "Wheel of Fortune," and spends the balance of her waking days shouting at stumped contestants. "Capistrano! They fly to *Capistrano*!"

Joseph goes into the kitchen and drinks milk straight from the carton, his eyes resting on a calendar that she never turns. He knows this is the Fat Moon month but Helene doesn't care either way. Noah gave her the calendar for Christmas, and her favorite picture was for the Blush Moon month, a waterfall in a place Joseph has never seen. It has been the Blush Moon month for a long time.

He is happy in her house, where the floor in the big room is soft like grass and the chairs smell of oil and the flowers on the sofa are forever bursting red and green. The kitchen reeks of lemon spray and is cool in the summer, warm in the winter, and Helene always has cold milk in her refrigerator.

Dinner scraps are still on the table—potato peel, eggshell, a slice of bologna and a mustard drip. She once told Joseph that as a child she was always so hungry she could have eaten the bark off a tree. But for years now she never thinks twice about food and eats whatever falls into her hands. Beets, carrots, red meat, fish. Noah drives into Wilma once a week and does her shopping for her. She used to give him a list of what she wanted and now she just tells him to get whatever he feels like, just so it's not in a can. Joseph takes the scraps out to her compost bin and shoves them under a mesh of dried grass, where blackened coffee grounds and humid vegetables give off steam. He washes his hands in the kitchen and wanders into the small room that once was his own.

Since Gaetan Avril gave him the house by the river, this room has gradually filled with riffraff that Helene either treasures or just hasn't bothered to throw away. He closes the door behind him to escape the noise of the game show. The room is warm and airless, sealed tight. Joseph steps over a bicycle with two flat tires and rummages through a stack of old clothing, frayed curtains, and worn dish towels until he finds the shoe box with the family photographs inside. Clearing a space on the bed, he balances the box on his knees and removes the top. The box is old and softened, its frayed edges Scotch-taped. He takes one photograph out at a time, careful not to run his fingers over the surface. Many are in color but most are black-and-white or sepia. There is one of his grandfather, Reynold Her Many Horses, in his army uniform and cap, squinting into the camera as if he was afraid of it. In another, Helene is standing next to an old car, one hand resting on the hood and the other holding an empty basket. On the back, someone has scrawled some words and the date but he cannot read them because he cannot read at all. There are several pictures he is told are of himself, color prints of a skinny, bare-chested boy in swimming trunks or jeans. There are many that show people standing in front of houses or trees or new cars. Helene has shown him each of these photographs, giving him all the names and the circumstances of the picture-taking. Reynold had a Brownie camera and Helene later owned a Polaroid, but the lens broke ten years ago and since then no one has taken any pictures at all.

Sifting through the photos with his fingers, he picks out the one he's looking for, a color shot of his mother before he was born. It is a picture whose story Helene has never told him. Whenever they look at the pictures together, she always skips past it and goes on to the next one.

His mother is sitting on a tree stump and her face is turned away from the sunlight as she smiles at someone outside the picture. She is wearing a shiny blue blouse and a gold heart on a chain at her throat. He has never seen this face of hers, these bright and lively eyes, the soft mouth, her skin the color of oranges. The woman he has seen has always been weary and pale, bone tired, but the woman in this picture she looks so young. Standing with her, one hand resting on her shoulder, a man stares directly into the camera, his mouth set into a forced smile. He wears a beaded shirt and his face is burned red from the sun.

Once, before Helene could turn to the next picture, Joseph asked who he was, this man.

Helene took a breath and then said, "He was a white man who wanted to be an Indian."

They were sitting in the living room. Joseph looked at the picture and then looked at his own face in the reflection of the dark television. His image smiled back at him with the same thin smile. "He looks like me."

"Don't talk foolishness. He doesn't look anything like you."

Years later, in the airless bedroom, he studies the picture for a long time before he returns the box to its place beneath the old clothing and goes back into the living room, where Helene sits leaning toward the television. He touches the top of her head and she looks up as if she's surprised he's still there.

"I'll eat the tomatoes tomorrow," she says.

The game show rages on. Joseph is out the door and is enveloped in darkness but can hear her from a distance.

"Coco Chanel, you idiot! Chanel!"

He wades east through the high fields, green wings of corn brushing his face and shoulders. He leaps a string of black wire and his feet touch on uncombed ground and buffalo grasses. But Joseph has never seen a buffalo.

He comes to a secret road, a strip that once led up from the river but now is cut off from the other roads by a cornfield. A few years ago, he'd found a place where lightning-struck trees had fallen in a circle. Inside the trees was a red car. There were canned goods in the backseat and a rifle resting against the steering wheel. The door was unlocked, and the keys were in the ignition and the rifle was loaded. Gil had told him that a battery dies if you don't use it from time to time, so he'd come back a day later with a gas can and charger from the country club and sparked the engine back to life. He comes back as often as he can to see if anyone's driven that car away, but it's still there, undamaged, that rifle in its place, the battery charged, and the keys still in the ignition.

Gil says you have to run a car now and then, so Joseph sits behind the wheel and turns the key. The engine shrieks to life and he presses the pedal to hear it bray. He turns on the radio and spins the dial until he hears music. Then he trips the brake and slips into gear. The car bumps forward onto the dirt road and he drives it straight to the the edge of the river. Stars swim in the black current and vanish when he turns on the headlights.

He climbs out of the car, shucks his jeans, and steps into the water. With cupped hands, he reaches to the bottom for the slick mud, and he spreads it until his arms and chest and face are covered. Then he lies down where the current is strong and the waters rub him clean. For a while he swims lazily on his back, his eyes searching for stars, and then climbs out and sits on a flat rock to dry.

The car radio crackles like a fire made from wet sticks. A man is talking and one of the words is a name that Joseph has overheard when the men are talking, a name they only whisper when he's there.

He quickly gathers his clothes and climbs, still wet, behind the wheel. Turning the red car around, he drives it back to its spot in the trees.

At Toby's, the men are arranged around the table, Noah Lame, Pete
Scully, Darryl Kills First, George Boy Kemper, and Frank Poor Bull.
But this night there are no pinochle cards, and they all look angry.
Frank Poor Bull has unbuttoned his shirt and his hairless chest is pale
below the bright red of his neck. Noah Lame is wearing his beaded
shirt and a clean pair of blue jeans over his worn cowboy boots. His
arms folded, he's telling the others they should listen to Gaetan Avril.

When Joseph comes in the door they grow quiet all at once, but
Noah Lame waves him inside.

"Is that a good idea?" Poor Bull asks.

"The secret won't last forever," Lame says.

Joseph nods his head in greeting, like he's ducking under a tree
branch, and takes a chair at the table.

"Another thing to consider," Noah Lame tells them. "Tyrone was
a veteran."

The room is clouded with cigarette smoke and steam from the
kitchen.

"So he killed men for a living. What's that supposed to mean?"

"He stole the bones back for us."

"And he was FBI." This from Poor Bull.

"We don't know that," Noah says. "We don't know anything at
all."

Jana brings a pitcher of water to the table and sets a stack of plastic
cups next to it. "Another beer, Frank?" He nods and she gets one
for him, taking the empty from his hand.

"I'm a veteran, too," Pete says. "I can understand something about
Tyrone."

"We knew better about Vietnam," Darryl tells him. "You was
fighting Nazis."

"Don't you remember," Pete asks, "when AIM started up, how
they was calling us all commies like we'd joined up with Castro or
something? Well, you add a vet to the group and that shuts them up
fast."

"He knew maps and strategy," Noah adds. "He helped us get our
thoughts straight."

"That might have been just to suck us in," Darryl says. "To get us
to trust him."

"All I know," Poor Bull says, "is I got a gun. I still got a gun and I plan to kill a man."

"What man?" Joseph asks.

"A want-to-be who's been in prison your whole life."

It looks like tears coming from Frank's eyes, but it could be sweat or from all the beer he's been drinking. He suddenly stands and glares at his friends, then, weaving slightly, he lurches from the bar. Outside, he hesitates before striding across the lot toward his house. Noah follows him out.

Joseph drinks from his glass of water. It's tap water and tastes nothing like the river. He takes a radish from his pocket and bites into it.

"It's time to face some bad music, Joseph," Pete Scully says to him. "Do you follow what we're saying here?"

Joseph nods but his chin turns to one side, a questioning look. He can taste the radish on his tongue, the beets and the corn. Pete is talking to him but all he can hear are the bats in the trees and the lapping of the river.

Sam Avril

When Sam was thirteen, his father took him on a jeep tour of their property, 19,000-plus acres of rolling Dakota grassland. He was liquored up, as Sam's mother put it, and drove like a madman over ruts and fallen timber, down gullies and back up stony paths, always in a tightening spiral. "Four-wheel drive!" he shouted. "Two hundred horses!" They started out early in the evening when the April sky was the color of a day-old bruise. The sun was long gone and Sam's hot terror had cooled to numbness and bone ache from the jouncing once they were again in sight of their two-story house with its fake Corinthian columns. "Just don't forget that all of this has been stolen," his father said. "A brilliant operation on your granddad's part, but thievery nevertheless. Before I'm dead, I'll give you a tiny piece, a place to relieve your bladder or plant some corn, but the rest I aim to give back."

Whom the land had been stolen from remained a mystery to Sam through his childhood, as did the fraction that was intended to be handed over to him. And his granddad didn't have any answers, laid up as he was in the Pine Valley Home with his eyes staring at the acoustic ceiling tiles. Paralyzed from the eyes on down after a fall from a horse named Said So, he lived almost ten years on tube meals and sponge baths. The nurses used to prop his head up and aim it at the television on the off chance that he had a yen to watch the soaps. They never knew. The only life they ever saw in him was an occasional twitching around the mouth, which could have just been his way of cursing them. When he died, his father said nothing was changed. "He's been in purgatory for ten years and from now on things only get hotter."

At the age of twenty-eight, Sam holds title to ten acres that are good for nothing but a constant yield of rich prairie grass, plenty of firewood, the capture of rain in various sloughs, and the ecological continuity of birds eating seeds and shitting those seeds in distant fields, insects being swallowed by frogs, and frogs being devoured by mammals. He lives in a widowed farmhouse. At one time the Averills had at least five of them, houses stranded without farms because all the land had been bought up by his grandfather. From where he sits, he can look south toward the rolling river or west, across a deep throw of trees that lead to Eagle Reach. The land is a concept he can almost ignore, but the house is two rooms too large for him, augmenting his loneliness with all its unoccupied space.

The furnishings are left over from his grandfather's time and his love of dark wood has left a gloomy signature: a sorrel armoire and mahogany writing desk, chairs the color of strong coffee, and a long dining table made from pine but stained the color of dried blood. He's added some Oriental rugs, floor pillows, a rattan coffee table with smoked-glass top, and has covered the walls with paintings that his father didn't have room for in his own house, gifts or purchases from his artist friends that sow visual confusion against the blue and yellow wallpaper flowers.

His father deeded the land to Sam when he turned eighteen and had a high school diploma. But Sam went away the following autumn to the University of Wisconsin, and then to Columbia, and most of those summers he spent a minimum of time visiting home. Although his field was European history, he studied the checkered history of his home state on the side and decided he would never live there. But a degree in history qualified him for little in the way of a career and when a research job lost its funding after eighteen months, he drifted from waiting tables to drug dealing. Pot, mostly. Hash on occasion. He'd thought of himself as a corner grocer, not a big wheel, but the police disagreed. An arrest set the stage for a return home, to this hideout.

At Columbia, he learned that all his father was doing was paraphrasing Marx's notion that all property was stolen. He also discovered that his father was a pale imitation of every hero he'd ever had. He hasn't lived life as he'd once planned it. The people in town think of him as a drunk, a crackpot, an Indian lover, and he admits to all of that but the drinking. He is eccentric and stubborn, and tends to say whatever he feels at the top of his lungs.

The summer is coming to an end and Sam's spent a good part of the day smoking pot and trying to remember whether or not he fed the dog. She's a bastard pup he accepted from Jana Johnson in a weak moment. Thus far, the dog's overriding inclination is to hide under the porch and whimper all day long, but for the moment she's sitting on the porch with Sam and staring into the yard. It relaxes her to hear human voices, so Sam turns on the radio and together they listen to the thin strands of music that drift around in the warm, still air.

The pot is homegrown, a kind of cultivation Sam knows like the back of his hand. The trick is to master the water supply and to recognize when to simply sweep the tops away and when, once the plant is thirsty and oozing THC, to cut the stalks down. He's on the run only insofar as New York State is concerned. Though he doesn't say as much to his father, he does not consider himself as altogether out of the marijuana business.

Gaetan kept the other half of his promise as well, and the land has been parceled out to the Lames, Kills Firsts, Poor Bulls, among other descendants of the Sioux nation. He kept only a few acres for himself, though he retained the lifetime right to take his jeep or his horse through any part of his former holdings. He doesn't ride much anymore. Instead he spends his days annoying the locals or tying imaginative dry flies or following the flight of his Titleists across emerald fairways. Gaetan loves western art, Walt Whitman, Jack Nicklaus, the painter Rauschenberg, and the poet Patchen. He is the prairie host to sculptors from Taos, choreographers from New York, and screenwriters from L.A. Though he resides in South Dakota, he donates money to ecology-minded politicos in New Mexico, Utah, and Florida. He recognizes no borders other than those between day and night. Just this afternoon, he called to ask Sam to dinner on Thursday night so he can meet "this woman I met in St. Louis who has a thing for historians."

He wants a grandkid, boy or girl. Someone to pull his chin with searching baby fingers. His hearty earnestness is fairly oppressive. Sam tells him that procreation takes time, not to mention the consent and collaboration of a female. What he doesn't tell him is that he hasn't been to bed with a woman in the year since he came back from New York, and not from lack of trying. Still, the bison were once nearly extinct but today there are herds of thousands in the western half of the state. Sam figures he was once nearly extinct, but here he is high as a Chinese kite on his own crops. He's only twenty-eight years old, sound of limb if not of mind, and the family tree might still sprout another branch. There is time. Time.

On occasion, he breaks down and drives into Wilma for a taste of living and the sound of human voices. But those visits tend to be short. He is usually poorly dressed and badly shaven, obviously unemployed, and his guess is that his eyes show how goddamn lonesome he's become because he tends to drive away even the friendly folks. As far as the people of Wilma are concerned, he would be an embarrassment to his father if Gaetan wasn't already an embarrassment to himself.

At the extreme northeast corner of his father's former property is the ruin of his grandfather's first house, burned to the ground in 1944. Local history has it that there was some sort of accident, a kerosene lamp tipped over or sparks from a blazing fire. But the deeds to the land were locked in a bank vault and most of Sam's grandfather's clothes and books were miraculously spared. "That fire," Gaetan once told him, "was about as accidental as the sun coming up."

Sam's mother is buried on top of a humble hill not far from Blue Eye Creek, where there are plenty of sunflowers. His grandfather is on the north edge of what is now Lame's property. The grave is right next to a corn-shuck dumping site that his father donated to the reservation farmers.

He can hear the dog beneath him, under the porch boards once again, whining to the tune of some old Hank Williams number.

Sam is drifting.

At eight in the evening, the sun hangs by a thread along the western swell of land and burns through the few trees within sight. At this time of year, especially when he's waiting for darkness to fall, he has the impression that the horizon keeps dipping lower and lower just to give the sun more room.

He has a neighbor close by, young Joseph, who has a tar-paper house across the road and beyond the trees. Gaetan gave him the house and a number of acres years ago, while Sam was away at college. In a lifetime that hasn't been rife with alliances, Joseph is the best friend he has. They cross paths irregularly but are always on the lookout. In the winter, Joseph left firewood stacked on Sam's porch. Sam, less woodsy, answered with a case of frozen beef.

Sam once asked his father how it happens that Joseph lives on what once was Avril land, and his answer was uncharacteristically evasive. "Just an old water-under-the-bridge deal between his father and me." But Sam's never seen Joseph's father, and has seen his mother on a handful of occasions. She has the lamentable countenance of a beauty gone to seed, her face often swollen from drink, her eyes losing their color, her mouth gone slack. Nevertheless, her beauty shines through now and then, like a painting beneath a painting, or a masterpiece badly restored. She's in and out of work and often on the move. She bounces between Pine Ridge, Wilma, Elk Point, the Black Hills, and here, although Joseph says she lived in Denver for a long time. For the past six months she's had a job at the Lakota Health Center in Wilma as a part-time typist.

Besides handing over that shack to Joseph, Gaetan arranged a job for him at Eagle Reach. "Your garden-variety white supremacists are all on the membership committee, but the personnel committee takes a more practical view of things. Besides, they only pay the boy minimum wages and he does the work of three. Plus, I started him out as a caddy, and he was the best I ever had. Strong, quiet, polite, never made noise or moved a muscle when somebody was bent over a putt. And you couldn't hit a drive where he couldn't find it, so you never lost your four-buck balls in his company."

"So what happened?"

"Hard to say. He knew the course inside and out, where the ground was hard and the ball would get a big bounce, which green would hold, and he could line up putts better than the club champ. But he made people uneasy, somehow. He looked them in the eye and they always looked away first. Put them off their game. So they put him to work as a groundskeeper and maybe that's for the best. At least the fairways don't burn out by the middle of July like they used to."

Sam's only other regular company is his father. There isn't much that they can talk about without lighting old fuses but Sam's begun to look forward to his visits, if only for the opportunity to observe his father's uneasiness in the sullen presence of his son. He wants to talk about the past, which Sam wants to burn to its foundation just like Grandfather's old house. Gaetan pours himself a tumbler of vodka while Sam fishes the rolling papers from his shirt pocket. Gaetan likes to point out that smoking pot is old-hat. His own invitation to lethargy is a vodka martini with a trio of olives. He meant to run with the wolves, he once said, and ended up jogging with the raccoons. All the same, he says, he's tried to have a little fun, even if it seemed like a feverish samba, whereas Sam's life has taken on all the sadness of a somnolent waltz in a hotel hallway. "There's a shotgun shell with your name on it, Sam. Unless you climb out of this hole you fell into, you'll be propping the barrel between your knees and wrapping your lips around the business end." Sam answered that he didn't have a shotgun and wasn't in any hurry to meet his maker. Gaetan drained his vodka and watched closely while Sam's fingers stiffened and curled and rolled a perfect joint.

When the sun is finally down, he's feeling hungry for the first time all day but unable to get up from his chair. It must be nine o'clock because the news is on, and despite the clouds in his head he hears *Sioux Falls* and *prison* and the name of a man that his father seldom shuts up about. They mention the war they fought when Sam was just a boy that never made the history books. Ninety-one degrees and humidity at forty-five percent.

He decides it's only right to take the news to his father. News like the olives he will drop, one two three, into his clear glass. He takes a long time to rise from his chair, as if his legs were drained of blood and muscle all at once. He fetches his car keys from the kitchen table, climbs behind the wheel of his Renault 5, and starts the engine. The dog comes running from the porch and at last he remembers that he hasn't fed her, so gets out of the car, returns to the house, and scrapes some meat from a tin can into her bowl.

At Eagle Reach, the first person he sees is Ted Roebuck, Albert's grandson, whose eyes take a disparaging inventory of him in the space of seconds. "So? Big night on the town, Sam?"

He's wearing jeans with a hole in the right knee and a shirt that he slept in last night.

"Just another lazy August evening, Ted."

"Found yourself a job yet?"

"Yes and no."

Ted gave up a promising law practice to become county commissioner and is rumored to be on the fast track for a job in Pierre. After that, he's let it be known, he's got serious plans to run for attorney general and it doesn't hurt that his mentor is former governor Bull Smedsrud. If this were Bolivia, Sam figures, he'd probably be an up-and-coming colonel. "Still and all, you'd think you might be able to spring for a necktie."

"There's no dress code here, Ted. It's a democratic bar, despite the dues."

"We'll take that up at the next steering committee meeting."

"You know, Ted, I once read that the study of law sharpens minds by narrowing them."

Ted swirls the ice in his drink like dice and doesn't take his eyes off Sam. "Your father's in the Elk Room with a queen of spades stuck up his right sleeve."

Sam orders a lemonade and ducks his head into the dining room, twenty round tables set for six or eight. Candles and condiments clutter the center spaces. The hostess, Irene, heads his way with a menu in her hand. "You want a singleton?"

"Petra working tonight?"

"No, she's on vacation."

"I'll pass."

"Her being gone won't spoil the food."

"I guess I'll just grab a burger in the grill."

Sam wanders down a hallway lined with golf plaques and photographs. He pauses in front of a trophy case and can see his reflection in the glass. Wide forehead, honest nose, generous lips, abundant brown hair. He'd be handsome if it weren't for his beady eyes and weak chin. With a pair of picture-postcard parents, he thought he would've turned out at least comely.

An elderly man whose name escapes him steps out of the locker room. "Evening, Samuel. Looking for your old man?"

"No, just out for a bite to eat."

"You'll find him in the Elk Room."

"That's what I hear."

"You tell him for me his time is up."

"What might that signify?"

"You just tell him."

On second thought, Sam doesn't want a burger, or the chicken or ribs or shrimp. What he meant in coming here was to sit at a table and smell Petra Andriessen's skin and perfume when she bent to fill his water glass or clear his plate. In his stoned state he is greatly relieved to have put his finger on what it is he wants, however unattainable that may be.

The wood-paneled walls of the Elk Room are lined with more plaques, deer and antelope antlers, an enormous painting of duck hunters aiming at the skies, and on a wall near the largest of four felt-topped tables, the immense head of an elk. His father is seated at his usual spot just below the elk, in a circle of four men roughly his own age. He is a head taller than any of them and his looks are still of the drop-dead variety that makes other men ill at ease. Sam observes in the first instant that his stack of chips seems slightly higher, and his martini glass is full to the brim.

He raises his eyes from his cards. "Son. You're just in time for the bloodletting."

Sam crosses the room and stands at his shoulder while his card partners nod in his direction.

"Albert," he says. "Jimmy, Calvin, Stuart." The saying of names counts as greetings in these parts.

His father is holding fool's gold, a jack of clubs, nine of diamonds, and three cards that don't add up to ten. They're playing five-dollar ante, single draw, a game Gaetan thinks he invented, and he tosses thirty dollars after his ante, asking for one card.

Calvin whistles. "Too steep for me." Stuart folds as well, leaving only Albert and Jimmy to call. Stuart deals two to Albert and three to Jimmy who pays the customary five bucks for that extra card. Gaetan barely glances at the card tossed his way but Sam can see it's a dead-end six of clubs.

"A straight fill," Stuart mutters.

"Or a flush."

"Two pair looking for full."

The others play with their cards fanned out in front of their faces, while his father holds his in a closed pack.

"To you, Gaetan."

He takes a long swallow from his martini, sets the glass off to the side of his chips, and puts fifty more in the pot. "The limit."

Albert eyes him dolefully. "You have a way of taking the fun out of this game, Gaetan."

"You can always sell another used car with a slippery odometer."

"That's slander, old friend."

"No friends at this table, Albert."

Sam has always figured that you'd have to have a screw loose to sit down to cards with Gaetan Avril. A cardplayer's best friend is a general disregard for money and if these ferndockers had half an idea of how little his father cares for the stuff, they'd pack up their chips and head home to watch color television with their wives.

Albert throws in his cards and, after taking thirty seconds to think it over, Jimmy does the same. Gaetan has just won eighty dollars for no apparent reason.

This isn't the moment to give him the news. What Sam heard on the radio would be of interest to all of them, no doubt, but it's his father he's come for. He watches another half dozen hands, admiring the way his old man, even in losing, keeps the tension at the level of gritted teeth. *No friends at this table, Albert.* You'd think they would've listened to him.

Sam says he'll be heading out and there is the same nodding of heads as when he arrived. He turns at the doorway and his father looks up, his eyebrows raised.

Sam's already in the parking lot when Gaetan calls after him, "I got the feeling you wanted to talk."

"The news on the radio. They say he's been released from prison."

Gaetan merely smiles. Sam thought his face would be like Christmas. "That's fine. Fine. Now you can meet him, Sam. We'll have him over and you two can sit down and talk."

This has been his father's theme this summer while waiting for news from the prison, that he should meet this man, though Sam doesn't for the life of him know why it's so important.

"Anything else?" Gaetan asks.

"About that dinner invitation. I don't think I can make it."

"We could make it Friday night if you've got other plans."

When he can't come up with an answer to that, his father says, "Listen, Sam. You won't believe this woman. She's a little on the hefty side but has a face on her as sweet as sunrise. You could take her out jogging and trim her up a bit. She's well-educated without being a pain in the ass about it—and even if she is a little older, what's five or six years? Give it some thought."

"I ran into a man in the club," Sam says. "He says to tell you your time is up."

"What man?"

"Don't remember his name. Skinny old guy with red pants and a turkey neck."

"Jack LeHavre. He's chairman of the membership committee. Hoo boy."

They can't kick his father out of the country club. The by-laws state that anyone with the right chunk of change can pony up and, anyway, Gaetan was one of the founders. There are rules about not going bare-chested on the fairways or pissing in the pool, but even those would have to be clearly transgressed for the membership committee to take action. It's been fifteen years since Gaetan gave his land to the Oglala families and for fifteen years he's been a straight-arrow member. He plays a lot of lonesome golf but laughs and says he can get in eighteen holes in half the time.

"Anyway, Sam, you changed the subject."

In his mind, Sam flips a coin and calls it wrong. "Do I have to wear a tie?"

His father's laughter is sudden and loud. "We're not much, Sam, but we *are* father and son. Maybe we ought to go riding one of these days."

"I never much liked horses."

"Then just drop by and we'll fry up some perch, drink from the can, and tell some Indian jokes."

Sam rolls his eyes and lets his breath out very slowly.

"Thursday night, then? Seven or thereabouts?"

"Just don't expect any fireworks, okay?"

"Well, Sam, you just may surprise yourself."

A few nights later, while his father fixes cocktails and serves them around, Evelyn from St. Louis sits close to Sam, smelling of rose petals and, faintly, cinnamon. When he can look without being noticed, he sees a face unable to mask constant surprise, a slight frame carrying twenty or thirty pounds too many, and round breasts that suggest a steady diet of corn and beer. In his lonesome and itching state, she would make a lovely mattress, and it would be pleasant to feel her breathy voice at his ear. But the solution to his desperation will not be somebody his father dragged him over to meet, no matter how enticing she may be.

There are seven of them there in all: Evelyn, Jack Simms, Noah Lame, Frank and Judy Poor Bull, and the Avrils, father and son. Simms is a trendy mystery writer on his way back from New York to his house outside Santa Fe. This is his annual visit, and the distant politeness with which he and Sam once treated each other has, through the years, slowly disintegrated into tolerance at best. His novels have few adjectives and no adverbs whatsoever, short tight sentences and dialogue as dry as the Mojave.

They are gathered on the back patio that looks out on a ruined garden. When his mother came back from Denver after staying away for close to three years, she tended three quarters of an acre in the English fashion, scattering seeds and tubers and bulbs in a fairly haphazard manner and letting the plants mingle and meld willy-nilly. There were onions, carrots, squash, pumpkins, frost-resistant ivies, cauliflower, strawberries, sweet potatoes, beets, radishes, tomatoes, and various berry-yielding shrubs amid a few cottonwoods and leaning elms. From year to year she harvested only sporadically. Or she would invite children into the garden in August or September, hand them lattice baskets and tell them to take whatever they wanted. At the end of each season the ground was a riot of rotting fruits and vegetables and in the spring, when the snows melted, that same ground would be black and matted with loam. She was married to a leper, a man who played golf alone, who drank alone. She shared his exile and her lifelong friendships withered like the leaves of a diseased elm. And when she felt a lump like a large seed below her left breast, she told no one. Untended, the cancer branched and flowered, like her wild garden, where they found her one fall morning, choking and weeping beneath a bronze sun.

He discovers Evelyn at his elbow, offering him a glass. "I was just passing through on my way to visit a friend in Toronto. Your father invited me ages ago, so this summer I decided why not." She holds her Tom Collins with both hands, like a chalice. "It's a fascinating place."

Sam nods. "Land of Infinite Variety, according to the tourist bureau."

"Variety?" Jack Simms snorts. "All I ever see here are cornfields and grasslands."

"West of here," Sam tells him. "That's where you'll find it all. Wind Cave, the Badlands, the Black Hills."

"Since when do you give a damn about South Dakota?" his father asks.

"Since lately."

"Bull. First chance you get, you'll be in L.A. or Philly or some such place where you can't park a car without slapping for your wallet."

Sam does a slow burn that is only slightly cooled by the whisky his father insisted he take. Evelyn touches his elbow and winks at him, though he's damned if he can figure out what secret they're sharing.

Gaetan has roasted venison on an outdoor spit. "Frozen since last winter," he explains as he carves. "George Boy Kemper got it with a bow and arrow out in the hills west of Breakneck Point and brought me half the carcass."

He has already uncorked three bottles of Spanish red wine. "It's a coarse wine," he announces, "not that silky business Jack favors. Brings out the taste of the meat without inspiring the gaminess."

Noah Lame just stares at his glass.

"Maybe you heard about Reese Lonetree," Frank Poor Bull says to Gaetan.

"Heard what?"

"Who's Reese Lonetree?" Sam asks, and immediately regrets it.

But his father spares him the usual withering glare. "Reservation council leader years ago. A real sonofabitch. What about him, Frank?"

"Heart attack. News says he's on his deathbed in some Sioux Falls hospital."

"That can't be right, Frank. Lonetree never even had a heart. Anyway, I suppose this means his son'll just step right into his shoes."

"The tribal council will vote tomorrow," Judy says.

"Young Lonetree had a mean streak a mile long," Noah says. "One of the top goons of our time."

"What's a goon?" Jack Simms asks.

"Guardians of the Oglala Nation," Frank answers.

"There's a joke in there," Gaetan adds, "like when the police said that 'pigs' stood for pride, integrity, guts, and service."

Evelyn looks blank. "I'm afraid I don't follow."

"Goons were BIA thugs," Poor Bull explains. "Indian police who used to prey on anybody who kicked up a fuss about reservation conditions. Or crossed their drunken path."

"That wasn't always the case," Noah says. "There was good and bad on that side of the fence. Sometimes it's just not easy to tell who's who. Look at Jerry Lonetree. Twenty years ago, he was one of the bigger goons around. Now he lives in Choteau and runs a filling station and there are no hard feelings."

"Nobody's forgot what he did," says Poor Bull. "But we forget about hating him like we used to."

"I guess I should know about these things," Evelyn says.

"No," Gaetan tells her. "There are some things you don't need to know."

There is a moment of silence as they start in on the venison. Gaetan might be great at cards, but the meat is overcooked and dry on Sam's tongue.

Evelyn suddenly looks up. "Actually, I used to work as a museum aide, so I do know a little about Indians. I was cataloguing, mostly. Indian artifacts."

"What kind of artifacts?" Noah asks.

"Pottery, beads, cooking utensils, religious objects."

"Any bones?" The old man gives her a hard glance, but she's looking at Sam's father and misses it.

"Yes, bones too. Kiowa, Wichita, Pawnee."

Gaetan coughs, then glances across the table at Noah.

Frank says, "No Norwegians or French?"

"No." Then Evelyn says, "I'm afraid there's something I haven't understood. Once again."

Gaetan stands and begins to pour more wine all around. "Jack," he says, "you still plan on driving over to Sioux City to check out that mare?"

"First thing in the morning. No, tomorrow's Friday. That'll be Saturday morning, if you can stand me here that long."

"If you can drink this wine without making nasty cracks about sediment and sulphur, you've got a bed as long as you want."

"I was thinking of heading west to see the Crazy Horse Monument."

When Sam's mother was away in Denver, his father took him on a vacation to the Black Hills. But when they got south of Rushmore the road was closed because the Indians were staging a protest over the blasting of a mountain into the image of Crazy Horse. Sam didn't understand why and Gaetan said, "The Black Hills are sacred to the Indians, Sam. Imagine the conniptions the Catholics would have if somebody carved the Dome of St. Peter's into the likeness of Elvis Presley."

"I'd pass it up if I were you," Gaetan tells Jack.

"Yeah, there ought to be other attractions in the area," Jack says to Evelyn.

She returns his smile with a certain heat in her gaze, and Sam figures he's off the hook.

After the cognac has come out, Jack Simms huddles in a corner of the patio with Evelyn, no doubt telling her about the sensuousness of desert life. Gaetan clears the dishes from the table and then invites Noah Lame and the Poor Bulls into the study. He wants to have a word with them, he says, and tells Sam he's welcome to join them. Instead, Sam wanders toward the far end of the garden. He smells onion, clover, and rotting tomatoes, and in the darkness he stumbles over a half-buried watering can. Prying it loose from the soil with his shoe, he recognizes it immediately and almost shouts out to his father.

It's only a watering can, but it was hers. An artifact. And what would he have said if he'd shouted and Gaetan had come running? His father has an image of him that Sam doesn't much like. When Gaetan's around, Sam keeps a lid on his anger and only shares the odds and ends that seem to have a smirk. His father thinks he's a cold fish. A few years after the cancer took his mother, Sam found his father brooding over it one evening, still missing her terribly. Sam suggested that he lighten up and his father replied, "*You* probably think heartache is a medical term."

At the far end of the garden is Blue Eye Creek, which in August is a thin bed of mud and slimy water that drains into the Missouri at a spot between Sam's house and Joseph's. When Sam was a child, he often followed the creek north as far as he could, looking for the source. But no matter how closely he hugged the shore, or even when he walked in the creek itself, he kept coming to a spot where the weeds and brush were too thick to push through. He had to climb up a low bank and no matter how carefully he circled that brushy area, he could never pick up the creek bed. It simply vanished.

He sits down next to the creek and digs in his shirt pocket for a joint he's been saving all night. The sweet smell of burning leaf fills his nostrils and he looks upward and studies the stars. On the other side of the creek, beyond his mother's grave, is a field of sunflowers at least six feet high. They bow to the least wind and in the darkness the field seems to be a living thing, a crowd of waving heads and hands, whispering, rustling. He finishes the joint and drops the last ash into the creek bed.

There are footsteps behind him and he is surprised to see his father crossing the tangled garden. He carries a cognac snifter in each hand and gives one to Sam before taking a seat on the ground next to him. "Jack and Evelyn have taken up residence in your old bedroom. I guess I was barking up the wrong tree."

"No problem," Sam says. "Strange dinner party, though."

"I wanted to mix it up a bit. You know, to take the pressure off you and Evelyn. Anyway, I wanted to see what the Choteau folks thought about Tyrone getting out of prison."

"What's all this business about bones?"

"History, Sam. Of a place that *I* call home. You know how much your granddad paid for that field out there?"

"Twenty-four dollars in beads and baubles?"

"Don't you ever quit? He paid thirty-six bucks for forty acres to a family of drunks name of Walking Horse. Thirty-six dollars in 1934 was worth about what, eight hundred today? Four months later there was another family knocking on his door and he got another fifty acres for about the same price."

"Am I supposed to feel guilty about this?"

"I always wished you'd take some interest."

He'd like to tell his father about the watering can but the old man's on his high horse again, going on about how *his* father was a land grabber. They haven't spoken of Sam's mother in years. Whenever the talk is of family, Gaetan always comes back to his father.

"We've been through this," Sam tells him.

"You did ask about the bones."

"I was just making polite conversation."

"Ever wonder why I won't hit off the regular tee at fourteen?"

Sam can't listen to any more of this. The Indians, the land, the ancient treacheries. He stands and his father follows him back across the garden and out to his car. When Sam's sitting behind the wheel, he taps on the hood and leans down to look in the window. His eyes are as sad as Sam's seen them in years.

"I love you, Sam, but the question remains: Don't we have anything in common?"

"Sure. We're both sons of a man named Gaetan."

Gaetan Avril

Pheasants, I was taught, take flight only when the ground cover is exhausted. They have to be flushed, as if they know instinctively that the sky's more dangerous than the earth.

But I can't flush out my own son, who can find endless cover. He doesn't listen to anything but what the wind tells him, which doesn't make him a nature lover. All he has to talk to in this world is Joseph, his dog, or me—and he doesn't say word one to me unless I start shouting at him first. Our conversations tend to be brutal and brief.

I suppose it's what comes from smoking weed on a daily basis. Loco weed, we used to call it, though when I was a boy you didn't see much of it around. Word was the Indians smoked it, but that turned out to be peyote, another pipeful entirely. I know it's shameful the way I keep sneaking up on my own son, but he leaves me no choice. I have to talk to him and he needs for me to talk to him. Nobody else does. And it isn't only family history I keep barking in his ear, it's *my* history. Even so, he has a way of shrugging me off, and in no time we're down to arguing about who washed the dishes last. I want to tell him the truth about his granddad and Tyrone, but more than that I want him to know that I missed his mother as he did and why I sent him off to that boarding school. He doesn't offer much in the way of a fight, though. Some sons would trade their stash to hear about their family's secrets. But Sam's holding a grudge that dates back to when his mother and I agreed to split up for a time.

He stopped by the other night to borrow some books and I laid it on him like in a fistfight, all at once. "Now that he's out of prison, I expect he'll be living in his old house."

"Fine, sure," Sam said. "Where's the Henry Miller?"

"You know he shot an Indian dead?"

Sam just ran his fingers over books on the top shelf.

"And the bullet caught Delores Her Many Horses while she was still carrying Joseph."

This stopped him cold for a moment. "I've seen the wound," he said. "Joseph said it was a birthmark." Then he grabbed half a dozen books and a six-pack just like that.

I followed him out the door to his car. "Come with me, Sam. I'll take you to meet him."

He smiled. "More local history to convince me to stick around?"

He drove away before I could cave in the windshield with my fist.

The nights are long when it's hot like this and every evening since Tyrone got out of the joint I get into my car and I drive as slow as I can on all the dirt roads between here and Wilma. Sometimes I tune in a ballgame on the radio if it's not too late and I take nips from a bottle I keep in the glove compartment. By midnight, I usually feel as if the pressure's off and I always go by Tyrone's place. He hasn't come back, though I was certain he would. The house is as dark as it's ever been and I remind myself to get a yard man out there to clear away the weeds and the debris. For years I kept the place up, but between the police and the Choteau people and finally the high school kids, it's pretty much a total wreck. I've asked around plenty and find I'm the only one who thinks he'll have the courage to come back and that's hard to think about for longer than a minute or two. So each night I end up driving home and looking at the books on my night table, wondering why I can't read them.

To pass the time, I've set up a putting carpet on the back patio and can build slopes by laying towels underneath. It's that Astroturf shit but close enough to the real thing. The object is to putt until I drain five in a row from fifteen feet. If I'm sober, it takes about an hour. It's a stupid game, golf. Superficially, that is. I've been playing it long enough to know. But any game looks stupid, broken down to its nuts and bolts—tag, baseball, bowling, darts. I used to hunt pheasants, then I realized how easy a pheasant is. You don't even have to aim, really, just lift the bore in the general direction of a slow-flying bird and pull the trigger to watch the feathers fly.

I prefer to play early in the morning, while the fairways are still damp from the sprinklers and the greens are slower and more for-giving. Golf is the only game I know in which it's me against myself and may the better man win. That's why I like to play alone. So it was something of a surprise when I got snookered into a threesome with Albert Roebuck and his grandson, Ted. They showed up at the first tee at nine a.m. on a workday and tried to make out like meeting me was pure chance. Albert suggested a best-ball tourney, them against me, for ten bucks a stroke. Taking Albert's money is a habit with me, so I knew something other than the pleasures of the links awaited me.

Albert was never very good and Ted always seemed to hit the wrong club. I was forty dollars up at the turn and then, just to rattle me, Albert mentioned that he'd heard Tyrone had been released from the pen and was headed this way.

"It didn't make the papers as far as I know," is all I said.

Ted said, "Well, I've got friends up in Pierre who keep me abreast of things."

"What's it to you, Ted? You're Sam's age, so that means you were about eight when the shit hit the fan. Now if you don't mind, I'd like to hit this drive."

And damn, I clunked the sucker all of one hundred feet down the right side. Everybody knows you keep your eye on the ball. Wild Bill Hickok would've been a terrible golfer, having to watch his back like he did. Still, after a big three-wood and a wedge, I had a downhill thirty-footer to save par. I'd lined it up and got into my crouch when Ted said, "Wasn't he one of those Indian activists, AIM or something?"

I like to win, to see the look on a fool's face when he has to peel money from his wallet like it's his own daughter's pink skin, so I never bet with anybody who has my sympathy. I held my breath for a moment and then let it out easily and put a good roll on it. The putt looked short all the way, but the greens were drying out and the ball paused on the lip and dropped in.

At fourteen I lost a stroke because I always refuse to hit off the men's tee. I've been hitting off the side of the tee as my *second* stroke for close to twenty years and nobody even bothers to laugh anymore. The Roebucks were still out forty for the match, and coming up to the green Ted said it would be a real shame if Tyrone Little had it in his head to come back to Choteau.

"Why's that, Ted?"

"Pulse of the public, Gaetan. That's my business, you understand."

"And what's this pulse saying, Ted?"

"They don't want any AIM people homesteading around here."

"AIM's finished, Ted, has been for years. Don't you ever read the papers?"

I took a bogey on fourteen and the shitheels earned twenty back. I quit talking to them after that. On the tee at fifteen, Albert gave me a short stare that I knew was coming. Fifteen and sixteen are uninteresting par-threes, a fact that still ticks people off. Back in 1971, the layout called for par-fours to bring the course up to a regulation seventy-two. But my lawyers beat their lawyers and those three acres adjoining the creek were stripped from the club and given back to me. I sat on that land for fourteen years and then turned it over to Joseph Her Many Horses. In the meantime, they had to settle on these dinky par-threes that screw up the rhythm of the course for everyone but me.

As we made our approach shots on eighteen, Ted gave me his version of the Roebuck look. "There's a rumor floating around the office, something about a marijuana crop down by the river. Kind of camouflaged, growing between rows of corn."

"Hell, Ted, I gave up farming years ago."

"Well, maybe Sam still suffers from a love of the land."

I was holding my five-iron and could have done some serious damage if I had a temper. "Speak up, Ted. Blackmail's nothing to be shy about."

"We'd like you to say a few words to this man Little. As a way of calming jittery nerves."

"Who's he making so nervous?"

"I don't think we need to mention names."

Albert Roebuck hitched up his pants and hit a three-iron shot that didn't clear a hundred yards.

I borrowed a tractor from George Boy Kemper and drove it out from under the shed and into the moonlight. It was a fifteen-minute ride down the river road, and when Sam's place came into view I swung left into the small field north of the house. There were four rows of sweet corn that stretched for fifty yards north to south and I aimed the tractor so the tires were perfectly aligned with the pot plants growing in the ruts between those rows. It had been years since I'd ridden a tractor and I was so taken with the noise of the engine that I forgot to switch on the little headlight. I was also shitfaced, so my driving left a lot to be desired. I'd just finished the first row and turned around to start in on the second when Sam came up the road. He was stark naked and I expected him to throw a fit, but he just stood there and watched while I finished turning his inventory to straw.

I cut off the engine and climbed down. Sam had put on a pair of jeans and was waiting for me on the porch. I bounded up the steps, still feeling the tremor of that tractor in my butt and legs. To my astonishment, Sam had whipped up a vodka and ice in a Mason jar and he handed it over while I studied the weird smile on his face.

"I had a visit from the sheriff this afternoon," he said.

"I'm not surprised."

"He had the impression I was a friend of your buddy Tyrone."

"So of course you told him you never met the man."

Sam nodded. "He kept grinning and was staring at the corn. I guess you got wind of the same suspicions."

I drank my vodka and tasted too much melted ice. "What I'd like to know is how you irrigated this dumb-ass little plantation."

River on the south. To the east, the Little Sky family had a number of acres wedged between the river, Blue Eye Creek, and our property. They farmed a small part and leased the rest to my father at prevailing rates. Although he'd made them a number of cash offers for full title, they'd been holding out for years. Half of that leased land relied on water from Blue Eye Creek, so my father's idea of damming the flow was going to do as much harm to his own income as theirs. Still, it was no surprise when the Little Skys kicked up a fuss, and one night my father decided it was time to have a talk with them just to set the matter straight.

We drove out together, father and son, to the south side of a long slope that led down the creek. There were a half dozen shabby gray shacks, a clapboard house, and some rusting machinery in a weedy yard. Not far from where my father parked was a lean-to for firewood, though there were only a few logs and sticks. "Look at that," my father said. "October already and you'd think they'd be laying wood in for winter."

An Indian I'd never seen before was in the farmyard when we pulled in. Though the evening was cold and a stiff wind was blowing from the northwest, he was wearing only a shirt with half the buttons undone and it looked like his pants were halfway down. He stopped and stared at the truck for a while and then wandered off behind the house.

I waited in the truck while my father went inside. It was just past sundown and the winds began to gust, lifting dry soil and dead leaves the air. I rolled up the window and watched two dogs chase the kens in the yard. The Indian we'd seen came back from behind house and stood a few yards away. He was carrying a beer bottle began to stumble in my direction. I wanted to lock the doors but s too scared to move. He came up close and leaned against the hood. I couldn't take my eyes off him. There were scabs on his face and his eyes were dead pools of milk with tiny red pupils. His front teeth jutted out and his jaw was slightly askew, as though it had been broken and badly set. He peered into the truck but couldn't fix his eyes on me. His body sagged and he slumped there, against the hood. The windshield and a foot or two is all that separated us, and I sat there still as a stone and studied the mystery of that godawful face.

Some minutes later, my father came out of the house and ran straight for the truck. He shouted something I couldn't hear through

"Simple engineering," he answered. "A slight diversion from the creek."

"You dammed it up?" I was hot all over again. "Goddammit, Sam, I told you about that creek!"

Half-crocked, I stumbled back through the cornfield, Sam dogging my heels, and after a hundred angry strides I came to where he'd stacked logs and mud so the creek formed a small pool. There were some stones laid across one side and all he had to do was pull them away to flood the corn rows. I'd just started lifting away the mud and logs when a pale spot of white downstream caught my eye. The moon was full and in the bleached light I saw what looked like silver just beneath the trickle.

"What might that be?" I asked him.

"You're the expert on this property."

I stepped into the water which didn't come to my shoe tops and bent down. What I saw was a human skull. "Sam, go get your shovel."

"Don't have one."

"A hoe, then. Don't argue with me."

While he was gone, I dug my fingers into the creek bed and moved the mud away. The water cleaned that skull until it fairly glowed in the moonlight. I had extracted the top of the skull and was just getting to the rib cage when Sam came back with a hand spade. "Best I could do," he said, a surprising tone of apology in his voice.

"Close off that trickle," I told him. "This water's making a mess of things."

He bent and shut the runoff with two large stones. Within minutes, the water ceased to flow and I found it easier to peel the mud away from the bones. The skeleton was bent at the waist and the legs emerged almost by themselves. "Shouldn't we call somebody?" Sam asked.

"Like the sheriff?"

A dead man on my property. Rather, Sam's property, since I'd deeded him these acres whether he gave a shit or not.

When the bones were finally free of the mud, I told Sam to let out some water to wash away the mud and leaves. He pulled away a log and water ran down over those bones while I held them in my arms. "That's enough, son."

He replaced the log and I set the bones back down. Five-eight, five-ten, it was hard to tell with that body bent like that. Two of the ribs were broken and the pelvis was badly cracked.

"What have we got here?" Sam asked. "Some lonesome pioneer? Maybe Crazy Horse?"

"Shut up." I sat down into the mud and just stared. There isn't much identifiable about ribs and pelvic bones, and most skulls are fairly anonymous to the untrained eye. But I knew who it was. There was no mistaking the neat hole at the top of the forehead.

Sam came to sit with me and there were the three of us, Sam, me, and the bones, resting on the muddy bank. "So who do you think it was?" he asked softly.

"Just a man I watched bleed to death."

I was eleven years old when my father dammed up Blue Eye Creek. He said he needed a watering pool for his livestock and planned on siphoning off some of the flow to irrigate a new field for alfalfa. If you check the records, no one was paying diddly squat for alfalfa in those years, which only compounds his guilt.

Water is money and without it, the land loses its luster in a hurry. And in South Dakota, counting on rainfall is like betting on acts of God and we know by now that the god who does or doesn't give rain is a touch perverse. Watching the So Dak sky in August isn't so much a religious rite as an economic one. When the clouds burst, you can almost hear the cash registers filling up. And when there are no clouds at all, you can hear the wind sucking the juice from both the corn and the checking accounts.

On and around our land, we had a number of water sources: the Missouri, Blue Eye Creek, and a slough that was mostly fed by rainfall or snowmelt. Four separate wells had been dug, though only two of them yielded much water. Compared to farmers to the north and even more arid west, we were water-rich even before the dams turned the Missouri into a faucet the Army Corps of Engineers could switch on whenever they wanted. But creek flow was another matter, and if a creek ran through your land and you decided to drain all of it into your own fields, there wasn't much your downstream neighbors could do about it. Blue Eye Creek was our east border at the time and was supposed to be shared. It didn't belong to any one person.

In 1943, all but a fraction of the Averill land bordered the Missouri

She quit the bridge club and returned all the library books. Fall winds shook the last crabapples from the trees and the pickup sat idle in the garage. There were long days to be filled and for a time she measured out the morning hours with drink and her afternoon lasted until dinnertime. If my father was away on business, the home would be dark when I'd come home from school. Cold chicken or ham on a plate was waiting for me in the icebox. In my bedroom, the next day's clothes were already laid out for me. When she was sober I was her little man. When she'd been drinking I might as well have been an orphan.

A week or so after we'd been to see the Little Skys, my father went up to Sioux Falls on an overnight trip. That evening, I found my mother sitting on the floor in front of the fireplace. A fat log was smoldering but wouldn't ignite, and coming closer, I could see wadded papers and a number of photographs burning in the grate.

"I don't understand it," she said.

"What?"

"The fire. Can you read it?"

I shivered.

"There are words in there," she continued. "In the flames. I can almost make them out."

The next morning, she drove into Wilma and made her confession at Sacred Heart. I have never confessed, so I don't know the particulars. All she told me when she came home was that she'd had a long talk with the priest and as part of her penance she'd be helping out at the Indian clinic. "I was a nursing student when I met your father. Did you know that, Gaetan? I was only four months short of my certificate."

I didn't know what happened to her. She took to the Indians even more than she'd taken to booze and I saw even less of her. In the daytime she worked at the clinic and at night she studied nursing books that she'd ordered through the mail. A full bottle of crème de menthe rested on her night table, within easy reach, but the seal was never broken.

Soon she was spending more time than my father liked over at the reservation. She was from back East and he'd assumed she would give more care to the setting of a table—the china alone cost him as much as three new acres—than to this half-assed attempt to play nurse for people who preferred to stay drunk and eat dog meat.

The first serious fight between my parents was touched off when my mother tried to rope in some other white women to donate old clothing. "Leroy Little Sky has opened a shelter and a food and clothing salvage. He asked me to help out."

"Our very neighbors," he said. "If you want to be a do-gooder in private, Louise, I won't stand in your way. But to make this a public deal . . . and with Leroy Little Sky of all people. Next thing," he said, "they'll be calling us all Indian lovers."

"I don't see any harm in that."

"Twelve years you've been living here and you haven't figured anything out?" My father shook his head.

"And I would appreciate it, Gaetan, if you'd remove the sign from the front road."

We had one of those signs that were common at the time: "No Dogs or Indians Allowed."

"Louise," he said, "don't press me on this. If you do, we're just gonna go round and round."

In late October of 1944, Dennis Little Sky drank a river of cheap wine and then walked two miles through the snow with a shotgun in hand. His first shot shattered the picture window in the living room and his second splintered the front door. My mother came rushing into my room and threw her body over mine. We could hear my father talking on the telephone to the sheriff in Wilma, telling him to make like lightning. My mother told me to get on the floor and stay there, then she straightened her nightdress and marched down the stairs.

"Dennis, you put that gun down and get yourself home!"

I got up and inched toward the window. The Indian was standing twenty yards from the front door, glaring at the house, and my mother shouted at him again to leave. I couldn't see her, but then I heard a gunshot and could see my father run off the front porch and fire twice into the air. My mother was holding him by the arms while he screamed at her to let him go. When I looked again, the Indian had vanished.

That same night, when the sheriff went out to arrest Dennis, his brother Leroy stepped forward and said he was the one who'd done the shooting. This confession only implicated him as well as his brother. My father testified it was Dennis he'd seen outside our house. When the courts offered Leroy as a bonus, he didn't argue. In court, my mother claimed she was upstairs the whole time with me and hadn't seen anyone. Leroy was sentenced to six months and Dennis a year for destruction of property and illegal use of a firearm, and the Little Sky family was instructed to pay for the window and wrecked door.

A few days later we found that the dam had been dismantled and Blue Eye Creek was flowing again. "Maybe we jailed the wrong Indians," my father said. He hired three men to build a new dam, this time using concrete. It was finished in a week and then winter came and the stream was frozen over.

For weeks on end, I didn't see any liquor in the house except for what was in my father's bar for visitors. All the same, my mother started hiding from me again as she had when she was drinking. My meals were waiting for me when I came home at night, and some evenings I found her in the living room with her sewing kit, stitching torn shirts or pants. I had holes in a few of my own clothes but these belonged to someone else. I sometimes caught her looking at me and when our eyes met I had the impression she was crying, but I didn't see any tears. She and my father didn't talk much. She'd come in the door at eight at night and my father would ask where she'd been. She'd say at the reservation school or at the Little Sky shelter, but she never offered details, only the name of a place.

One spring night she announced that she'd sold the DeSoto. "It was in my name. I tried to give the money to June Little Sky but she was too afraid of you to take it. Leroy's getting out of jail next week." She laid three hundred dollars on the table. "I plan on turning it over to him."

My father looked at the money and then at me, as if I somehow understood more than he did. Then he looked at the ceiling for a long time and said, "Why on earth, Louise? Why give money to Leroy Little Sky?"

"He's got his sister June to look after. She's only eleven years old. Now that you've stopped up the creek, he'll be needing to dig a new well. That's at least three hundred dollars, according to your own ledgers."

"God, Louise." He sighed. "I sometimes wish you'd go back to the crème de menthe."

She gave him a look that was neither hard nor soft. "That's very loving of you, Gaetan."

"Oh, hell, you know what I mean."

Later that night I heard his car. I got up and went to the window and saw that it was one of those blue clear nights when the stars look wet. The moon was like a penny hanging in the trees and I was squinting at it when I heard my mother's voice.

"I knew you'd be up. We must make it hard for you to sleep nights."

I kept my eyes fixed on that moon and it turned into a dime. "Where do you think he's gone?"

"Into Wilma," she said. "Or else a card game at the bar in Arthur. I never thought it was possible to know everything about someone, but in his case it's the truth." She sat on my bed and gestured for me to sit next to her. I don't know why, but I resisted. We sometimes spurn what we know will do us the most good. We cling to our aches because they lend a sharpness to life that we need even more than comfort.

"I'm not going to turn you against your father," she said. "The truth of what he is will be evident enough for you as time goes by." She looked at her hands as if at something handwritten. Then she said, "I guess this isn't what you expected me to say."

"Are you going away from us?"

She took a deep breath. "You've already guessed? I thought I was going to have to say the words."

For my birthday, my father had given me a lamp with a painted porcelain base in the form of a cowboy swinging a lariat and the lampshade was made of cowhide. The lamp rested on a little table next to my bed and when my mother reached to turn it on, she knocked it over. The lampshade was only bent but the porcelain cowboy had broken into a dozen pieces, an arm here and a chunk of lariat there. My mother was on her knees and her nightdress came open. I was sitting up in bed and could see her breasts as she tried to piece the lamp back together. "A broken cowboy," she said. I didn't know what to do but knew I had to get away, so I turned and ran downstairs onto the front porch. Moments later she was there as well, reaching her arms around from behind me to pull me close. I could feel the heat of her through our thin clothing.

"The hard words, Gaetan. You have to hear them so you won't wonder about me. They start with me telling you I don't belong to him. I'm not your father's anymore. I've read the book of him and closed it for good."

I pulled away from her to avoid her skin. She thought it was because of what she'd said. There was a long silence, and my heart was beating a stampede. I couldn't imagine the end of life as it had been lived up to that night. Father, Mother, me. With Mother in between.

"You can think bad thoughts, but I hope you won't say them to my face."

I was going to answer her. I was going to tell her to go upstairs and get dressed if she wanted to talk to me like that. She hadn't said the hard words I wanted to hear, to admit what I could see pretty plainly in her eyes. I wanted to tell her I could smell the man she was loving. But I didn't say anything and then she was gone. I stood alone on the porch until the cold finally drove me inside and I lay in bed for hours without sleeping. I could hear the dogs, Ace and King, yelping and howling. They had something cornered or treed, a raccoon or maybe just a squirrel, and I was hoping it would get away without being torn to bits.

When I woke up the next morning it was too late to go to school and the house was empty. My father came home at five o'clock and didn't even ask where my mother might be. She was gone for three days and when she came home, she locked herself in her room and would open only to me.

The next few days she went to the reservation early in the morning and returned late at night. Then she was again gone for a week and when she came back to the house her clothes were muddy and her hair was wild. My father sent me to my room and though I listened from the top of the stairs I couldn't hear what they said.

It isn't only the Indians who've been stripped of their past. For the past twenty years, antiques dealers from either coast have been coming out this way and attending the auctions at bankrupt farms. The houses were filled with brass and silver and gold, porcelain and marble antiques, wooden furnishings and knickknacks brought over from Europe and lovingly maintained for three or four generations by Swedes, Norwegians, Irish, and Ukrainians.

Years before the practice was common, my father got into the habit of visiting families that were socked by the Depression and therefore willing to part with fragments of their heritage for very small sums. Our house was furnished in a mishmash of European and Scandinavian styles and the overflow filled half a barn. The bed I'd slept in every night was bought from the Ingersolls in 1937 and was said to have been made in Göteborg. My mother's dresser came from Orléans in France and my father claimed it was close to two hundred years old. Our tableware was made by English silversmiths, and when I was nine I broke a Limoges coffeepot.

But it was my father's private room that held the greatest treasures, so I waited until he'd gone off to his office and my mother was at the reservation. Then I went looking.

It was the room of a man of Dakota means. The rug was brown and rust red with little amber curlicues and green leaves woven into it. One of the walls was covered floor to ceiling with books and another was lined with a wet bar and a massive oil painting of early Dakota settlers that hung over the shelf holding glasses. A huge red leather swivel chair sat behind a high wooden desk with carved scrolls and lines on the drawers. There were six drawers, three on each side. I sat in that chair and felt small and stupid, and I thought it might be best to just stay that way. But I had to find out why my mother was leaving, so I stayed.

There was nothing damning in any of the left-hand drawers, just papers and pens and check stubs. In the top drawer on the other side was his gun. My father had at least eight hunting rifles, one for rabbits, one for deer, some shotguns for pheasant and duck, and a few old-style collector pieces. But the pistol in that drawer, a Colt, is what he called his gun. Everything else was a rifle or a sidearm. It occurred to me right then, or maybe it was much later, that my father was right-handed, so it made sense for the gun to be in a right-hand drawer. It was loaded, so I carefully set it aside and rummaged underneath. There were only some old engineering books and notes and a box full of keys, so I closed that drawer and started through the last two. Nothing.

I spun the chair around so I was facing the window that looked out the front of the house. Thick green curtains had been pulled to either side and the window was open wide to let in the spring air. In the far corner, half hidden by those curtains, was a wooden chest. It was my father's service trunk from when he was in the Corps of Engineers and it was secured by a padlock the size of my fist. I swung the chair back around and got the box of keys, then tried one after another, even those that didn't look right, until the padlock sprung open.

Inside were legal papers and accounting books in my father's hand-writing, a loose scrawl you'd have to be a member of the family to decipher. I didn't read anything carefully that day. There wasn't time. I had two of the large leather binders on the floor in front of me and had just opened the first of them, marked 1927–1932, when I heard a car on the road out front. I put the binder back in the chest as my father's car pulled up to the house. He got out and was standing there, looking off in the distance. I moved closer to the window and could see Leroy Little Sky coming up the path toward the house. My father shouted at him to get off our property, but he didn't stop. He was wearing what must have been his best clothes, though they were still pretty raggedy, just brown pants and a white shirt and a leather vest. I had seen him before. He didn't have a smashed face like his brother's. His skin was smooth and his eyes so brown they were almost black. He was taller than most of the Indians I'd seen and had a way of walking with his back ramrod straight. They were too far away for me to hear what they were saying, but it was obvious my father didn't want Little Sky to get too close.

Little Sky looked tired, as if those months in prison had sapped his strength. While he was speaking, he held both palms upward as though to show that he'd come as a neighbor. My father turned suddenly and walked toward the porch. Little Sky followed him and I could hear the front door open. Footsteps were coming toward the room and there was nowhere to hide except behind the trunk. I nudged it a little farther away from the wall and squatted down, pulling the curtains in front of me.

The door opened and my father walked in with Little Sky right behind him.

"You don't listen, do you?" my father was saying. "I try to give you a fair shake and you send your brother to my house to shoot out the lights. Don't tell me you didn't send him, Leroy. He wouldn't have thought it up by his lonesome." He moved behind his desk and picked up the telephone. "Get me the sheriff's office."

"No," Little Sky said. "No."

My father spoke into the phone, telling the sheriff that he should come out pronto. "I got a trespasser right here in my office." Then he laughed and said, "Sure, I think I can handle this buck." And he hung up the phone.

Little Sky said, "I'm here to ask you to take down that dam."

"We've been through all this."

"We need the water. You know that. I've got six people to feed."

"You've got the land, Leroy. And a few wells, if I remember right."

Little Sky shook his head so hard I thought it must hurt. "The water from those wells isn't enough."

It was a good fifteen minutes from the sheriff's to our house, so my father gave Little Sky a convoluted explication of water rights, property boundaries, and the terms of the lease deal he'd made years before with Leroy's father. Leroy was staring down at my father, his eyes growing darker by the sentence.

My father opened the top right-hand drawer and took out a sheet of paper. "Right here, Little Sky. The contract that says I own water rights to the tune of one hundred percent for Blue Eye Creek anywhere south of the highway. Go on, give it a read."

I couldn't tell if it was genuine or if it was a grain inventory or a letter to the editor of the Wilma *Sentinel*. Whatever it was, Little Sky refused to read it.

My father set the paper on his desk with his left hand. His right hand was resting next to the open drawer.

"Our seed is dried and dead in the ground. You're starving us, Mr. Averill."

"I made you a proper offer. You keep that trashy house of yours and get four thousand dollars cash plus another five hundred for the implements. Considering that your tractor's worn to shit, that's almost charity."

Leroy shook his head. "I can't sell," he said. "The land's forever."

"Damn shame," my father said, glancing at his watch.

Leroy said, "We're going to starve and that's all you've got to say?"

"No," my father said, and there was smoke in his voice. "No, what I wanted to say is I'm not the fool you take me for."

The color left Leroy Little Sky's face. His lips formed the word *why* but he didn't say it aloud.

"Word is, your brother's been acting up in that prison. You know how he gets. I could always put in a good word, though—"

My father didn't finish his sentence. Leroy Little Sky lunged forward and stuck his face over the desk. "Break the dam! Break it! Give back the water!"

"There's also the more personal matter of"—my father raised the gun—"my wife."

The gun went off. The first bullet was a surprise to both of them. The noise of it stopped Little Sky in his tracks and then he reached a hand to his neck. A thin line of blood trickled down on his white shirt, but he was only grazed. I was amazed at his strange smile, the way his lips stretched over his teeth. "Missed," he said.

The next shot hit him in the chest and knocked him backwards. He struggled for his balance, shifting his feet against his weight. He was about to advance again but my father fired once more and Leroy fell backwards and landed on the floor. He lifted his head and for a second I could swear he was looking right at me. Then his head dropped to the carpet. Stepping around the desk, my father stood over him. He held the gun straight downward and pulled the trigger. The bullet hit Leroy Little Sky in the forehead. For a moment both of his legs were twitching and then he was still.

My father looked at the body, still pointing the gun. Satisfied that Little Sky was dead, he opened the chamber and took out the bullets that were left and dropped them in the drawer. Then he put the gun in the drawer and closed it.

I crouched where I was and watched the blood leave Little Sky's body until it covered half the rug. My father sat quietly at his desk and swiveled the chair around to face the window when the sheriff's car pulled in. I tried to slide behind the curtains but he saw me there and froze. I jumped up and started shouting, "I saw you, I saw you shoot him, he's dead!"

My father opened the door. The sheriff walked in with Albert Roebuck and two men I didn't know. All of them had guns. Roebuck looked down at Little Sky. "So, Gaetan, it took you three shots."

My father nodded. "The first one's somewhere in that wall."

At a sign from the sheriff, the other two men hauled the body out of the room. There was a trail of blood, like after a pheasant hunt, all across the floor.

I stepped up to Al Roebuck. "I saw the whole thing. Little Sky didn't have a gun."

Roebuck looked across to my father as if to say what the hell, then he turned to me. Like always, he was wearing a string tie with a silver clasp that had his initials. "You must be mistaken, son," he said. "There's no one here." Then he and the sheriff went outside.

I was slow to understand. Sunlight coursed through the two large windows onto the floor, where the blood was still wet. I turned to my father, who sat down behind his desk and stared back.

The men came back half an hour later. Their sleeves were rolled up and their boots were dirty. I noticed that Roebuck's string tie was loose and the clasp wasn't there anymore. One of the men nodded to my father and they bent and rolled up the rug and carried it out of the house.

So the bastards buried him just below the cement dam my father had built, where the water from Blue Eye Creek should have been flowing into Little Sky's north fields. I blew up that dam twenty years later, and then along came my stoned son to build a new one. And by now all the gravediggers except Roebuck are long dead.

I can smell rain but it doesn't make sense. The sky is as clear as my memory. I know I can't just sit there in the creek mud, but am too juiced and shook up to go anywhere right away. A long time passes while the moon moves through the trees overhead. I sift my fingers through the mud in search of a slug, or Roebuck's tie clasp, but all that happens is I grow filthier by the minute.

When I give it up, I'm surprised to find that Sam hasn't gone home yet. He normally likes his comforts, but for the moment he sits close by me and next thing I know we'll be growing roots.

Then he says something, and I take a while to make sure I heard him right: "Tell me who Tyrone really is."

"The people in Choteau think he's a want-to-be," I say. "But they never were clued in to the truth of the matter."

Sam is silent and I have to look at him to know he's still there. We're both covered in creek mud and in the moonlight he looks like a young boy again.

"I'm not an anthropologist, Dad," he says. "I'm trying to add this up."

"Leroy Little Sky," I tell him, gesturing to the bones at our feet. "He was a friend of your grandmother's."

Delores Her Many Horses

Her 1982 Skylark is parked in the Save Rite supermarket lot across the street from her apartment building. She doesn't have the right to park there and doesn't remember doing so the night before. *Unauthorized vehicles will be towed at owners' expense!* But this time they didn't catch her and she starts the car and pulls out of the back exit to avoid being seen by the checkers near the wide front windows.

The Skylark is the best car she's had in some time, purchased in May with five hundred dollars down and twenty-four installments of fifty-three dollars a month to Sioux Valley Bank. The engine is sound and the rust that had accumulated over eighty-eight thousand miles has been sanded away. She can overlook the hole in the back window and the fact that the heater doesn't work at all. She'd discovered this fact during a cold night in late May while driving home from the Red Rock Lounge. Just turned the temp to Hot and cranked the fan to Max and felt a blast of cold air on her knees. Myron back at the Red Rock took a look the next night and said, "No coil in there." When she'd asked what that meant he said he could make a fortune selling cars to women and Indians. "Didn't anyone ever tell you to never buy a car on a sunny day?"

She drives east out of Wilma on Highway 50 with both front windows rolled down and the wind is hot against her face. The alarm was set for ten o'clock, but she slept past noon and then struggled from the bed and ran a hot bath. Stepping into that water was like stepping into her mother's womb and she fell asleep again. When she awakened, the water was clammy and the soap that she'd lathered on her shoulders had hardened on her skin.

After half an hour of driving she's on the edge of Choteau and can see Helene's trailer on the other side of some trees and a car with no tires. She hasn't been this way since last spring. The town's too lonesome and the only place to get a drink is at Toby's, where the old men still gather to drink and scrape at the rust of ancient grief.

She turns right onto a dirt road that gets worse the farther she goes. The last three hundred yards, it's only a pair of tire paths with tall weeds between them and then it runs out just before the river.

Joseph is waiting in front of the house. He is wearing jeans and is barefoot and when she gets out of the car he grips her hands in his own. Blue flies circle them and she can smell the cattle from George Boy Kemper's pasture.

"The house," Joseph says, and she follows him across the high grass and through the trees.

It's a crackerbox, twenty-two feet by thirty with a sagging front porch, no basement and no attic. The government built hundreds of them in the forties for council Indians who had lost their allotments. The foundation is a slab of cement poured onto the flattened earth, and the house a pine two-by-four frame covered with plywood and sealed with tar paper. Joseph's place has a living room, bathroom, and kitchen, but no bedroom. He doesn't use the kitchen much and the bathroom not at all. Through the year he moves the bed between the window and the fireplace and its placement serves as kind of a calendar. It is August so the bed is by the window. In late September or early October it will be in the middle of the room. By Christmas it will be close to the fire.

The room is neat and ordered, free of dust. There is the bed, a table with two wooden chairs, and a low bookshelf that holds the coffee cans he fills with golf balls. Because he never leaves food to waste, there are few flies to bother them and Delores smells what she takes to be freshly cut cucumbers. Joseph offers her a chair at his small table, then goes into the kitchen. When he returns he is carrying her box. Inside the box is a glass, a bottle of whisky, and a pack of Winstons. He pours out some whisky for her, and then lights the cigarette with a stick match and hands it to her with a smile. He's been doing this for years and it always puts a deep dent in her heart. She takes a puff from the cigarette and finds it dry. A wicker basket of vegetables is on the table and Joseph says she should eat.

"From your garden?" she asks.

"I don't have a garden," he says. "There's a place over by Gaetan's house where everything grows wild. Potatoes, cucumbers, tomatoes, even strawberries."

"Cucumbers don't grow wild, Joseph. Not in this part of the world."

"They do," he says. "They grow. And carrots, onions. More."

When her glass is empty, he looks at the bottle and then at her. She says, "Yes, thank you, just a little."

"You're tired," Joseph tells her.

"No," she says.

"Or hurt."

She has difficulty looking into his eyes. His gaze is so certain, so unflinching. When she looks into the eyes of the people in Choteau, it's like looking at a house about to collapse. She knows she has a talent for making others avert their eyes, but with Joseph it's just the opposite. When she looks at him she's fishing in deep waters.

Joseph tells her he's seen snakes in the river and many shed scales on the banks. This is strange because normally he finds those scales in the spring. "And George Boy Kemper put white paint in the river, which is dumb."

"Is that why you called me? You said you had something to tell me."

When he doesn't answer, she knows he's trying to remember. He has no sense of cause and effect and little understanding of before and after. But he is not the imbecile they said he would be. When he was four or five years old and she was in jail in Denver, Helene would send her his drawings. In one, a high hill was circled by eagles and two of them were carrying a woman off into the sky. In another, a bear and fox had burrowed a tunnel to a space deep in the earth where a woman was tied to a stake. He was rescuing her with crayons and Lakota myth.

Noah Lame is the one who started the talk about Joseph being a holy man. Then Pete Scully and some of the others picked it up. She had come out of prison to find them all casting around for signs and she resented that they were taking his silences and staring for trances. "He's a boy," she would tell them. "A boy like any other, only with thoughts that go up and don't always come back down." But at least they saw him as something special. To the whites he was only a lamebrain who couldn't even write his name without putting the *p* before the *s* or adding letters that looked to him like birds. The *i*, a sparrow; the *g*, a heron.

She chooses a small tomato from the basket and places it whole into her mouth.

"Frank Poor Bull," he tells her, "wants to kill a man."

She swallows the tomato. "What man?"

"I don't know him. Pete Scully says he has never seen my face."

"Did Frank say a name?"

"No, he just said he was a want-to-be who was in prison all my life."

She drives her Skylark with her foot pressed to the floor all the way in from Choteau. At that speed she expects that any bump or curve in the road will undo her, the least wind will blow her off the highway into oblivion. But her tires hold fast and she feels a curious mixture of relief and disappointment when she arrives at the Red Rock Lounge.

By six that evening, her lower lip is numb from where she slipped and banged her face against the bar. No one took special notice except Myron, who came over and took her by the elbow. "You're in a hurry tonight," he said. "What're you drinking, Everclear?"

"I just slipped is all, Myron. And it's my face that's hurt, not my tit. Is there blood?"

"Not that I can see. Want anything for that? Maybe an ice cube for the swelling?"

She reaches into her purse for a Kleenex but doesn't have any.

The Red Rock Lounge, two miles north of the Wilma city limits, is only half full. It's a Sunday-night crowd, a mix of people with no television to occupy their time, farmers reluctant to head back home, and those like Delores for whom every night is Saturday. Management has recently installed the electric five-card stud machines that are all the rage now that limited gambling is legal. Three of the machines are occupied by white women who pass their fingers over the screens as though sifting sands for slivers of gold or silver as the machines monotonously repeat their computer tones for win and lose. Delores has only played once, slipping her dollar bill into the slot and feeling it pulled away from her fingers. Deal and then draw and kiss your dollar goodbye. Ever since, she saves her money for beer or whisky or car payments, whichever shows up first.

A group of whites come in the door, four men and two women. This isn't their first stop.

"What can I get you?" Myron asks her.

"Beer and a Wild Turkey."

"I meant for your face."

"Same thing. For my face, Myron."

He orders for her and she thinks he'll want some of her female mercy before the night's over. It shows in his eyes and the way he dotes on her as if he knows she's drunk and in no mood to police his hands. She's had more than enough and not enough. The Wild Turkey looks black in the shot glass and she gives it a long stare before drinking it down. The first six or seven shots have left a rut in her throat and she can barely feel the burning.

"My car," she says to Myron. "The Skylark."

"Right, the one without a heater."

"You want to buy it off me?"

"Talk to me next spring."

The whites have crowded her end of the bar. One of the men, a ranch hand called Durrant, glances at her. He's a good-looking man with bright blue eyes and straight white teeth and a way of wearing his hat that says he's ready for a good time. But that smile of his can turn mean like the sun going behind a dark cloud. Hang a sign on him: moody when drunk. He was accused of rape by a girl from the Clay Creek Reservation, but there was no way to prove it and the charges were dropped. Delores has run into him on more than one occasion and the hatred between them has begun to smolder like burning hay. Male and female, white and Indian. She knows she might have slept with him if she hadn't heard that story about the reservation girl.

The woman closest to Delores is yelling that she's come all the way from Sarasota. "That's Florida, not Iowa. Doesn't that deserve a drink?"

Myron tells Delores to go home and sleep it off. "I can drive you if you want. Do you want that?"

Her stomach is empty of anything but whisky, beer, and the to-mato she ate. When she'd slipped and cracked her face against the bar, she'd been surprised she hadn't broken like an egg. The least wind, she has been thinking all evening. The least wind.

"Sarasota, *Florida*. On the Gulf of Mexico. I took it south through Louisiana going ninety all the way and then cut north after Texas."

Delores leans over and whispers in her ear, "Just between you and me?"

The woman turns to face her.

"Just between you and me, a slut from faraway places is still a slut."
Then Delores turns and steps around the tables to the Ladies', where
she throws up the tomato and twelve dollars' worth of good liquor.
She rinses her lips and throat with cold water, slaps her face twice,
and goes back into the bar. The woman from Florida is getting her
tit squeezed by Durrant, who is smiling at his own reflection in the
mirror.

She has no feeling in her fingertips and doesn't remember how
much she's had to drink. Myron has given up on her and wandered
over to a video poker machine. She can see him from behind, his
head bowed to the glow, and can't tell whether he's winning or losing.
She means to sit on a barstool and finds she is already sitting on a
barstool. Then she is in space for a half second that seems longer.
When she looks up, Durrant is smiling down at her, his teeth like a
dog's, and she knows she's on the floor. She pinches her thighs with
all her might to get the feeling back in her legs and stands just long
enough to reach for the edge of the bar. The woman with Durrant is
saying something to her but she can't make out the words. Nothing
pretty, is all she knows.

Joseph, color me an eagle to fly me away.

When she steps outside the air-conditioned bar, the heat folds
around her like a blanket. She is going into a trance, she tells herself.
Not the spirit trance. She doesn't see her ancestors, the lance, the
bearskin, the winter count. She sees a new pair of shoes, her father's
hands gripping a screwdriver as he bends over a broken radio, her
neighbor's mad dog that needs shooting, the Sno-cone she had at the
county fair, that movie she watched a week ago at two a.m.

Her car is parked on the other side of the street and that is too far
away. She slumps against the building and then finds herself on the
cement. She calls out for Myron but the white man is still inside.

She looks up and sees Tyrone standing over her and nothing she
can say to him will cool the hell that is in his eyes. "It's OK," she
tells him. "We both lived." But when she squints, nobody's there.

She rises from the cement and finds her keys at the bottom of her
purse, then staggers to her car. She reaches into the glove compartment for Kleenex and her hand closes over road maps of South
Dakota, North Dakota, Colorado. She saves these maps from car to
car and Tyrone's first letter, scrawled in pencil: *Delores Her Many
Horses, General Delivery Choteau S.D.* Beneath the letter is a tissue

that she wipes across her lips and chin. The Skylark seems to glide of its own power, though twice she feels a jolt when the tires hit the curb and she's certain that she ran a red light back at Fifth Street. She parks in the supermarket lot and climbs steep stairs to her door.

She had left the radio on, tuned to a station in Sioux Falls, and the music is nervous, pulsing, a dance beat. She walks in circles for a while, then goes into the bedroom. She drops to her knees and reaches under her bed for the box of letters. The last of Tyrone's letters arrived nearly a year ago and she hasn't even opened it. Lifting the box, she digs her hands inside and swirls the letters like leaves, feeling their weight and their weightlessness. She doesn't read the letters so much as look at them. In the first few, the handwriting is bad, pencil on yellow ruled paper. The letters that came after the third or fourth year show improved handwriting and the pencil has been replaced with ink. The most recent are typewritten, single-spaced, and some-times run to twenty pages or more. One of them, she has counted, makes forty-three pages. She figures that forty-three pages is the sum total of all the thoughts in her head.

The music stops and there is news on the radio. She sifts through the letters in search of the third one, or maybe it was the fourth, the one she read three times and then spent years trying to forget. The newscaster is droning on but then she hears a name that makes her sit up suddenly. And all at once she leaps upward and staggers into the next room to turn up the volume. The highway patrol is on alert and a manhunt is under way across sixteen counties. John Fire Smith has escaped.

Noah Lame

Until the cataracts, I managed just fine. But now I've taken to walking with my hands out in front of me to spare myself harm. I still know day from night and have long since memorized the routes from kitchen to living room to bathroom, but when a fly circles my head, I'm helpless to swat it. I no longer have enough squint to clean the fish that Toby brings by after a day at the river, so I leave that chore to Joseph. When I watch him use the scaling knife, it's like watching my own hands. We have the same long fingers, he and his mother and I. I call him grandson, but so do most of the other men in Choteau. We're all of us grandfathers to all children, that's an Indian sentiment, and Helene says I shouldn't make too much of the fact, even to myself, that this bloodline's straight as a new sapling.

The day after John Fire busted out of that holding room in Omaha, Helene comes by with an onion, a handful of radishes, and two fat tomatoes. I don't know how she does it in a little garden that's only as long as her trailer. But once or twice a week she's at my doorstep with more. I asked her once what she put in her compost and she said, "Nothing fancy. I have my ways." She sure does.

I put the vegetables in a basket with the others and sit down at the kitchen table. I'm wearing my glasses but I might as well have whisky bottles strapped to my eyes for all the good they do me. Helene's hair has gone gray, but through the cataracts I see the same woman I've been seeing for years. A woman who always stares back hard if I so much as glance in her direction. She moves around the kitchen, wiping up what I can't see: toast crumbs, coffee stains, flakes of onion skin. "Any news on the radio?" she asks.

"I just woke up. You can turn it on if you want."

She tunes to KELO and we hear music instead of chatter. She turns the volume down low and sits next to me at the kitchen table. Besides the food, she's brought the Sioux Falls *Argus Leader*, the Omaha *World Herald*, and the Wilma *Sentinel*. "Delores brought them out after reading for herself. Shall I read the articles to you?"

I nod.

First she reads the stories about his escape, and it sounds like vintage John Fire. There's even a disagreement as to who screwed up worse, the feds or the Omaha police. John Fire was supposed to be cuffed but since they were three floors up, someone got careless and unhooked his hands. He jumped over a desk and went right out the window. One article says he landed on a car and another claims he fell into a dumpster. There are lots of side articles rehashing everything and my name shows up six times in the *Argus Leader* and twice in the *Sentinel*, always in connection with that Fargo trial. I'm the one that got off with six months when John Fire's been put away for life. Helene folds the *World Herald* crosswise and passes it over to me so I can scan the photographs. There's a recent one of John Fire so we'll all know who to turn in if he shows up. There're also some old pictures of Willard Bent, those FBI men who got killed, and a "panorama" of Choteau from a 1974 FBI flyover. But the picture Helene especially wants me to see is the one of me wearing her cracked glasses. She's still mad about my busting them.

I become light-headed, certain that this time John Fire will get clean away. He has the gift. It makes me remember what it was like taking Joseph to the river to teach him to swim. He was five years old and we tied him into a red life jacket. He looked up at me and I could see he was disappointed. "I float anyhow," he said. And he took that life jacket off and slipped into the water before I could catch him, and went under. I waded around thrashing my hands in search of him, but then he surfaced downstream, showing me a big smile. And he swam back to shore as if born to it.

"How's Delores taking this?" I ask.

"She's too scared to drink. That's something. You know, there's Bingo tonight at the VFW."

I pretend not to hear the last part. I gather up the newspapers and stack them on the counter by the sink, then I take the biggest tomato and reach for a knife. "I could watch your card as well as mine," Helene says. "I still see twenty-twenty with these lenses."

It's the tomatoes I'm most grateful for. Onions and radishes leave a sting in my mouth where I lost a tooth, but the flesh of a tomato goes down like sugar water.

"We could win a toaster or an electric blanket."

From the kitchen I can see across the field to Poor Bull's house and the sweat lodge out back. It looks like smoke is coming out the top of the lodge but that might be the cataracts. It's been a rainy summer and the weeds in that field are as tall as men. When the wind blows, I see ghost dancers. That leads me to thinking of Herman, who is still not dead to me. He is at my side every minute of the day.

Then I feel something biting my hand and when I lift it to my face all I see is red. I must be yelling because Helene's at my side in no time. She takes my hand in her own. I have sliced my own flesh instead of that tomato and it hurts like hell.

Helene looks up at me and I give her a squint. It's like staring at lit matches and it's strip poker all over again.

"It's only blood, Noah," she says. And she takes my hand into her mouth and sucks away what grieves me.

Joseph Her Many Horses

Near sundown, as the last golfers abandon the course, Joseph rides his cart to the shed near the twelfth tee. The fairways are losing their color fast, the grass turning the color of sand in the heat of a single afternoon. There is no breeze and the golf cart kicks up dust along a path that leads to the shed. Inside are the gears and dials for the sprinkler system. Joseph uses his key to set them to a ninety-minute soak from ten-thirty to midnight.

That morning he'd found scuff marks at the fourteenth tee and signs of digging, as though the grass had been stripped and put back. Stepping from his cart, he'd bent low to the grass and saw that a seam had been cut across the sod and patched over. Back at the clubhouse, he'd asked Gil if he'd laid down new sod on the tee box and Gil had just looked at him as if he was drunk.

He tosses his Eagle Reach shirt and cap on the seat of the cart. Though there's no sign of rain, he covers the golf cart with a tarp and heads for the river carrying his shoes. The river glides away from him as he walks downstream, his eyes sweeping the banks for lost balls. Blue flies shimmer in the dying light and a walleye surfaces just offshore. Weeds have sprung up where the water has receded. Then he sees a ball wedged like an egg in a nest of red loam, and another by a snake hole.

He wades along the bank until he comes to the sandy spot near his house and he knows immediately that someone has been there. The sands have always left a message for him and now they are scarred with footprints leading to and from the water. He studies the boot-marks and decides there was only one person, almost certainly a man. He came from the path that leads from Joseph's house and turned downstream for a few yards before circling back to this spot, where he stood, shifting his weight from one foot to the other as if he didn't know where to go next. Then he just turned and went back the way he'd come.

Joseph has never seen any footprints other than his own on this sand. He follows them back into the trees, losing the trail where the earth is hard and covered with leaves, then picks them up again not far from his house. They lead off the path toward the house, and then around it, before leading right up to the kitchen window. It could have been Sam, who sometimes gets lonesome after smoking his weed. But these marks are made from boots and Joseph has never seen Sam wearing anything other than tennis shoes.

He has never tracked a man. He has followed the hoofprints of cattle, the forked prints of deer, the flat pads of rabbits, and the dotlike tracks of raccoons. When he was young, Pete Scully showed him how to tell which way a rabbit would turn when it came to a tree. And once, a long time ago, he found Frank's lost dog by following his trail from the house all the way to an empty cornfield three miles away. It was in October and the dog was dead from buckshot probably meant for a pheasant. Old Pete had never taught him how to track a two-legged man, but from here on, it was easy. The man followed the road.

The sunlight fails and a half moon casts shadows of trees and cornstalks along the road. Past Choteau, at a fork where the road continues north and a new road heads east, Joseph drops to his knees and sees that the prints lead east. He's on the road they named after Gaetan Avril and the tracks are thin. The road has recently been oiled and steamrolled to stop the dust from blowing. Joseph walks slowly, his eyes cast downward. For moments at a time he cannot see the least trace, though he senses the man wouldn't have turned off into the cornfields on either side. Ten steps later, there's a heel mark, and then another. The moonlight shrinks his vision and, feeling a dizziness wash over him, Joseph holds his breath against the stench of that road oil. Up ahead on the right is a house that is surrounded by trees. He has been there once before and found only ruin and sadness, so has avoided it ever since. South of that house is where the red car is hidden in the circle of trees.

Then Joseph sees a car parked along the road. A man stands next to it looking at the house. Joseph crouches down so his profile won't show against the moonlit sky and steals closer. He can see it is a white man in a golf shirt and slacks. The man shifts his weight from time to time, then gets into his car, and drives away to the east, away from Joseph, without turning on his headlights.

Joseph follows the bootmarks off the road onto a dirt and gravel drive, where they are as easy to read as if they had been chiseled into stone, beckoning him. He follows the drive for a hundred yards and then the house comes into full view. A smashed-up car is in front, along with strewn junk and weeds as high as his chest. A path has been cut through the weeds, and there is a pile of leaves and sticks and garbage near the porch steps. One of the downstairs windows is yellow with light.

Joseph drops to his belly and snakes forward. He peers through the grass toward the window, watching for signs of movement inside, and then rises to his knees and holds himself as still as a tree. He fixes his eyes on the window and waits. An owl sweeps from the trees behind him and vanishes. Joseph leans his weight on one foot and very slowly rises up. The window is just above his head and he lifts himself on his toes to look inside.

A single lamp burns in a room filled with shadows. Close by the lamp, a man sits on a wooden chair reading from a stack of white pages. He makes a note on the page, then sets the pen on the table. The room is empty except for the chair and the table, which is piled with books. Joseph watches for a long time as the man turns pages and now and then lifts his pen to write something down. He is fascinated by the stillness of the man. His only gestures are to turn a leaf of paper or to scratch out a word or two. It's as if he is bound by ropes to the chair.

Suddenly the man coughs. Joseph can hear it from the other side of the glass, a rasp like bark being torn from a tree. Then he coughs again and heaves in the chair, dropping the book and rising to his feet. He puts a fist to his mouth and shudders, but the seizure won't stop and between coughs he gasps for air. He whirls, wild-eyed, and Joseph drops down and crouches by the side of the house. When he edges back up to peer into the glass, the man has fallen to the floor and is gasping for breath. Joseph claws at the glass and then bends and searches the ground around him for a stone. Lifting his arm to break the window, he sees that the man is standing again, bent over with his hands on his knees, taking short breaths. His face is red but he now is calm. He stands there for a long time, just breathing in and out.

Joseph lets the stone fall from his hand. He feels the wind begin to rise. It blows the weeds around him to one side and then the other. A dry wind, a rainless wind.

He turns and runs as far as the road. And then, as the smell of that oil rises to his nose, he begins to cough as well. His nose and throat burn and he runs off the road, leaps over the barbed wire and races into the high corn. Above him, the stars are starved and thin. Moonlight has picked them clean and he sees that there is no wind at all. The tall stalks are motionless and the night is heavy with silence. He returns to the road and puts bare feet to the oiled dirt. It is a hard road, low and flat and without the ruts of dried mud like the road that leads to the river. It has been smashed flat like a highway where nothing will ever grow again.

He takes a heavy step, leaving a clear print in the dirt. Then another, and another. His walking is slow and he stamps each footprint with all his strength. The night grows with the corn. The earth is still. He leaves his mark with each footstep all the way back to his house by the moving water.

Tyrone Little

And when he comes home, the doors and windows are boarded shut and a thick beard of weeds and brambles covers the porch.

He stands and gazes at the glorious ruin of the house while the breeze runs through his fresh-cut hair. The wardens insisted on a haircut both coming and going. He kept the blue blazer and the shaving kit they gave him, but threw the necktie in the trash in the Sioux Falls Motel. He stayed there ten days, getting slowly accustomed to his new freedom, and then came here.

The shell of his Delta 88 rests beneath the largest of four elms. He cranks the door open and sees that the rear upholstery is gone. That backseat probably served as a couch in someone's shack, or the stuffing was used to refill a sagging mattress. But the engine is still under the hood. He looks it over in the moonlight and decides it might be salvaged.

He closes the hood and glances around the property. Clouds shroud the moon and he's not used to being outdoors in the dark. He finds an old steel fence post half-buried in the ground and uses it to pry loose the old, dry boards. When he touches the front door, it simply falls off.

He takes a step forward and then stops. The years are an explosion of dust and cold ash. The darkness is almost total and he reaches for a light switch that is no longer there, but his eyes gradually adjust. He has spent years in shadowy interiors. The large table is gone and the bookshelves have collapsed. The roof has fallen open to reveal a jagged oval of sky, and the floor below the hole is covered with dust and mud mixed with beer cans, paper trash, and broken glass. The walls are watersoaked but intact. When he reaches his fingertips to peel a strip of loose wallpaper, it comes away easily and flutters to the floor. He always hated that wallpaper; what he hadn't done the years have done for him.

He can feel the ropes tighten around his chest and he begins to cough. It takes a while to subside and then he just breathes in and out. If he's going to live here, the first order of business will be to clear the air.

He steps through mud into the kitchen and is shocked by the familiarity of the room: the white shape of the refrigerator, the pine shelves that rise to the ceiling, the pattern of the yellow linoleum. Rainwater has warped the floorboards beneath the linoleum and there is a film of skunk crap that stinks to high heaven, driving him back to the main room.

From behind him, the house fills suddenly with light and he turns and sees a car in the front drive, its beam turned high. The law, he assumes, but when the lights go out only a single figure emerges from the car. "That you, Tyrone?"

"Gaetan?"

Tyrone steps outside as Gaetan Avril climbs over the weeds and broken boards onto the porch. They face each other in the moonlight and then fall into a silent bear hug.

"I should have come up to Sioux Falls to get you," Gaetan says. "Never mind what you said in your letter. I've been coming out here every night for a week thinking you'd show up. You hitch or take the bus?"

"The bus," Tyrone says. He coughs once but catches his breath quickly. "Hitching's illegal in this state, Gaetan."

Gaetan sweeps a hand toward the house. "I'm sorry about this, Tyrone. I fixed the place up two or three times but nothing ever lasted. First the feds took the rooms apart looking for guns or whatnot, then Fast Horse and his friends—"

"I know," Tyrone says. "I heard about it."

"And through the years, the kids around here . . . Hell, you know how that goes. I came by about three years ago and could see it was hopeless. Ever since, I've been counting on your staying at my place. I got a room already made up."

"I don't think so, Gaetan."

"Well you can't stay here, that's for sure."

"What's to stop me?"

Gaetan considers for a moment. "Frank Poor Bull?"

Tyrone laughs and coughs at the same time and the sound is frightening.

"I've asked around. The Choteau families are mighty confused about how to take you. They still don't know which end of the stick you're holding."

"No, I imagine not."

They step off the porch and pick their way around to the back of the house where refuse runs twenty yards into the field—a steel sink, bedboards, mattresses, chairs, lampshades, unidentifiable pieces of metal. Tyrone steps over to a high mound of what first look like dead leaves but turn out to be books. A sodden volume falls apart in his fingers.

"You want to be an Indian," he says, "you gotta have an Indian house."

"If you'd have left me to tell them about you, get the truth out—"

"I'm obliged you kept your mouth shut, Gaetan. I'd like to borrow some tools, if you don't mind."

"Take whatever you need. But first of all, come to supper. I got some other visitors I'd like you to see, including, touch wood, my wayward son."

"Thanks, Gaetan, but no."

"But, I was hoping—"

"And Gaetan? I just need tools. No visiting and no visitors. Time to myself."

"You'd think you'd had enough of that."

"In prison? There's no such thing as being alone."

The clouds move away from the moon and the yard and house are bathed in pale light. They return to the front of the house and Tyrone leans against the hood of his car. "Another thing," he says. "I'd appreciate it if nobody else knew I was here. In this house, I mean."

"Done. Day at a time, right? Which reminds me." He reaches into his back pocket for his wallet.

"No handouts," Tyrone says.

"This isn't one. The boys at the club took up a collection of sorts." He pulls out some bills. "If I mentioned their names you'd be tickled pink." When Tyrone hesitates, he says, "All right then, twist my arm. Albert Roebuck, Calvin Denton, Jimmy DeWare, and Stuart Baumgartner. I couldn't entice that lowlife Jack LeHavre to the table or there'd be more."

"Albert Roebuck?"

Though Gaetan can't see clear enough in the dark to be sure, he imagines Tyrone is smiling.

"But I don't need the money," Tyrone says. "My attorney's all paid off."

Gaetan picks his way over the weeds to his car and opens the door. "Delores is living in Wilma these days. She's got a place on Third Street across from the supermarket, if you remember where that is."

"I think I could find my way."

"She's drinking too much and her looks are gone. But the boy lives where I told you, in a shack down by the river."

Tyrone nods.

"You plan on seeing them?"

"Drive carefully," Tyrone advises. "Crazy Indians on these roads."

Once Gaetan leaves, Tyrone climbs up into the loft that was once his bedroom and then collapses on the top step, short of breath. The four-poster bed has been disassembled and the chest of drawers is gone. But the roof is intact and the room is dry and warm. There is a mattress on the floor and a pair of dirty blankets, a pillow without a pillowcase. Yellowed magazines, the usual beer cans, newspaper, and discarded Trojan boxes.

Downstairs, he finds a crusted broom in the kitchen, takes up the fence post and climbs the stairs again. He bangs at the mattress with the broom to get the dust out, and then in anger he sweeps the floor clean, leaving a pile of dirt and trash in a corner by the stairs. His chest tightens and his head spins. Enraged, he takes up the fence post and flails at the planks over the window until they bend, then crack, and finally splinter away.

The sweet night air, smelling of grass and the river, rushes into the loft. He sits on the mattress and breathes it in until his head clears, then notices his hand is bleeding from where he'd gripped that fence post. Sucking blood, he decides that no amount of years will stanch the bleeding. He's out now but might as well still be in.

His first morning, he wakes up in the loft bedroom and sits for a long time on the bed, just staring at the door, before remembering it isn't locked. He stands, crosses the room, and lays his hand on the doorknob, turns it, and steps out to the stairway. But he can go no farther than the front porch. Beyond the trees out front is a vision of prairie endlessness that sets his heart to beating wildly. But when he thinks of leaving the house, he feels anxious and his palms begin to itch.

He moves from room to room and does whatever comes to mind to repair it. One day he sweeps the dirt and spiders from the living room and the next day he strips off what's left of the wallpaper. He puts new glass in the downstairs windows and clears the chimney, scraping the blackened brick with a metal brush and lighting a high, hot fire to burn away the debris and the bird's nests. He props up the sagging porch with four-by-fours. When he aims a hammer at a nail, the head crashes down on his thumb. One hand is trustworthy and the other should still be locked up.

He covers the hole in the roof with plywood and tar paper, then nails the slats into place before the first rain falls. Gaetan has come by twice already with groceries, tools, supplies, and books.

His third visit, Gaetan brings the news of John Fire's escape.

"He was being moved out of that high-security joint in Marion back to the pen in Nebraska, so they had him in a holding room in downtown Omaha and he jumped out the window. Three floors is all, and you'd think they'd have remembered who they were dealing with."

Tyrone spends a long time studying the newspaper articles.

"He won't come this way," Gaetan says. "The country sheriff already came to visit on some bullshit errand and I told him why didn't he just look in the closets and under the bed. As if he'd be dumb enough to hide out at my place. Where do you figure he'd go?"

"North," Tyrone answers. "Through Standing Rock into North Dakota and from there to Canada."

Gaetan nods. "It's getting to be like old times again. Visits from the sheriff, FBI reports, and John Fire's picture on every front page."

After his third week in the house, the parole officer drives down from Sioux Falls. Although she's not in uniform, she wears a holster tight against her right hip. She shakes his hand with a stonelike grip but her perfume is overpowering and he guesses she doused herself before getting out of the car. He offers her a chair and they sit at the small table in the living room.

"You're surprised by something," she says.

"I expected a man."

"I'm twenty-seven," she says, "and I'm not new to this. If you'd prefer someone—"

"I've got no preferences whatsoever."

She nods after a moment, as if some sort of deal has been struck, then looks down at the documents spread before her. "According to the conditions of your release, we are to meet once every month either here or at my office. I assume you're clear about the terms of your parole."

"Sure."

She gestures to his file. "The psychologist says you have a martyr complex. And maybe a latent death wish. 'Stored rage,' is how he puts it. Like you're a walking threat to society."

"I've seen the file," Tyrone tells her. "He just wrote what they told him to. I even gave him some help with the spelling."

She gives him a long hard look, wondering if she should believe him. "You're my first case of this kind," she says.

"What kind is that?"

"Long-term sentence. Mostly I handle people who've been in for two, three years."

"Is there a difference?"

She avoids his eyes. "According to the books I've read, there's bound to be."

After half an hour of answering her questions about work and rehabilitation, he breaks down and brews a pot of coffee. His hands are sweaty and he drops a coffee cup and is astonished when it doesn't break.

"Am I making you nervous?"

"No." He is used to the company of men at close quarters. Muscle and beard and the smell of sweat, not rosewater and skin like butter.

"The report says you tried to have a book published a long time ago."

"They took it away from me and I wrote it again. I doubt anybody wants to read it."

"Your pre-release questionnaire says you'd like to find a teaching job of some kind."

"It can wait."

"What?"

"A job. I've got other things to take care of first. Like this house."

She drops a cube of sugar into her coffee and looks around the room. "So this is where you lived before?"

He doesn't answer.

"With that woman." She pauses. "The file says she still lives around here. And the boy, too. Do you plan on seeing them?"

He stands and reaches for the coffeepot, then sets it back down.

"It's not for my report. There's nothing in this file that forbids you from seeing them. I was just curious."

"Stay curious," he says.

To his surprise, she reaches a hand across the table and touches him. He has not felt the fingers of a woman in years. He waits until she retrieves that hand and then wishes she would touch him again.

They both sign her visit slip and he opens the screen door.

"You don't have a phone," she says. "If you don't have one installed, you'll have to be the one to call me."

"Why would I do that?"

When she drives away, he returns to the book he was reading. But ten minutes later she's back at his door, her face flushed.

"My boyfriend is one of those good-looking brutes who figures I'll always be there no matter what he's up to."

He doesn't know what to say to this, so he says nothing.

"He goes to those fern bars in the south part of Sioux Falls, you know, where the women wear pastels and have big tits. I sometimes think about getting even with him."

Tyrone moves inside and leans against the bookshelf where he has arranged the books and newspapers Gaetan brought him.

She follows him through the door. "Are you listening to me?"

This, he decides, is a test of some kind, an exercise from her textbook or research for an article she wants to write.

"You seem lonesome," she says.

He can sense the hook beneath the bait and shakes his head. She sighs and offers him a smile that looks rehearsed. "I guess I'm forgetting myself. I suppose I could search the place for things that could be overlooked. A shotgun under the bed, a pistol in a toilet tank. But I don't want to force you into anything."

"Leave it," he tells her. "You're forgetting I shot the last woman I ever made love to."

"Not to mention Harold Bad Hand," she says, her eyes cold.

"Yeah, him."

"I'll see you next month," she says, going out the door. "On the fifth."

"I'll be here."

The next day he dresses in jeans and the new boots that Gaetan bought for him, and early in the afternoon he walks to the edge of his backyard to the treeline and gazes into the distance. The winds have shifted and to the west the sky is darkened with blowing dust. Then he feels something like a hand at his back and steps forward out of the trees and strides into the grassy field. He has taken twenty steps before realizing that he is out. Sky surrounds him on all sides. There is nothing to lean against other than the earth.

Some miles away, he can see the dust kicked up behind a pickup. Grackles are screaming in the trees at his back. For the first time in years, he wants a cigarette. He has a memory of the taste of Scotch whisky.

He begins to walk again and, after clearing the oiled road, cuts south on the dirt road that leads to the river. He is light-headed, grinning from ear to ear. The road is as worn and uneven as ever, and he steps over the dried-out tractor ruts until he comes to the part of the creek Gaetan told him about, where the dam used to be. The water flows unimpeded and he follows it downstream, past a ruined cornfield, to where they buried the girl's bones. He nearly walks into the water and his boots sink deep into the clay. He backs up onto on a sandy stretch, then he turns in small circles, trying to remember exactly where he was standing when John Fire gave him the eagle feather.

The wind smells of the river, of fish and grass. The woman wanted him to jump her and melt into her like hot wax. He's sorry now to have said no. She can have him, what she wants of him. First he will bathe her and get the perfume off her skin, scrub her down until she smells like this river and these trees. The trees were here back then. This river and this sand and this wind from the west. Nothing in nature is changed.

Back in Choteau they'll be waiting for him, but he will find them before they find him. He will sit down with Poor Bull and Noah Lame and tell them who he is and why he never explained before. They will sweat together in the lodge and his skin will come clean, his sorrow will fly through the roof with the smoke.

He circles back to the road and heads toward home. To his left is the tar-paper shack and his feet lead him off the road and through the trees. He stops at a distance and it's minutes before he finally gives in to his curiosity. Through a window he sees a room that looks as though no one has ever been inside.

In prison, he wrote letters that no one ever answered, except for one, in his first year. Delores wrote, *The bullet cut off his oxygen and they say he will be stupid but I don't believe them. His name is Joseph. I think he looks like you but I don't say so aloud.*

All at once Tyrone feels the weight of where he is and his boots are as heavy as stone. He quickly turns and scrambles through the trees onto the road, where his footsteps are faster and his smile is long gone.

At home, he sands away the remaining traces of wallpaper from the living-room walls. When his arms begin to ache he is calm. The sun is down and he reaches to turn on the lamp, then takes a stack of typed pages from his shelf and sits in the wooden chair by the table. For a long time he reads the book he has written himself, the story of the Bones War. He is scanning the pages when he feels in his chest the explosion of a gun.

His breath leaves him all at once. He stands and flecks of blood appear on the fist in front of his face. When he reaches for the table it is too far away and he stumbles to the floor, gasping, until the first whisper of breath returns to him. He sees red and then white. His shallow breath deepens and he struggles to his knees, his head pounding. At last the wings of his lungs spread outward, and when he opens his mouth the rattle has ceased.

The following morning, he sees that a trail has been trampled through the weeds from the front drive all the way to his window. He searches the road for tracks and to the east he finds the tread of car tires and a number of footprints. That would be Gaetan, watching over him. Tyrone is about to head back into the house when he sees footprints in the oiled road ahead of him. In the white daylight, the road shines and the prints of bare feet are clear. He follows along with footsteps of the same length, placing his boots over each of them, but doesn't have the courage to follow them to his son's house by the river, so he turns and heads back to the house.

The glass is still shattered, the upholstery scarred, the body dented and rippled. But he dissects the engine and files its parts clean, oils and polishes and fits them back together. When he turns the key, the engine beats like a new heart and nothing is solved for him except for that sound.

He is busy stitching the upholstery when Sam drives up in his French car. For a moment, the two of them stand ten feet apart. Tyrone notices he's is shorter than Gaetan by six inches and doesn't have his father's steady gaze. Sam's eyes drift to the car.

"You fixed it?"

"Not all of it. Some things you can fix and some you can't."

"I came to warn you," Sam says. "Frank Poor Bull has a loaded gun."

"I know that, Sam. But he won't use it on me."

Tyrone invites him inside. His house is transformed, the large room warm and clean, the wood freshly stained and polished, the floors covered with deep rugs, one wall lined with books, a table with a typewriter in one corner. The walls are still bare and Tyrone says he intends to leave them that way. The last thing he wants to see in his life are photographs. "Prison walls are covered with them."

"When I was in high school," Sam says, "we all used this house for parties or a place to bring girls." Then he adds, "You've been haunting this place my whole life."

Tyrone is forced to smile. "Haunting?"

"My father's spent years trying to tell me all about you."

"What's he said?"

"Mostly he starts by trashing everything about my grandfather."

"And you don't listen."

"Not until lately. But I still don't know any more about you than everybody else knows."

"What is it everyone thinks they know?"

"That you were a plant for the FBI. Then you shot and killed Harold Bad Hand and wounded Delores."

"Why would I do that?"

"Vietnam syndrome. Jealous rage. What's your version?"

After a long pause, Tyrone says, "Ask your father. He's got a better memory than I do. And he knows where all the bones are buried."

Sam nods. "A few weeks ago we found some bones in Blue Eye Creek."

Tyrone nods.

"My father says it's Leroy Little Sky, and he acts like it had something to do with you."

Tyrone is looking out his kitchen window. "If you want the whole story, listen to your father. I'm out of the habit of testifying." Then he strides out of the kitchen and through the living room.

Sam follows and finds him on the porch. "I thought you should know. Joseph's my neighbor. And the only friend I've got."

For the first time, Tyrone looks him in the eye. "Tell me about him."

"What do you want to know?"

"Has he ever talked about me?"

"He doesn't talk much at all. He works and he wanders around. Everyone loves him in Choteau. Why don't you go see him?"

"Like I said, some things you can fix and some you can't."

"I thought you were talking about broken glass."

"I was." Tyrone points to his car. "Gene Fast Horse and Harold Bad Hand did a little body work on the car the night they threw me out of town. Anyway, at the pen, we all had these ideas of what we'd do when we got out. Buy a car and drive all the way to the coast. Eat a fancy meal with French wine and white tablecloths and candelabras. Screw a two-hundred-dollar whore. Hold our sons or daughters in our arms until nobody could breathe anymore. Some guys had ideas that were a little strange. Jimmy Arnt just wanted to go to a bookstore and buy a book, it didn't matter which one. Jeremy Changed Bear said he'd sleep a week in a bathtub filled with beer. My idea was to come back here and fix that car."

"What happens when it's finished?"

"I drive it away."

"Where to?"

Tyrone shrugs, then he laughs. "Hell if I know." He's thinking of a man he knew years before coming to Choteau, a drunk who always wanted to fly a plane. "He stayed sober long enough to complete the lessons and get his pilot's license, but after that he never once took a plane up. He went back to drinking and, when I asked why he wouldn't fly, the man said, ' 'Cause there isn't any goddamn place on earth where I'd want to land.' "

Unlike his father, Sam can't hide his uneasiness with small talk. Pretending he's due somewhere, he takes his leave, offering Tyrone an awkward handshake. Once he's gone, Tyrone gets behind the wheel of his car and starts the engine. He lets it idle for a few minutes, then shifts into gear and turns right onto the oiled road and drives slowly toward Choteau. The sky is dark as he cruises past the Lame house and then the trailer court. At the end of the road, the lights of Toby's are lit. Three cars, two pickup trucks, and a pair of motorcycles are parked outside. The early September air is wet and smells of diesel fuel, rotting apples, and the vague but haunting perfume of the Missouri. He drives past, daring only a glance, and sees men gathered around a table playing cards. One of the men looks up from his cards and Tyrone drives away. When he looks in the rearview mirror, Noah Lame is out in front of Toby's, watching his back.

He doesn't stop until he gets to Wilma, where he parks in front of the Save Rite. The clock on the dash is broken but he guesses it's about eight. She won't be there, he decides. But he waits in the car, the window rolled down, and watches the front door across the street.

In front of the supermarket, a young Indian is banging on the candy machine with a flat palm. "Give it!" he yells, and slaps the machine again. "Damn!" The boy stumbles drunkenly and reaches into his pocket for another coin, which he slips into the machine. When nothing comes out, he bangs it, then kicks it, but the candy won't fall. Finally, aggrieved, he walks away. When Tyrone turns again to watch the door, she is standing in front of it. Her back is to him and she trips on the first step. He wants desperately for her to turn around and then prays that she won't. She unlocks the door and is swallowed up inside. He stifles a cough, then opens the car door and puts a boot to the pavement. Then he lifts his leg back in and closes the door.

A police car pulls alongside and a young cop says, "No parking here, mister. This is a loading zone."

Tyrone just shakes his head.

"Move along," the cop says.

The engine sparks and he pulls away, slowly gaining speed, past the filling station, through a red light on First Street, past the Gem Bar, forty miles an hour, the True Value hardware, Kinney's Shoes, fifty, the town hall, until he is back on the open road. And though he presses the pedal to the floor, the wheels hug the road, and it will not take wing.

The parole officer spreads her hands across his kitchen table as if to show him there are no rings. But she is not without adornment. Her nails are painted fire red and the top buttons of her uniform are opened below the throat. She should lose some weight, Tyrone thinks. The flesh is too slack across her jawline though her legs are fine.

"This isn't a routine visit, Mr. Little. John Fire Smith is still a fugitive."

"It's in the papers every day."

"Ten days. Do you suppose he's made it to Canada by now?"

"If that's where he's headed."

"You haven't seen him, then?" Her smile is a straight line.

"Not since 1978."

That was the year they moved John Fire from Lompoc to the maximum-security facility in Marion. He was transited through the South Dakota State Penitentiary, which raised a lot of eyebrows around the state, but came as no surprise to Tyrone. A Minnesota Sioux named Richard Deer had recently been transferred from Stillwater to South Dakota, and John Fire was assigned to the same cellblock. Deer was serving a life sentence for murdering a policeman and was said to have previously killed a Chippewa woman with a rifle at close range. The day John Fire arrived in Sioux Falls, the authorities tipped their hand by becoming lax about security. John Fire was given recreational privileges that had previously been denied, and he was allowed to participate in spiritual meetings and pipe ceremonies. George Brings Yellow and Pete Scully were permitted to visit him for the first time in three years. The prison guards, still assuming that Tyrone was an Indian hater, hinted to him that his old enemy was in range.

Tyrone and John Fire were kept apart, but the grapevine was smoothly functioning. Short of tom-toms and smoke signals, Tyrone passed on word that John Fire should beware of killdeer and please sign that message "Wannabe." By this time, Deer had already attended a number of meetings with him and had even offered his services as bodyguard. One freezing winter evening, a number of inmates sat down for a pipe ceremony and when the pipe was passed to Richard Deer, one of them reminded him that you were supposed to smoke with a clear heart. They were all watching, and Deer understood. Throwing the pipe to the floor, he leaped up from the bench and started screaming for the guards. A week later, Deer was returned to Minnesota and John Fire continued on to Marion. All Tyrone ever saw of him was his back as he was escorted to a squad car.

The parole officer is working him like a machine whose gears and levers she doesn't understand. He has dreaded her coming back to his house. He even called her to say he'd come to her office in Sioux Falls, but she said she was obliged to inspect the premises. "Because of this John Fire."

Like the fear that takes hold of a child before the Ferris wheel starts, his dread is mingled with a fluttery excitement. He feels the rage and ache of enforced abstinence, eighteen years' worth. With the woman so close, he feels himself lifted from the chair and can feel a pounding of blood at his temples.

She reaches for her purse and takes out a pack of Marlboros and a plastic lighter. "I've made some inquiries in and around Wilma. Joe Merchant tells me that he's seen you around town."

He nods and watches as she lights the cigarette, willing the smoke to blow elsewhere. His eyes drift to where her buttons are undone and she catches his gaze. "Grocery shopping," he says.

"And a few trips to the library." She lifts her head and blows smoke toward the ceiling. "Would that about cover it?"

"Pretty much."

"Have you had any visitors here?"

"No." He doesn't see any need to tell her about Gaetan, whose police record is long enough already. The truth of the matter is that he comes by at least twice each week and Tyrone is no longer uncomfortable in his presence. Nor does he tell her about the gifts he finds each morning on his front porch: tomatoes and onions, sweet corn and radishes. The clear prints of bare feet. Once, when he got back from Wilma, the weeds in the front yard had been cut down and the dead branches pruned from the elms. In return, he'd taken his toolbox to the shack by the river and repaired the torn screen on the front door and straightened the sagging porch planks, the hammer in his hand swinging downward and driving perfect nails.

"You must be lonely," she says. She is purring now and her head is circled in blue smoke. "Perhaps you could use a job."

For the first six years, he was alone in his cell—for his own protection, he was told: a man who had killed Indians, surrounded by Indians. But he wore a handstrap of buffalo hide and a look on his face that told them all to go to hell. Even in prison they called him Wannabe.

At first he worked in the machine shop repairing what was broken or flawed, but his hands seemed to fly too loosely off his wrists and he no longer trusted them. The right index finger that had pulled the trigger. He could grip a screwdriver but couldn't drive the screw, so after four months he was transferred to sanitation. Prison garbage was identical from week to week.

Gaetan sent letters, books, and money, but Tyrone had nothing to purchase except pen and paper and, after his fourth year, a manual typewriter. In 1978, Tyrone could not pay the taxes on the thirty-four acres of farm and grassland around his house and sold them to Gaetan. He tried to give the money to Delores, but she turned him down and the full sum has been sitting in a bank all these years. Now that he's out, Gaetan wants him to take back the land at the same price, but Tyrone says the name on the title doesn't matter as long as he can stay in the house.

The parole officer has finished filling out her forms and she slides them into a black briefcase with a combination lock. "All that's left, I guess, is the inspection of the premises. I hope it isn't too much of an inconvenience."

He knows she's lying. No inspection is required unless he's shown cause. All the same, he rises from the table and follows her as she opens and closes kitchen drawers and cupboards and then moves into the living room. "The heat," she says, touching fingers to her throat. "Another Indian summer."

He follows her up the stairs to his loft, where the bed is made and the sheets are clean. He knew she was coming and he knew where she would take him. The open window offers a thin breeze and the musty smell has long since been cleansed from the walls. She lingers for a moment in front of the dresser upon which lay his wallet, comb, car keys, and bone choker. "Have you seen the woman?" she asks.

He comes behind her and presses himself against her, pushing his face into her hair. His hands move upward to her buttons and he begins to undo them.

"Wait," she says. "The gun."

He steps back and she turns and removes her holster and drops it to the floor. Then she swiftly strips off her uniform and settles naked to the bed. "You can do whatever you want," she tells him.

He plunges and writhes, already wishing it to be over but unable to stop himself. Close up, she smells of tobacco and coffee and he likes the feel of her nails on his back. She pulls free and tries to move her head down his body but he doesn't want that and yanks her back into his embrace. He closes his eyes and conjures Delores, though the images below his lids are moving and vague, blurred by the film of years. The woman is too fat and makes noises that remind him she is there. "Quiet," he tells her and pushes himself deep. He begins to rock and feels a sudden surge of pain in his chest. His lungs empty and he lifts himself by the arms and throws back his head. When he opens his eyes, he sees only white and then red. The woman is shouting at him as his chest cracks open and the coughing begins. He stumbles upward and hauls himself to the window. The ropes that bind him grow tighter and his coughing turns to a dry wheeze. The woman moves behind and reaches for his shoulders, but he shakes her away. The coughing stops and he takes tiny breaths, in, out, in, until slowly his lungs clear. When he turns, the woman is buttoning the shirt of her uniform.

"You need a doctor," she tells him.

He watches her breasts disappear beneath her blouse and shakes his head.

"Maybe we can try again next month," she suggests.

He can't speak. Words deplete the oxygen.

When she is dressed and holstered, she turns toward the stairs, her bra in one hand. "Aren't you even gonna walk me to the car?" she asks.

He can't make it down the stairs. He is still without wind and his legs are weak. He sits on the edge of the bed and offers a small wave of the hand. Disgust fills her face and then melts to disappointment. She descends the stairs and he can hear the door closing, the roar of her car engine. Moments later, he hears the front door open again and footsteps coming up. She's desperate, he thinks. And she's the steep hill he can't climb anymore. He summons the strength to stand and then crosses to the door where he is about to slip the lock, but a hand on the other side pushes the door wide open. The hand is dark-skinned with long, delicate fingers. Tyrone falls backward and John Fire Smith, in a blue prison shirt and brown pants, catches him before he hits the floor.

Gaetan Avril

The Titleist Three is nestled in a patch of high grass in the worst part of rough, still a hundred, hundred ten yards from the green. I'll have to bring it in high to clear the sand trap in front, and of late my nine-iron has gone south on me so I consider dropping to wedge for extra lift. My third shot on the par-four thirteenth hole. Albert Roebuck is lying four on the front edge. He owes me fifty-five dollars through twelve holes but you'd think he was ahead by the look on his face. I slip the wedge from my bag and waggle it a bit. It feels heavy and that's the price of being hungover.

We're having one of those course meetings, Roebuck, his cretin grandson, Ted, and myself. Joe Merchant, the retired sheriff, has joined us to make it a foursome even though he barely knows the game and is happy to score eight on a par five. He's lost four of his orange balls already and is relieved to be out of the wagering.

We're playing hard-ass rules today so I can't even give myself a decent lie. I'll have to swing hard to get any club on the ball, and with all that grass I could either skull it or hit it fat. There's a slight breeze at my back that won't make any damned difference. I settle my feet, dig my spikes into the hard ground, and swing the club back and down. The ball flies out like a flushed pheasant, too high, and drops hard into the sand.

"Bad luck," Ted Roebuck says as I catch up to him.

I ignore him and take the sand wedge from my bag. The others are waiting, putters in hand, above me on the green. I haven't had to answer any questions yet. Ted and Albert are sharing one cart, and Joe and I the other. I actually like to pass the time of day with the sheriff, and I'm still grateful to him for past kindnesses, but golf conversations tend to progress slowly, punctuated as they are by looking for balls or lining up putts. Most of the chatter takes place on a tee where the four of us have already gathered thirteen times. I'll keep them waiting until the last three holes, I figure. And in the meantime I'll take as much of Roebuck's money as I can, though today it's small consolation for the unpleasantness of his company. What they want, still, is for me to carry a message to Tyrone.

I step down into that bunker as if into an enclosed room and the ball is half-buried in the sand. I've been here before. Since the course opened, I've played more than a thousand rounds and have been in this same trap at least fifty times. Even so, I catch too much sand. The ball clears the lip but makes it only a few feet onto the green.

"Good out, Gaetan," Albert says.

I'd like to tell him to shut up. He's wearing lime green slacks and a lemon yellow shirt with "Eagle Reach" embroidered on the front. With his white shoes and belt, he looks like he could glow in the dark. I tried to get Ted to play for cash, but he just laughed and said his old man would lose enough for the both of them. We're all such goldarned pals.

Albert, putting out of turn, jabs the putt instead of stroking it but gets a good break downhill and the ball slides up three feet from the hole, a gimme for him. Ted nods to Joe, who bends over his ball in such a way that you'd think his back was hurting him. He mutters "Shit" even before the ball stops rolling, then taps twice more before holing out.

"Another three-putt," he says as if telling the time.

I'm away, so it's time to putt. I've got twenty feet or so uphill with a slight lie to the right. I don't want to think it to distraction, so I just put a decent roll on it, ending up two feet short.

"Nice up, Gaetan."

Ted drops his five-footer and I hole my short putt for a double-bogey six. Albert's only down fifty bucks.

I drop the putter into my bag and settle into the cart next to the sheriff. He looks sillier in golf clothes than most of us, perhaps because we're used to seeing him in that tan uniform with the dignity of his hat and badge. He looks as peculiar when out of uniform as priests do when they dress up in civvies and leave the collar on the dresser. "Quite the game," he says. "I think I started playing too late in life."

We cruise to the fourteenth tee and I unholster my driver. The hole is a par five, 516 yards that look tougher than they really are. The fairway has a downhill bounce that adds forty yards to your drive, and there's plenty of room on your right. But I always lose a stroke because I won't play from the regular tee.

Albert Roebuck sidles up near to me, but not so close as to remind us both that he's six inches shorter than I am. He hates looking up into my face. "We know he's back, Gaetan. He's been into town at least five times. At the supermarket, the library, the filling station."

"So? He's entitled."

"That's right. It's a free country and he's served his time."

"Then what's got you by the throat, Albert?"

"The Bones War, Gaetan. It's been eighteen years since you gypped me out of a sixth of my land."

"The courts didn't see it that way, Albert."

"Water under the bridge, Gaetan. I stopped hating you for it years ago. You're a crackpot is all, and I'm not the only one who thinks so. Plus you got a hero complex. Your whole life you haven't had any friends in this entire county and you just stay and stay and stay. Don't you get tired of eating lunch all by yourself?"

"Are we talking about something here or just shooting the breeze?"

"Tyrone Little's a dangerous man. Everybody in Choteau's riled up ever since he came back. Talking about the bones again, keeping loaded rifles around the house, telling the same old stories."

"They've got their own way of seeing things in Choteau. They think Tyrone worked for the FBI."

"But we know that's bullshit, don't we? More like he was working for you, Gaetan."

Joe Merchant swings his driver like a baseball bat and his ball shoots low along the ground and bounds down the hard fairway about two hundred yards. Ted says his grandfather is up, but Roebuck just waves him off. "You hit, Ted. I'm talking here."

Ted sticks a yellow tee into the flat ground and lays a Maxfli on top of it like he's lighting a candle.

"Ted and I are having this disagreement," Roebuck says. "He was just a little boy back then and doesn't remember the marshals and feds crawling all over everything. But he's been in touch with the bureau office in Denver on the subject of Tyrone Little."

I'm already wishing I was alone in the clubhouse with a drink in one hand and a scorecard in the other, winnings on the table, remembering my best shots of the day while Petra Andriessen asks me what I'd like for lunch. "Let's get to the point, Roebuck. I want to know what you're after and why the hell we're playing golf together when it's obvious we hate each other's guts."

"All's I want is a meeting. You and Tyrone tomorrow in my office. We've got an offer to lay on the table."

"Pay him off to leave town?"

"We can be generous, can't we? To avoid all the complications of lawmen and vigilantes."

Ted takes four practice swings before stepping up to his ball. "Give it a ride!" Albert tells him.

Golf isn't much of a contact sport. Hockey players tend to do a lot of damage and a baseball player with a bat can sometimes make a pitcher mighty nervous. And here I am holding a driver in both hands and wanting to clock the old man with it, though a five-iron would probably be more efficient. I catch myself talking through my teeth. "Why don't you goddamn drive out there and see him for yourself?"

"Because I want everything done in the clear light of day, Gaetan. In public, in town. Not out beyond those treelines where you can't see what's happening."

Ted hits his drive a little high but with plenty of distance, and it takes half a dozen bounces before settling in the middle of the fairway. He looks over at us with a smile that shows how much toothpaste he uses.

Albert tees up his ball and then gazes down the fairway as if into a sunset. "One more thing," he says without looking at me. "Sheriff here got Sam speeding last night. What was it, Joe? Forty-five in a twenty-five-mile-an-hour zone?"

"Forty-seven," Merchant says.

No one is looking at me, even though they're arrayed all around me.

"That's not all," Ted says.

I knew it wouldn't be.

Sheriff Merchant clears his throat. "There was, uh, some controlled substance in the glove compartment."

"Weed," Ted pipes up.

"About half an ounce is all. But there was lots of seeds. You can always grow more from seeds."

It wasn't enough that I plowed over that field. Next I'll have to take a vacuum to Sam's car and probably under his bed as well. I take one look at Albert and he doesn't bother hiding that thin-lipped smile of his. Then I turn to Merchant. "I thought you were retired, Joe. You haven't worn a badge in over five years."

"I'm still empowered, though," he says. "When I come across a felony or misdemeanor."

"We don't want Sam," Roebuck says. "We want to put a stop to Tyrone. Gil Dunham says he's seen him strolling across the golf course late at night."

This is news to me but already I understand. "He's not strolling, Roebuck. He comes out here for a reason. To pay his respects at this spot right here."

"Pay his respects to whom?"

"How does it feel, Albert?" I ask him. "Standing there with your cleats dug into a gravesite?"

"What are you talking about?"

"About a resting place for I don't know how many ancestors of the Choteau crowd. Don't give me that look. We both know you found more bones and told the crew to just cover them right up. You think I won't hit off that tee out of respect for the people who *used* to be there?"

I watch the lines in his face go north and south while his eyes move from east to west and back again. Then those eyes rest on the high grass to the back of the tee. "It isn't hallowed ground. They weren't Christians."

"No, but they're buried here. Imagine the din in the clubhouse if word got around Eagle Reach."

"Who'd believe you?"

"All it would take is a shovel and a few minutes of digging."

"You wouldn't dare."

Albert's face is as red as a tomato. Sheriff Merchant turns on him. "Is that true, Albert? There's more bones buried here?"

I point a finger at the back of the tee box. "About a week after they came across the white cemetery and the bones of that Oglala girl, the crew moved the tee right here, ten yards to the east. That's why this hole plays so hard to the left. And that's where they found more bones. When they figured out they were only Indians, they just shoveled another ten feet of dirt and called it good. Anybody ever wonder why this is the highest damn tee box on the course?"

"He's lying, Joe."

"Albert knows where *all* the bones are, Joe. Ask him about Leroy Little Sky. Jog his memory a little."

Now the sheriff's bewildered. "Who in the world is Leroy Little Sky?"

"I found his bones just last month, on my own property."

Suddenly Roebuck is pale. "So where exactly did you find him?"

"Right where you buried him, Albert. Below where that dam used to be on Blue Eye Creek."

"What makes you think it's him?"

"He's right where you put him in 1944, after my father got him with three shots. One to the neck, one to the chest and a clean hole in the head."

"You got no proof it was me who buried him."

"Not yet."

Sheriff Merchant says, "Gaetan, I can't say I understand what you're talking about."

"Albert understands. He lost his tie clasp that day. I figure it'll show up once the mud dries."

"That's going too far, Gaetan. I'd advise you to shut your trap."

I was lying through my teeth. I'd sifted through a ton of mud and gravel around that creek bed and come up empty, but nobody knew that except me. "Nothing stays buried forever, Albert."

"Are you threatening me?"

"I want you to lay off my son. And leave Tyrone alone. Or you'll see me out there with a shovel and a dozen witnesses with perfect eyesight."

"I can overlook the speeding and the seeds and all," Joe says. "But

I ran a computer check and it turns out Sam's wanted in New York State. That's something I can't sweep under the rug."

"You're retired, Joe. Don't you think it's time you climbed out of Albert's pocket and got some fresh air?"

The game is ruined for me, spoiled as it can be by corrupt company or bad weather. And if I can't hide my hatred, I shouldn't be playing with the shitsuckers. While Roebuck stares at the white ball on its tee, I stalk back to the electric cart, stab my driver back in the bag, and unstrap it from the cart.

Joe Merchant hurries over. "Listen, Gaetan. Why can't you just enjoy yourself a little? Your old man's dead and buried. All you're doing is help the bad Indians piss on the good ones."

"Is that how you see it, Joe? Those nights when you stare at the ceiling and add up how Albert's generosity keeps the roof from caving in?"

I turn my back on all of them, sling the bag over my shoulder, and head for the clubhouse, knowing that my days of being a golf monk and the country club oddball are over. I will never play golf at Eagle Reach again.

In the weeks after my father shot Leroy Little Sky, I lived alone with the ghosts of parents. My mother was either locked in her room or gone. My father spent most of his time at his office in town. After he left in the morning, I'd find money on the kitchen table that I assumed he intended for me. As the weeks passed, he continued to scatter bills around the house like letters to me, coded messages. I collected all the money and hid it in a drawer.

In Choteau they organized a search party for Leroy Little Sky. My mother lent her car and two weeks later, when it was returned in good condition, my father couldn't hide his astonishment. They didn't find any sign of Little Sky and my mother said they feared he was dead. Her lips were white. "He wasn't the type to leave his family." I didn't tell her what I'd seen, but she could read my father's face well enough to be suspicious. For a time I erased the memory—or, more precisely, buried it. If I'd told her, what would have been changed?

I had the feeling that our house had grown larger, the rooms expanding and a wind blowing down the hallway that linked our bedrooms. It was rare to find my parents in the house at the same time, as if each could tell when the other was gone. My father would rise at dawn, run his bath, shave, and drink his coffee. Once he was out the door and down the road, my mother would come in the back way, wearing the clothes she'd slept in, and go straight to her room to change. I never saw her take anything to eat but she never left the house without carrying dishes, silverware, clothing, or even furniture with her. I would follow her from room to room while she gathered whatever caught her eye. "Are you well?" she would ask, and I'd say I was right as rain. The empty house grew emptier and when her car had disappeared, my father would return from Wilma. Before long, the silence changed from manic to brooding.

I taught myself to cook—fried bologna, apple sandwiches, hot milk poured over dry bread. And as time went by there were more than a hundred twenty dollars in the envelope in my drawer. I didn't have the heart to do my schoolwork, though each weekday morning I trekked the half mile up the road to the bus stop and sat in a classroom like a statue all day long. November blackened the sky and three days of rain stripped the leaves from the elms that circled our house. I opened my history book to read about the pilgrims and the Indians sitting down to eat corn, and the words were no more legible than those leaves.

One windy afternoon, I returned to the house to find my mother's bedroom completely empty. The bed, nightstand, dresser, mirror, and rug were all gone. Only a couple ragged dresses were hanging lifeless in the closet. A lone earring lay on the floor, cracked mother-of-pearl that I bent to retrieve and then changed my mind. I was standing in the middle of that room, dumbfounded, when Dennis Little Sky appeared in the doorway. He had the same crooked jaw and wandering eye but was sober, if bent around the shoulders. Without that stoop, he was almost as tall as my father. He wore brown pants over a green lumberjack shirt with the sleeves rolled up to the elbows and his forearms looked strong. His black hair was combed straight back to show off his forehead and one eye bore into mine with neither affection nor malice. I saw fear in his gaze and I answered it with a glare of defiance. He took a step forward. "You know who I am?" he asked.

I was afraid to answer. There was too much to tell him. That I knew who he was without wanting to know. That I had seen my father shoot his brother. That my mother no longer spoke to me except to ask if I was well. I said, "Her bed is gone."

"Yeah," he said, and surprised me with a smile. "Gone."

"Dennis?" She appeared at the door and looked at me over his shoulder. She was wearing long pants and a man's shirt and her pale hair was tied in braids. She was already crying when she stepped into the room and then rushed to take me in her arms.

"Pack a suitcase, Gaetan. With your shirts and pants and underthings. An extra pair of shoes. Hide the suitcase under your bed so he won't see it and keep this door closed. Don't go to school tomorrow. Tell your father you're not feeling well. We'll come back for you as soon as he leaves."

"Where are we going?"

She gave me a look that made me feel old. "Dennis busted out of jail to come here. We're going to help him get away."

Dennis went back down the stairs and waited in a truck that was parked out back. I followed my mother to the kitchen where she was packing things into a box—a spatula, baking tins, a potholder with blackened edges. "I don't know why I'm taking all this," she said. "I just, I just . . ." She held a wooden candlestick in one hand and a dish towel in the other as if she couldn't decide which to put in the box first. Then she shook her head and looked across the table at me. "You may never forgive me," she said. "If you come with us, you'll be poor. You've never been poor, Gaetan."

I shook my head.

"All of this. This life. It's not really ours. It's been stolen, Gaetan. Nearly everything we thought was ours. I found the papers, your father's dirty secrets, and I wanted to give everything back. Now those papers are gone and I don't know where to find them. So I have to give back what I can. The things in this house. You don't understand me, do you?"

I nodded. "We stole the toaster. And the potholders."

She laughed aloud, and that frightened me more than her crying or her tying her hair in braids and wearing a man's shirt. "Yes, Gaetan. And the cups and saucers and all the rest." Suddenly she was serious again, her voice quiet. "I think there's something about

Leroy that you haven't told me. Is there something you want to tell me?"

I was looking at her but pretending I wasn't even there.

"I suppose he's told you by now about Mr. Little Sky and me."

Until that instant, I hadn't understood what my father had said to Leroy Little Sky before pulling the trigger. And the way my mother was looking at me, I could tell she didn't know he was dead. I nodded.

She turned away and added the salt and pepper shakers and a gadget she used to grind onions or garlic to her box. There was no room for anything else.

"Pack your things when I'm gone. Use the suitcase with the broken strap, the brown one. It's big enough for what you'll need. I'll come back for you tomorrow morning."

"He has a gun," I told her.

"Everybody has a gun," she said. Then she lifted that box of kitchen junk and carried it out the back door. Dennis jumped from behind the wheel and helped her load the box into the back of the truck, where the bed and dresser and armoire were already tied down with thick ropes. Then I took a key from the kitchen wall and climbed the stairs. I locked her bedroom door, then hid the key under the hallway rug so my father wouldn't know she was gone for good.

It was late when he came home and the house was dark. The wind had blown leaves across the porch and his feet scraped through them to the front door. He went straight into his office and stayed there for a long time. Looking out my bedroom window, I could see the spill of yellow light from his window in the front yard. When that went out, I returned to my bed and listened as his footsteps mounted the stairs. He stopped in front of my mother's room and tried the knob, then came to my door and opened it.

"Little G? You asleep?"

I lay still, my head turned away from the door.

"Playing possum again?"

I didn't answer.

"It was self-defense, son. You don't understand that, you didn't see everything that went on. Leroy would have killed me. With a knife or with his bare hands. He was strong enough and none too bright."

He'd been drinking and his voice was cracked. I lay as if dead, listening to his heavy breathing.

"This Indian thing, there's more danger than you know. Leroy Little Sky wanted to break us up. Like the family was just a stick in his path. It was him that made her like she is." He stopped for a moment, out of breath. "His brother Dennis broke out of the pen in Sioux Falls, and if he shows up here there'll be more trouble. I wish to God you'd stop blaming me. Life goes on a long time, Gaetan. We have the same name and the same blood. Think on that." I thought he was gone, but he said, "I know you haven't told her, so I guess I can count on you. I *can* count on you, can't I?"

It wasn't until the next morning that he discovered the kitchen. Rain had blown the door open and the floor was wet and covered with leaves. I dressed as if for school and came downstairs where my father was standing next to the gas oven with all the burners going. He was staring into flames, then he saw me off to the side and gave me a crooked smile. "It looks like she doesn't know who she's dealing with."

Then he turned off the burners and went out back. The dogs answered his whistle and he threw them some scraps, then went over to his car. But instead of going out the drive toward town, he pulled around to the back of the house and parked behind the garage. Then he came back into the kitchen and locked the back door. "She's got a paper," he said. "A legal document she thinks is a loaded gun. I put this house in her name years ago, to avoid taxes. That was stupid, I guess. Do you know she means to kick me out? Did you know that? Some lawyer from Yankton says it's her house and I have to leave."

I didn't tell him he was wrong. It would have been enough to show him her bedroom, how nothing was left.

He took a letter from his pocket and handed it to me. It was a court order and I couldn't understand the language.

"Eight days," my father said. "I have eight days to vacate the premises. Christ almighty, she doesn't know who she's dealing with."

"I don't feel good," I said. "Like the flu or something."

"All the same," he said, "things could get hot around here. You better go to school."

"I might throw up."

"And you might not."

I went to my room to fetch my book bag and took the envelope of money from my drawer, then put on my coat and left. The main road was about three hundred yards with open field on one side and a grove of fruit trees on the other. When the school bus came by, I didn't get on. I waited under a tree by the road as the sky darkened and a cold rain began to fall.

I had no way of warning them. After an hour or so, I saw the truck coming and stepped out from under the tree. The truck only had one headlight working and the rain fell in gray slants across the windshield. I got to the road but in the rain they couldn't see me. I stumbled in the mud and fell twice. Dropping my book bag, I raced down the road and leaped over a wide ditch. My right foot caught in the mud and when I pulled it free, I lost my shoe. I ran through the stubble cornfield and when I came to the fruit trees I heard two quick shots and then a third. I hurried ahead until I was in sight of them. The truck was going up the road away from the house, but I'd cut across the field and was two hundred yards away. I shouted and chased them across the field but the truck turned east and finally disappeared in the rain. She was gone.

When I got to the house, the dogs were lying dead in front of the porch. King had tried to crawl under the steps, and Ace had a neat hole in his head.

My father was sitting behind his desk. His eyes were like white holes and his face was pale. "He shot the dogs," he said. "That bastard Dennis. I didn't even tell them to attack." He sat motionless in his chair. "I don't believe it. She actually thought you'd go with her."

"Where?" I asked. "Where's she going?"

"Hell if I know. She's with that Indian, son, but you don't have to be afraid. I can protect you. I can protect both of us, I guarantee you. Anyway, they won't get far."

I left him alone and for the rest of the day I stayed in my room. He was stalking through the house, digging through drawers and rummaging in closets. By evening I was hungry, but there was nothing in the kitchen to eat so I went back up to my bedroom. And though I watched out the window for that one-eyed truck, all I could see was the wind in the fruit trees and the gray sky that stretched all the way to Canada and beyond.

When my father woke me, I was sleeping by the window. He shouted at me to get outside in a hurry. I was still dressed in my school clothes, and when I ran after him into the hallway I saw smoke coming from under my mother's bedroom door.

"Run out to the orchard and stay there!"

I obeyed. When I turned to look back at the house, flames were coming from an upstairs window and my father was on the front porch. He was bent over and I couldn't make out what he was doing. Suddenly the porch erupted in a blaze and I could see my father running toward me. He was breathing heavily and rested his hands on his knees while he caught his breath. I could smell gasoline on his pants and shoes.

"Phone's out," he said. "We have to hope someone sees the place burning and calls the fire station."

The winds whipped the flames upward and the roof on the west side collapsed. Straightening up, my father curled an arm around my shoulder and held me close against him. I don't know how long we stood and watched the house burn. After a while we heard sirens to the west, and a few minutes later two fire trucks and the sheriff's car came tearing up the drive. The firemen hooked their hoses to the well pump out front and aimed the spray into the center of the house, but it was no use. The wind blew veils of fire around the entire house, and by dawn it had burned to the foundation.

The hoses were shut off and the men were milling around the trucks or looking for a place to sit down. Someone had wrapped a blanket around me, but I still felt the cold. I watched my father and some other men as they walked slowly through the debris, and then they stopped in front of a charred mound where the porch had been. The sheriff was pointing at the ground.

I shed the blanket and slipped into their midst.

"Those prints are fresh," the sheriff said. "Judging from the size, I'd say a man and a woman." He knelt down to trace the outlines of the footprints with his finger and nodded at an empty gas can a couple yards away.

I looked around for the bodies of the dogs and realized they weren't there anymore.

"It looks like arson, Gaetan. You got any idea who did this?"

He was staring at the mess of char and ash and took a long time before answering. I wanted him to look at me first and he must have known, because he turned his head to the side.

"Yes, sheriff. I sure do."

. . .

There was a warrant out on my mother and Dennis Little Sky, but neither of them could be located. My father sent me to stay at the Roebucks' for the winter. He couldn't start building a new house until spring, so he took a hotel room in town. I saw very little of him and he knew well enough to avoid me. What I remember of those months is obscured by a sorrow that has never grown lighter or more bearable. I had headaches for no reason and couldn't hold down my food. Roebuck's wife tried to take me to a doctor, but I was convinced they'd poison me to shut me up, so I wouldn't go. I knew what I had seen, and so did Albert Roebuck.

In early spring, I found a note taped inside my school desk. *Come to the launderette in Choteau* is all it said. I said I was sick and went home for my bike. I was afraid my father or Roebuck might see me, so I kept to the dirt roads where mud made it hard to pedal.

I'd never been to Choteau alone and didn't know where to find the launderette. I was terrified. The whole town seemed lifeless, like the site of a battle long since lost, and even the people I saw walking from place to place seemed to be going nowhere in particular. I rode the bike down a dirt road that led to a tiny church next to a cornfield. A man was sitting on the steps, but I was afraid to ask him for directions. So I rode around until I saw a white stucco building beneath a pair of leaning elms. The cardboard sign in the window was so faded I couldn't read it clearly, but I heard the rumbling sound of a washing machine, so I leaned my bike against the wall and stepped inside.

The room was long and narrow and smelled of sweat and mildew. A dim bulb was burning at the far end where a woman stood behind a table piled with laundry. When she saw me come in, she glanced up and then turned back to the shirt in front of her. "Little Gaetan," she said.

I wanted to turn and run. The woman looked crazy, and I didn't want to be alone with her. But I stood my ground, unwilling to either advance or retreat.

The woman placed the folded shirt on top of the stack in front of her. "Does your father know you're here?"

"No. Did you send the message?"

She looked me straight in the eye. "Jesus," she said. "He sent it."

Then she lifted a bony hand and gestured for me to step forward. "The walls of this town have ears, boy. Come closer."

When I was standing across the table from her, I could see she was wearing a rosary around her neck. I'd never seen anyone wearing one like that, as though it were a necklace.

"Do you know who I am?" she asked.

I shook my head.

"Good. You don't have to know my name, do you?"

"I guess not."

She lifted a hand toward her neck and with fingers white as chalk she grasped a rosary bead between thumb and forefinger. Her lips were moving but I couldn't hear what she was saying. Then she looked me in the face. "You been baptized?"

"My father's a Lutheran."

She let out a long sigh. "Your father has turned his back on the Lord."

There was another shirt in front of her and she crimped the sleeves, folded them backward, and tucked the waistline. I had never seen anybody fold a shirt so quickly. Then she stepped from behind the table and came close to me.

"Tell me about my mother."

"There's nothing to tell."

"Where is she?"

"I can't tell you that." Her hand moved from bead to bead, down toward the little cross at the end. "Come once a month," she said, "and don't wait for my message. I'm always here. Do you understand?"

I nodded. "Is she coming back?"

"No," the woman said. "She can't ever come back. But when the time comes, maybe you can join her." Again her lips were moving silently and I realized that she was praying.

My father had chosen a spot south of our old house, not far from Blue Eye Creek. The foundation was laid in late March, and by the end of May the walls and floors were completed. Once again I was living with his silence and his rage. And each month through the early summer I biked out to the dark launderette for the letters my mother sent, or small gifts that I wouldn't have to explain to my father. On my fifth visit, there was a card with a prayer printed on the back and a picture of some saint on the front. "Saint Francis," the woman told me. "An old Indian favorite."

I can read upside down. It's a gift of sorts, but generally not very useful. The woman was careless that day, and when she'd passed me the card, she left the envelope faceup on the table. I gazed at Saint Francis until she started folding the laundry. Then I glanced down at the envelope and I memorized the return address and I have not forgotten it to this day.

The next morning, while my father still slept, I dressed and slipped out of the house. It was a three-mile walk to the gas station that served as a bus stop, where a man with oil on his hands counted out my change and handed me a ticket. At Sioux Falls I took another bus to St. Paul. My father was still in the habit of leaving cash around the house, and I didn't even bother counting what was left when I got into a taxi and gave the driver the address. He drove me through downtown St. Paul, past buildings that were three and four stories tall, across the railroad tracks and a bridge that went over the Mississippi. The farther we went, the worse the houses looked. Many of them had junk scattered out front like the houses I'd seen in Choteau. Then the driver pulled up in front of a small house with peeling yellow paint and a broken rainspout that hung from the eaves of the roof like a cowlick. A German shepherd barked when I got out and I could hear a man shouting for him to shut up from inside the house.

The taxi drove away and Dennis Little Sky came outside. He didn't say a word. He just stood with his back against the door to hold it open and waited for me to come inside.

I could smell pine oil and lemon and the faintest odor of something I couldn't place, urine or vomit or just stale vegetables. My mother came in from another room and stood staring at me, trembling, as if I was the miracle of the month. Then her arms were around my neck and back and her lips covering my hair. Her eyes were shiny with tears, and she was still wearing her hair in braids. But the mourning was gone from that face, the mourning I'd seen ever since she started hiding in her room for days at a stretch with her crème de menthe.

"You're safe? You're well?"

"Right as rain."

"And your father doesn't know you've come?"

"I didn't tell anyone, not even that scary woman who gave me the letters."

This confused her for a moment. "You mean Pauline Lame? She scared you?"

Dennis Little Sky laughed and covered his mouth.

I looked around. The walls were drab and spotted with water stains, bare except for the wooden cross hanging from a nail over the couch. One of the windows was covered with plywood, and strings were poking through the couch. My mother took my hand and led me through the kitchen to a small bedroom whose window looked out on a trashy backyard. The walls were freshly painted white, and I recognized a lamp from our old house. My mother squeezed my hand fiercely and then let go to reach into a crib in the corner. She lifted the baby and held it out to me. "Don't be afraid," she said.

I'd never held a baby in my arms before, and I awkwardly raised my arms as if to hold firewood. She laid the struggling body against my chest. It was as weightless as a falling leaf and I closed my arms around it and felt its puny warmth.

"Leroy Little Sky is his father," she said, her smile brighter than I'd ever seen it. "He's your brother, Gaetan. His name is Tyrone."

"We didn't know where else to go," my mother explained. "We tell people our name is Little, but obviously we can't sign up for welfare." She had spent the past ten minutes banging around the tiny kitchen looking for the toaster. "It's a Sunbeam. You remember? It can toast four slices at a time."

The baby was crying and that distracted her.

"I find work sometimes," she said. "Housecleaning. Day jobs. My hands." She looked at those hands and then at me, and I didn't know which sight caused her the most pain. Then she picked up Tyrone and her mood brightened. "Tell me about Choteau. Is there any word of Leroy?"

It was like asking the wind to stop blowing, or catching pieces of it in your hands and holding it still. I turned away when she offered Tyrone her breast. Her nuttiness terrified me, and if I told her what I'd seen, she'd fall over the edge for good.

I was saved by Dennis, who blew in the door and weaved for a moment before landing faceup on the couch. His eyes were glass and with that skewered jaw his breathing was labored.

"Dennis!" She handed me the baby, who squiggled like a sunfish in my arms, then kneeled down by the couch.

Dennis rolled over and buried his face in the cushions. He mumbled something I couldn't hear.

"What'd he say?"

She got up and brushed the dirt from her knees, and reached to take Tyrone back to her breast. "He said he's sorry. He's sorry he drank the toaster."

My father located me in less than a week. He paid off somebody in Choteau and didn't even have to come get me on his own. A Ramsey County sheriff drove up to the house at suppertime and said he was looking for Gaetan Averill Jr. I was eating soup and by the time I set down my spoon, Dennis Little Sky was out the back door. One of the deputies went after him, but the sheriff's eyes swept the room and latched on to me. "You don't really want to stay here, do you?"

He had my description on a sheet of paper—height, weight, color of eyes. He asked me to roll up my sleeve and show him the birthmark on my right forearm.

The deputy came back without Dennis, who'd disappeared. I thought they'd arrest my mother, but it was me they'd come for. She wept while a deputy pried me from her arms. She'd find a way, she kept saying. She'd find a way.

The sheriff held me by the arm and dragged me through the dirty snow to his car and I never saw my mother again.

They put me up overnight at the Ramsey County jail, and the next morning I was put on a bus with a woman in a uniform. We rode all the way from Minneapolis to Sioux Falls and my father was waiting for me at the bus station, his eyes like fists.

During the drive back to Wilma, he reached into the glove box and pulled out a brochure. Kennebeton Military Academy, in northern Wisconsin. On the cover was a photo of a boy in a blue uniform brandishing a saber.

"You'll like it there, son. You get a swank uniform and three squares a day. They play all the sports and you'll learn more about taking care of yourself than most men ever will. And after a year or so, you'll see I was right to bring you back. Trust me on that score. You're an Averill and it's better to live with your own kind. You're not Indian even if your mother thinks she is. But if you ever run off like this again, I'll call the police and she'll be in prison until you're an old man like me."

But I also learned that day that I was his blind spot. Since I still hadn't told my mother about the murder, he assumed I was on his side. He couldn't see me for what I was. And if I ever hoped to repay him, I'd have to stay as close to him as a loyal son could be. So I went off to Kennebeton where I squinted at the crosshairs and every target fell with a single shot.

Until the Bones War, I had him snookered. But when the marshals found me sitting on Poor Bull's toilet the day of the shoot-out, he finally saw my heart. By the time they captured John Fire in Washington, I decided to stop dancing around. I loaded the jeep with the documents I felt would state my case and drove down the road to my father's house. I no longer had access to his offices or files. Locks had been changed and Janet Orbach wouldn't even type my letters. All the lines we needed had been clearly drawn in the dirt.

It was a blustery March morning, the sky churning and the soggy fields still pocked with leftover ice and dirty snow. All the same, to calm my nerves I drove with the top down and felt the cold wind in my face. I found him out by the stables,where he kept three horses. There was a bridle in his hands and it appeared he was going out for a morning ride. I parked in the yard and on second thought left the box of documents sitting in the backseat. I didn't plan on holding a conference with the old man.

The first thing he said was, "You read the papers?"

I nodded.

"Indian turned him in, a Pullyap. How about them apples?" He laughed without mirth and I shrugged. I'd been counting on John Fire. While he was still on the wing, a legend formed around his name that gave comfort to a lot of people. And now he was caged like all the rest and there was no one left to capture.

I stood there ten feet away and waited him out. We had the same face and it was like looking at my future. Nothing could break him. Like a cottonwood tree, he bent to every wind and then regained his upright position. I would have to tear him down branch by branch and leaf by leaf.

I used the words I'd long since chosen to inform him of my plan to turn all of the land over to the Choteau families. Without his knowledge, I'd already ceded forty acres to Pete Scully. "Since June Lame died, there aren't any more members of the Little Sky clan, but Pete's sister was married to a cousin of theirs. I figured that was about as close as I could get."

"Start counting your pennies," my father said. "I'll rewrite my will down to where you won't see a pinch of Averill dust."

"No can do, actually. Not since you incorporated the whole ball of wax. We're tied together, you and me: Gaetan and Gaetan, just like you wanted. You can scrape the second Gaetan off your letter-head, but we're financially wedded for life."

"That's insane."

I explained in detail what I had in the way of deeds and titles, all that paperwork he'd long since forgotten. Some of what I said was just made up to make him uneasy. I'd gone out there wanting to erase his satisfaction over John Fire's arrest, but once I got going, I wanted to erase a lot more than that. Though it wasn't a long tirade, it was hot. At the end, I added that I hadn't overlooked his part in putting Tyrone Little away. "And don't bother pretending you don't know who he is."

"I didn't know," he answered. "Not until after the FBI took a deep shovel to his past."

"He's a war hero."

"He's a bastard half-breed."

"And you're a murderer and a goddamned firebug."

I had him stripped; there was nothing left to chew on but the roots.

"What is you want, Gaetan?"

"I've got some papers I want you to sign."

"What kind of papers."

"Concessions, surrender, capitulation."

"And if I don't?"

"I've got a cardboard box in the back of my jeep that would give the taxman a hard-on for months."

"What are you talking about?"

"Tax evasion, mostly, and the distinct probability of you showering with the Indians out at the pen."

He turned his back and strode into the stables. He led Said So out and saddled him, though he wasn't thinking straight and must have left the belly cinch loose. I thought he'd ride into town but he headed off east, where rainclouds were gathering, and I jumped into the jeep to go after him.

The cornfields were down to stubble and the horse kicked up clots of mud. I had to swing around a stand of cottonwoods and for a moment I lost sight of him. But when I circled left onto the road, we were almost parallel. He saw me and whipped Said So into a full gallop. I was coming to the narrow bridge over Blue Eye Creek to the land I'd just given to Pete Scully, so I slowed down a hair and didn't look back until I got across the bridge. My father was riding with his knees flailed out, not tucked like he should've, and was almost standing in the saddle going hell-bent for the creek. Then he sat back in the saddle and lowered his head, and I realized he was planning on jumping it. But Said So was an old horse and hadn't been ridden like that in years. Twenty feet from the drop-off, she shied and then bucked, her forelegs hitting the ground, and the cinch on the saddle opened up. My father rode that saddle into the air and landed just short of the water.

After my last stand at Eagle Reach, my first thought is to get to Sam's. My second is to wonder where I'll play golf from now on.

Pulling down the mud road toward Sam's house, I don't see his car. I get out anyway and bang on the door. There's no answer, and when I try the knob, the door's locked. He must be spooked because that door hasn't been locked in years, even when the house was empty. I step down from the porch and notice there are tire tracks leading across the yard into the weeds north of the house and I follow them to where the Renault 5 is pitched into a ditch. As I approach, Sam straightens up from his crouch on the other side. His eyes are wild and he has a rifle in his hands.

"That's for killing gophers, Sam."

"Are you alone?"

"I'm always alone. It's kind of a habit with me."

"I thought you might be the FBI. They're coming for me, I can tell. Last night I was stopped in town for no good reason and the sheriff went through my car."

"That's what I hear."

"It was a setup. I wasn't even speeding and those seeds he says he found were planted."

"Quit barking, Sam. The town boys don't give a shit about east coast felonies or marijuana in the glove box. They just tabbed you as a suitable rabbit to bait me and Tyrone. Now get your shoes on and let's get moving."

"Where're we going?"

"Eagle Reach. But first I got to get out of these golf duds and over to Tyrone's. You can ride along and listen to what I've got to say, and when I'm done talking, you've got a choice. I'll bankroll a run to the Canadian border, if that's what you really want. Otherwise, you can face the music and ride shotgun with me out to Tyrone's."

"What for?"

"Family business."

Tyrone Little

For a long time I play among the stars and moons and circles and small faces. Everything I stare at seems to grin. But when I am upright and taller, I see that world for what it is: drippings of paint, old stains, scratches and bootmarks on the kitchen floor. My mother shows me abc in a big book with animals. B is Bear, D is Deer.

One morning, I watch her cross the room. She is wearing a pink bathrobe with torn pockets. I lift a Cheerio to my eye like a monocle and see through the tiny hole as she steps to the mirror and throws her face at it. Louise Little. Dennis pulls her away and I can see the bleeding. We can't do this, can't live like this. Hell, Louise, ah hell.

Delores, listen to me. I don't know what happened. There are files somewhere, but I don't want to read them and never asked Gaetan what he found when he had the nerve to paw through them. All Dennis told me was that she was put into the state hospital. There were no stitches, no open wounds for her to point to. We waited long months for a thaw that wouldn't take and it was finally us who melted away.

Dennis packs food, my clothes, and my abc books into a car and drives us in circles. He says over and over, *This heap's on its last legs.* North of Milwaukee we settle into a shack not far from the cold lake. The roof is tin and the walls are plywood with a few scraps of tar paper. Dennis finds moving and hauling work as long as he keeps his mouth shut and takes cash.

He teaches me to drive and how to light a fire with trash—what will burn fast and cold, what will burn slow and hot, and what will just make smoke. Cornhusks are good for lighting and corncobs make great embers. I throw an empty wine bottle into the flames and learn that glass will not burn at all.

In the winter, we sit close to the stove and watch the coals burning while he talks to me. I learn words wrong from his crooked mouth. We'll get a new ker, Trone. Ker, car. Pess me them metches. He has trouble with words that want an oval from lips that can't form one. He tells me we should never go to South Dakota. Garden anvil, he says is there. When the fire is hot, he talks about California. In California, he says, you can sleep on the beach without so much as a blanket to cover you. And you can pick fruit from the trees, no need of a ladder, those branches bend to your eyes and the fruit says take me. He reaches his blackened fingers into the bin for another chunk of coal. In California, Trone, they got evocados. I never ate one but I hear they're real good.

He drinks, always has. Wine makes him puke but the juice from Sterno cans sews his eyes shut. I know when he's had Sterno because his face goes black as toast and he can't even cry. He lies faceup on the cold ground, so I roll him across the cardboard closer to the fire. In the morning his clothes give off smoke and he tells me to tear off that shirt and stop the burns.

We are having supper. I stir hot water in a can and Dennis measures out the hard brown chunks in a pan. Adds a lump of grease fat and when the fat is melted in, he tells me to pour the water. I stir it in slow like he showed me and the gravy bleeds from the chunks. He can't read more than Stop signs and asks which bag is that, the collie or the German shepherd?

In the store, he palms a can of sausage with his big right paw and a lady comes from behind her register to stop him at the door. He shows his empty palms and when he smiles, his teeth scare her. I slip out the door with my arms full of beans and sugar and creamed corn and the pint of Wild Turkey he asked for.

We have to leave Milwaukee. The police aren't chasing us, my father's chasing himself. Waukegan, Green Bay, St. Cloud, Duluth. Left and right swings with a constant veer to the north where work is harder to come by and winters colder and Dennis drunker. Back south for no good reason. Hennepin Avenue in Minneapolis. Wet pavement I watch like a blank page while I wait outside the diner across the street from Shinder's Bookstore. Dennis enters slim beneath his coat and comes back out heavier by a thousand pages. We go back to the warehouse and he opens the coat to show me. He chooses my books by the pictures on the front. The first one has stacks of dollar bills and is called *Investing in the Post War Economy*. The other one has a woman with a red dress so torn she's almost naked and a gun in her hand. We burn the pages of the dollar book to stay warm while I chew over unfamiliar words in *The Tramp Twice Dead*.

We're stealing horses tonight. They're corralled inside a chain-link fence. Fords, Buicks, Pontiacs. Pick us out a pinto, Trone. Sumpin wild. I am ten, eleven. My fingers are screwdrivers, my thumb a crowbar. The ice of the door cracks open and we slither inside. He lays the wires together and we buck out into the street, the car rocking like a bronco. We drive out of the city, through miles of stars, and he pulls over in the country where there's a gas station and a roadhouse bar. It's summer and I sleep in the backseat with the windows rolled down. When I wake up, the sun is high but my father's gone, so I pull on my shoes and walk to the roadhouse. The doors are locked and when I look in the window I only see an Indian girl with a broom. He's not at the gas station either. After walking left and right a long time, I find him beat up behind the gas station. Flies are stuck to his face and when I touch his arm I can tell it's broken. I run around to the front and tell them to come quick, my father's hurt, and they follow me out back into the weeds. They look down at him and one of the gas men says, he isn't your father, he's a fuckin' deadbeat Indian.

He drives with a crooked arm south to St. Paul and I shift the gears. I don't remember the place but Dennis takes us there and slides the car into a parking slot. At a window in the lobby I ask about my mother. Her name. The woman takes one look at me and reaches for the phone, so I show her my blade. She puts down the receiver and says, "Take it easy, young man, you might hurt someone."

"Louise Little," I repeat. "I want to see her."

She shakes her head and says, "Who are you?"

I say, "Tyrone Little, her son."

Her eyes get softer and she starts breathing again. "We've been looking for you." And she tells me that after five years in that hospital my mother died of pneumonia. "She took to sleeping without a blanket, exposing herself to the cold. We tried everything, but it was as if she couldn't feel anymore. I'm sorry." The woman says there's a young man who came and left a note for me. In case I ever showed up. Mr. Av-reel, she tells me and I ask, "From South Dakota?"

"I believe so," she says.

I turn and run out the door to the car, "Drive, Dennis, drive. He's been here, let's go!"

They catch us with that car in St. Cloud. Dennis goes to jail for three months and I skip out on the place they take me to and live with a family of Indians. The two women fight all the time over the man who runs the house, and I share a mattress on the floor with a little girl who spends whole days in dirty pants. One of the women hits me with sticks and calls me names. I can eat only when I've finished whatever work she dreams up for me to do. I can't wait for Dennis to get free and come get me, but when he's out I find he's half-cracked in some new way I don't understand. He starts to mixing his talk with Lakota words I don't know and don't want to hear. I drag him from bars, I break up his fights. He isn't alive to me anymore, he's a smoking stick and I just grow taller and stronger.

We ride the rails, jumping flatcars in good weather and boxcars in bad. Dennis is still fighting whatever moves and breathes, but I do my best to get along with the other passengers. One summer morning, we join several others and hop a flatbed between Madison and Eau Claire. A man settles next to me and offers a snort that I refuse. "Don't drink. That's good, that's real good. You got any money?"

I shake my head and he says, "Okay, that's okay." Then he nods at Dennis, who is sleeping over in a corner. "Watch out for him," he tells me. "Indian'll cut your foot off to get the money in your shoe."

"He's my father," I say.

"Like hell he is. You ain't no Indian. Not unless . . ."

I hear the word *half-breed* for the first time. Sitting on a flatbed somewhere in Wisconsin as we pass a lake I don't know the name of.

In Omaha, I pick out the track that leads to Denver and help Dennis into a boxcar. Our things are still back in the weedy lot, our blankets and canteens and some books I still haul around. "Stay here," I tell him, "and don't fall out the door." He leans his head down on the pillow of that crooked arm and sleeps. I run back to the lot and a man's going through our stuff. I yell at him and he takes off with our blankets flapping after him. I slip on the ice and go down hard on my chin. Then I get up and run after him to an empty warehouse. Without those blankets we could freeze to death. I can't see a thing in the darkness and stop still, listening, but the man has disappeared, so I turn and run back to the railyard where the Denver train has already pulled out.

I search three dozen cities and towns between Denver and Chicago. Omaha, Council Bluffs, Des Moines, Ottumwa, Grand Forks, Mandan, Fargo, Sioux City, Mankato, and Eau Claire. Every town has its ghetto on the other side of the rails, and that's where I look for him, where Indians go, trying to live invisibly on welfare or odd jobs that don't pay lunch, or whatever they can steal. I have it all over them, I think. I can read and write and I don't drink cheap wine. And once when I'm in a bar and a woman is looking into my blue eyes, I know she isn't seeing Crazy Horse or Red Cloud or any of the maroon shades of Dennis Little. She takes me to her bed and afterwards I tell her I'm a half-breed, and she moves her head off my chest. I learn to wear those blue eyes like a pass into a nation where they count.

After I become white even to myself, it's easier to find work. People tell me I'm handy but mostly I find myself moving furniture, hauling trash or wreckage, or doing jobs that involve a shovel. I meet a black man who can take apart a broken radio and fix it by himself, so I pay him to show me how. I learn to gather the voices that call out. Stars are too distant but radio waves skim the earth close by.

In Mankato, Minnesota, I become a dishwasher in a truck-stop diner. A dollar seventeen an hour plus lunch less fifty cents for every plate I break. My fingernails are clean as peeled onions. I buy myself a knife meant for gutting animals. Lots of the men I see have knives like that, and alone in my room I swing it and stab at shadows and practice passing it from hand to hand. The room smells like tar and ash from a fire and I cut at the walls and find the charred wood beneath the paper. I wonder if I could ever turn that knife on a person, to rust the blade with blood, and then think about throwing it away or selling it. Though one time I misplace it and am heartsick for the rest of the day. When I find it the next morning, stuck between the cushions of a chair, I weep from the relief and then know I'm cracking up and will never find Dennis, that he probably froze to death and got pushed out that boxcar like a log into the weeds.

After ten years I stop looking for him, and for five years after that I avoid Indians and the places where Indians go.

In Sioux City, Iowa, I see a sign in a window that lists the benefits of army life. I'll need a GED, they tell me, and I figure they rigged the score when I'm handed a high school diploma. In the army, nobody knows I'm an Indian. I forget about it as well. My enlistment papers say I'm Caucasian, blue eyes, black hair, six foot one, no dependents. I signed on hoping for radio work, but they're sending me to a jungle with a gun in my hand. "If you die, who do we contact? Come on, son, you got to fill that box in like everybody else."

No, Delores, I didn't count my kills like some of the others. Though there are two that I'm sure of, having seen the bodies curl and drop on flat terrain. But I send enough scared fire into the brush and jungle around me to murder a whole town. It makes no sense to me, shooting into the light and the dark. Men, cattle, birds. Time passes, days tipping over into weeks. Everyone is younger, and they look at me as if I'm fearsome. After six months, I have a new commanding officer, who calls me Ty and leads me into a field blanketed in a yellow-orange fog. That night I can smell mustard on my hands and my tongue is dry as pavement no matter how much water I drink. I think it over for a long time before I get the drift of what's happened to me. Then I get up from where my unit is camped, cross a ridge, and shoot a water buffalo because it's standing there.

. . .

The air around my face is heavy and dry. I crave dampness and cold and have a yen for darkened rooms where my brain doesn't feel squeezed like fruit inside my skull. I have a lung condition and have been at the VA hospital in St. Paul for six months, sucking on respirators and reading old magazines. I watch television reruns in the lounge with a legless guy who's been there for seven years and has a thing for Lucille Ball. A doctor tells me that I probably got bit by something in that jungle, some exotic insect, and there's a virus in my lungs. I know he's lying through his capped teeth but don't call him out.

After close to a year, I'm in the TV lounge when a nurse says I've got a visitor. When I tell her I don't know anyone on earth who'd come to see me, she says he drove all the way up from South Dakota. The guy with no legs tells us both to shut up. "Send him away," I say. But he's back the next day. "He looks like a nice man," the nurse says. "Why not give him a minute of your time?" I look at my hands and there's free time written all over them, but I still shake my head. The nurse leaves and comes back with a note. *My name is Gaetan Avril and I've spent years looking for you.*

I crumple up the note and leave it inside the fist that I use to cover my coughing. The air is bad and I choke a little and when I look up from my chair he's standing there. He's a good bit older than me, but his face is familiar in a weird way. I get a chill seeing his blue eyes and the first thing he says to me is he'd hoped to find me in better shape.

I get up and walk away, but he follows me down the hall to my room. He keeps saying he can help me, and I tell him he's barking up the wrong tree.

"I've got money that belongs to you," he says, and then I snap my head up and look him in the eye for the first time. "Unless, of course, you aim on pissing away your life in a bathrobe in front of black-and-white television."

"When I feel better," I say, "I plan on going to California. Ever eaten an avocado, Mr. Avril?"

"Tyrone," he says. "If you want to pass for white, that's okay by me. But stop pulling the wool over your eyes about the rest of it."

"What do you mean, 'pass for white'?"

"I mean your Indian side. What you got from your father."

"I lost my father at a railyard when I was twelve."

"His name was Dennis, maybe?"

"Yeah, Dennis Little."

"Well," he says, "it used to be Little Sky, of the Oglala Sioux. That man was your uncle. Your father was dead before you were born."

I lead him to the cafeteria where he gets a coffee and I spoon honey into my hot tea. He tells me a long story that ends where I begin.

I walk by myself up and down the halls of the VA hospital, and when I get back to the cafeteria he's still sitting there with a full cup of coffee in front of him. I ask him why he came and he describes his plan for getting back at his father and turning the land over to the families who've been swindled. He also offers me some land and a house. "There aren't any avocado trees, but what do you care?" He pauses. "Since we're brothers, you have as much right to that place as I do."

It takes me a week to check out of the VA hospital. There are more tests and the doctor gives me a sheaf of prescriptions for inhalants. I have my army savings and spend twelve hundred dollars on a used car in a lot off Wabasha Avenue, a powder-blue Delta 88 with white leather interior. I drive slowly out of St. Paul, feeling a tug of gravity that doesn't let go until I'm past Shakopee and on the open road. I drive faster, through Mankato, Windom, and Luverne, to the South Dakota border. In a gas station in Sioux Falls, I step into the men's room and study my face in the glass. I scrub my face and still can't see the Indian anywhere.

Heading west from Yankton on Highway 50, I change my mind and pull over to the side of the road. The chain around my chest tightens and the respirator doesn't help. I've never even seen a reservation Indian. I feel white. I am white, *Iyeska*, half-breed. Being an Indian isn't a matter of skin or blood or the shape of your nose. And I'm not about to start freeloading on a heritage I've been denying for years.

While I'm sitting behind the wheel, a trooper pulls in behind me. "Car trouble?" he asks when I roll down the window.

"I just stopped to catch my breath."

"Where you headed?"

"Choteau."

He looks at me closely for the first time, his lids closing like pliers. "That's on the reservation," he says. "You a half-breed?"

"Take a look at my eyes," I tell him.

"I don't subscribe to eyesight."

I drive on but he doesn't follow. Two hours later, I turn left off the highway and park in front of a house with fake columns across the front porch. Gaetan runs out and clasps my forearms. He's been waiting for me, and after pouring a few drinks, he drives me out to the house and shows me around.

Before leaving me there alone, he reminds me that I am technically on the Clay Creek Reservation and, although I now hold the deed, it's all Lakota land as far as the eye can see.

I walk the rooms of that house, running my fingers along the wood and plaster. I test the walls with my fist, tap my knuckles on the windowpanes, kick at the new yellow linoleum spread like butter across the kitchen floor. I open and close the door on the first refrigerator I've ever owned. There's a radio on the shelf over the sink. I plug it in and turn it on but hear only a hissing sound. So I take it off the shelf and sit down at the table with tea and honey, pliers and screwdriver, and remove all the parts and spread them across the table.

The people in Choteau get used to my being there the way you grow used to a bad haircut. I work with them, play cards with them, drink with them, and sometimes sit with them at the supper table. But no one bothers asking me to join them in the dancing or singing or the sweat lodges that are springing up around us. And when I slide into a chair at Toby's, the talk dies down. But if I ask, Frank Poor Bull or Pete Scully tell me the stories about coyotes and turtles and the deeds of warriors from a hundred years ago, none of which squares with what I see around me. The people are poorly clothed, poorly fed, and get drunk and start fighting every Saturday night just like the city Indians. I tell Gaetan that I don't see how giving them land is going to make much of a difference.

I live in a country of my own, neither Indian nor white, on an edge of the reservation. Gaetan senses my unease and visits often, bringing books and drink and treated chips for the fire so the smoke won't bother my breathing. He hopes I can gain the Indians' confidence. He has his father like a stone over his head and none of them trusts him farther than they can spit. "I'll take care of the legalities," he says. "It's up to you to convince the families to go along with us. They'll trust your blood, Tyrone. The part of you that's theirs."

But I don't trust my blood at all, and I'm still not convinced I want to be an Indian. "Don't get your hopes up," I tell him.

It was with you, Delores, that I truly wanted to be. You drove me wilder than the March wind, so I stole back those girl's bones from the statehouse for you. Our homemaking left a lot to be desired and the house looked like a wreck—an Indian house with beer cans and cigarette butts and empty food cartons here and there. But you had those books, lots of them, you read secretly and never told anyone about how much you read or how much you knew, not even me. I heard you had a reputation as being easy, and at first that shook me to the bone, the thought of you and other men before me. Then I just let it go, it was me you came home to, and when you kissed me, you bit. When you held me, you left red scratches where your fingers dug in, and I wanted to bleed Oglala for you. I felt it was my blood you were reaching for.

Gaetan shouldn't wonder why I couldn't tell anyone who I am. I had to know for myself before the words would come. There were countless times, Delores, that I meant to tell you. From week to week the need to tell you grew, usually late at night after loving you and feeling my limbs like water and the furnace of you so close to me. Wherever I turn I only see versions of Dennis instead of what I want to see. It will take someone who loves me to the bone to know the difference. I think always of my mother, the last I ever saw of her, throwing her face at the mirror in disbelief. I want you to recognize me, to see the Indian in me for yourself. Maybe then I'll be more than Tyrone Little the Wannabe and the Sky will be restored to my name.

John Fire and Tyrone

Sunlight streams through the kitchen window onto John Fire's bare back. He is cut in a dozen places where his flesh caught on barbed wire. Tyrone cleans the wounds and dabs Mercurochrome, then applies a white scar cream.

"You're covering red with white," John Fire tells him.

He hasn't changed much in eighteen years, during which time he's become the Indian version of Nelson Mandela, his pictures in all the newspapers. The poster that's displayed in the post office and shop windows in Wilma makes him look older and more dangerous than the man sitting in front of Tyrone, but the hair and teeth and slim smile are the same, and the way he squints his eyes even in soft light. Tyrone tells him to sit very still and hold his breath, then, with a clean knife, he cuts a half moon around the black shape in John Fire's left upper arm. The blood that flows is viscous and yellowed. He points the knife, pries, and lifts the slug out like a black seed. "A twenty-two," he says. "How long you been hauling this?"

"Three days. It didn't hurt all that much till this morning."

Tyrone holds the blade of his knife over an oven flame. When the tip is red hot, he lays the blade flat against the bullet hole to cauterize the wound. John Fire howls and, once Tyrone removes the knife, breathes hard in and out. Tyrone cleans the knife and slides it into a wooden sheath. "The radio says you were spotted in Yankton. Some newspaper has you up near Bismarck, headed for Standing Rock, and Gaetan figured you were in Canada by now."

"I was in Yankton," John Fire says. "After I got clear of Omaha, I hooked up with friends and hid out for about a week. Then I got to feeling housebound, like I was still in the box, so I went for a stroll and ended up on the run." He nods in the direction of his wound. "That was a farmer hunting rabbit north of Yankton. Good thing he wasn't hauling a shotgun around." He lifts and stretches his wounded arm then lays it back on the kitchen table. "It took me three nights to walk here. I was waiting outside in the trees, watching, since near dawn. I wanted to be sure you were alone and then that policewoman showed up."

"She's my parole officer," Tyrone says quickly.

"That's all?"

"Meaning what?"

"Well, she didn't look all put together when she came barreling out the front door."

Tyrone gets up and puts water on to boil. He wants to ask John Fire why he has chosen his place to hide out. But he has long since lost the habit or ease of asking questions. "I'll have some lunch ready in about an hour. You want a beer?"

John Fire nods, and tries to look carefree when Tyrone tosses him a can and he pops the top on his first beer in eighteen years. "Who knows you're here?" he asks.

"The whole town. But no one comes except Gaetan."

"You been to Choteau?"

Tyrone stares at him.

"Place must be crawling with feds about now."

After washing the knife he used to extract the bullet, Tyrone slices the two onions that Joseph left for him the day before and tosses the thin circles into a frying pan.

"How about Delores?"

Tyrone takes this question the way he once took a shank to the butt when one of the Indians in the pen caught him with his guard down. He'd felt surprise before pain. "She's in Wilma. Got a job there I guess."

"She know you're back?"

Tyrone adds butter and stirs it around the onions with a wooden spoon. "The trick," he says, "is not to scald the onions. To not be careless."

John Fire tips the can to his lips and drains the last of the beer. "How safe are we here?"

"We're not safe anywhere."

For a while they fall silent. The strangeness of being together has not left them. John Fire sits at the table while Tyrone works at the stove. "You did me a good turn on that Richard Deer business."

Tyrone keeps stirring the onions.

"You weren't the informer, were you? During the Bones War."

The flame burns low and the onions brown slowly.

"I figured that out in prison. It was Bad Hand. That's why you shot him."

Tyrone lifts the frying pan and drops the onions into a pot of boiling water.

"I could be in Canada by now. But I wanted to come here first, to tell you that I figured it out."

Tyrone takes the bread that's hardened on its shelf and breaks it into twenty pieces that he drops into the water. Then he lowers the flame to a thin blue glow.

"They used to feed us onion soup at Marion," John Fire says. "But it sure didn't taste like this."

The sun is down and they eat by candlelight. Tyrone pours coffee into two large mugs and hands one to John Fire. "Same thing at the state pen in Sioux Falls," he says. "Every year some farmer used to donate his leftover crop and we'd eat onions by the truckload. When I got out I wanted to find out how they'd taste cooked right."

They share a long silence that Tyrone knows will lead to talk of the Bones War. Men in prison tend to puzzle over the events that put them there, sometimes to the point where distraction and madness set in. And getting out doesn't change a thing. Tyrone's last thought before sleep each night is of the sound of his gun in that bar in Blunt. "What did you think about most in prison?" he asks.

"When I escaped that time in Lompoc," John Fire says. "I let them take me alive. That won't happen this time."

"You'll need a place to go."

"I made a lot of friends in prison, people I can trust, and some are on the outside now. If I'm going to get north of here, though, I need a car that doesn't have 'runaway Indian' written all over it."

"You could always take mine."

"That Delta Eighty-eight?" John Fire laughs. "I wouldn't make it past Sioux Falls." He pauses a moment. "If you help me, you're an accessory."

"What am I if I don't?"

Hearing a sound, Tyrone turns toward the window but can see only the reflection of the candle.

"So if you weren't FBI," John Fire says, "what made you come to Choteau?"

They both hear the noise of a car on gravel and John Fire goes up the stairway while Tyrone snuffs the candle and moves to the front door. The headlights blind him briefly, then they're switched off as the car pulls up to the front and stops. Gaetan Avril and his son, Sam, get out.

"Rivers of shit are flowing this way," Gaetan says. "We've got to talk."

Tyrone leads them into the kitchen.

"What's the matter with the lights?" Gaetan asks.

"I'd rather keep the house dark," Tyrone tells him.

Sam sits by the window and Gaetan close to the stove. Tyrone stands in the doorway that leads to the stairs as if to guard the passage.

"I brought Sam along because this time around he's a part of things. He tells me he's already been by to see you."

Tyrone looks at Sam who is staring at him across the candlelight.

"Dad's told me the story," Sam says.

Tyrone nods.

"Listen, it isn't me they want. Roebuck and the others. But they can have me if it comes to that. I seem to be the only way they can get to you."

Tyrone says, "I don't understand."

Gaetan says, "There's a warrant out for him in the state of New York. Old business that will become fresh news if you don't meet with them."

"What do they want?"

"They want to pay you to leave town," Gaetan says. "For the longest time I didn't understand just why. Roebuck fed me a line of bull about Indian agitation and such."

"Who wants me gone?"

"Jesus Christmas, Tyrone. I can't even see my nose in front of me. Turn on the lights or fire up some more candles."

"I asked who."

"Roebuck, of course. He knows we found your dad's bones and I figure he's on his way to dig them up. Thing is, I already moved them."

Sam says, "Would somebody please fill in the last of my blanks?"

"Delores never knew," Gaetan says. "No one knew that Tyrone had the same mother as me and his father was an Indian named Little Sky."

From the stairway comes a whoop, then a yell that sends Sam to the wall. Gaetan reaches to his pockets as if to find a weapon. There are footsteps behind Tyrone and Gaetan leaps to the wall switch.

"You sonofagun! An Indian! You're a goddamn redskin!"

"I guess he was listening in," Tyrone tells them.

Gaetan finds the switch and in the pale yellow light of a sixty-watt bulb sees John Fire with one arm around Tyrone and his bandaged arm hanging on a sling. He thinks at first that they're fighting, but John Fire is holding Tyrone in an awkward embrace, then their foreheads come close together and touch.

Joseph Her Many Horses

At sunset, the western sky is the color of dried blood and the clouds the shapes of tongues. There are cars in front of Toby's and the outside lights are already on. He knows they will be inside, Noah, Pete, Frank, and the others. They will be talking about John Fire Smith. Since he escaped, they all are always talking—his mother, Helene, the men at Toby's, the people at Eagle Reach. He has seen a picture of John Fire posted at the country club. He has long hair, like Noah Lame, but he is younger and his eyes seem to look at nothing. He is wanted, Gil has said. They all want him, the whites and the Indians. Gil says he shot some white people but his mother and Helene say no, he's innocent. The people in Choteau are hoping he's in Canada by now, up north where they say he will be safe.

He walks east along the road below Toby's and can see boot tracks leading in both directions. He knows the way now and doesn't need the tracks to lead him there. Since that first time, he has come each evening to watch the man from the photograph in his grandmother's box. During the day, while Joseph works at Eagle Reach, the man comes to his shack and fixes what's broken. They have never spoken, nor looked upon each other even at a distance. He turns off the road and shimmies under a line of barbed wire into a field of ragweed, then climbs a low slope to the wooded area where the red car is hidden, the rifle still resting against the steering wheel. Then he cuts through the trees to the river and follows it upstream before cutting inland at the south edge of the Avril land. The tomatoes have all rotted, as have nearly all the strawberries. But the food that grows into the ground like roots is still edible. He bends and scratches in the earth and pulls up three fat onions and a handful of radishes. The ground has grown hard and the food bitter. The leaves of trees are losing their color to the wind and closer to the river the mushrooms have grown fat and black. Soon he will no longer have to cut grass at the golf course. Gil Dunham will spill chemicals behind the tractor and Joseph will wrap cloth around the tender trunks of new trees to protect them from the winter cold. They will drain the swimming pool and put up the snow fences to keep the course from flooding in the spring. Once winter comes, he will not wear the starched shirt again or feel the cold where the grasses grow crazy. He will gather his firewood and stack it close to his house to keep it dry.

But in the winter he will no longer have this place for food. He will have to take his food from cans and cook it over wood fires. And when he walks the empty fields, he will find the spent red and yellow shotgun shells, and dead pheasants that the hunters failed to retrieve.

He turns back toward the river, to where the ducks gather and foxes stalk them from behind the high grass. Crows circle the treetops beyond the grass and within those trees the owls sit silently awaiting darkness. Once Joseph saw an owl drop out of the tree like a stone, then it soared back upward with a kit fox stuck in its talons and Joseph could barely hear the sound of its wings beating. He has seen a lot of killing in this spot, none of it with guns.

Coming to the river, he bends to read the shore. But there are no signs for him in the green-and-white muck besides mosquitoes that rise like smoke toward his face. The creek isn't flowing. He stands, frightened, and hurries to Sam's house. But Sam's car is gone and the house is dark. The dog is barking and Joseph hears the voices of men. He lies flat against the ground, his fingers like roots in the soil. Then he crawls forward and can see them. They have stopped up the creek with lumber and stones and two men are digging in the mud while another is giving them orders. "It can't be too deep," he says. The man walks around the others as they work and Joseph recognizes Albert Roebuck.

"You sure it was here?" Joseph sees the sheriff.

"Right below where the dam used to be. You ought to be hitting into bones any time now."

The sheriff and the other man continue digging, growing angrier by the minute. Roebuck is shouting and cussing at them, and then he takes a shovel from the sheriff and begins to dig. He flails at the ground with the shovel and flings dirt into the air. Then, exhausted, he throws the shovel to the ground. "There's nothing here!" He stomps toward his car and takes a rifle from the front seat.

Joseph crawls backward through weeds to where the darkness gathers him in and swallows him whole. Then he leaps up and races to Choteau. Where they are afraid of him because the wind blows in his eyes, where they love him because he carries a bullet from their war, where they feed him soup in the winter and bend low and place their fingers on the scar for luck or blessing and everyone calls him son and every man is grandfather.

North

Helene and his mother sit in the tiny kitchen, Helene peeling apples for a pie while his mother smokes a cigarette and drinks. He steps in the door and feels shorter beneath a ceiling than he did beneath the sky. His mother's face is tired from whisky but her eyes burn at the sight of him and she reaches to pull him closer. "Joseph," she says. When she says his name it sounds like a wish she is making. "What have you brought? Onions?"

He takes two onions from his pockets.

"Always onions," Helene says. "I don't know where he finds them all."

Helene sets down her paring knife and stands to put water on for the corn. His mother takes a deep drag from the cigarette and stares out the window toward the road. She's wearing a clean white blouse and jeans torn at the hip as though someone has taken a bite from her.

He swallows air and says, "They're looking for bones."

They don't appear to hear him. Helene tears green shucks from the corn and his mother turns to look at him. "What bones, Joseph?"

He shakes his head. "There's a man I go to see. He barks and drinks at the air and falls down."

"Coughing?" His mother asks. She coughs. "Is that what you mean?"

"Yes. Coughing."

"What man, Joseph?"

He goes into the bedroom beyond the sitting room and turns on the light. Helene's boxes are stacked everywhere and he has to step over them to find the shoe box. He carries it back to the kitchen and sets it on the table. Then he passes his fingers through the photographs until he finds the one he's looking for.

His mother looks at the picture for a long time. "I forgot about this," she says.

"He's been looking at it for years," Helene says. "Like he knows."

"Have you met him?" Delores asks him. "Talked with him?"

"We watch each other," he tells her.

"What do you mean?"

"With our tracks. We visit. I always see him through his window or at his place by the creek."

Helene rips a hank of husk. "Do you know who he is?"

He looks at her and her eyes are hard and gray.

"After all, he does have a name."

He feels the name like a seed on his tongue. "Tyrone."

His mother stands awkwardly, balancing her weight half against him and half against her chair. He slips his arm around her waist to hold her upright. "He was in prison," she says, then goes into the living room where the television is showing a cop show with the sound turned off. She sees herself in a nearby mirror and looks away.

"He comes to the creek to pray," Joseph says. "Every night, I hear him talking to his father. Now the men are there with shovels."

"His father?"

Joseph nods. "He calls him Little Sky."

While Helene runs to Toby's, Delores races her car through Choteau and down the rutted road, but when they arrive at the creek the men are gone. Delores spins the car around and pushes it to its limit back to the highway and east toward Tyrone's house. She is dizzy from whisky and lack of air. The taillights of a car flash in front of her and she races around them. Fluorescent orange cones are lined along the highway and up ahead she can see a roadblock. She slams on the brakes and when the car begins to spin, she yanks the wheel to right it. "Too late," she says. There are sparks at the corners of her eyes.

Then Joseph is speaking to her, his voice as ever calm. Through her tears she can barely hear him. "What did you say?"

"Let me drive," he repeats.

She nods, benumbed, and they change places in the car. She didn't know he could drive.

"At Eagle Reach, I drive the tractor," he tells her. There's a smile on his face she's seldom seen, and in the watery darkness of the car he has the look of a grown man.

"Put your head down," he says.

He spins the car down a ditch and into the cornfield. Cornstalks go down like men before them as Joseph wheels around the roadblock and then veers back onto the highway. Tyrone's house is just ahead and Joseph swings his mother's car into the weedy yard. The house is dark but instantly the front light comes on and John Fire Smith is at the front door. Tyrone, holding a carving knife in his hand, steps in front of him.

Tyrone looks stricken. He glances down at the knife, then turns and offers it to John Fire. Gaetan and Sam Avril come out on the porch. Delores reaches for the door handle. It sticks and she has to bang it hard. She wants to get out gracefully, but her feet are tangled and she slips and falls into the weeds.

"Men coming," Joseph says, then bends to help her up. Her eyes scan the dark and then she sees Tyrone on the porch. His eyes blaze at the sight of her. "You didn't have to write so much," she tells him. "I knew all along you didn't mean to . . ."

"It's John Fire!" The first shot hits the ground between them and then more erupt from the trees along the highway. Sam Avril takes two steps toward the car and stops, shaking his head. Then he falls and crawls in a circle. Tyrone hits the ground and starts to slither toward Delores but stops when a hail of buckshot raises the dust in front of him. Delores, crouching low, hurries to Sam's side. His knee is bleeding and horribly bent. Gaetan scrabbles toward them, half running and half crawling as Joseph reaches the front porch and Tyrone drags him into the house.

Three men come running from the trees, Roebuck trailing behind them, and one of them stops to fire at the house. Delores is still shielding Sam and Gaetan is screaming at her to get moving, but suddenly they are surrounded by rifles.

"We're sunk," Tyrone says, peering out the window.

John Fire shakes his head. "Where's your gun?"

"Don't have one."

Two men are coming toward the house from either side, while Roebuck covers Delores, Sam, and Gaetan.

"You're one dumb Indian, Tyrone."

The yard fills with light as cars and pickups pull in. Frank, Pete, and a dozen others leap out with rifles and Roebuck drops his gun, but the other two men make it to the porch steps.

Joseph rises from his crouch and looks out to where Helene gets out of a pickup and hurries to Delores. "I have a car," he says.

They stare at him as if he'd said he could fly.

"This way," he says, and they follow him to the kitchen and out the window.

They can hear the men crashing into the house as Joseph leads them across the field beyond the elms in back. Thirty yards farther on, they come to a dirt path overrun with summer growth, itchweed and ragweed and high grasses.

"There's a road up ahead," Tyrone tells John Fire. "But it doesn't lead to anywhere but the river."

Another hundred yards west, the path crumbles into sand and rock and then forks. Joseph stops for a moment, looks at the sky as if for guidance, and then turns onto the branch that leads away from Choteau. Up ahead, in a clearing, fallen and partially burnt timber forms a rough rectangle open at one end, a natural shelter. Tyrone stops and looks inside at the dented red Thunderbird.

Seeing the car, John Fire bursts into laughter. "You know what that is?" he asks.

Tyrone shakes his head.

"It's Gene Fast Horse's T-Bird!"

Slowly, Tyrone remembers. "The one they tried to repossess."

Joseph opens the door and climbs behind the wheel. The key is in the ignition and he pumps the gas pedal twice.

"Shit, it's been almost twenty years."

The engine roars and Tyrone and John Fire climb in. Joseph switches on the headlights and the car leaps through the darkness and heads straight for the cornfield. They bounce and rock across the dried furrows, then burst across the ditch and onto the highway.

When they are clear of Choteau, John Fire takes the wheel and cuts from dirt roads to gravel and mud and occasionally over flat fields. Now and again the roads run into creeks or straight to private land, a farmhouse or shack, and John Fire has to circle back. Tyrone is stretched out in the backseat, his head propped on the armrest, and his coughing is nearly constant. "Drop me here," he says, "and get yourself to Canada. I'm going back to Choteau."

"They'll put you right back in prison, Tyrone."

A hundred miles to the north, on a dirt road between Fedora and Carthage, the engine begins to sputter and John Fire says they'd best pull over before that tank goes bone dry. He slows down and turns the wheel to the right, stopping beneath a leaning elm tree. They get out of the car to stretch their legs and Tyrone takes shallow breaths of the night air. They've been in the car for four hours and it's the first time he's been able to look at Joseph's face, at the bridge of the nose and the arc of his chin and the lower lip that juts forward. His eyes are loam brown, hooded like Delores', but what Tyrone can't get over is how tall he is.

"Can you show me?" he finally asks, and Joseph understands. He unbuttons his work shirt and exposes his chest. All these years, Tyrone has imagined an immense yellow wound, but the scar is the size of a dime and barely visible in the moonlight. He resists the want to touch it. The bullet can't be removed even by the man who put it there. "Do you feel it?"

Joseph says, "I don't know how it's supposed to feel."

When they briefly turn away from each other, John Fire is gone. One minute he was checking under the hood of the car and the next, thin air.

Joseph looks startled, but Tyrone laughs. "Don't worry. He's got a nose for gasoline. He'll be back."

They recline on the warm hood of the car and watch the stars without speaking. Tyrone's coughing has eased and he leans his back against the windshield and closes his eyes. He feels himself drawn downward by fatigue and slips into sleep, but then his lungs are bursting again and he snaps awake.

Joseph is at his side. Together, they watch the sky. The stars hang there, tightly fastened. Turning slightly, Tyrone looks at the muscles on his son's bare arms. It's the first time since Delores walked out on him that he hasn't felt himself alone. "Come on," he says, sliding his feet to the road. "I just thought of something we can do."

He picks up a handful of sand and gravel and starts rubbing the car with it. "They'll be looking for a red car," he says. He scrubs harder and the red paint goes from pink to the color of pale skin. Joseph nods and joins him, and together they rub away at the car until it is no color whatsoever.

Near dawn, with a whoop of triumph, John Fire shows them a plastic jug of gasoline. "I'm parched. It's been a while since I tried this and my siphon didn't take. I ended up with a mouthful of gas before getting the hose down." He pours the gas into the tank. "This won't get us all that far."

"I'll go fill up," Tyrone says. "I can still pass for white."

John Fire looks at him hard, and then Tyrone breaks into a grin.

While Joseph and John Fire wait in the field, Tyrone drives into Carthage and pays for a tank of gas and a quart of oil, then drives back out. They decide it's too dangerous to drive in daylight, so they pull into a stand of trees down the road, and take turns sleeping throughout the day.

When darkness gathers again, they head north, John Fire driving, while Joseph sits in the passenger seat and Tyrone, his breathing still difficult, is sprawled out in the back.

John Fire and Tyrone, their raw nerves soothed by sleep, want to know about Choteau, about the eighteen years they missed, and Joseph tells them what he can. That Frank Poor Bull loses his temper at the sounds of gunfire every hunting season and that Jana and Toby still can't make babies so they went to the reservation services office for an adoption. That the stuff George Boy Kemper dumps into the creek turns the water white. That Noah goes to the sweats every day and talks with himself, alone in the hot darkness with only the coals to answer him. That he's almost blind now and Helene has to drive him into town so he can do the grocery shopping.

Tyrone stifles his coughing to listen to that voice. For years he thought the bullet had made his son a half-wit. *He's more alive than I am*, Delores wrote. *The bullet cut off his oxygen and they say he will be stupid but I don't believe them. His name is Joseph. I think he looks like you but I don't say so aloud.* But except for the dryness in his voice and occasional moments of self-doubt, he's fine. He's a miracle.

By ten-thirty they make it to the North Dakota border. An hour later they're in the lakes region and haven't seen another car the entire time. John Fire begins to tire and Tyrone insists on taking the wheel. There's a cloud cover and the sky is a starless, moonless gray slate. Rabbits and insects leap across the beam of the headlights and onto the windshield. For the next few hours, as Joseph listens from the backseat, Tyrone and John Fire swap memories of Choteau before the Bones War and exchange small jokes, acting as though the years have been easier than they've known them to be. "What has long black hair, brown skin, and a shitload of money?" John Fire asks.

When Tyrone says he doesn't know, he gives the answer: "A Sioux Indian." Then he adds, "I lied about the money."

After a time, though, they talk about being locked up. They each felt their limbs had been stunted by the tight boundaries and confines, the low ceilings and cramped quarters. Inmates learn early on to duck their heads and to move slowly. John Fire is six feet tall but says he felt a foot taller in the pen. As Tyrone drives northward, they soak in the boundless prairie space, the wheat and grass fields that can't be framed or fenced by simple eyesight.

Then John Fire says, "Since you're stuck with me in this car, there's something else I want to get off my chest. It's about Delores."

Tyrone coughs into his fist, craving the respirator, and grips the wheel.

"We never talked about this, so you couldn't know I didn't love her like you did. I would've married her if you hadn't shown up, but I felt like I just was going through the motions, doing what was expected. I stopped being mad at both of you almost right away."

"That's good to hear," Tyrone says.

"Everyone figured I'd end up dead or in jail, and I guess I believed them. It didn't make much sense dragging a wife into a life like that."

Then Tyrone has another coughing jag. He barks and chokes, and in fear he moves his foot off the gas.

"You gonna make it?" John Fire says softly.

"Just got to find the, ah, rhythm. There's a breathing rhythm. It comes and goes."

John Fire takes the wheel and drives one-handed. Tyrone rests his head against the window as the silver wheat fields part before his eyes. John Fire says, "How many Indians does it take to change a flat tire?" but Tyrone doesn't have the wind to answer. He can feel a hand on his head, Joseph's long fingers touching his hair. "Three," John Fire tells him, but he doesn't hear the rest. Closing his eyes, he finds the rhythm, a taking and a giving, a swallow and a sigh. He thinks of Delores standing across the weeds from him. The weeds become a river and he steps into it. The ropes around his heart loosen, and he and Delores climb into a boat that's drifting between them. Her face is close to his. The ropes unravel and fall away. He coughs blood as the boat rocks its way to swifter waters.

Dawn lights up the horizon and they are high up in North Dakota when they stop at a gas station in Dunning, a very small town slumbering beneath a grain elevator that rises above it like the spire of a cathedral. A grizzled old man in overalls and tractor cap watches from his seat near the garage while Joseph swings the lever and feeds gas into the tank. John Fire swipes a dirty rag across the windshield and kicks the sluggish tires.

Tyrone is slumped with his head against the window, but the money that's left to them, fifty-six dollars and change, is in his wallet in the glove compartment. John Fire takes twenty and crosses the lot. He and Joseph fill four empty Coke bottles with tap water, then John Fire pays the man, who takes the bills without speaking or taking his eyes off either of them.

Starting back across the lot, Joseph stops a few feet away. The door is open on the passenger side and one of Tyrone's legs is sticking out, the boot resting on gravel. His head is tipped forward and his chin rests on his broad chest. His eyes are closed and blood is mixed with spittle on his lips. They don't have to touch him to know he is dead.

There are two worlds, Joseph's mother told him. The first world is as whole and evident as the wind and the second, well, the second is less whole.

John Fire drives west and then north beyond Antler, North Dakota, and stops within a few hundreds yards of the border. A weak sun pokes through rainclouds and scatters shadows at their feet. Birds scream from the tall pines as John Fire and Joseph lift Tyrone out of the car and stretch him out on a bed of grass.

John Fire points north. "There's a shallow river on the other side of those trees. Once you touch the water, you're in Canada. But you don't want to go there, Joseph. You want to get back and look after Delores and Helene." He holds out Tyrone's wallet, but Joseph won't take it. He repeats what Noah Lame once told him, that after the Custer battle, the money found on the dead soldiers was turned over to the children and they made play tipis with it. John Fire laughs, then counts out half of what's there and presses it on him. He leans his face close and says, "I look at you and I see them both. After long years spent looking at a blank wall, that makes me believe in something besides saving my own hide." He reaches into his pocket and takes out a book of matches. "The fire has to be high and hot. Make sure the smoke is white."

Joseph doesn't want the car. They argue about this for a few minutes and finally, feeling short of words, Joseph turns and heads down the road. The wind picks up at his back, pushing him south. A little while later, he hears the engine start, and an explosion of gravel. When he turns around, the car has vanished into the treeline.

He picks his way through the woods, gathering willow sticks an armful at a time and taking them back to where his father is laid out. He uses Tyrone's shoelaces and strips torn from his own shirt to bind the sticks into a litter. His hands move swiftly, and when he bends to lift the body onto the litter he feels the first raindrops on his exposed back. Gathering kindling and dry leaves, he makes a mound of firewood and drags the litter close to it. Then he takes the matches and lights the dry grasses.

The first world you have to search for, Joseph, you have to listen for it, you have to close your eyes and seek it below your lids. The second world is always there, all the time, whether you want it to be or not.

The wind comes up strong and bullwhips the flames. Willow sticks catch and throw off white balls of fire. Raindrops crash and spit through the embers. The willow bark burns away like paper and the burning wood is red while white smoke rises in rich plumes toward the roiling sky.

Noah Lame

I was maybe the only one in Choteau who was happy to see the snows come early. The earth is quieter in wintertime and the only racket I have to live with is the one inside my head. I step out the back door and walk through new snow to the sweat lodge, and when I come back out I can't find my footprints. I know the word: senile. I was a schoolteacher one year and taught American History to those black kids in Chicago. That's what I sometimes dwell on in that sweat lodge. The foolishness that lasted me my whole life long.

Frank Poor Bull is convinced that nobody will play golf at Eagle Reach anymore. The bones we never knew about, along with Leroy Little Sky's, have all been moved to the spot by the river where we buried the young girl's bones so many years ago. That sandy soil is

Indian land and they can turn the dams on and off all they like but the river still flows right past.

Frank's wrong about Eagle Reach. Scandals like that don't last any longer than the leaves on trees, and I figure membership will pick up again in the spring. Folks like their swimming hole and that game of golf, though they'll have to do without their best yardman. By the time Joseph made it back from North Dakota, barefoot and half-starved, his job was long gone, but I don't think it mattered to him at all. There was something about cutting grass that always rattled him. He still lives in his shack by the river and sometimes he comes into town to help out with firewood or housepainting or whatever Toby finds for him to do at the bar and grill. We don't think of him as our child anymore. He's outgrown us in ways none of us can put a finger on. You try to measure the height of a tree and you tend to forget the depth of the roots.

When Joseph came home from his long walk, Delores moved in with him for a little while. There were things she had to say to him, and I imagine the two of them alone in that tiny house, Delores tipping whisky for courage and Joseph keeping the fires going. She couldn't stay there, of course, any longer than she stayed anywhere, so right after Thanksgiving she took off. We don't where to yet, but Helene says a postcard will come. She's guessing Denver, though I wouldn't lay a bet on it. Indians can end up almost anywhere and still find other Indians wherever they go.

When we gather at Toby's, we tend to imagine John Fire living in Saskatchewan or Manitoba, hunting, fishing, smelling the air that isn't tainted from four walls and a low ceiling. And though we argue about Joe Merchant, I always take his side. It was his word that kept us all out of jail for helping John Fire get away. Roebuck tried to make it look like he knew all along John Fire was hiding out at that house, but with Sam Avril laying there with his knee blown off, Joe Merchant climbed out from under Albert Roebuck's thumb and acted like a man. We were all hoping to see Roebuck bunk down in the state pen, but my guess is he'll get slapped with a probation of some kind. But Gaetan Avril's got some pretty sharp teeth and the price of his boy's knee could be sky high.

Gaetan's told us the whole story of how his father shot Leroy, and in the sweats we think hard about Tyrone Little Sky and it's as though he's among us at last, shrouded in the darkness and the heat, asking us the question: What makes a man an Indian? His blood or the heart it flows through?

From my kitchen window, I can see Gaetan Avril's car pull into the trailer court. He's going to see Helene but that trailer's empty now. Time is a circle, as John Fire liked to say, and all of us will meet again. Helene's TV is in my living room, against the wall that has the pictures of Herman and June and my mother, Pauline. Her dresses hang in the closet next to my shirts and a suit I haven't worn in years. At night she rubs her cold feet against my legs and that always wakes me up, but I don't mind. I only wonder how she warmed her feet all those years she lived alone.

One night, an ice storm pelts the house and I can't sleep. I'm thinking again of the night we drove Tyrone out of Choteau and I end up kicking the bedcovers until Helene wakes up. She makes the kind of fuss that old women make, telling me how selfish I am to disturb her beauty rest. To make amends and put her back to sleep, I decide to tell her a joke.

"Helene," I say. "How many Indians does it take to change a light bulb?"

"What's that hand doing there, Noah?"

"Warming itself in your good graces. So, how many?"

"I don't know."

"Sixteen. One to rob the liquor store for the money to buy the light bulb. One to spend the money he stole on liquor. One to beat up the guy who spent the money on liquor. One to drive the beat-up guy to the hospital."

"That's only four, Noah."

"The other twelve are in jail."

I pause and fall deeper into light and love and female mercy.

Helene gives a little gasp. "Noah? What about the light bulb?"

We struggle under the sheets and there is the dust of beating wings.

"What light bulb?"

A NOTE ABOUT THE AUTHOR

Michael Doane was born in South Dakota and now lives in Montecito, California, with his wife, Claudine, and his children, Guillaume and Sarah. His previous novels are *The Legends of Jesse Dark*, *The Surprise of Burning*, *Six Miles to Roadside Business*, and *City of Light*.

A NOTE ON THE TYPE

The text of this book was set in Simoncini Garamond, a modern version by Francesco Simoncini of the type attributed to the famous Parisian type cutter Claude Garamond (ca. 1490–1561). Garamond was a pupil of Geoffroy Tory and is believed to have based his letters on the Venetian models, although he introduced a number of important differences, and it is to him we owe the letter that we know as old-style. He gave to his letters a certain elegance and a feeling of movement that won for their creator an immediate reputation and the patronage of Francis I of France.

Composed by Crane Typesetting Service,
West Barnstable, Massachusetts

Designed by Brooke Zimmer